THAT WHICH BITES

CELIS T. RONO

Cover Designed and Illustrated by Shane M. Tyree
http://ireforge.embarqspace.com

This book is a work of fiction. Any resemblance to actual events or persons, living or dead, is entirely coincidental.

"That Which Bites," by Celis T. Rono. ISBN 978-1-60264-384-0 (soft cover) 978-1-60264-385-7 (ebook).

Manufactured in the United States of America.

To Theron

TEN YEARS PRIOR…

A PALLID, MALNOURISHED GIRL of twelve sniffed and blew her nose. It was her second viewing of *Billy Jack*, a tawdry vigilante movie from the 1970s she had come upon in the Flower District. The badly acted and shoddily directed B-movie affected her like nothing else.

"It's time you took matters into your own hands," she lectured herself, borrowing from the movie. "You're out of cereal, Nutella, vitamins, and Cheez Whiz, and you need to get some rainwater from the roof. Don't just sit here dying of thirst. Be brave for once in your life!"

She kicked a shoebox full of gems, diamonds, and gold jewelry out of her way. They were nothing more than shiny trinkets as useless and garish as Barbie dolls.

The girl named Julia Poe gathered three empty plastic gallons and made her way above ground from the hotel basement. She climbed the stairwell to the rooftop, leaving her winded with a powerful stitch to her side. Eating expired food from tin containers and lack of cardiovascular exercise would do that to anyone. She vowed to get fitter.

Inflatable swimming pools and pails, drably painted to match the nearby mid-rise buildings, littered the rooftop to collect rainwater. She submerged the plastic jugs until bubbles no longer surfaced. Julia disliked leaving her bomb shelter if she didn't have to. She was developing more phobias as the years slugged on that made it tougher to perform everyday tasks like shopping. Watching movies was the only activity that got her up in the morning.

"Maybe I'll see someone today," she whispered quietly. "I'm tired of talking to myself."

Feeling emboldened by the film, Julia walked to the edge of the roof and peered down. Little Tokyo didn't look so bad with the exception of skeletons strewn like Dia de los Muertos dolls minus the sombreros. They left it alone mostly. Maybe it was the close distance to Skid Row that made living in the area unattractive. A mere block away, the famous mecca of the dispossessed was speckled with rusty, corroded cars – their owners' skeletal remains still waiting for the traffic lights to change.

While a supermajority had choked and sputtered on noxious gray mist, an inordinate number of Skid Row homeless initially survived. Most likely their constant state of infection desensitized them to the filth that contaminated the lower atmosphere. The new powers-that-be, however, didn't think kindly about the mentally unsound walkabouts, the shake-inducing cheap smack, or the stench. The survivors on Alameda Street didn't make the cut and were slaughtered. Poe witnessed the carnage from the same roof. She could almost hear the screams as they were flushed out.

It was first of many declarations that came to be. Sampling transient blood anywhere in the city was determined unlawful. Not shortly after that, human cattle of darker complexion or pronounced ethnic features were set aside for the dirty jobs. Their blood, slightly higher grade than that of the homeless, was deemed 'for emergency use only.'

"Pay attention," she told herself. "Don't think about the bums."

Everywhere else, rabid dogs that had been lucky enough to dodge vampire fangs now overran the once bustling streets surrounding her hotel. Jagged concrete chunks, tall weeds, and broken glass littered the road, causing a mess during the rainy season when muck ended up in the already clogged storm drains. The filthy infrastructure flooded and emitted putrid vapors that could offend even the toughest of the supernatural.

From the corner of her eye she saw him down Alameda Street.

"A halfdead," she said, fear catching her throat.

He was chasing after a pack of dogs and flinging rope at them. The white blur wearing a Hawaiian shirt and khaki shorts could outrun the fastest four-legged creatures. He was toying with them, purposely dogging their steps like a gunslinger from the Old West. Only, this guy was no Clint Eastwood. Dry mouthed, Julia watched him lasso in a Rottweiler and bury his fangs into the dog's neck, tearing its flesh brutally, unnecessarily. Like an empty soda can, he tossed the ravaged mutt over his shoulder.

"Evil son of a bitch," Julia said quietly, shuddering at what she'd witnessed.

The git was a halfdead, a rare stuck-in-the-middle vampire that could sunbake all day if he wanted. He may not have had the immortality of a vampire, but he had all the other perks. The creature lassoed six dogs and dragged them back to the heart of downtown. The more they resisted, the harder the ropes dug in their necks, cutting off their air. He was the fifth day-vamp she'd seen since the Gray Armageddon.

"This is no good," she mumbled, swallowing bitter-tasting fear. "Next thing you know, Nosferatu will be knocking on my door at one in the afternoon."

The silent film had pounded serious fear into her spine a few years back. Just the memory of the strange demonic face of Max Schreck made her nose and upper lip bead with sweat.

Back in the bunker, Julia shoved a seven-inch stake in her coat pocket along with small glass vials and an empty plastic gallon. She took along for safety measures a sharp kitchen knife endorsed by Iron Chef Morimoto himself. It was a mean nine inches in length.

"The mummy can't hit what the mummy can't see," she recited, quoting Muhammad Ali, one of the three people she'd have liked as bunker mates, with Bruce Lee and Gandhi rounding off the list.

After double-knotting her shoelaces, she headed down to St. Vibiana's, the old cathedral that was replaced by a gargantuan edifice on Temple and Hill. Built in 1880, the original church was two blocks away. It had been gutted and turned into an art center and loft housing for the hip and moneyed. The bug-eyed statues, grotto, and fountain were kept intact for more exotic appeal. The courtyard fountain spouted water considered holy. At least that was what she was told as a child.

"Get outta my way, dogs!" she hissed. Haggard dogs gave her wide berth as she brandished a daunting walking stick taller than herself. With nervous eyes and shaking hands, she walked briskly to the former church. She normally only slinked out like a coward for food. This was her first attempt at vigilantism.

For strength and luck she wore her matching long johns, Adidas shoes, and beanie – all black – that coordinated with her dark hair and eyes. She figured there was no harm in looking like Bruce Lee in *Enter the Dragon* when he stealthily infiltrated Han's opium lab.

"Please no halfdeads or regular vampires until I get some holy water," she said under her breath and looked at her watch. She still had a couple of hours until sunset. "Mom, I hope you're watching over me right now, 'cause I don't feel so good. I plan on killing vampires with holy water. If I don't, might as well give up and join you. It's no fun being alone."

The church spire loomed ahead with its moldy, antiquated bell. A compulsion to ring the bell to alert any remaining humans in the city took hold of her. "I won't do it, Dad. I'm not that stupid."

Human-size statues of the Virgin and St. Bernadette welcomed her inside. Their painted eyes followed her every step. When Julia looked closely at their faces, she could see actual eyelashes fanning out of the plaster like fly legs. Creeped out wouldn't have been accurate enough to describe the goosebumps that speckled her skin. Her teeth chattered noisily when cowardice begged her to go home.

It was dark inside the vestibule which she had to cross to get to the fountain in the back garden. Of course, she had forgotten to pack a flashlight. She didn't waste time in the dark and ran to the garden in triple time.

"Eeesh!" came out of her mouth. "Goopy and green!"

The three-tiered fountain bubbled to life on occasion like the tar pits of La Brea, emitting raw gaseous smells. The water had the consistency of NyQuil, and baby aquatic mosquitoes swam around like royal sea monkeys.

There was nothing for it. Julia submerged her hands and began filling the small bottles and a dented gallon. Chipped stone angels fit for decaying cemeteries surrounded her. She focused her eyes on St. Francis in a cassock followed by his animal entourage.

She didn't mind him at all. Without much notice a familiar voice in her head told her to buck up. It was then that she sensed them.

Eyes were boring down. She could feel them. The hairs darting straight up on the back of her neck proved it. Slowly she eased the plastic milk gallon from out of the water and waited. She remained still for what seemed like centuries. A small frog jumped from one lily pod to another, believing the still girl to be part of its world. Julia nearly screamed.

"Just a frog," she said in a low voice instead. "Nothing to worry about."

Before she could draw another safe breath, "Fudge!" escaped her lips. From behind her, a gigantic raven swooped down and captured the little frog in its beak. Julia's heart hammered so hard she saw spots.

Bracing her hands on the fountain seats and the gallon container, Julia rebuked herself out loud. "Bad time to lose it, Julia. Think of Ali. Think of–"

From the reflection of the swampy fountain water, she could see the garden wall where a row of ravens chattered and took it easy. The sun was almost down. "I've changed my mind," she whispered to the thin, wide-eyed girl staring back at her. "I can't kill vampires. I'm not ready–"

She saw him on the watery reflection, eclipsing the image of the birds. She tried to blink him away, but the new image stayed. The immense creature opened his arms wide like he was going to scoop her from behind. Her only lasting memory was of her throat itching something powerful. The irritation triggered Max Schreck in her mind. Before the reflection touched her, she turned around quickly and whacked the looming vampire with the gallon of holy water, crying, "Die!"

There was no acidic hiss upon contact. Unlike the holy water sprinkled on Christopher Lee, the damp vamp before her was neither melted nor singed. The voluminous undead from the reflection in the fountain water was quite manageable in size, only a few inches taller than her.

Pausing in disbelief, the creature looked from the scrawny girl and back to the fetid water on his coat.

"What the–" he began, wiping the swampy liquid off his black Mickey Spillane coat and Jesus and Mary Chain t-shirt, appalled for even daring to touch it. "You stupid kid. This shit is disgusting!"

Julia's jaw dropped as the youthful undead wiped away the stagnant water from his person. Realizing that cleaning the coat was futile, he trained his eyes on her.

"You're dead, kid. You know how hard it is to find a trench coat in this town? It's on every dead's list. The newly turned have claimed them all. I'll to have to walk to the Americana in assfuck Glendale to scrounge up a new one!" Like most ordinary vampires, the young dead had the strength of three strong men and the inability to die the easy way. He, however, did not have the skills certain powerful vampires possessed, like the ability to fly or walk under the sunniest of skies without getting incinerated.

"Maybe you can w-wash it?" suggested the scrawny girl.

"I don't do laundry," the smallish, whacked-out version of a young Christopher Walken spat. "I'm a vampire."

With wounded aplomb, the Walken look-alike took a predatory step toward her and bared his fangs. She watched his incisors elongate into two-inch carvers. His hand reached behind her head before she had time to blink. With her eyes still focused on Cujo teeth, Julia dug for the stake from inside her jacket.

Because the vampire was so close to her, she couldn't hit anything other than the side of his neck. The stake plunged a few inches in his neck but the wood was too stout to lodge any deeper. Cartilage and vocal chords barred any further progression.

Enraged, the vampire slashed Julia's face with his middle fingernail, the only one that grew long and solid as petrified wood. Poe hit her head on the side of the fountain from the impact and couldn't quite get herself to stand up. She was dizzy, and blood oozed from the diagonal wound from her forehead to cheek. From the feel of the scratch, the vampire must have scooped at least half an inch of flesh.

The smell of her blood and the darkening of the skies brought intense panic as she watched the vampire extract the stake from his neck. The infuriated undead fixed her with fevered eyes.

"We've been feeding on rationed refrigerated blood for years now 'cause there ain't enough breathers to go around," he gasped, holding on to his throat. "You're going to be my first human kill, and believe me when I say you're going to suffer for the privilege."

"Mom and Dad, help me," Julia whispered as the vampire lunged for her. Before he could lay a hand on her, the ninety-pound girl reached from behind and brandished the kitchen knife she'd brought. With a powerful sweep, Julia Ginsu-chopped most of his left hand's fingers.

Ignoring the hair-raising scream that came out of his mouth despite his vocal chord damage, the girl lunged at the vampire, and he fell on his back.

"Quit moving around, asshole!" Julia screeched from atop him. She took advantage of his temporary shock at losing his fingers and pinned his good hand with her knee. At several attempts later, she finally succeeded in slicing off the remaining fingers of his right hand as well. His oozing limbs pushed off her bucking body.

With the memory of her parents' very violent end from the fangs of a gang of young vampires, Julia found the strength to straddle Christopher Walken's youthful doppelganger once more. Blinded by her own blood and pounded by his stubby hands, she concentrated on stabbing his heart nearly a dozen times and ending the massacre by hacking off his head. The feel of bone getting severed by a sharp knife felt right to Poe.

The youthful vampire, no more than eighteen when he turned, stopped moving. Bloodied and shell-shocked from her first kill, Julia made her way back to her hotel without further attack. Living near Skid Row had its advantages.

As she locked the hotel door carefully behind her, she whispered, "Thank you, Mom and Dad." Then and only then did she allow herself to collapse in a faint.

CHAPTER 1–STUTTER AND SCRATCH

AT THE PRE-ARRANGED TIME, Sister Ann and Goss scratched the secret knock on her new metal-enforced door carted away from the Japanese American Museum down the street. The original had succumbed to rust. Even knowing in her gut that the people standing outside were her friends, Poe had to fight the bile that rose from her throat.

"Breathe from the umbilical and exhale like you have all the time in the world," the robust nun had told her time and again. She was breathing from the umbilical alright, but she was still gulping air like she'd just climbed Mt. Fuji directly after trekking the Inca Trail.

"No Nosferatu. No Nosferatu, please," Poe prayed fervently to her parents. The creature from the silent classic film was the face she gave to the terror above ground. Seizing the nearest semi-automatic pistol, Poe unlatched the bolt and thought, *The hell with Goss, that snail! I'll put in the peephole myself.*

She yanked open the door.

Sure enough, her most trusted friends, a nun and a giant, stood outside with patient grins on their weary faces. As usual they were literally armed to the end of days.

"Holy Jesus, girl, it took you six minutes to answer the door. That's a record low," drawled Goss, practically crawling inside because of his super-size-me height.

"Well, if you h-had put in a peep h-hole like you said, I would've let you in sooner," Poe countered, disgusted by her stutter. She had been getting better for a while there. Now the h's, w's, and occasional p's tripped her tongue ignominiously.

"Yes," Sister Ann agreed with Poe, her sweat-stained wimple bobbing. "You've been promising to drill a peephole in this child's door for nearly a month now. Que pasó? And Goss, even though Armageddon's dropped its ugly face upon us, don't use the Lord's name in vain. At least not around me. You know how much it aggravates me."

Goss bowed his head in exaggerated penitence. "Sorry, Sister. Must've slipped my notice that you're the last practicing Catholic in town. Next time I come, I promise to bring my best drill."

Something was off. Poe could feel it. The three usually hugged like it was the last time given the cosmic odds against them. Goss insisted on open affection because he could not stand repressed feelings.

"Only a handful of us left," he lectured often, directing his words to the fifty-five-year-old nun who preferred to fondle rosary beads to embracing. "On no account should we hold back sentiment because any day now one of us could get killed or worse, become blood cattle."

The plump yet powerfully dense nun brought Poe a new waterproof pack with lots of pockets to store ammo. With a leather bandolier filled with shotgun shells crisscrossed around her shoulders and a heavy wooden cross dangling upon her chest, the Carmelite looked like a silver-haired bandit from Emiliano Zapata's time. Her saintly countenance screamed purity and love, clashing most wretchedly with her soiled and blood-crusted uniform of eradication and death. Poe loved the nun with the dirty habit and a Tennessee twang but had always suspected that she wasn't quite all there.

"Shoot it in the heart, girl!" the nun instructed fiercely on Poe's first raid. "Shoot the dang thing in its Godforsaken heart! Do it now for heaven sakes!" The memory left a bad taste in her mouth.

Sometimes Sister Ann confused vampire killing with her beloved but dead religion. Instead of Holy Communion, the creepy crawlies left behind by the gray days received blessed bullets through the head and heart.

Goss, a six-foot-seven black man with a pro wrestler's body, handed Poe *Black Belt Jones, Rally Round the Flag Boys,* and a bootleg Pixies concert DVD – all rare gems. He knew how much she loved Gloria Hendry, Paul Newman, and especially the Pixies, which was one of her mother's favorite bands along with the Clash and Sonic Youth.

"Thanks, Goss," she said as she patted his bulky jacket. "This is a h-hard-to-find Paul Newman! Four more and my Newman collection w-will be complete."

Goss taped a perfectly cut Boondocks strip from old Sunday funnies on Poe's busy wall. The comic strip was growing on her. It served up history through the point of view of children with attitude. She didn't particularly understand the dated political angle, but the jokes were hilarious anyway.

"Hmpf! I told you what I think of that nonsense," the nun said, gritting her teeth and fingering the cross hanging upon her chest.

"Yeah, Sister, I heard you." He carefully smoothed the taped ends to get the bubbles out. Goss was a tad fastidious. "I heard you say that it was nothing more than a racist piece of propaganda. But

Poe needs to be infused with something other than the still prevalent white pop culture in these dark times – even if she is the last one of her kind. She's got to feel some pride."

"Like *Black Mama, White Mama* or the other gems you're so fond of bringing her? In case you haven't noticed, she's not black. She's all kinds of other complicated things, God help us! Her mother was Japanese and Filipino and let's see...her father was Scot-Irish and Mexican or something difficult like that." She squinted at Poe whose long and deep diagonal facial scar turned white from the attention.

"Exactly! That constitutes multiracial, and therefore she qualifies as an honorary sista!" he reasoned, looking at Poe who stood mutely as her friends tried to outdo each other. It wasn't the first time the two clashed. The girl held up her hands and silently conveyed, "Don't look at me!"

"And really, if she gets captured up there, they might declare she's not white enough to be cattle. Her black hair, dark eyes, and curious features, not exactly Caucasian and not altogether ethnic, might just get her in trouble. She might end up changing bedpans and wiping ass for dying vamp snacks and incinerating corpses like I did."

"At the risk of sounding like a cold-hearted bitch," Sister Ann stated with much strain as she tried her hardest never to swear. "I'd rather Poe shove bodies in furnace chutes than be laid narcotized on a cot getting bled and molested by leeches."

"A nun, envoy of the most high, sound bitchy and cold-hearted? Never!" said Goss with a rancorous undertone. "I suppose you're right. It would be better for Poe to be a custodian, but seeing that she's light-skinned and pretty, barring the scars – sorry Poe – chances are they've already busted out a cot with her name Sharpied on the pillow. And if she's ever unlucky enough to meet Trench, he'll surely poke a hole through her head. He'll spit blood into it to turn her into a vamp and add to his retinue of pretty people."

There were two ways of turning humans into vampires. The speedier method involved pouring vamp blood through a hole in the skull. The second was through repeated biting over several days.

Sister waited for the flesh of her face to stop jiggling. So upset was the nun that her entire body shook. "Everyone's up for grabs, as we all know," Sister Ann said levelly when her composure returned. "According to my contacts, many farms have started milking their minority custodians as their white cattle die off. Even you, Goss, with your inky blackness aren't safe."

"I've always thought I looked blue-black myself, Sister." His smile didn't reach his eyes. Poe hated these moments when the subtleties of race and language divided her friends.

"Maybe these master vampires realize it's not wise to have so many educated slaves running around. They might revolt," continued Goss. "This is California after all. Home of the black bear, Mexicans, movie stars, plastic surgeons, the tired, the weary, the huddled masses. I'll be the last to go then since my skin's so inky. The Last Chance Ration. Isn't that right, Sister?"

Before Sister Ann could retort, the nun's eyes bulged at the movie playing on Poe's dented television. Poe, who didn't notice the nun's discomfort until Goss nudged her to attention, bolted toward the coffee table and madly searched for the remote.

"Hijo de puta!" the girl cried when she bumped her head on a hanging punching bag, bringing on a prickly headache.

The pile of DVDs, magazines, books, empty cans, and paper plates didn't make the search any easier. Try as she might, the television wouldn't turn off. The power button always got stuck. Her slim back shielding the screen couldn't cover all of Tad Wanky's endowments. The giant poster of a grinning open-shirt Jim Kelly directly behind the television seemed to be laughing at her mortification. She really shouldn't have pinched the poster from the movie rental store next door, but she loved Kelly's cotton candy hair so. Out of desperation, she resorted to yanking out the cord from the small generator.

"And how do you defend that one, Goss?" Sister asked sarcastically. "I suppose that's more pop culture she needs to be exposed to?"

"Don't look at me, Sis," he said, waving the responsibility away. "She's been watching that crap since she was eight – years before we ever found her." He cleared his throat, "The girl says she enjoys the background music."

The two of them trained their accusing eyes on Poe, still guiltily clutching the remote control in her hand. At last they found something they could agree on.

"The m-music," Poe said lamely, avoiding their disapproving look and cringing at her own speech impediment that sometimes came and went whenever it suited itself. *Boku no shiri ni kisu siro,* she thought, conjuring up her knapsack of Japanese curse words and coming up with a lame 'kiss my ass.'

The nun was right about certain things, though. The dialogue and storylines were pretty weak, and the men looked nasty. But those were the best things about dirty flicks because they made Poe laugh by grossing her out. For a minute or two, she could forget that everyone she knew or loved was dead. And no, she would not give up her movies as easily as the confiscated video games Sister claimed would damage her eyes and wrists.

Truth was Poe simply loved the Superflyish background music of certain films from the 1970s. Later, she got into repetitive techno beats from really bad 1980s and 1990s San Fernando Valley-produced videos. She popped them in while she trained and read, to occupy all the years of dead silence living underground. It wasn't because she was sex addicted. On the contrary, the tapes never acted as a stimulant but were more like a boring commercial people watched because there wasn't anything else on TV. In this case, she'd burned through all the movies worth watching.

"Anyway, here's some Tommy Dorsey and Count Basie for you as promised," Sister Ann said as she handed Poe the CDs. They were from the nun's private collection. "Consider them an early birthday present."

She would have listened to the emo and indie-rock bands her older brother Joseph used to like, but her friends would never take the time to sort through the mess in a cobwebbed record store to find her any. Even her mother's late-1970s and early-1980s punk band favorites would have sufficed. Instead, Sister Ann and Goss tried to indoctrinate their own tastes upon her. She smiled and accepted them for she found that Louis, Billie, and Ella weren't so bad. In fact, they had a knack for improving her mood when life was in the toilet.

Not to be outdone, Goss excavated some Thelonius Monk and Coltrane from his jacket.

"A pre-present before your birthday bash."

They had differing views on how to civilize the girl and an unspoken rivalry that kept Poe wary of choosing between the unbranded survivors left she personally knew of. The only parenting skill they had in common was to outfit Poe with guns and ammo.

"Thanks for the goodies, Sister and Goss," she said, perusing the CD covers capriciously.

Sister Ann once told her that love was the most powerful amulet against life's travails. In a sense, she was right. Poe got another chance at life because two people loved her enough to teach her guerilla tactics. Goss energized her with his zest to bring down the fanged powers-that-be. Sister Ann shared the dead aim secrets her family had passed down since the Civil War.

Fending for herself in an eerily silent city since she was eight years old gave her a skewed view of the world. Poe knew that love meant squat next to fear, hunger, and hate. Her bunker contained thousands of pilfered videos and DVDs, many of which were about love. Love soothed and so did friends. But they weren't enough.

"How can I take Sister Ann's advice when the woman of God stuffs three sawed-off double-barreled shotguns under her habit for a living? Preaching to me about love while staking hearts and decapitating vampire heads with a crazy smile on her face is too much," she'd complain to the television when alone.

Besides, love could not kill Kaleb Sainvire and Quillon Trench, leaders of the two most powerful vampire factions in the city. Fear and hate, however, would do the trick. Poe was banking on those emotions for the courage to shoot their dead hearts, if she could only force herself to swallow her phobia of leaving her bunker and infiltrate their well-fortified domain.

Unlike Sister Ann and Goss, she had never caught even a glimpse of these two master vampires. No matter.

"Trench has set up another blood bank on Sweatshop Alley," Goss announced, taking off his jacket. "There're about a dozen cattle, a handful of leeches, and two janitors – one of them's my contact. Time to clean up the filth."

"What happened to your arm?" Poe asked, noticing for the first time his bandaged arm stained with blood. She'd never seen him injured in any way.

"It's nothing," he shrugged. "Just some canvasser trying to mark my building. I blew his head off before he could decide that he liked the place. Getting back to Trench, his blood farm will be destroyed today so get your gear ready."

"Heard anything about Sainvire?" Poe asked quietly, a finger tracing her five-inch scar from forehead to mid-cheek. They only spoke of the master vampire living in the Central Library when they thought Poe was out of earshot.

"Nothing at all," Sister Ann answered.

"We have to focus our energy on shutting down Trench's newly sprouted farms. Right now," Goss insisted.

"But Sainvire's more dangerous, w-we ought to–"

"Not now," Goss cut in. "Trench is priority one. He's the one with LAPD cops working for him."

Trench had a thing about turning police officers and magazine-cover stick people into his personal blood brigade. The master vampire, an advocate of creating more vampires through old-fashioned hunt, bleed, and feed, was famous for thinking with his many appetites. Brawn and beauty were known to be his worst vices. At least he didn't discriminate on that score. Anyone eye-catching, no matter the skin color, he would gladly add to his entourage. More than once he defied the Council's decree of zero vampire creation.

"Sorry, Goss. You said to question everything, and that's what I'm doing." Poe stood her ground, her stubborn streak igniting. Even her stutter seemed to have taken a hike. "We've been on Trench's trail for almost nine months now. Only makes sense to take another angle to throw some slack off our operation. Trench is getting nervous. I mean, he's planting random new farms around downtown to throw us off. Doesn't it make sense that one of them could be a trap? Maybe it's better to let things cool off and hound Sainvire for once."

"Always good to voice your opinion, Poe," Sister Ann said, patting her back lightly, patronizingly. Briefly the nun met Goss' eyes and an unspoken agreement was made between them. "But I agree with Goss. Quillon Trench is certainly more dangerous at this juncture than Sainvire."

"How can that be when Sainvire was the one who came up with cattle milking?" Poe insisted, the back of her throat starting to hurt.

Kaleb Sainvire was the vampire who convinced the Council to ban the addition of new minions a few months after the confounding gray matter carried by the Pacific winds wreaked death and devastation, razing almost the entire human population on the spot. As they were now the majority, the vampire underground came out of hiding, rejoiced, and feasted indiscriminately on the human populace that survived the Gray Armageddon. Sainvire, however, reported to the Council that the few humans that survived weren't enough to quench the hunger of the new vampire realm. So he developed the self-sustaining process of systematically "milking the cattle".

"You'll have to settle for getting Sainvire next time," Sister said rather politely.

"Now's not the time, Poe," added Goss who sat cross-legged on the floor to be more level with the women.

Poe nodded, swallowing hard. She hated it when they didn't include her in the decision- making.

"Don't just hook your pepper spray on the side like that," Sister loudly pointed out, shaking her head. "Really irresponsible," the nun muttered. "How're you going to detach it if a leech attacks you?"

"I won't be using pepper spray," Poe muttered under her breath, shoving the spray in her pocket. Shooting would be too easy for leeches. In many ways they were worse than vampires. Humans who did the bidding of vampires, including bleeding cattle and storing blood during the day, deserved to be pistol whipped and castrated at the very least.

"What was that you said?" Sister asked, cocking her head toward Poe.

"Just saying you're right as usual, Sister." Poe forced a mirthless grin and concentrated on packing incendiary materials more carefully into her new pack. She could see nothing godly about the nun at that moment. A ruler-wielding school principal, yes, but Sister Ann was no sweet, old bride of Christ.

Goss gave her a "be patient" squeeze on the shoulder, which lightened Poe's mood ever so slightly, but she was still sore at them. Her extremely tall friend could always be counted on to douse water onto heated moments.

"Now, Sister," he began in a very eloquent TV commercial voice. "Remember that it will be Poe's 22nd birthday a few hours from now."

"Hmph," was Sister Ann's only reply. The smile that transformed her heavily lined face belied her grumpy pretense.

It had been nearly eight years since she had met Sister Ann and Goss who slowly coaxed her out of her safe underground world of cinematic fiction. Poe had already known how to read, write with both hands, view movies "borrowed" from the Black Yella Bruthas video store two buildings down, play video games, and forage for food during the day. Of course, she also knew a handful of Japanese, Spanish, and Tagalog words she had learned long ago from her irascible cousins who were probably all dead. And yes, she was good at hiding. Burrowing like an animal was how she survived without her parents all those years

Goss and the Catholic nun introduced her to the life of vampire killing and cattle running. These activities gave her a smidgen of self-worth and fired up a palpable desire to seek revenge for all the years alone underground – with nothing but the replay of her parents' and siblings' deaths for company. The nun had to teach her to handle guns, distinguish between flashbang and fragmentation grenades, make bullets and bombs, and understand the evils of nudie films.

Rounding off her education, Goss had brought some proper jujitsu, tae kwon do, jeet kune do and a dollop of other no-holds-barred martial arts DVDs to learn from. The training was hard going since her bunker had limited space from wall-to-wall stacks of movies, books, toys, dead chia pets, and magazines. Having had no sparring partners to practice difficult maneuvers with didn't help either.

Goss, who was a tree compared to Poe and most everyone for that matter, was of no use as a partner as he could just sit there like Kareem and kick out his long legs at her stunted ass. Fortunately she had a sharp mind, keen imagination, and was a quick learner. Her senses were quick and shooting skills honed, all from years of playing video games. If Sister Ann and Goss hadn't come along when they did, Poe believed that she would have lost the ability to speak as well as the will to live.

———

Her mind often revisited what happened the first hours when the world became a cesspool of vampires. Shortly after watching her brother and sister's insides turn to mush outside the Museum of Neon Art atrium, puss oozing out of every orifice as they suffered morbid deaths, Poe had to endure her parents' screams as they tried, futilely, to fend off a gang of starved, newly turned vampires. What a time to find out she was immune to the poison in the air.

"Run, Julia, run!" her mother shouted while overzealous bloodsuckers tapped every artery.

Hiding behind a deformed, glowing metal slab that had once been referred to as an acclaimed plug-it-in sculpture, Poe was far too small and unappetizing to be of interest to the sated undead as they tore her parents apart. Perhaps a lingering paroxysm of guilt kept them from making her into an after-dinner mint. She ran and kept on running while the unfortunate folks around her convulsed their last breaths.

Theories abounded about what the Gray Armageddon could have been: The last world war. Germ warfare gone awry. Alien crafts unloading their septic tanks. Who knew? The point was, nobody cared anymore. The survivors of the poison were too busy trying to fight off anemia from their narrow cots while blood was sucked from their veins intravenously every three days.

Eight was a bad age to be left alone, especially since the bogeyman from Grimm's tales actually walked the streets at night. She was living where the wild things were. Rabid, terrified dogs creeping out of their hiding places during the daylight hours to forage for food kept her on pins and needles. She was old enough to know that rabies could kill.

Downtown was mostly foreign to her, as she and her family had lived in the Sawtelle neighborhood of West Los Angeles, half an hour from downtown without traffic and ten minutes from the Santa Monica and Venice beaches that she could still vividly picture. The Central Library was the only downtown site she knew with GPS preciseness as her parents had made a point to take the family there every other Saturday.

The whole family came downtown to attend a reception thrown for her mother, Beatrice, at the museum where her paintings were interspersed with neon lights depicting the seedy side of the city in a contemporary, loopy sort of way.

"It's the type of exhibit that is so ludicrous that it is bound to be a hit," her grandpa George had said.

Instead of having a fun night out, the gray clouds appeared and infected her brother Joe, her sister Sirena, and almost the entire population.

The holdovers couldn't have left downtown even if they wanted as a permanent traffic jam created by survivors trying to escape by foot and automobile made the roads impossible. All the drivers could do was honk their horns and await an excruciating death.

It took her months to find a long-term refuge and feel a modicum of safety. In an obscure city preservation book she serendipitously read about a forgotten Cold War bunker under a nondescript three-story brick hotel in Little Tokyo. The isolation also brought on a not-so-unreasonable phobia of the outside world.

"You look green," she'd say to her reflection on a chipped mirror. "Time to sunbathe on the roof and get some groceries."

The Gray Armageddon killed off her family and friends, but vampires completed her imprisonment. Caged and isolated, she learned to hate Sainvire and Trench.

Any information gleaned about the two came from the semi-lucid cattle they were able to rescue and from bitter custodians forced into post-apocalyptic slavery due to the hue of their skin, the size of their nose, and the shape of their eyes. A rift had opened between the two opposing heads of the city.

"Trench fancies himself a connoisseur of flesh. He has a weakness for perfect-ten women, and you know he has a thing for pigs because of their penchant for hitting first and asking questions later. An ideal force for a fickle vampire," a tall, curly-haired smuggler named Morales who smiled too much told Poe when she was sixteen.

Goss and Sister had asked him and a fellow smuggler to bring Poe up to speed. He and Megan had both suffered as cattle. They were the lucky few who had escaped.

"To find Trench, all you have to do is follow a trail of be-mustached vampires and emaciated looking waifs that looked like they A-Ha'd their way out of a fashion magazine," added Megan, a startlingly luminescent smuggler with guarded eyes and red hair. She nearly gagged at the warm, fizzless root beer she'd been sipping.

"Sainvire's another matter," said Morales, massaging his temple. It was a tough thing trying to explain the powerful vampire in simple words, but he did it anyway.

"He's cautious, logical, efficient. Our biggest danger. For the past ten years, the human holdouts were hunted and eventually herded into Union Station – you know the cool passenger train depot near Chinatown. The Vampire Council and titled undead divided the cattle and took them to buildings around the downtown area that were snatched up by master vampires. They're fed, watered, encouraged to squeeze out babies, and of course, used intravenously to satisfy the hungry vampos."

With her face blanched of color, Megan added, "The more important undead were able to hook up their own straw attachments. They feed directly on human sushi to savor the warm blood without the chance of contamination."

"Sainvire was even nice enough to set up a vitamin regimen for human cattle with a large dose of iron tabs to stave off anemia. Other masters followed. If the rumors are spot on, he came up with liver and onion Thursdays, too. He's a true saint," Morales fumed.

Always fascinated by the deft fluidity of her friend, she watched Goss check and re-check his Uzi, armalite, and cadre of "small" guns. Poe's mother and father had many friends who used to frequent their house, but none ever looked like Goss. It wasn't just his height and muscular body that set him apart. It was his sense of deep loss.

"How many people could actually claim they found their soul mate?" Sister asked one day. Poe couldn't even begin to explain what the term meant.

The closest thing she could come up with was Westley's relationship with Buttercup in *The Princess Bride*.

Goss used to be an attorney and the director of the regional Gay and Lesbian Alliance before the world teetered to an end. He watched his partner of many years bleed to death to feed Trench's brood. Under a stupor similar to being gagged and drugged, Daryl lived the rest of his short life like a zombie. Two tiny punctures in the neck were potent enough to turn victims into drooling cattle for a year.

"Daryl died because some substance-addicted leech forgot to unplug the IV from his vein. He was literally sucked dry," Sister had told Poe years ago. "Perhaps the trauma of seeing his life mate die drip-by-drip shook Goss out of complacency. He escaped by hiding out in a wheelbarrow for the dead with Daryl's corpse piled up with others until they were all thrown into the body pit on the outskirts of town. Crawling out of a pile of vermin and rotting remains, Goss rose from the pit vowing to avenge the death of his only love."

Out on a rare daytime hunt, Poe was thrown to the street by Goss on their first meeting. She had no idea a human lived in the great emerald Eastern Columbia building in the old Broadway Theater District, let alone an ugly coarse-hair terrier that bit her ankle and a pathetic three-legged hound named Legs. Goss refused to leave home, an impressive art deco tower crowned by an enormous stopped clock, for a more secure hiding place.

"Do you have an extra bottle of holy water, Poe?" Goss asked to lighten the awkwardness brought on by Tad Wanky and the subject of Sainvire.

"It's in the fridge."

Sister Ann insisted that they call the garlic and water concoction "holy water." The term stuck. The nun never stopped trying to link God's divine plan with the struggle against the new blood-letting order. It was no wonder that she sometimes suffered from mental episodes. Most garlic-related wounds proved to be fatal. The allicin in garlic reacted like plague to vampire flesh and prevented wound healing, causing eventual decay.

Poe stuffed her new pack with bullets filled with garlic oil supplements, two sturdy stakes that she hardly ever used for their dangerous inefficiency, a jagged Rambo knife, holy water in Windex spray bottles, and freeze-dried food. She wore around her neck a slender cigarette-shaped silver whistle, keys, a beaded rosary Sister Ann had given her, talismans, and all sorts of mostly useless gadgets.

Everyone knew crosses, Stars of David, fat Buddhas, and other emblems did nothing to vampires. Such protection was simply movie lore thought up by the superstitious. She wore them anyway just to please her friend. And it was the same with the stakes. Shooting vampire hearts with garlic marinated bullets was the short, uncomplicated version of staking the heart without getting too close. How could she go against the wishes of the good nun?

Contrary to old beliefs, a truly dead vampire didn't implode into dusty nothingness. Their bodies remained intact but decomposed at a faster rate than a human cadaver.

"It takes about two days for the vamp to liquefy into sludge," was one of the first things Goss had taught her. "Don't get too freaked out if they are still looking at you after a kill. If the stares bother you, go ahead and chop off their heads." Hence the meaty bone slicer in her pack.

Poe stuffed extra bullets, clips, and dated candy bars in the side pockets of her dark green army cargo pants and kneeled to double-knot her Adidas sneakers.

"You really ought to wean yourself out of that compulsion," said Sister Ann, who watched Poe with a frown. "It could cost you your life."

"Yes, Sister," the girl answered weakly. She swore under her breath, "*Kuso baba*." Poe had always been paranoid about her shoelaces coming undone while in flight. It didn't matter if the laces were double-knotted; she had to give them a tug to be sure.

"Don't think I don't know you're cursing me in one of your people's languages, Poe," the nun said with bite. As if talking to the air, Sister Ann added, "See that, God? The only thing she remembers about the language of her ancestors is filth."

Once her Walther PPK, aptly named James, and her 9mm Beretta, the only two guns she could handle easily, were safely tucked in her black shoulder holster, Poe's escalating heartbeat slowed. Back in the days when humans ruled, Poe would have looked like a typical kid: black t-shirt, olive army pants, and long hair in a disordered ponytail. Instead of going to a Radiohead or Death Cab concert, however, Poe and her friends were about to embark on their weekly raids.

While her companions re-checked their gear, Poe opened her battered Bad Batz Maru Velcro wallet and touched the picture of her parents and siblings to her lips. It was a nice shot of the family at the dinner table. Her two older siblings, Joe and Sirena, were making throw-up faces, Poe was grinning and missing two front teeth, and her mother and father were pretending to gobble down food like hogs. Poe inherited her mother's semi-wavy black hair, dark brown eyes, arched eyebrows, and slim but sturdy frame. Her father's nose, full lips, dimples, and light skin that browned easily completed her looks. Poe remembered them very well. With reluctance, she placed the wallet in two protective zip-lock bags and slipped it in her back pocket. She murmured her usual prayer for courage, "Please don't let them get me."

Poe was lucky to be young enough not to remember downtown Los Angeles in all its glory. The silence and emptiness of the streets didn't depress her as it did her two companions.

Downtown was one big, looted disaster area, not at all like Sister Ann and Goss remembered it. The museums were the first to be ransacked by discerning undead, leaving nothing but the most puerile contemporary pieces for the slowpokes. The Jewelry District came a distant second. Free diamonds were nothing to scoff at, even in death. The staking of buildings came third. Many a vamp died a second death fighting over the Walt Disney Concert Hall, an undulating metallic symphony hall shaped like artichoke leaves.

"Yuppies started buying loft housing along these streets." Goss shook his head, keeping his voice down. "These rich clowns had buses re-routed to other streets, just so they could have extra street parking. And the poor bums. Baton-happy cops harassed them to fringes."

"It's the lack of familiar smells that gets me," Sister Ann changed the subject, her eyes glazed from remembrance. "I remember buying sliced mangos with lemon, salt, and chili along street corners. The old aroma of tamales, roasted buttered corn, and Italian sausage at the Grand Central Market destroyed my diet. Believe me, Poe, I was much heftier fourteen years ago."

"Daryl and I would shop the flower and fashion districts racking our brains over where to have lunch – Mexican food at Olvera Street, okonomiyaki in Little Tokyo, dim sum in Chinatown, or plain old smorgasbord at Clifton's Cafeteria," Goss said quietly.

"Now it's just a matter of w-which expired can of rusty tasting SpaghettiOs to open," Poe said, feeling like she ought to contribute but could remember nothing much about downtown.

The busy downtown of the past slowed to a stop, covering many of its buildings with tar to keep the sun out for their new tenants.

"Here we are." Goss looked up indicating the early-20th century three-story brick building that later housed a sweatshop for clothing sold at Wal-Mart. "Poe, you climb up the fire escape. Sister, you take the elevator, and I'll take the stairs." The two nodded. They knew the drill. Sometimes it was just too easy. "Watch out for leeches."

Poe hated leeches almost as much as bloodsuckers. In exchange for keeping their blood intact, these human traitors agreed to be watchdogs over cattle during daylight hours. They supervised the intravenous bloodletting for delivery, making sure the bottles were dated and refrigerated properly.

As an extra perk, they could harass, rape, and torture any humans they wanted so long as they didn't abuse the livestock too much and weaken their blood flow. They were also allowed to keep whatever loot they could find out on the street. These thugs were usually heavily armed, as they spent their days shooting at cans and vermin to keep from dying of boredom. As heavy drug users, leeches tended to be slow to react and easy to subdue. They glittered with the gold they'd pilfered off of skeletons and nearby loft units.

According to Goss, who had scoped the brownstone building for a week, six leeches patrolled the blood farm. After climbing the last rung, Poe hid as best she could on the ledge and waited for the signal. Daytime raids were seldom in the favor of the one sneaking around, but it was either leeches during the daytime hours or vampires at night. She preferred to deal with her own kind.

She peeked inside a broken window and adjusted her eyes to the dim room within. Rows of mostly empty cots lined the walls. About half-dozen gaunt souls with unhealthy greenish hue slumped vacuously on thread-worn chairs. They were indifferent to others laying on stained beds connected to dextrose hoses, transferring their blood into plastic containers. One corpulent leech was busy crumbling dried marijuana leaves onto a torn page from the Book of Mormon, letting his partner do all the work. Every single finger was chocked with obnoxious diamond-encrusted horseshoe rings.

A particularly emaciated old man with a whoosh of thinning white hair sat pathetically on a bloodstained cot. He was having trouble inserting a needle in his vein, especially since a rock star-thin leech, high on glue, was screaming, "Old man, stick it in, or I will!"

The outburst only made the poor man shake even more, puncturing bruised flesh and bone rather than mangled veins. From the looks of him, they hadn't given him his yearly stupor bite. Maybe he was too old.

Gritting her teeth hard, Poe protested under her breath, "The man should be sunning himself in Florida instead of giving his last blood reserve to seedy vampires."

She had a fondness for older people, after all. She had seen *Cocoon* when she was twelve and couldn't look back. The blood cattle reminded her of her own sweet grandparents. To see the elderly in such dismal conditions made her furious.

"Touch him and I'll blow your head off," Poe threatened in a whisper, screwing the silencer into the nozzle of her Walther PPK. She hadn't salivated over killing a human quite like this before.

A flick of the wrist brought out a four-inch Faka knife from her sleeve. She deftly placed the spine of the knife between her right thumb and index finger in a pinch grip and kept her wrist stiff.

Poe thought of herself as disgustingly useless with lots of hang-ups and phobias but hardly any skills to boast of. However, there was one odd expertise she didn't mind having. Whatever weapon she wielded seemed to find its mark.

"Dang, child," said Sister Ann, who had been greatly confounded during a weapon rundown eight years ago. "You've got yourself a dead aim, and my Tennessean tutelage had piddly to do with it. I've questioned God daily since we found you why he left such an innocent lamb in a den of fiends. Now I know he didn't leave you entirely without a skill."

A scream reverberated from the floor below, momentarily obstructing the ranting of both the skinny leech with sparkling studs in his ears and the pathetic apologies of the old man. Chubby Toker paused, mid-lick of sealing his spliff. His white tongue and swampy teeth indicated that the man had given up brushing long ago.

With a deep breath, Poe snapped her left wrist and simultaneously fired the gun with her right. The blade trekked on with force, burying itself in the fat leech's neck while the bullet caught the emaciated leech in the temple. Before he even clutched his neck, the thin man toppled onto the whimpering cattle while his partner fell, face down, onto his crumbled loco weed.

"Sometimes it's hella great to be ambidextrous," she said under her breath.

Poe unsheathed a second gun and climbed in. She put the slim end of her gun to her lips, silencing the stunned human cattle as she ambled toward the door.

"Fuck," she muttered with annoyance. She hadn't seen the third leech sleeping on one of the cots and clutching an open canister of rubber cement until the old cattle pointed at him with a shaky finger.

Poe placed one of her guns on the floor and drew a six-inch jagged knife from her belt – the one she referred to as Rambo's Own that was given to her by Sister Ann as a birthday present. Without flinching, she yanked the unconscious glue sniffer by his oily hair and sliced his neck from ear to ear until his gold chains slid one by one into the gaping crevice.

In a hurry, Poe approached the portly toker clutching at his throat. She quickly pulled out her throwing knife from his neck. The thin wound oozed like lava flow, yet the man still lived. With a grunt, Poe wiped the small blade on his filthy shirt, placed an Adidas foot on the pothead's throat, and put all her weight on it. The cracking sound disturbed her, but she waved the feeling away.

"Fucking leech," she muttered, picking up her gun and turning to the old man. "C-collect your things and get everyone downstairs." She had a terrible compunction to kick herself for stuttering.

Mayhem continued on the floor below. The sounds of scraping furniture and large objects thrown against the wall compelled Poe to hightail down the stairs to investigate.

"Mom, please let Sister Ann and Goss be alright," she prayed, gripping her weapons mercilessly.

Sister Ann was down, her stained habit hiked up to the knees, exposing lightning feelers of blue and purple varicose veins. An enraged bruise quickly spread its red-blackness over her forehead. Her sawed-off shotguns lay ineffectual beside her on the floor.

The sight of the indomitable and seemingly indestructible nun on the floor was a stab at Poe's lungs which seemed to plunge to her stomach. Her organs took further nosedives when a halfdead massaging his knuckles spotted her from the other side of the room.

Sister put up a hell of a fight.

Before she could even raise her guns to the daywalker, something long and eel-like snaked up to snatch the guns from her hands. Fishy slime passed over her flesh. When Poe realized what the pink tentacle was, she nearly fainted, a first in her eight years of cattle rustling.

The tongue tossed her weapon recklessly to the floor. She'd heard of certain vampires with peculiar abilities such as flying, crawling on walls, and superspeed, but never one who possessed a tongue like pulled taffy. Poe shuddered at the anomaly and wondered what other grotesqueness was in store for her.

"Ah, a girl," the creature said with a smile once he retracted his tongue. "I thought this nun was my boon for the day. Everyone's itching to get their hands on pain-in-the-ass rustlers who've been stealing our cattle. Come here, lovely, so I can inspect that whopper scar of yours."

The redhead vampire had been turned in his forties. His earlobes proved to be more interesting than his bland face. Tattooed on each lobe in black ink was an iron cross. The oversized jersey he wore sported a Public Enemy logo in the center.

Great, thought Poe. *A neo-Nazi that listens to rap.*

Poe's eyes flickered from the vampire's eyes to his ear. The man nodded in understanding. "Oh, don't worry about my tats. They're just for effect. Fads borne out of boredom among day managers. And this city is so damn boring with everyone interesting drugged out of their fucking minds. Even rape has gone stale like the rotten breath of these cattle," he said, indicating the two slumbering women in crusty PJs.

Do not stutter. Not now. Please.

"How do you do that thing with your tongue?"

"Dunno. But my tongue's become superdooper long after I turned. Cool, huh? Would've been cooler if my little man got the extender power, too. Shoulda seen this guy I met last year. His eyeball balloons and can actually lift him up to places. Almost as good as flying."

Poe repressed a shiver. "Nice sweatshirt you have there," she said, carefully enunciating each syllable in her husky voice. She swallowed nervously when the man began to walk toward her. "My cousins liked old school hip-hop," she lied.

"So do I. There's nothing better than Slick Rick, NWA, and Too Short." He cracked a sweet smile once again and traced the scar on her face. Sheer will alone kept Poe from turning tail. "Too bad about this. You're such a beauty, too."

"Yeah, it's just too fucking cruel," she concurred. In a blink, Poe snapped a knife from her left wrist and buried it into the vampire's ear. His scream died in his throat when Poe took a step back and let him have two thunderous kicks in the groin. Before she could embed her other wrist knife into his heart, the poser-Nazi snaked his tongue to coil around Poe's arm.

The wet, sandpapery feel of raw muscle holding her arm hostage more than disgusted her, but she ignored it.

"Ou soopid mutt itch," he croaked, unable to speak ably with his tongue far removed from his mouth.

"Uh hmm," Poe nodded. "All that and worse."

Poe yanked the grip of flesh around her arm until the day vamp's head wrenched forward. Angrily he pulled back and uncoiled his tongue for some slack. Reaching behind with her free hand, she extracted Rambo's Own from her back sheath and sliced off his tongue in one stroke.

She shrugged off a five-pound lump of tongue and threw it in his face. Black ooze poured from his mouth. His animated eyes flashed with a mix of fear and undiluted loathing as he backed away and tripped on Sister Ann's shotguns. Desperate to end the ghastly moment, Poe picked up her weapons and shot the vampire in the head and heart. The garlic-oiled bullets destroyed his vampiric immune system. Nazi man died a very painful second death, which suited Poe just fine.

"Sorry, Sister. I gotta find Goss," she told the unconscious nun. Left with little choice, Poe sped downstairs in search of her friend.

The blood farm was too quiet.

"If they have another day vamp then we're really screwed," Poe muttered quietly.

She found him taped flat upon the cot with his extensive legs dangling to the floor. The noise the bed made while he struggled against some very steadfast duct tape was loud enough to wake the sleeping vampires in the basement. Two leeches lay dead by the door, no doubt stabbed to death by her friend. Goss' janitor informants blinked at her from the ground not far from where the murdered bodies lay. They were likewise duct taped around the wrist and ankles and gagged.

"Quiet, Goss," she said, peeling the tape from his mouth. "I'm here now." With a few strokes of her blade, Goss sat up and unpeeled his bonds, wincing as his body hairs stuck to the tape. He gave Poe a powerful whack on the back and collected his weapons. He quickly freed the janitors who emptied bedpans, fed cattle, and cleaned up after tweaker leeches.

"I'll make it to your birthday yet," he said, shaken at being caught and bound. "Where's Sis?"

"Upstairs. She's unconscious but alive."

"What about the daywalker with the tongue?"

"I killed him."

"Good on you, kid," he grinned. "I'm very proud. Now we gotta take out the vamps downstairs then get Sister. Javier and Reuben, look in on Sister, will ya? And get all the kids up and ready to skedaddle from this hell hole."

Pull yourself together! Poe berated silently. She followed the yoga breathing exercises Sister Ann had taught her, breathing as deeply as she could, holding her breath, exhaling slowly through her teeth while they made their way to the basement.

"You first, Poe," Goss instructed after she put on her headlamp.

Poe hated wearing it because in all of the vampire movies she had seen, no Dracula killers ever wore nerdy mining torches on their foreheads. *Remember, they're hard to wake up.*

As soon as Goss stretched his on, the two moved inside with weapons ready to fire. Three vampires were reposing on queen-size beds. Poe quickly claimed sleeping beauty, the closest to the door, by pointing the nozzle of her silencer to the woman's chest and pulling the trigger. The undead's longlashed eyes fluttered open in mute annoyance until true death descended.

Goss passed by a corpse that was so hairy, he looked more like the Wolf Man. From his pack, he took out an axe that quickly descended on the hairball's neck.

"Hurry up so we can get out of here." He took out the big flashlight slung in his belt and double-checked closets and niches. "Head's up," he said, tossing a six-inch stake at Poe.

Poe spiked the heart of what would have been Sister Ann's kill with a weapon the nun would have used.

"I don't have to recite the Lord's Prayer, do I?" she asked, confounded. "Cause I'm stumped after '...who art in heaven...'"

"Nope." He hewed the head of Poe's kill just in case. He smirked at the sound of head hitting the floor. "Just make sure to hack off my head if one of these bastards ever bites me."

The two doused the basement with holy water until the place stunk like garlic marinade.

The execution took less than five minutes. Typical vampires needed considerable effort to waken during the day. It made killing them a cinch in the daytime. The partners made their way to the first floor and were greeted by a ragtag group of cattle in hospital gowns ready to follow a groggy Sister Ann who had taped up the mouths and hands of two very nervous leeches found hiding in the attic. Two custodians, one Latino and the other Thai, wearing matching blue overalls shook hands with Goss.

"My hand's still shaking, my friend," said the man named Javier, who was only a few inches taller than Poe. "Ten years of this shit because I got Montezuma's nose and dusky skin. I don't know how to thank you all."

"There's a halfdead missing," Sister blurted out. "Javier here tells me you were all tied up by a female halfdead. Any ideas where she could be?"

"No, Sister," Reuben, a tall gaunt Thai American fellow with sad droopy eyes answered. "She must've snuck out, maybe to get reinforcements."

"Let's get out of here pronto," Sister said, breathing heavily and shooing the dazed cattle to the door. She was nauseous herself from the blow to her head.

The nun had the urge to slap the unfortunate heaps of humanity until they gave a good enough imitation of a live person. Instead, Sister Ann took out a bag of protein bars and handed them to the nearest lucid cattle to distribute as she prodded them outside the building.

"Jesus, save us," Sister muttered when she spied a hugely pregnant cattle wearing a stained hospital gown. Her backside dotted with bedsores was exposed for all the world to see. The nun wiggled a voluminous slip from under her habit and stepped out of it. The slip used to be pristine white; now it was dirty-water gray. Quickly she put the slip over the pregnant woman's head and secured it on top of her belly.

"The rate these goons are going, future children will all be fathered by contaminated, hophead leeches," commented Reuben. "And the kicker is every single Ritalin tab's expired."

"That's all we need, more trash slavers with ADHD," said Goss.

The trek to the edge of Main and 2nd Street by foot took longer than expected because some of the cattle could barely walk. Two semi-tranquilized leeches connected by rope to Goss' muscular shoulders were sometimes tugged by force to keep them moving. The designated intersection was at the clearest street where a driver could actually maneuver through the zigzag of abandoned cars. They halted before a battered blue pickup truck, blocked by a heavily dented Harley and a shiny, completely out-of-place guacamole-green moped.

"C'mon, get up there," Goss said firmly but quietly. The buildings had eyes and the missing day vamp could have been following them. He assisted those who couldn't lift themselves onto the truck bed.

True to their name, the cattle filed in the back of the truck without resistance. Pitiful though they appeared, Poe couldn't find it in her heart to ridicule them. They were snake-bit Gumbys for vampires to mold and bend at their choosing. Very few defied the venom by shaking off its effects within days to a few months instead of the usual year.

The leeches that had once abused the cattle now had to suffer being sat on like benches by derrieres not completely shielded by hospital gowns. Deflated though the tires looked, they were able to chug along to the team's satisfaction. Sister Ann hopped on her Harley that had been muted and took the lead, shotgun resting on the crook of her arm. Goss drove the truck and Poe followed in her Vespa, automatically switching on a movie in her head.

"I don't want a jackhammer between my legs," Poe had complained to Sister, who was insistent she choose a proper Honda or Harley motorcycle.

A Vespa, on the other hand, had footrests perfect for easy cruising. The green model she chose had a basket and plenty of storage space for snacks and weapons. Besides, the Vespa dampened her irrational fear of her shoelaces getting caught in the motorcycle spokes.

With everlasting traffic blocking every which turn, the caravan took a while to reach 4th Street at the Los Angeles River. Poe insinuated herself into *Cool Hand Luke*, where Paul Newman was having an egg-eating contest. Poe pictured herself among the prisoners, banging on the table and screaming, "Go, Luke, go!!! Swallow them eggs!"

Daydreaming was a dangerous habit to have in the cattle smuggling business, as Poe was well aware but often indulged in. "Grow eyes on the back of your head for the buildings have many spies," warned Sister Ann.

A voice in her head warned, *Be vigilant. There are others*. But as usual, she ignored the voice that often saved her hide.

She failed to notice two black blurs that kept about 50 meters behind the slow procession. Poe could have easily spotted them had she not been lollygagging. After about an hour, midway across a Los Angeles River bridge linking downtown to East L.A., the caravan stopped. A beige carpool van backed up a few feet from the truck, and a heavily armed man and woman emerged.

Sister Ann blessed both newcomers with the sign of the cross and kissed them, her left hand still holding the shotgun upright.

"You cattle, get down now!" Goss ordered, effortlessly lifting the cattle nearest the rear. Poe turned off her Vespa and helped the disoriented, stiff-limbed humans down.

"We could only bring one van today, but I see that won't be a problem," the built, bowlegged man by the name of Sam Morales laughed, amused at the amount of people crammed in the truck. As usual, his dark, perfectly barbered hair was gelled for a Saturday night excursion. He air-punched Goss, who was about seven inches taller than him, and he nodded at Poe, throwing her a smile that made her feel awkward. It was as if he knew she watched *those* kinds of movies. For ex-cattle, he was sure bursting with exuberance.

Poe had never really had a conversation with Morales, not because he was a terrible guy; it was just that he looked way too nice to be a breather, and he knew it. Dressed like a realtor replete with polished Italian shoes, Morales looked like he was off to a business lunch and not a cattle pick-up. His suggestive smile and confusing flirtatiousness intimidated her. And truthfully, she didn't want to appear the geek by stuttering a reply to his many questions. So she left the relationship with the dark charismatic man at a minimum, merely nodding and saying yes or no. Also, she had been warned by Goss and Sister Ann not to ask too many questions about cattle smuggling.

"H-hiya, Meg," Poe greeted with a smile. Her friend was quite plucky in a quiet, steady way. She loved the serious redhead with bulging triceps to death. She could always be relied upon to transfer refugees to safe havens all over the state.

"Hey, Poe," Megan said with a grin as she hugged Poe. She looked tall and lean in her jean overalls. "Did you get a chance to watch *Freaks and Geeks* yet?"

"Yeah, funny stuff, but I forgot your DVDs."

"Don't worry about it. I have three sets at home," she winked, scratching her freckly nose. The woman tanned in freckles.

Pico Rivera, a city southeast of downtown Los Angeles, was where Megan lived with five other smugglers. They turned the ramshackle and almost non-existent Pio Pico Mansion, the historic home of the first Mexican Governor of California, into a halfway house where rescued cattle stayed to recuperate for a few days. Afterwards they exported the breakouts to real country farms where they could shake off the vampires' yearly bite and begin a new life in a closer-to-normal environment.

Even Poe, Goss, and Sister Ann weren't told where those communities were located. As cattle rustlers and sometime vampire hunters, their jobs weren't exactly the safest. They risked capture, torture, and mauling by vampires, leeches, or wild dogs alike. And similarly, Sam and Megan remained blissfully ignorant of the three's whereabouts downtown.

When the human cattle were safely squeezed inside the van and the leeches flat on the floor as footstools, Megan took out a tiny box from her pocket and handed it to Poe.

"Happy 22nd birthday tomorrow, Poe."

"You remembered," Poe muttered, reddening. She opened the little box containing tiny peridot earrings. She thanked her friend with a hug, even though she wanted to throw the useless present on the ground and stomp on it.

"Figured it'll match your moped there," she said, indicating the avocado Vespa with her bright eyes, barely refraining from laughing.

Poe frowned, flinging her friend an affected smirk. "Now I'm dead certain that you'll never get to p-pierce my ears in this lifetime." The redhead had been on her case about poking holes in her virgin earlobes. That was one thing Poe was sure would never happen. She didn't like unnecessary pain.

"No one told me it was your birthday," Morales complained, giving Megan a sharp look only intimate friends or lovers would engage in. "I suppose this sack of garlic will have to do until we meet again, Poe."

Poe's light-hearted demeanor changed to serious again. She mustered a 'thanks' and stuffed the sack of stinking bulbs in her basket. She had always wondered if Megan and Sam had a relationship that was more than a professional one.

"What, no hug?" Morales flung his arms wide, offended. For a grown man, he sure pouted quite often.

Poe dropped her pack with a sigh and gave the pushy man a tepid pat-pat hug. Morales, having none of that, gave her a tight bear squeeze that lingered a little too long.

"Our little smuggler is a woman now," Morales declared, rubbing her back and adding, "And quite a woman she is, too." The look he gave Poe made her ears burn and her nostrils flare as his eyes lingered on the scar that began on the left side of her forehead and crossed over to her right cheek. Brashly, his gaze dipped lower to her chest. All she could think of were those cheesy swinger flicks from the 1970s starring chest hair and gold chain guys like Bam Boozle and Ram Martini.

Megan pried her friend from Morales' grip, saying, "Do I have to douse you with ice water, Sam?"

Poe so wanted to chew out the presumptuous Morales if only she could utter a stutter-free sentence, but Sister Ann interrupted.

"A halfdead is missing from the farm."

Everyone quieted down.

"I hope these sun-proof vamps aren't growing in numbers," Megan said, fingering the silver cross of the rosary the nun had given her, and she unconsciously rubbed it against the fang bite scar on her neck. "Last week, I was followed by one. If Morales hadn't been there to shoot the bastard, the HQ would've been compromised."

"We have to discuss a different pickup route. We can never be sure who's watching and who's following."

At Goss' words, everyone looked at each other. All operations would have to be suspended at least a month for precautions. A new route would need to be planned and debris cleared strategically. They would have to stealthily execute the plans with precision and without alerting enemy eyes. Poe couldn't help but look over her shoulders and feel malevolent eyes staring back. She should've listened to that pesky voice in her head for just then a peroxide-haired day vamp and her reed thin companion emerged from behind an overturned truck.

Poe reached for her Beretta, alerting the others. Sister Ann cocked her shotguns. Goss, Megan, and Morales unslung their semi-automatics.

"I wouldn't shoot us, if I were you," said the blonde vamp with overkill makeup and earth mother hips. "None of your guns have silencers on them. One bango and poof, a whole buncha sun deads are gonna rain down your rickety van over there."

"I don't think that'll happen," Goss said. Can't you hear gunfire all over the city? Your leeches are bored, and they're shooting up old skeletons."

"You have a point there, brother," said the femvamp. "You're too smart to go back to being a janitor. We're just gonna have to drain you. I'm sure Trench and Sainvire won't mind since you're a threat to our way of life. Big guy like you ought to be enough for the two of us. We'll even overlook your skin color since we haven't had a human kill in years."

"Just you try, Elvira," said Goss, gripping his semi tighter.

"But getting back to the point, how do you know we didn't bring reinforcements? "Because you two don't exactly strike me as being very bright," said Sister Ann.

"I heard about you, nun. You're a pest. And if you think Romeo and I are alone, then why don't you take a shot at us right now?"

Sister's eyebrows furred. She couldn't take the chance.

"So this is how it's done," said the toothpick of a vampire before Sister Ann could reply. "These rustlers take 'em outta the city from this bridge."

"A black, a bean, a nun, a redhead, and a girl mutt. These are the people that've been stealing our livestock, Romeo," commented the undead with wide hips. "How pathetic is that?"

Romeo inched toward the van, opened the door, and looked over the cattle inside until he chose the pregnant one. He helped her down the van like an anorexic gentleman. "Very pathetic, Charlene."

"Leave her be," said Sister Ann in her harshest Mother Superior voice.

"You talkin' to me, nun?" he said, shaking his head. "I could strangle you with your rosary, you know."

"Not before I scatter your skinny ass with my bullet," said Goss.

Romeo smiled before punching the pregnant woman in the stomach and jumping back as bullets flew around him. He and Charlene skipped from one stranded car to another like hopped up ballerinas, dodging bullets as they moved.

Sister Ann helped the whining cattle off the ground and into the van. The woman had wet herself.

"Morales, Megan," Sister yelled over the din of gunfire as she slammed the van door closed. "Get these people out of here now!"

Megan's eyes widened with fear when the skinny dead brashly landed next to Goss from five cars away and smacked him on the head before disappearing in a blur. She didn't want to be taken as cattle again so she dropped in the driver's seat and started the engine.

"Sister–" began Morales.

"I don't need your lip today. Do as I say!" She waited until the van drove off before turning back to deal with the Cirque du Freak vampires.

Goss' arm muscles bulged as he rained fire over the halfdeads who were obviously toying with them. Sister glanced at Poe. The girl's sidearms were down to her side. She'd stopped firing altogether, her eyes carefully following Charlene's every move. Inhaling deeply, Poe raised her Beretta and fired once. The haze that was Charlene slumped face down on the roof, writhing for a few seconds until her body stilled.

Sister felt a chill through her body. She'd always thought the girl was an instinctive shooter, but hitting a vampire that was a mere blur with one bullet in the heart should have been impossible.

"Charlene," cried Romeo who watched his partner get killed three car roofs away. He looked at Poe, baring incisors that grew three inches in length. He leapt, easily dodging Goss' indiscriminate fire. The giant's clip was nearly empty. The cheeky vampire landed in front of Goss, yanked his semi-automatic from his hand so hard that the strap gave way. With a grunt, the vampire slugged Goss in the face until he slammed against Sister's Harley.

"Fuck!" Romeo screamed when Sister's shotgun blast hit. His right shoulder hissed from the garlic burning its way into his flesh like acid. Pissed and high on undead adrenaline, he jumped into the air with the intention of squishing the nun like a spider.

The downing of Poe's colleagues happened faster than her eyes could register, but when she saw the vampire leap to crush Sister Ann, her nostrils flared and all concentration went to exterminating the dead once and for all. She fired twice, shattering the vampire's head and puncturing his neck. Romeo fell square on Sister Ann. By the time Poe untangled the vampire from her, the nun was drenched in vampire sludge.

"No communication for a month," said Goss when he came to, his cheekbone and eye swollen already. "Don't go to your homes. Hide in other buildings and basements, the ones where we hid canned goods and such. Do this for a month. Assume we're tracked."

"We'll celebrate your birthday on the fourth week Poe," said Sister Ann.

"We'll bring weevil-free cake mix and we'll have a party."

"Promise?" asked Poe, dreading being alone downtown for four weeks.

"We promise," said Sister, embracing Poe voluntarily for once. "God bless you, child."

CHAPTER 2–CORNED BEEF, YAM, AND A PINT OF RED

SHE SPENT HER BIRTHDAY by herself, eating a can of sweet yams in a shed in Chinatown. All night she craved something salty because of the sickeningly sweet canned root that smelled of rust. Worse, it gave her terrible gas.

"No more yams for me," she vowed.

During the day, Poe foraged for water. The thought of undead eyes following her every move ate at her, cutting her outings short. These were the times she ignored her preference for non-animal food, gulping down expired Spam, rancid corned beef, and slimy Vienna sausages from cans placed by Sister Ann and Goss in various hiding holes. She sorely missed the safe, cool bunker containing her favorite movies. It was like reliving the nightmare of being homeless the first few weeks of the Gray Armageddon.

The darkness of the streets was the worst for it made her hideaway more tomb-like. Streetlights, their bulbs long expired, were only towering relics of days long passed. Otherwise, the moon, flaming metal rubbish drums, and flashlights were the only light sources at night. The city truly became dead after sunset.

Not once during the weeks under metal slabs, inside janitorial closets, and semi-buried below the earth did Poe avoid hearing the garbled, gleeful sounds of vampires hunting four-legged beasts.

"Look how low we've been reduced to," the bitterest of two voices complained from below a dark attic hideout where Poe could clearly see through the uneven floor slabs. "Man, we're the top of the food chain, but we hunt dogs and vermin for something warm to munch."

"That dickhead Sainvire and his farms! He can just shove his microwaved plasma up his ass!" his friend exclaimed, kicking a malnourished dog that barely yelped. The shorter, rounder vampire picked up the medium-sized beagle-spaniel mix and began plucking its neck fur. Once a clearing was formed, he sank his lengthened fangs into the dog's neck. He handed it to his disgruntled friend after a couple of sips to drain what was left of the blood.

"The hell with cold, bottled blood! I want to hunt and kill people again!"

Many wished for the good old days when vampires hunted for their supper. The vampire life had once been romantic and noble. Being on the blood dole sucked, and they were extremely bored of it.

"Too much Anne Rice would have every undead thinking leather and lace, Goth sex, and the titillations of drinking blood," Goss had said some time ago. "These vamps are missing out on their lusty New Orleans heritage. If they only knew that their favorite author became a born again Christian. Not that there's anything wrong with that, mind you."

A nervous old dog followed by two cats and a rat slinked up to Poe's half-buried hiding place. In normal circumstances, these beasts would've acted like the cartoon characters of old: Tom the cat, Jerry the mouse, and Spike the dog. Under vampire rule, however, the lesser beings bonded together in an alliance of convenience, companionship, and protection – or perish. On some nights Poe needed them as much as they needed her. Oily fur, fleas, and the bubonic plague didn't even occur to her as she snuggled wearily against the trembling animals that were worse off. At least she was only homeless for a few weeks while street critters fended for themselves in the wilds of downtown Los Angeles all their brief, terrified lives.

When the days were up, Poe bounded back into the old three-story brick hotel in Little Tokyo surrounded by the stench of garlic bulbs planted almost in every garden, pot, and planter around the block. She thanked the Great Ali for keeping her neck fang free and her cranium intact. Poe entered the hotel with relief after careful inspection of an undisturbed single strand of her hair strategically taped on the door. The descent to the basement where the latch to the bunker was hidden was not as terror-free as she had imagined, however. Every creak and shadow from her flashlight evoked an image of old Nosferatu.

These were the times when her mantra needed to be uttered. "I am Bruce Lee's daughter, Muhammad Ali's niece, and Xena's clone. I fear no one!"

Chanting, she let herself down to her cozy bunker. Now it seemed like a prison. Her favorite films no longer held her interest. As for her jeet kune do workouts, she almost always had to force herself to strengthen the calluses on her shins and knuckles just to please Goss. The kicks and hits she bombarded the punching bag with no longer felt solid.

Thai kicks were considered the most lethal in the world. Even Bruce Lee incorporated them into his own martial arts style, jeet kune do. The video she often watched for guidance showed kickboxers hitting metal tubes and concrete posts as if they were mere foam.

Poe could never follow through correctly because most everything she did was half-assed. It didn't matter.

Yet deep down lingered the knowledge that JKD mingled with Thai boxing and other fighting styles would be no match against immortal vampires that could lift her Vespa with one finger while drinking a bucket of human blood.

Six weeks after the cattle drop, she still hadn't heard from her partners. She knew something was wrong. If they had been captured, or worse, killed, then it was up to her to either free or bury them.

"Get your butt off this futon, dummy!" Poe yelled in frustration, punching a pillow. The outburst was supposed to be an order and a challenge, not another excuse between bathroom breaks. The thought of losing her family of nearly eight years made her want to vomit.

"Let them be alive," she prayed to no particular god as she put on her lucky Pixies t-shirt.

————————

The lukewarm feel of late-November rain against her pale, scarred face nearly drove Poe back into the sanctuary of her underground home. The last time she was above ground, everything was warm to the touch. Now the world was saturated. Even the patented California sun was gone, leaving the city in a dampened gloom. The rats scuttling away from the overflowing sewer onto the cracked asphalt streets gave her a sense of foreboding. The day was too gray, reminding her too much of a grisly time. But she had to go to Goss' home on Broadway as she did not know Sister Ann's permanent safe house. Her tall friend was the only one privy to the nun's convent of one.

Poe took comfort in imagining Sister Ann living in a downtown church, scared to death of the life-size statues of bleeding saints and wide-eyed angels that resented her.

"And that's for still considering me unworthy of your secret even after eight years of friendship," she fumed. "I hope the statues march around like they did in *Exorcist 3*."

She walked a couple of blocks to the Japanese American National Museum and retrieved her Vespa. The old building was a safe place to stash her moped. Even the baddest vampires around couldn't abide the depressing pictures of Japanese Americans interned in Tule Lake, Manzanar, and out-of-state camps during World War II. They generally left the place alone. The Hotel New Otani in Little Tokyo was another matter. High-class undead repeat-debutantes and movie stars were known to frequent the posh hotel at night. Poe swore that she spotted the Governator late one night snogging Paris Hilton, both looking like well preserved pickles.

Vampires who enjoyed something more gritty and banal could be found in the outer blocks of downtown. Gambling, live and illegal suckage, and whatever naughtiness anyone wished for were located in one of the many warehouses in the industrial zone. The decaying distribution centers were purported to attract the darkest denizens of the city. Even the master vampires and ancient undead gave the outskirts a wide berth.

"Under no circumstances will you go anywhere near the warehouses," Goss admonished one day when Poe attempted to take a shortcut home but got lost in the maze of oppressive concrete-block buildings.

"Heed his words, Poe," Sister seconded. "At least in the city there are still some rules left standing, however corrupt they are."

Quillon Trench lived in the Los Angeles City Hall with his LAPD sycophants, but ran a nightclub for creatures of the night at the famed tubular glass towers of the Bonaventure Hotel. Kaleb Sainvire, known for his quieter tastes, inhabited the Los Angeles Central Library and used the beaux arts Biltmore Hotel as his official business space at night. Poe smiled grimly at the thought of these vampires having such high times at the expense of human misery.

"I'll blow up your glass showcase someday," Poe vowed.

Because it was a habit she hadn't yet licked, Poe berated herself, *This compulsive behavior has really gotta stop!* She bent down anyway to inspect her shoelaces once more. Her self-reprimands went nowhere.

Only when she was satisfied that they were double-knotted did Poe hop on her Vespa. She placed an Uzi in the basket, adjusted her two guns of choice in her shoulder holster, rearranged her backpack over her trench coat, and pulled the hood more securely about her face. She turned the key, and the engine sparked to life at once. *Good ol' reliable Vespa.*

The darkening sky quickened the beat of her heart. Just to satisfy her many compulsions, Poe checked her watch. It was a little after one. She should have left earlier, but she took hours to psyche herself up to leave the bunker and get her ride. The cloudy skies made her nervous.

The thought of Goss' friendly three-legged hound named Legs gave her a warm feeling. Instantly it vanished because Legs' face was replaced by an image of Penny, Goss' other dog, a ratty-looking terrier mix with the coarsest dirty-white hair there ever was.

"I wouldn't mind seeing that little rodent drained of blood," she sniffed. "I still have a loud scar on my ankle from her bite eight years ago."

So deep was her animosity toward Penny that Poe soon forgot her fear of the outdoors. Her little Vespa, easily maneuverable through the blocked streets despite the partial floods, fractured asphalt, and massive weeds, delivered her to the Eastern Columbia building in no time. The rabid street dogs milling about the intersection scampered to the shadows. They did not like the buzz of the engine.

Poe parked her bike round the corner from the building. She put the key, strung on an extra long shoelace, back around her neck. She could put her idol, Mr. T, to shame with the array of necklaces she wore. She pulled out an ancient breath mint from a pillbox around her neck and popped it in her mouth. As a force of habit, Poe kissed the rosary cross Sister Ann had given her for luck even though it didn't do squat to vamps.

She clamped a hand over her mouth.

She saw her startling reflection on the window of Goss' tower and instead of a vampire killer, Poe looked more like a vampire chump. The bulky pack on her back gave her a Quasimodo bulge, and her wet and scarred face made her look depraved. She held the small Uzi at the ready and hurried into the green deco building.

Goss was as paranoid as Poe when it came to home safety. A year earlier, he had booby-trapped thirteen flights of stairs and rigged all but one elevator to be permanently disabled. In order to get it to open at the bottom floor, a code had to be entered correctly.

"You're a hundred times more paranoid than me, Goss," she accused.

If incorrect numbers were punched, the elevator would open and deposit the invaders onto the thirteenth floor where Goss would be waiting for them, or climb back down the emergency staircase, booby-trapped with exploding holy water and shrapnel. Only the three knew which steps to avoid down the thirteen flights. Poe had suffered dozens of nightmares about forgetting which stairs to dodge in the dark.

She stood in the lobby and entered the over-the-top sixteen-digit access code. The asthmatic wheeze of an old descending elevator filled the silence. Just in case, her finger touched the hammer of the Uzi. Her ears stood at attention and burned with fever.

"No fucking gits, please," she prayed.

Her prayers were answered as the doors opened to an empty elevator car. She stepped in and blew out a shaky breath. Goss lived at the floor where the giant clock was perched. The elevator rose and opened to an almost cylindrical room tastefully decorated in a Danish Modern motif, where a sprinkling of pilfered Diebenkorn and Picasso paintings hung on the walls. She had helped him pick out the Diebenkorn at the MOCA museum. Apparently none of the vampire looters thought much of such a plain painting. The strange feeling of nostalgia was so acute that Poe clutched the rosary around her neck with a ferocious grip.

"Mess with my friends and I'll kill you slowly," she threatened the elevator.

Instant relief washed through Poe as she spied the dozing head of her friend, his giant feet draped over the couch arm. She was going to give him the biggest kiss ever. Then Poe realized that Penny and Legs were nowhere to be seen. They may have been a raggedy couple of canines, but they were excellent guard dogs. Their barking and snarling usually alerted Goss to the elevator's every movement.

The Uzi shook in her hands, but she prayed to her patron saints, Bruce, Ali, and Xena, for courage.

"G-G-Goss," she called, butchering his name in stutterspeak. She cleared her throat and tried again, at the same time sweeping the room with her eyes. "Goss. The boys are w-waiting downstairs. You'll never believe how big and muscular they've become. They, um, only eat chocolate steroids these days."

Her friend didn't even stir. "They brought the flame throwers and bazookas." She walked closer to the couch where her friend looked to be asleep. At least, she prayed that he was sleeping.

"They'll be up here any–"

She gagged. Her friend's face was ashen. His left arm hung lifeless to the floor. Blood trickled from the needle in his arm onto an overflowing makeshift container. A ballooning stain on the vanilla rug gave Poe pause. An unconscious Sister Ann lay where the coffee table used to be. Her mouth was open as if she couldn't gulp in enough oxygen. Her habit was tainted with splotches of blood. Legs was dead, his head twisted in a strange angle. Penny, the dog she had cursed, was the only one of the group to acknowledge her with terrified eyes. She had two broken legs, and blood trickled from her mouth. The attackers had cut off her tongue.

Even before "Jesus!" came out of Poe's mouth, an undernourished halfdead with Gatorade strength fell from the ceiling, landing feet first between her unconscious friends. The ceiling dweller hissed, showing a mouthful of missing teeth but for two yellow fangs. From the kitchen area came two gold encrusted leeches carrying machetes and guns. Another emerged from behind the powder blue curtains.

"Don't even think about it, little chick. You're outnumbered," the scrawny, pockmarked halfhead with a tan warned. *Who ever said vampires were attractive?* "If your big friend here and his Chilly Willy chum couldn't take care of us, what makes you think you or your imaginary m-m-muscled boys can?"

Poe looked down at the two friends she considered family, and for some reason she did not care anymore. If she died, big whoop. There was nothing left for her. Then the inimitable voice in her head said, *Snap out of it!* and the self-pity ended there. If she was going to croak that day, she was going the JKD way and take out as many as she could. She would not be made into cattle or a stinking vampire. Hell would freeze over before she lay bloodless and dead on the floor next to her friends.

She nodded, trying to look scared which wasn't hard. "W-what do you w-want me to do?"

The leader smiled, pleased by her quick acquiescence. "That's a good girl. Just drop your gun, and you'll be treated like candy."

"I'll do whatever you say. Just d-don't hurt me," Poe said in her most childish voice, which came out as a croak since her voice was quite deep for a girl.

"Can't wait to re-slice that caterpillar of a scar," said one of the stoner leeches, but the tanned halfdead quickly silenced him.

"You're not slicing anything, leech. You, girl, put your weapons down on the floor," he ordered. "Slow like a snail."

"Y-yes. Please don't shoot me."

"You're the freshest dish anyone's come across in years. No one's gonna do no shooting, girl," said the halfdead gallantly.

Poe lowered the strap of the Uzi, as if to lay the weapon on the ground. With a whip of a hand, the Uzi snapped into her palm, spraying a round of bullets. The halfdead was showered first, his chest and head eviscerated. The leeches, not at all slow to react, dashed behind the marble columns and shot at her from every direction. Poe, invigorated by fear, adrenaline, and hate, dove to the ground, making sure not to step on Sister Ann and the dogs.

Peeking from the floor, she spied an ankle and fired. A body fell clutching at his splintered anklebone. Poe finished him off before he ruined her eardrums. Two left. Her Uzi locked, refusing to fire. *Jesus, Mary, and Joseph, not now!* She took out her Walther PPK and Beretta, cursing the wretchedly unreliable Uzi. She sat up, careful to keep her head low. A squeak of pain nearly caused her to jump and be a human target for leech heshers. She had accidentally stepped on Penny's injured foot.

"Sorry," she whispered apologetically to the suffering dog.

Poe touched Penny's neck with the tip of her smoking Beretta and vowed, "If I get out of here alive, I promise I'll take you with me."

"You're done for, assholes!" she declared. She lunged and ran at the two leeches, guns blazing. With her right hand she shot leech one dead center in the forehead. With her left, leech two got it in the heart and eye.

Like a crazed hyena, Poe ran around the suite, checking out the ceiling, bathroom, columns and nooks. Only when she was sure that the home was secure did she re-sheath her guns and put a new clip in the Uzi. To make sure, she looked under the king-size bed. Instead of vampires, she found a gift-wrapped box with her name written on it. The sight almost undid her. Shaking, she brought the box to the living room and placed it beside Goss.

Poe pulled off Goss' intravenous drip that was pumping hardly more than air, and she checked for a pulse. Her most brave and tender friend was dead. She turned her attention to the nun, who lay unmoving on the floor. On her arm were days of needle marks. She, like Goss, was lifeless. Not since her parents' and siblings' deaths did she feel this awful, so awful that she wanted to puke her entrails out. She was alone. Again.

Sister Ann and Goss, her second family, had taught her how to fight back in this horrific city overrun by thugs and bloodsuckers. They treated her like kin. Poe had the urge to shoot herself. If she had left the safety of her bunker days earlier, she could have done something to help her friends.

"Fuck me and my goddamned phobias!" Poe cried, smacking her forehead with her palm several times. She wiped an errant tear. She didn't even deserve the comfort of a good cry.

Poe stroked Sister Ann's icy neck. Unlike Goss, she had not been bitten. Sister once said that no creature of the dark would dare bite a nun. She turned Goss' head and found marks.

"Jesus Christ!" she cried in frustration.

It was then that Sister Ann blinked open, a hoarse sound emitting from her throat.

"Holy God," said Poe, pulling out a bottle from her pack and pouring some water into Sister's open mouth.

"Do not," began Sister, coughing. "Do not use the Lord's name in vain, Julia Poe," she said tiredly.

"Sorry, Sister. Are you alright?"

Sister shifted her position and attempted to sit up. Poe helped her. "I feel like hell. Go slice some lemons.

They're in Goss' cupboard." She stared at the discolored face of Goss.

"They'll be back soon," said Sister Ann when Poe came back with four sliced lemons. "Better cut off Goss' head. He'd a wanted it that way."

"But there's no hole in his head."

"Doesn't matter. They'd bitten him several times. I'd do it, but I'm weak."

Remembering the pact with her friend, Poe swallowed her disgust and shot Goss in the heart with a holy water bullet.

"Sorry, doggy," she apologized to Penny's tongueless whimper as she pulled out a battery-operated meat carver from her pack. With numb efficiency, she cut off the head of her friend. She flung the bespattered carver once the deed was done. Lifting the heavy bloodless head of Goss put a permanent frost in her heart. She placed the head in a pillowcase and covered his body with a sheet.

"I'm so sorry, Sister, for being a coward," Poe said as she dropped Goss' head down the garbage chute. "Sorry, Goss. I let you down after all you've done for me. I'll be brave from now on and kill as many of them as I can." She listened to his head banging against dirty metal as it made its way down the shaft.

"Don't take it so hard, child," said Sister Ann, gulping down the rest of the water. "Goss knew it would end bloody."

Poe sniffed, crouching over Penny. "Hold on for a while longer," she said to the dog with wiry hair. "I'll get you out of here, I promise!"

Poe could do nothing about the dog's tongue. All she could hope for was that the bloody wound would coagulate on its own. She wrapped the shaking dog in her trench coat and stuffed her in the pack, scruffy head sticking out.

Sister got unsteadily to her feet and held to the arm of the couch. "Better scoot. They're bound to check on their friends. They know you're here by now."

Because she didn't deserve a present from a friend whom she had betrayed, Poe left the unopened box on Goss' stomach. She doused the body with holy water and sprinkled the rest all over Legs. Penny whimpered, tightly bound inside the pack.

"Sorry about being mean to you before, doggie," Poe apologized, feeling awful for the injured scruffy dog. The dog whimpered again in response, turning her head toward the elevator, almost as if in warning. Eyes widening, Poe dashed to the elevator, placing her palm on the cool metal surface. Sure enough, she felt a vibration.

"Oh shit," she groaned.

"Give me a gun," said Sister Ann. She deftly caught the .22 Poe tossed her way.

"You're not fit, Sister. Get by the staircase and let me handle this." Before the nun could protest, Poe shook her head. "Don't fight me now, Sis. I need you safe. I can't be alone again."

Reluctantly the nun struggled to the emergency exit to the west side of the pad. She was dizzy and shaken from her ordeal. "I'll watch you from here."

Slinging the pack over her shoulders, Poe pointed her Uzi at the elevator and prayed that the gun wouldn't jam. Her left hand slid down to the Velcro pockets of her green army pants. She had at least three rounds per handgun in each pocket.

"Nice work leaving the incendiaries underground," she chided herself. Realistically, explosives would most likely have left everyone permanently dead, including herself in such a confined space as Goss'. Her eyes quickly darted down to her shoes. Just fine. She was ready.

Hate and guilt overpowered her fear, and when the elevator door opened, she let the eight halfdeads and leeches have it. Shrieks and cursing accompanied the sound of her bullets ricocheting, hitting steel and flesh alike. She didn't know the body count because the bullet-ridden elevator door closed again. Not waiting for their return, Poe said a quick goodbye to Goss and the loyal dog, Legs.

"I'm sorry about this. If I had just left sooner..." She stopped to pick up an old picture I.D. of Goss on the floor and sped down the emergency staircase, which Sister swung open for her. She was flabbergasted to read that Goss' real name was Fred Beaver.

"A dorky name," Poe said to no one in particular. "I'd change my name, too."

"Who's a dork?"

"Goss' name, Sister. Very funny sounding."

"Can't help that. In any case, you've done fine, Poe. You've done me proud," said Sister Ann, accepting Poe's arm as they made their way down the stairs. She patted the stake in her pocket she'd found at Goss'.

"Shoot! This whole booby trap thing is confusing!"

"Just remember not to step on the first, third, sixth, and eleventh steps between landings," warned Sister.

The trek down was difficult since they were on the thirteenth floor, and the one energy saving light bulb per floor made the journey dark and perilous. One false step and she and Penny were goners. She had to rescue Penny and Sister so she could redeem herself in Goss' estimation.

An explosion two flights above let her know that vampires and leeches were in pursuit. Soon after, a halfdead or leech tripped a booby trap a few floors beneath. The enemy was above and below them. The feeling of panic burgeoned, getting more pregnant by the second.

"I'm going to be sick," she said to the nun, swallowing a heave. "I try to only battle sleeping vampires."

"You did a damn fine job a few weeks back," muttered Sister, breathing erratically. Twice she'd paused to vomit and steady herself. "Not to mention today."

The darkness, smoke, and explosions were making it horribly difficult for Poe to concentrate on counting the stairs accurately, let alone practice her breathing exercises while swallowing bile. Twice they had to retrace their steps to start the count all over again. She was almost hyperventilating from sheer terror.

Penny stopped squirming inside her pack. "Please don't be dead."

She prayed to whoever was listening to keep the little dog alive and Sister conscious. It was vital to have friends during trying times.

"I need a reason to stay alive," Poe gritted under her breath. "Watching all the movies ever made and killing vampires doesn't cut it."

On the eleventh floor, a raging halfdead missing a nose nearly sliced Poe open with a twenty-inch machete. She wouldn't have seen him had his blade not reflected the weak glow of the light bulb.

"Watch out!" cried Sister Ann as she slipped on the landing.

Poe hung left to avoid the menacing steel as Sister Ann let a torrent of bullets hit the creature. If he wasn't dead yet, the trip-switch his body fell on did the job, exploding a round of puncturing nails and broken glass.

"No!" Poe shrieked as an errant nail lodged into her left thigh, causing her to almost fall back onto the rigged stairs. She waited for the ringing in her ears to stop then dug out the rusty four-inch nail and shoved it in the left eye of a dwarf vampire that abruptly appeared from between the stairwell grates. "What's this? A Fellini hallucination?"

The little creature covered his eyes and shrieked, "Fuck you!" to Poe over and over. Poe had the urge to give Sister Ann a hug for the nun had insisted that she forget her needle phobia and get rabies and tetanus shots, all good for ten years.

Sister Ann plugged the dwarf with her remaining bullets to shut him up. "I need more bullets, Poe."

With shaking hands, Poe handed the nun a Ziploc full of .22 bullets.

"What the heck do we do now?" Poe asked, lightly smacking her ears to get the ringing to go away.

"Let's hope that's the last of the little people."

"Crap. I forgot the count."

Either the explosion or the pain in her leg distracted her enough to forget the stair count. It was too dark to count the steps up and the steps down below. She gripped her Uzi, briefly thinking about strategy, when Penny's whimper prodded her to keep going. The dog was still alive! The little mite was encouraging them.

"Hold on, little Penny. I'm gonna get us out of here real soon. Sister, do you think you can slide down the handrail without toppling over?"

"No. But we don't have a choice now, do we?" The nun looked spectral in her bloody wimple and habit in the tiny light of the staircase.

"I'll go first so I can stop you from falling over."

"With my bulk? It'll take a miracle." She straddled the railing after Poe and slowly, shakily, made her way down the next level. Poe slid down until the end of the curve and the beginning of a new flight of stairs was distinguishable by feel. She jumped down at the landing and caught Sister Ann. Once again, they started the count.

Nothing untoward happened, only an occasional explosion above the stairs brought on by trip wires to unsuspecting vampire minions, until they hit the eighth floor. There a vampire actually flew at her, catching her by the throat, nearly dragging her to the wired eleventh step. She blasted the flying vermin in the leg, but the injury to the enemy only fueled wrath. Sister, fighting dizziness, couldn't take a shot.

"Kid, don't you know the golden rule?" the vampire with a unibrow asked.

"No, Frida," Poe managed to squeak out. "I guess I don't."

"You can't just go around shooting vampires." The vampire backhanded her with such force that she ended up flat on her butt with a resonant thud on the seventh floor landing. Unlike the moderate body temperature of halfdeads, this vampire's hand was cold to say the least. She tasted warm metallic blood on her lips and ran an investigative tongue over her teeth. Complete and cavity-free teeth were very important to Poe.

"Ouch, that hurt," she said to the dog who kept silent. Only when the vampire's dark high heel shoes floated next to her forehead did Poe realize that the

Bert creature was a woman. Frida Kahlo's eyebrows looked tame in comparison to Berta's caterpillar brow.

Woman or not, Poe shot her private parts, heart, and head from the ground, showering herself with vampire fluids and hot shells. She knew she would be extremely bruised and sore the next day – if she survived that long. A sickening thought came to her. *Why would a full-blooded vampire come out this early in the day?* Without wanting, but knowing she had no choice, Poe pressed the chrono light button on her limited edition Iron Giant watch. It was 4:49pm.

"Jesus, where did the time go? Is it Double-Daylight Savings Time?" she asked the dog while wiping gut from her person. They were moving too slow. She climbed up once more and helped Sister descend the stairs.

"Did I hear you use the Lord's name in vain again?"

"Sorry. Couldn't help myself. There was this hairy woman and–"

"Poe, this is your soul we're talking about!" complained the nun.

To keep from getting annoyed, Poe took out some holy water in a spray bottle and dangled it from her belt, making her look like a window washer. Her Rambo knife was hooked on her belt already. Poe looked down at her shoes, but couldn't see well enough to check if her laces were still in position.

Two vampires flew down at them. Poe managed to shoot one dead, but the other was too quick. It slashed Sister Ann's shoulder as it landed on the steps, drawing blood.

All Poe remembered was the cry from Penny as the two of them were thrown against the wall, landing with a groan on a platform. Her Uzi, cut in two by vampire nails, lay on her stomach.

"Sorry, Penny," Poe whispered. Her jaw hurt.

Death was so close, Poe could taste it. The movement was too quick for the human eye. The vampire's tongue had snaked out to lick the blood on her cut lips, and he smiled at her. When the bombastic undead's white face lowered to her neck, his reddened mouth parting for a bite, Poe was just able to grab her holy water and squirt it into his throat. The vampire's scream sounded like a pig being butchered in the PETA video she had lifted two years ago. *Faces of Death* had nothing on undercover PETA exclusives. The scream was terrible, but Poe preferred it to the sound of her blood slowly drained by fanged muthas. Her James Bond gun ended the squeal.

Respite was not to be had by Penny, Poe, or Sister Ann. At the hand of five, all the lights in the building went dead, even the sickly one-bulb lights in the stairwells. With shaky hands, Poe fumbled for the much-maligned headlamp in her pack. Without it, Poe knew they were dead. Vampires had excellent night vision. She did not.

"Sister. Do you need me to come get you?"

"Eleven, twelve, thirteen," the nun counted to the next landing. "No thank you."

"Sister, you're bleeding!"

"It's nothing, girl. I've been cut worse before. Lead the way with that light."

"You know, doggie," Poe said softly to dispel her fears. "I've been a full-fledged smuggler for years, but nothing like this has ever happened. This is a nightmare."

"Don't be negative, Poe. Nothing good ever comes out of negativity."

Even with the miserable headlamp, she could scarcely see the gun in her right hand. She stopped talking to Sister Ann and the dog. Between trying to see, trying to count, and trying to aim at anything that moved, Poe was a basket case. Like an errant fly buzzing too near her ear, Poe waved away the thought of the lobby waiting outside the door of the stairwell.

Since no further incidents plagued them, Poe was able to concentrate on counting down the sixth floor, then the fifth, then the–

"Crud!" screamed Poe, whose scalp felt like it was on fire.

A pudgy male paw grabbed at her hair from the air until her feet no longer touched the ground. She clutched at the cold hand and tried to pry the dead fingers away. She was going to go bald, Poe thought absurdly. Then she remembered the present from Sister Ann on her 17th birthday – her Rambo knife.

The fall to the third floor was nasty after she hacked at the intractable hand. Her funny bone hit the railing and she screamed out a family of expletives. The severed hand continued to pull at her hair from sheer reflex. Pissed, bruised, and on the verge of insanity, Poe grabbed her spray bottle and blasted away at the squirming digits.

"Get off me, crummy hand!"

The hand hissed with exploding pustules and left yet more ooze on Poe. She flicked the smoking flesh off her head and watched out for a single-handed vampire. The creature did not come, but another did. Still holding the spray bottle, Poe neglected to grab her gun. The only thing she could do was spray ineffectually at the hovering vampire until she could unsheathe the weapon. With a flick of the vampire's hand, both the Beretta and the spray bottle clanged on the marble stairs. The container fell on a trip-wired step and exploded, spraying holy water at Poe and her vampire companion.

Poe thanked whoever was looking out for her and jumped on the smoking fallen vampire at her feet. She lunged at the undead with the full force of her five-foot-two-and-three-quarter frame and drove her wrist knife into the creature's dead heart.

"See that, you ass wipe!" Poe screeched, slashing away. "You mess with me, you die a one-time death!" She was on the verge of tears and hysterics.

Her headlamp was smashed somewhere on the steps, and she couldn't see an inch ahead.

The Rambo knife and the beloved Beretta were lost. Poe wiped away cowardly tears. She felt silly to fret over lost things. After all, they could be replaced. "Sister? Where are you?"

"I'm here," she said, sliding erratically down the handrail.

Poe caught her voluminous rear end and helped her down. The handrail, Poe noticed, was slick with Sister's blood.

Poe reached for the two weapons she had left, her faithful James, the Walther PPK and her Faka knife. She transferred the extra magazines from her leg pockets to her waist and handed the wrist knife to Sister.

"Sorry, but there's only one gun left," she said miserably.

"Don't apologize, child. You've always been a better shot than me, even when I wasn't seeing double."

"So if we open that door, it'll be *Butch Cassidy and the Sundance Kid* time. You know that, right, Sister?"

"I've been ready to die since this whole Armageddon started. Don't worry about me," she said, clutching her stake.

"Remember, doggy. Shoot, release, and reload," Poe said, voice quivering. She knew she had to keep her shit together. There was more than a good chance that they would be overtaken. If so, she had to be brave enough to shoot Penny, Sister Ann, and herself.

"Just don't let us be bloodsucker fodder," the nun intoned in her Tennessee twang.

"You said it, Sis. And um," she began, finding it difficult to speak. "I'm sorry for not coming sooner."

"Child, you're here now. I thank you for that."

Feeling for the last of the holy water in her pack, Poe was heartened somewhat when Penny licked her hand. She patted the dog's head and doused her with holy water. She sprinkled Sister Ann and herself as well.

Her pack again secure on her back and the rosary cross kissed, Poe hobbled down the last steps with an exhausted Sister Ann. Her gun was drawn and her bottle of garlic water was in her other hand. She took a deep breath and stepped into the lobby of the Eastern Columbia Building.

Blinded!

The sudden emergence into a brilliantly lit room hurt more than her eyes. Defending herself became a problematic. Her eyes, wet from the lights and possibly from defeat, were forced open until they adjusted to the bright hotel lobby.

"Motherfu–"

Surrounding them were over two dozen children of the night and their leech groupies. Some grinned while others cast looks of contempt. They had not forgotten the murder of their friends. An especially belligerent, thickly mustached undead had to be restrained by two vampires from attacking her.

"I'm going to squash that little shit!" he gritted. The vampire was missing a hand that would never regenerate because of Poe.

We're dead, thought Poe. She gripped her gun and spray bottle even tighter, shielding the nun with her back. She flicked her eyes about the group. Close to the end, Poe's most significant thought was, *Some of these vampires are really, really ugly. Whoever said they were–*

Her scattershot musings were interrupted when a mixed diaspora of vampires, humans, and subhumans parted dramatically, making way for an immaculately attired vampire in a black turtleneck and his entourage of mustached Village People wannabes.

"Oh no," groaned Poe. "Quillon Trench and his LAPD goons." They were truly dead. She swallowed. Her throat was parched from all the killing and dodging. She stayed quiet and alert, not daring to make any threats or beg pathetically for her life. They would not understand a word she would say anyway. She was so nervous that only rat-a-tat stuttering would come out. To top it off, she was on the verge of urinating. If only she had packed explosives.

Trench dared to approach, undeterred by Poe's spray bottle. He was a pleasant looking man of the Velvet Underground variety. He broke the mold by not being as malignantly hideous as his minions. In his perpetual thirties, the man exuded an aura of arrogance. His mid-neck reddish-brown hair was gelled back, leaving a few well-placed curls to escape.

"Sister Ann," he nodded at the nun trying her hardest not to look woozy. "I see no one had the balls to puncture your neck. It must be the habit."

"Must be my superpowers," said the nun, tracing her cross and clutching the stake with her other hand.

"And you're the human that's been causing all this commotion, the one we set this elaborate trap for. You see, we had a feeling you'd be coming back for Goss and the nun." He looked the girl up and down like she was for sale then tapped his nose. "And from the smell of you, one of my favorite women is dead." He came closer as if for a better sniff, but Poe would not have it. She thrust her gun at the slick vampire to warn him that he was close enough. At this, Trench's lips trembled as he tried to keep from laughing.

"Jasmina. You've killed my beautiful Jasmina. Great dresser but for the shoes. Never understood her fondness for Walmart."

"The unibrow," Poe answered automatically.

"What can I say?" Quillon shrugged his shoulders. "She's of Eastern European stock." A smile lingered as he spoke. "Am I to believe that you are the supposed leader of an underground network of hundreds of human survivors? I expected someone larger."

What the freak are you talking about? Poe thought silently. She wanted so badly to turn to the nun and ask what the fuck was going on. She allowed Quillon to do all the talking.

"Do you deny this, little girl?"

Again, Poe didn't say a thing. The head vampire sighed, giving her another once over. She hated being called *little.* In her mind, she was five-foot-seven, for crying out loud.

My folks were decent-sized. If it weren't for poor diet and stress, I'd tower over Mr. Turtleneck.

"Your friend, Fred Beaver, also known as Goss, told us all about your little network. Over two hundred humans in our downtown playland." He looked pointedly at her. "Your fat nun told us the same thing. They must be telling the truth. Nuns don't lie."

The vampire's blue eyes darkened, annoyed at Poe's silence. "I assume you're the leader now since your Goss is dead and the Flying Nun there is about to keel over."

Poe bit back a pain in her throat that could at any second betray her. She inhaled deeply, willing her voice not to fail. Slowly enunciating each word, Poe finally spoke.

"There's no network. Just the three of us." *There. I did it. No stuttering gibberish whatsoever.*

"Ah, so our little rebel finally speaks. And what a voice she has for one so young." His own voice was caressing, but Poe wasn't fooled. He had referred to Sister Ann as fat. She was stocky and muscular, but she wasn't fat. *And even if she was, who gave a fig!* The standards of vampires were worse than all the magazine diet gurus combined that still beleaguered living room coffee tables.

"She's Julia without a surname, isn't she, Ann? The mythical secret weapon you were telling us about."

Sister Ann merely narrowed her eyes, not saying a word.

Poe winced at hearing her first name. No one called her Julia anymore. Only Poe, her last name.

The vampire, tickled by her obvious surprise at his vast knowledge of the underground, including her name, laughed.

"Well, Julia, stop acting the ignorant bumpkin, and let us know where we can find your other friends. I am most anxious to retrieve my stolen cattle and add a few more to my stock."

"I told you, there are only the three–"

"I'm hungry, I'm bored, and I'm quite tired of this conversation. Scar and all, I want to have you for dinner tonight. What a treat to have someone so obviously untouched and deliciously young." The smile on his lips turned into a tight line. His eyes glinted. Poe would have retreated a step if it weren't for the emergency door at their back.

"I would dearly love to have you replace Jasmina. You have a pleasing figure and face despite the mark, but I'll have no problem turning you over to Clyde and Bergman over there." Trench indicated a leech and vampire with unhygienically long mustaches that arched chinward.

Poe, who had been conjuring Butch, Sundance, and Cleopatra Jones inside herself, couldn't take it anymore. She was not going to be turned into a vampire slut or a luau centerpiece.

"Fine. My blood tastes like chewed aspirin, and my feet are way too wide for high heels," Poe said, her voice strong. She couldn't afford to stutter and appear weak. "There are over a thousand of us in the city, even more in the 'burbs." She let this sit for a moment until the faces of Trench and his pals turned from grinning buffoons into nervous jackasses.

"Some are straight-away human, some recovering ex-cattle. They're all well armed like me." Her cheeks were hot and her palms sweaty, but she had forgotten her speech impediment. Too bad she had one lousy gun to her name.

"They have acres and acres of garlic bulbs." She permitted herself a slight smile as some of the so-called immortals shuddered. For effect, Poe raised her own brow at the goon on Trench's left. The vamp scooted back as quickly as an undead could. "Our plan is to hose down vampires with garlic water as they sleep during the day. Maybe decapitate a few heads."

"You are sorely exaggerating, *Julia*. A mere two hundred were mentioned by your friends. Now you say there are thousands."

"I didn't say thousands, *Quillon*. I said over a thousand." Trench's surprise at the use of his first name was well worth dying for. The strength in her voice pleased her. "My death will only piss them off since they see me as a sort of leader, and I feel sorry for the dingbats who sleep in attics all day."

"Nun, is what she says true?"

Sister shrugged tiredly. "She's the savior, and saviors don't lie."

"Well, Queen Julia, you won't die so easily. You might just prevent me from becoming bored the next ten years until I find another pretty face with guts. I am rather looking forward to putting a hole in your skull, my beauty, and spitting blood into your brain." As if to grind more salt in the wound, Trench added, "But I'll be on the lookout for a face without a scar."

Maybe it was the mention of her scar or the spitting blood in her brain part that did it, and she really did not care. She shot Trench in the chest and sprayed his face with holy water.

"Ahhh!" he screamed, clutching his burning face. "Kill her!"

Quillon's screams were awful, indeed, but she didn't have time to dwell because bedlam reigned supreme. His bodyguards carried him a distance away from the melee. Poe high-kicked the Lou Reed poser to the sidelines. Some vampires took to the air while the rest bided for an opportunity to get at her. The leeches and halfdeads scattered to desks, couches, and whatever solid lumps of furniture they could hide behind. Every single undead wore the expression of livid hate.

"Sister, keep close to me," she whispered behind her. In a booming voice Poe taunted, "You idiots wanna follow your leader, huh?" Teeth, pallor of skin, and the rise and fall of the chest distinguished the creatures before her. She shot two vampires, two leeches, and another suntanned halfdead in succession. She knew that replacing the magazine was going to be tricky because her spray bottle would have to cover her.

When the gun clicked empty, she released the clip. Before she could reload, a vamp flew at her and kicked at the gun but missed. Sister Ann rammed her stake into his back.

Poe's chest burned as it absorbed the brunt of the blow. She almost collapsed but had the foresight to replace the magazine first. By the time another vampire appeared, Poe was ready.

"Fucker!" she screamed, shooting the vampire's foot and kicking him in the chest. For a second there, she thought she heard ribs breaking. Poe finished him off when he fell on the floor squawking like a mallard during Wisconsin duck season.

The stairway emergency exit door flung open and a halfdead with a rosy complexion jumped out, grabbing her from behind. Sister Ann tried to kick his leg from under him, but she was too weak. Fuming, the creature embedded his index finger into Sister Ann's left eye socket. Poe did not see the nun crumple to the ground.

"You stupid little cunt! I'm going to–"

Poe stomped her right shoe down the tender part of his foot as the "Grab Twist and Pull" self-defense video had taught her, and she rammed her elbows into his ribs.

"I hate the c-word, asshole!" Poe squeezed out. Once her arms were free, she shot the bastard in the face. "Just so you know. For future reference and all that."

From the corner of her eye, she witnessed a vampire carrying Trench outside. Another vampire locked the front door as soon as their master left the building. They were going to execute Poe and Sister Ann in the lobby. *Jesus, Mary, and Joseph!* With her back to the wall, she moved away from the stairwell.

"Sister, keep close to me!" she ordered. When the nun didn't respond, she looked behind her only to see Sister Ann twitching on the ground. "No! Sister!"

The body went still, blood oozing from the socket.

Poe released a strangulating screech, so full of grief and frustration that the creatures present gave her a temporary berth. Again, the voice in her head set her right. *It's not over yet*, it said. *Buck up. She doesn't want you to die this way.*

She pulled her gaze from Sister Ann's body, looking up, down, sideways at anything that might aid her. Vampires were moving toward her from every corner.

Then she saw the glass wall on the west side of the building. Her moped would be right around the corner. *I could either die in this miserable art fucking deco building or die outside in the rain.* She'd take the outdoors anytime. Blasting her gun and squirting her bottle, Poe ran for it. Two shots cracked the window into tiny veins. With her remaining strength, Poe booked it and slammed the side of her body against the spiderwebbed window, praying it would shatter.

"I'm sorry!" she bellowed to her dead friends.

She fell hard on the wet pavement outside.

Penny whimpered once in the backpack and quieted down again. Shards of glass lodged in Poe's skin made getting up difficult.

"Ouch!" Poe belted out. Vampires soared out of the jagged hole she created and hovered above her, followed by the humans and subhumans who couldn't fly. Poe shot at the first two vampires that flitted toward her and chunks flew everywhere. She inhaled sharply as her bleeding shard-infested right hand pulled the trigger.

With much effort, Poe hobbled over to where her Vespa was parked. She reloaded the last of her Walther PPK cartridges and sprayed the final few drops of garlic water onto vampire legs that dared scoop down too close. The bottle, completely empty, she tossed at the nearest halfdead who hopped back fearfully. The creature's face would have made her howl in laughter a week before, but not then when she was about to die. She switched the gun to her left hand, the less injured of the two.

"*Hijo de puta*," escaped her lips. Her heart banged gong-clangs, for her beloved avocado green moped was nowhere in sight. She and Penny were truly dead. She had less than nine bullets left and at least a dozen vampires and their minions were still in pursuit. Best case, she could shoot seven of them, saving the last bullets for Penny and her.

"Give up, bitch!" Pengle, the one-handed vampire she had hacked, screamed. He hid behind a group of leeches. "Your life's over. Might as well face up to it."

"That's telling her, Pengle," somebody from the crowd seconded, laughing.

"Are you listening to yourself?" Poe spat. "You're the one that's dead and can't admit it. Go back to the grave and let the worms have you!"

Enraged, Poe shot in his direction and killed a leech instead. A fresh recruit of vampires wearing Kevlar vests marched boldly toward her, unafraid of her gun.

"Fucking cops," she muttered.

Without even cringing, Poe shattered two vampire heads, a kneecap, and a neck before the rest scattered. Zombie Hunt and Sister Ann, the dead aim from Tennessee, had taught her well.

One bullet left. She prayed that Penny was already dead because the remaining bullet was hers alone. Without further ado, she placed James, the trusted gun, to her ear and fired.

CHAPTER 3—A NEW WORLD UPSIDE DOWN

A SWISH OF WIND smacked her face. Her trusted James clanged on the sidewalk, sliced in two like her Uzi.

When Poe opened her eyes, the same raging vampires hissed malevolently. The gun she held to her head lay by her feet in pieces, and a tall man she'd never seen before stood inches from her. His middle finger that looked more like a mini-sword retracted into a regular size digit.

He cut up my James! thought Poe with annoyance, her fear momentarily overshadowed.

He gave a cursory glance at Poe before turning his back. But it was enough. It was as if his strange eyes branded her synapses, leaving them etched in her mind.

"Go home, all of you," the looming figure said with a quiet voice resonating with authority and power. Only Pengle had the audacity to protest.

"This is none of your affair, Sainvire." He dragged out the name as if it left a trail of sticky dirt in his mouth. "She shot Trench and killed a score of our people. We have first rights."

"Wrong. I was the one who stopped her. She's mine," Sainvire answered tranquilly.

"You just got here," Pengle said as he shook his fistless hand at the master vampire. His face contorted with rage, and a perceptible trembling began from his knees to his bulky shoulders. "We were on the verge of capturing her."

"You mean her corpse, don't you?" His expression mimicked a smile that didn't quite reach his eyes. Without pomp and preamble, Sainvire pointed at the girl's Walther PPK on the wet pavement. The litter of bodies on the street that led to the hotel was not quite so easily forgotten. "As I understand, vampires can't lap up a dead human's blood. It would kill us."

"I lost my hand to that bitch," Pengle roared, raising his maimed left hand for effect. "So lay off."

"Sorry about your hand, Pengle, but if you have a problem with my claim then you can take it up with the Council," Sainvire retorted coolly, his expression benign. Pengle immediately took the look as insolence and arrogance that came with being a master vampire.

"The Council! Screw that! Why are you nosing around other people's business? Don't you have enough fresh necks for your straw? You have a library full of them," Pengle accused, dribbling with hate and envy.

Sainvire considered his words before saying, "Yes, I do have many necks to choose from. But not one this young."

Pengle's enhanced olfactory sensory neurons could smell the warm, iron tang of blood on Poe's injured skin, and he felt entitled. Most vampires were insulted by having to sup on cold refrigerated blood. He was one of them. He especially resented the privileged few who imbibed warm blood through straw attachments each night. Like many, Pengle believed in the thrill and excitement of the hunt. It was an innate right of the undead and shouldn't have been banned by the Council and irritating vampires like Kaleb Sainvire.

"You," Pengle bellowed, too angry to do anything but make a fist with his remaining hand. "You greedy–"

"Think what you want, Pengle, but she's leaving unharmed." He turned and faced Poe. The girl still reeled from pulling the trigger on herself. Even in the dimly illuminated street, she was startled by the silver-gray intensity of the notorious vampire's dark-rimmed eyes. Only the white line running vertically from the top of Sainvire's upper lip to his nostrils interrupted her perusal.

Before Poe could make sense of what was going on, Sainvire spoke. His voice was purposely low so no undead could overhear. "The moped is behind a garbage truck. Second alleyway to your right."

Poe stared mutely at him or rather his cleft scar. She felt like she ought to belt him one but was distracted by his nice manners. The vampire's mouth twitched in amusement. "Plenty of time to stare later, Poe. You've got to get out of here."

Her face immediately warmed. Without turning back, Poe ran, ignoring the wound in her thigh and the shards still embedded in her skin that burrowed deeper with every movement.

True to his word, the green Vespa was parked behind a garbage truck a short distance away. Poe took the key from around her neck, her fingers fumbling.

"Quit shaking, nincompoop," she ordered herself and hopped on her trusted vehicle. The Vespa's dependable engine burst to life. Maneuvering the little moped out of the clammy, cockroach-encrusted alleyway was cake.

"Penny girl, hope you're still holding on. Forgive me for wishing you dead back there. I meant what I said about needing a reason to live," she cooed tiredly to her new pet. "I'll treat you real good. You can't leave me."

The slick road wasn't as easy to manage in the dark, however, especially around the water-swept areas. Poe had no idea where she was going. It was too damn dark. She couldn't go directly to her bunker because she was sure an undead was on her tail already. She decided to lead whatever was following her down to Santee Alley, in the heart of the Fashion District.

"The whole world's a Skid Row cesspool," Poe whispered to the dog.

The freezing rain added to the physical and mental beating that left her blue and shaking. Her waterproof trench coat wrapped warmly about the little dog. Poe had nothing on but her black Pixies t-shirt full of holes and soaked army cargo pants. With no weapons of any sort, only candy bars as hard as shin bone, Poe almost wished that the vampires would just hurry up and finish her off.

She could have ended it with a bullet had it not been for Sainvire's interference. The creature was not ugly enough to be a wretched vampire.

"He didn't even look pasty!" she grumbled. She'd never heard of a vampire with healthy skin color unless they were halfdeads. Even Trench had the complexion of bleached rice.

"He knew the name I go by," Poe gritted, realizing too late.

Sainvire hadn't called her Julia like the contemptible Trench vampire. He called her by her last name – a name only Goss, Sister Ann, and a few smugglers knew about. Her two friends were dead.

Maybe Sainvire ordered their torture. Was he there when Goss was bled to death? The thought made her insides boil. She stopped being cold, her body shook with rage.

"You're dead, Sainvire," she promised, vowing that she would kill the bastard before offing herself. Poe cranked harder on the gas.

"Why didn't he let me kill myself or leave me behind for Pengle?" she asked the rain.

She knew the answer. He believed the horseradish Sister and Goss had spread; there were hundreds of organized humans waiting to stab, behead, and hack to pieces the city's vampire population while they slept. A vampire's worst nightmare to be sure. Her friends' only means of making their deaths meaningful was by chiseling away the undead's sense of safety.

They were able to fool Trench and Sainvire into thinking that they would be summarily executed. Very smart. Why, even Trench easily believed the hogwash she fed him about underground guerillas numbering over a thousand. To her knowledge, the outfit consisted of about three dozen, seven of whom she'd personally met.

She could feel it in the back of her neck. Somebody was following her, probably after some extra brownie points. Having the reflex of one acquainted with a two-wheeler late in life, Poe cranked the throttle nervously, causing the moped to skid into a pool of murky water that stank like shit marinade. The Vespa fell on its side and pinned Poe's injured leg. In that helpless position, two vampires advanced. They jogged. Some vampires had less impressive powers than others.

A golden-haired undead with a drawn-on pockmark on his chin hissed and roughly grabbed Poe by the shoulder. He wore a delicate cotton shirt with fluted 18th century buccaneer sleeves. Only the last few buttons from the mid-abdomen down were clasped, exposing his chesty hair. He wore red lipstick to boot.

"Great. Anne Rice fans," Poe muttered under her breath and rolled her eyes to the crying sky. His companion, a breathtaking Asian vampire with long, curly hair, appeared at his side. Her lacy bodice pushed up her ample bosom, barely covering her silver-dollar nipples. Silky lingerie from Frederick's of Hollywood completed her look. It was no wonder they let the non-white vamp hang around instead of giving her ethnic ass latrine duty.

"What did you utter, wretched girl? I didn't quite hear you," she said in a very affected British accent, her fangs elongating in the half-moonlight. Poe could swear she detected a Valley accent under the facade.

"I said," Poe answered hoarsely, attempting to unpin her injured leg, "you guys are swell. So original."

"It's very foolish of you to mock us," Lestupid butted in, running his press-on nails lightly along Poe's scar. He sounded like Keanu destroying Macbeth.

"Very foolish, indeed," Asian Marie Antoinhack hissed, licking her luscious lips.

"When did you guys turn? In the '80s? '90s? Somewhere in Encino, right?" Poe shook her head, far from being afraid. She'd cut off Goss' head and watched helplessly as Sister twitched her last breath on the lobby floor. These ridiculous posers in silk and velvet hardly incited fear in her. She just wanted to go home or be dead already. "So stupid. Pamela Anderson and Jean-Claude Van Damme could probably do better–"

The blond vampire buried his hand in Poe's hair and lifted her up like a rag doll. The moped made a watery thud sound as it fell to the gurgling asphalt when Poe's leg was freed.

"Iza, take the right. The left is mine." He indicated the throbbing pulse on each side of Poe's neck. He lost the shoddy English accent.

"With pleasure, lover," the woman purred, baring her fangs.

"I wouldn't d-do that if I were you," Poe stammered now that she realized she didn't want to be drained to death after all. At least not yet.

"And why not?" the gorgeous vamp asked, her rain-soaked nipple peeking.

"Because I ate stacks of garlic for lunch," she answered lamely. If only she had followed the ruckus in her head and actually chewed some garlic before heading out to Goss', she wouldn't have been in this situation.

"Cream of broccoli soup," the woman declared with a laugh. "And crackers. You ate soup and crackers."

"You can't fool my Iza," Blondie said. He shook his head in admonition. "She was a chef at Ginza Sushiko and knows her food."

"She's got broccoli flowerettes in her teeth," Iza stated flatly, clearly annoyed at her man. "And I told you to stop telling every jerk we encounter that I was a goddamn cook!"

While the two lovebirds bickered, Poe searched for the broccoli bit in her mouth with her tongue. *I can't believe I'm actually embarrassed by vamps that ransacked Hot Topic, the lamest commercial chain store of its kind*, Poe thought. Truly unpunk!

The two turned their attention back to her – their Double-Double Burger for the evening. This time they looked with malevolence and a united front. Poe closed her eyes, waiting for the twofold bite as she felt the couple's cold mouths descend on either side of her neck. *This is it? Dinner for two?*

Once again she was wrong. Instead of getting four fang holes, Poe simply fell onto the submerged pavement. She scrambled out of the way as the left half of Iza rained down from the heavens. When Poe looked up, she witnessed Kaleb Sainvire crack Blondie's head with a head bunt and stab the vampire in the heart with a fingernail, sharp as cut diamonds and lengthened at least twelve inches before her eyes.

Sainvire's nail reverted back to its natural length as soon as Blondie's twitching body splashed down on the wet ground. Like an eager mouth, the groove of his finger absorbed whatever juice kill clung on the nail.

Arm yourself, stupid, the voice in her head bullied. *His erector nails are bad enough, but he's Kaleb Sainvire*. She spotted a broken wood beam riddled with lengthy oxidized nails on the ground and picked it up. Before Sainvire could turn her way, Poe leaped and whacked the vampire across the back, grunting, "Take this!"

The vampire cursed.

Great. He's some sort of uber-vamp, Poe thought distractedly. Something was off about the master vampire, but she couldn't quite place her finger as to what it was.

The man staggered, touching his left shoulder as if in pain. "You better quit that, Poe," he said, his polite warning laced with menace.

"Go bury your face in your asshole," Poe spat, high on the pungent combination of fear and adrenaline. She struck him again on the skull, this time jumping higher to reach the tall man's tousled, wet head. The scattered nails sunk their rusty points.

Sainvire shook and turned to look at the soggy, undersized vampire rustler with a piece of wood in her hand. The head of a pitiful looking dog peered out of her backpack. Avoiding the vampire's angry gaze illuminated by the headlights of the Vespa, Poe lunged again, aiming for the face. Sainvire had enough.

"No more!" he ordered with barely controlled cool. The imposing vampire intercepted the beam and broke it in half on his knee, leaving Poe with a handful of splinters.

That's really it. The shithead Sainvire is going to finish me off. Her messed up JKD moves learned from DVDs seemed laughable at that moment. She wished for her lost Uzi. In an epiphany, Poe remembered the dart thrower around her neck containing whittled down toothpicks dipped in garlic oil.

She put the device in her mouth and blew. The first dart hit Sainvire's forehead while the second hit his neck. The vampire caught the third with his deft fingers mid-air.

"Enough!" he roared with the tone of a man truly annoyed. The scar above his lip was as white as her own. Poe obeyed, defeated. It occurred to her what was off about the vampire. His right shoulder was slightly warped and stuck out a little too forward.

The rain pounded harder than ever, eviscerating the scent of waste and animal feces. Sainvire pulled the pathetic darts and flung them threateningly to the ground.

A weak "Shithead" was the only thing she could think to say.

She assumed the fighting stance that almost all the martial arts disciplines taught in the numerous videos she had studied. Left leg lifted slightly for a block or parry, Poe cursed the man silently, vowing to go down fighting. She didn't kick her punching bag and metal rod in the bunker thousands of times over the years to cultivate leg calluses for nothing.

"C'mon," Sainvire commanded. "We've got to leave this place."

Unable to order the vampire to go jump in the dirty L.A. River without churning up a bout of stuttering, Poe punched at the rain and kicked at the flooded street.

"F-fffuck off!" she managed to say. Short, sweet, and to the stuttering point.

Anger left Sainvire's face, replaced by a patient, Andy Griffith smile. His expression further pissed off Poe, who believed the vampire was making fun of her speech impediment.

The near grin left his face, however, as the squalling of a flock of livid vampires filled the air. What happened next was a blur. Like a bad Sam Peckinpah movie, Poe watched Sainvire efficiently hack to pieces five undead with his elongated talons where they stood, leaving a litter of heads and limbs on the flooded ground. She couldn't help but notice his teeth growing to monster size in the hazy light of the moon.

"Scary fucker," Poe said under her breath as she watched him demolish Trench's brood.

Before the corpse of a fifth vampire even ate cement, Sainvire secured his claws around Poe and propelled them both skyward.

Dizzy and in awe of the fight, if it could be called that, Poe held on to the vampire's marble arms. Her bladder threatened to burst.

"P-put me down, or I'll kill you," Poe threatened feebly, her hand automatically reaching for her only weapon, the candy bar in her pocket. Her stomach was in her mouth.

If his fellow vicious dead failed to scratch Sainvire, what made her think she could? It was common knowledge that vampires couldn't carry another human in flight. They could drag them up a few feet from the air a short time. If Sainvire could soar over the city like Superman with an embittered and suicidal Lois Lane as baggage, then Poe was truly screwed.

"Afraid I can't do that right now," Sainvire explained. "You'll go splat if I do."

She said nothing else. The flight and the burning tightness around her ribs from the pressure of the vampire's hold brought on vertigo and something akin to claustrophobia.

Within minutes, Poe caught a view of the pyramidal tower of the Los Angeles Central Library that bled into a long and deep structure of eclectic Egyptian Mission design. The massive library, over 100,000 square feet, had been a monumental part of her childhood.

Her parents had religiously taken them down most Saturdays to tinker with the computers and listen to volunteer grandparents read boring stories years below their grade levels.

The inside had been a mix of state-of-the-art technology, modern art, and a splattering of contemporary architectural hodgepodge. Even though she hadn't been inside since she was eight, she could still picture every single detail in her head, including the great escalators that festooned the library from top to bottom and the three-dimensional papier-mâché art hanging from the ceiling.

Her visit to memory lane was cut short as they descended toward the front entrance of the library. An angular and chiseled Asian undead met them, his black head of hair falling in unruly waves around his smiling, strangely likeable face. He wore no shirt despite the rain, showing off his slim yet muscular build as well as the massive dragon tattoo that covered his entire back. The handsome man with full red lips grinned at Sainvire, his fangs showing.

"Joseph," Sainvire said, returning the medium-height vampire's grin and clapping him on the shoulder. "How goes it this evening?"

"Just fine, Kaleb." Joseph inclined his head then opened the door for the two. "Just the usual, you know. Like, say, a couple dozen infuriated cops banging on the doors demanding a certain someone's genitals."

"Wonder who that unfortunate creature could be?"

Sainvire let Poe enter first. "I see you brought trouble with you," Joseph dropped casually, his eyes scanning the girl's exposed wounds.

The sight and smells of the oh-so-familiar foyer brought a stab of memories. The place still hinted of plaster, Pine-Sol, old books, and crayons. Only now, a strong antiseptic smell dominated. The corner where the information booth used to be now housed a vampire of South Asian descent clicking away at an old computer. The checkout booths seemed the same except for the intimidating looking group of black and Vietnamese undead futzing around behind the counter and giving her the once over.

I thought minority vamps are out of vogue unless they're purty. Are those Latina humans handling firearms?

The little gift shop to her right displayed antique weaponry dating back from the French and Indian War to the American Civil War, no doubt pilfered from museums. Three middle-aged Latinas continued their conversation in Spanglish while cleaning and loading modern firearms. Their eyes never strayed from where she stood.

"Trench isn't going to like this one bit," she heard Joseph comment.

She looked over her shoulder and found the two speaking more quietly, obviously talking about her.

"I wonder if those muskets still work," she muttered to herself. "What I'd do to use them right now."

Risking it, Poe hung right while the Sainvire and Joseph chatted. The walls, once bedecked by black and white city photographs and questionable kids' art, now boasted Chagall, Christo, Kandinsky, Miro, Dali, Maholy-Nagy and other paintings she vaguely remembered seeing at museums like LACMA and the MOCA with her parents. There were at least fifty paintings on this floor alone.

Her reverie was interrupted by the low voice of the master vampire startlingly close to her ear.

"Have you an interest in art, Poe?"

Poe frowned. Her mother was a local artist. *And what an incredibly stupid question from the man who single-handedly turned humans into heifer!*

"Who doesn't?" she answered snidely. Then she remembered complaining along with her siblings, Joe and Sirena, that they were tired of looking at weird, ugly paintings over and over again, and they wanted to go to the movies already.

"Hmm. Good point. Lousy ice-breaker I chose there." He ignored Poe's scowl. Instead his gaze lowered to the pool of water and blood collecting on the floor. "You need to dry up and get that glass out of your skin. The wound in your leg is hampering your steps."

Hot from feeling like a dirty, dripping plebe with broccoli in her teeth, Poe intentionally shook her wet hair, splashing some of the precious paintings. She stomped on the pool of rain and sewer. "You're right. I better be dry and clean before you drink me through a straw."

She just had to piss him off in some way. Deep down, however, she felt her parents' disapproving scowl at her irreverence to the art they had so admired.

The vampire didn't even blink an eye. He merely indicated that she follow him up the escalator.

"Um," Poe began slowly, trying hard to speak clearly. "If you're gonna drink my blood, you better axe my head. 'Cause if I turn vampire, I'll make sure to return the favor. And if I end up as cattle, I might just snap out of my stupor one day and stab you in your sleep."

"I'll give it some serious thought."

Poe touched the key around her neck, imagining gouging the vampire's disturbing eyes with it. They ascended each floor without speaking. Poe noticed more paintings, even in heights where no ordinary human could reach.

Poe could barely contain her foul mood, until she figured out where they were heading. The painted sun dome loomed above their heads, and the children's literature wing was only a few steps away. Memory was bittersweet.

Then she remembered Penny. The poor dog was still in her pack probably soaked and shivering while she toured the goddamn museum with an evil and calculating dead guy.

She unslung her pack, lowered it to the floor, and found that the dog was not in her bag. *Jesus, the poor dog must have fallen from the air!*

"Oh, no!" Poe cried, imagining vampires making a bony meal out of her.

"I deserve to be butchered, no doubt about it," she said quietly. Slumped in defeat, Poe covered her clammy face with her bleeding hands. She had forgotten about Sainvire until he placed a hand on her shoulder and spoke. The vampire was kneeling next to her.

"Penny is being taken care of."

At the mention of the dog, Poe stood up and looked down at the master vampire. She itched to stab his eye out with the rosary cross dangling from her neck.

"Where's my dog?"

Sainvire rose, looking limbless in his black coat. Wordlessly he pointed to the children's wing. Poe forced herself not to run, motioning for him to lead the way. With her heart beating like a demolition ball descending upon a condemned building, she followed.

The last thing on her mind was to glance around the familiar place with the giant tapestries and murals of Indians and settlers on the walls. Her family had attended a lecture once where California historians tore apart the murals because the headdress depicted was a typical feathered stereotype instead of an accurate representation of west coast Native American attire.

Poe ignored the familiar carpet with happy chickens and gleeful barnyard animals.

Sainvire turned a corner, into the wing where the carved puppet theater still stood. On the stage crouched Joseph and a human. Between them lay an unconscious Penny on a bed of soft yellow comforters and pillows.

Poe noticed the tray of syringes next to the dog's head and immediately flew into a rage.

"What the –"

With a pole vault leap, she charged at the human leech holding a hypodermic needle. The move was so unexpected and silent that both Sainvire and Joseph were genuinely taken aback by the attack. Poe launched herself at the human girl, taking her over the edge of the stage and onto the carpeted floor with a wallop.

"You wanna bleed my dog, you gotta go through me first," she hissed.

Like a maniac, Poe repeatedly punched the petrified taller girl in the face while screaming nasty epithets she had learned from *Scarface* and *Clerks*.

Sainvire and Joseph looked at each other, silently agreeing the spectacle was invigorating despite the violence. It wasn't every day that two attractive women wrestled on the ground. When Poe stabbed Samantha's thigh with the syringe, however, Sainvire had seen enough. Like a puppy getting carried by the neck, Sainvire lifted the still-kicking Poe by her t-shirt. He unceremoniously deposited her on the floor, her gutter mouth still rattling non-stop.

"You goddamn vampire. I'm going to suffocate you with your crushed nuts!"

When his order for silence fell on deaf ears, Sainvire had no choice but to clamp a hand on Poe's mouth.

"Poe, be quiet!" he commanded. "You're giving me an unforgivable headache, and last I heard, my kind doesn't get headaches." He kept his hand clamped on the smuggler's mouth. "How's Samantha, Joseph?" Sainvire asked over the sound of Poe's muffled curses as she tried, unsuccessfully, to capture his arctic fingers with her sharp teeth.

"Beaten up and sedated," he sighed, shaking his head. "She'll be black and blue tomorrow." He pointedly stared at the wriggling Poe on the floor. "And to think, she was just trying to patch up this ratty old dog." Poe stopped her struggling, feeling guilt suddenly.

"How's the mutt's tongue?" Sainvire inquired, knowing full well the answer.

"It stopped bleeding," said Joseph, again flashing Poe a quick accusatory look. "I watched Sam here stitch the serrated wound closed."

"Must have been quite a job."

"Yup." Joseph lifted the brown-haired Sam, making sure to pause in front of Sainvire and Poe for dramatic effect before walking away. "I told her to let me just do a mercy killing and break its neck, but Samantha wouldn't have it. She just wanted to help. Tsk tsk."

At this point, Sainvire's hand fell away. Poe avoided eye contact with him. Instead, she crawled to the dog's makeshift bed. She looked at Penny's well-bandaged legs and peeked inside the dog's open mouth. Sure enough, Poe could see neat black stitches. Shamed but tremendously relieved, she swallowed the urge to hide behind the puppet stage. She had beaten a human who had tried to patch up her dog. She was no better than them. A tear threatened to fall, but she quickly wiped it with the dog's soft ear. And she had thought Penny was coarse all over.

She inhaled a shaky breath to clear her throat as well as her mind. Something nagged at her. The whole thing was wrong. Why didn't Sainvire leave her as a vampire snack for Trench's people? Why the annoying rescue at the risk of pissing off Trench and his thugs? *Why didn't he drain me dry? And how did–*

"How did you know my dog's name is Penny?"

Sainvire appeared across from her in a flash and kneeled before the dog. His large hand smoothed Penny's coarse stomach hair. Poe's injured hand resting on the dog's ear looked puny and filthy next to his bigger and more immaculate hands. Just thinking about his retractable nails gave her the creeps.

"I'll tell you," he paused, making sure their eyes met, "after I take the shards out of your skin." When

Poe didn't answer, Sainvire went on, eyelids slowly descending on his dark-rimmed gray eyes, perfect for a walking corpse. "Unless of course, you're afraid of me."

Damn right. I'm scared shitless of you, thought Poe acrimoniously. *You're one scary mofo that can slice all of me like thin salami.* Sainvire was the baddest, most powerful vampire she'd ever had the misfortune of meeting. There was a reason why he had saved her hide, and it made her sick to her stomach to think about it.

"I'm not scared of your ugly mug, Sainvire. Go ahead and do your worst," she enunciated. Her quip would have been more effective had she spoken faster and with more boom instead of moronically slow to avoid stutterspeak. What else could a girl who had survived an onslaught of idiot vampires do?

"Then come with me."

Poe followed Sainvire to the wing across the domed hall. Her squelchy Adidas desecrated the quiet. Her muscles ached. Her soaked clothing didn't help either. Limping slightly, the nail wound in her thigh caused discomfort. She could feel every shard and splinter lodged in her flesh as they sliced deeper with every step. The vampire slowed his long gait to accommodate her. She detested him for it even more.

If memory served her correctly, the rooms within had been a gallery of sort. It had held The Wizard of Oz exhibit at one point.

Sainvire waited for her to enter the room then closed the heavy door behind them. The spacious exhibit space was gone. In the center of the room stood the biggest bed Poe had ever seen, although that wasn't saying much because most of her years had been spent sleeping on a ratty futon mat. The impressive streamlined bed of the late Art Deco period was dull silver.

The long room had an assortment of intricately carved desks and divans. The place had a feel of Metropolis from 1940s DC Comics. Only a dash of paintings appeared on the walls, mostly the minimalist abstract impressionist work of Rothko and Newman. By the window, Poe noticed an arresting nude painting of a dark-haired woman, eyes shut, painted in warm orange-brown tones. Below the painting, Poe read the name, Amedeo Modigliani.

"You'd think she was painted by Gaugin, wouldn't you?" Sainvire asked, noting Poe's appreciative, open-mouth scrutiny.

Her examination of the woman ended then. Berating herself, Poe silently swore. She had been staring at a naked picture of a woman in the lair of a vampire. *How Rat Pack is this?*

To save face, she voiced the first artsy thought to enter her mind. "Right. The guy who painted fruits and naked Tahitians, right? Then he molested them all afterwards."

"Not exactly," said Sainvire as he indicated a table laden with medical supplies. Poe sat on Sainvire's right, placing her arms on the clean cloth covering the table.

"This shouldn't sting so much," he assured the girl.

"Well don't hold back on my account," Poe gnashed.

Shrugging, the vampire poured hydrogen peroxide on her wounds until they fizzled, and with deft hands, picked up a pair of tweezers. One by one, the sounds of glass dropping into a tin container filled the uneasy silence.

Color drained from her face. Each extraction hurt like magnified paper cuts, only deeper, wider, and with a squeeze of lime. Poe forced an immovable cattle rustler veneer.

"You want me to stop?"

"No. Doesn't bother me," she said, lying through her teeth.

Despite the warning her brain shouted, Poe snuck a tentative look at the vampire before her. This corpse with dark hair that rivaled her own, fastidiously plucking shards from her arms and palms was dangerous. He very well could have tortured Sister Ann and Goss. And yet, why did Poe find herself having to feverishly work to despise the guy? The vampire mystique was wreaking havoc in her already addled mind.

She didn't encounter a decent-looking vampire everyday. The ping of glass hitting the tray echoed in the room. Poe marveled at his black coat, completely dry already. Did he have some sort of inner dryer function to go with the retractable digits? And how was he able to get Penny out of the pack without calling attention?

Again she stole a look at the vampire. For such a little thing, the harelip scar was pronounced. *He could never be handsome*, she thought. *Not with a nose that looked like it was bashed in by the great Ali himself.* But who was she to talk? Her face bore a deep vampire slash that dwarfed Sainvire's twenty times over and could never be hidden with cosmetics.

Despite the facial quirks and the deformed shoulder of the undead before her, Poe had never seen anyone so striking. Each defect came together to form an interesting visage. Outside of movies, he was the most interesting-looking person she'd ever met, except, of course, her father, Goss, and Morales. But those men never made her feel strange. Goss was gay. Morales was an arrogant prick.

Long black eyelashes feathered his smooth cheeks as Sainvire carefully ministered to a particularly nasty cut near Poe's elbow. His touch was mortuary-cold, but he was peculiarly warming, like the feeling in her gut after two swigs of whisky.

"Sorry. My hands are cold," Sainvire said, like he'd read her mind.

"That happens when you're dead."

No wonder he wore a lot of black. It wasn't to perpetuate the cliché vampire look or to veil his gnarled shoulder, but to complement his dark hair and eyelashes that truly seemed like hairy tarantula legs. His high, slightly twisted nose had a tiny bump on the bridge, making him look menacing and of this earth at the same time. He could have been a poster boy for all the beaten up and downtrodden Roman soldiers of old. And then there were his lips.

His lips weren't cursed like the majority of leeches and vampires she'd killed who unfortunately had thin lines for mouths. His were simply lush and riveting. The more she sat staring, the more interesting the thin upper lip scar looked.

Stop it! The words in Poe's head halted further musings, forcing her to look away.

Your friends were killed today, for chrissake! Legs is dead and Penny is tongueless, she admonished herself. That no-good Pengle had called her a bitch – a first in her lifetime. *It's sick to drool after the one vampire that could've set up the torture and death of my friends. He's a regular Mengele. He's the one who came up with cattle milking.*

"Did I hurt you, Poe?" Sainvire asked, concerned that he had tugged too hard on a piece of glass shaped like Florida.

"No." Poe couldn't help herself. "Look, why don't you just suck my blood? Get it over with. This Frankenstein patching before eating me is sick."

Sainvire looked up briefly from his ministering, shocking her yet again with the wintery tint of his eyes. The vampire lowered his gaze and dug out a fat piece of glass lodged near her left thumb. "I've already had my dinner, but I'll take you up on your offer one of these days." To further his point, he threw her a suggestive smile and licked the bloody shard with relish.

Poe looked away muttering in a low, cowardly voice, "You try it, and I'll pull your guts out through your eyes and feed them to Penny."

The vampire succeeded in spooking the socks off of her. Needing to know the truth, Poe broke the quiet by asking shakily, "Did you have Goss for dinner?" The memory of her comrades drained of blood twisted her empty stomach into a knot.

Sainvire blinked slowly, never leaving Poe's volatile gaze. "No. I didn't."

"H-how do you know Penny's name and mine if you didn't torture them?"

Sainvire dabbed the last cut with ointment and applied a Band-Aid. He wiped his stained hands with a cloth and smiled at Poe. "There. All done." He stood up and pointed to an open door. "I'll tell you what you need to know after you get out of those wet clothes and take a hot shower." He handed her a bottle of peroxide. "Make sure to put some of this liquid on the wound on your left leg. You don't want the infection to get worse."

"I don't want to take a shower," she said, purposely ornery.

"It's up to you," he shrugged. "But you're covered in foul water. If you're into bacteria and disease, then more power to you. In any case, you won't get any answers from me."

"Why the hell not?" Poe demanded.

"Because I refuse to sit in a room with you another minute." He presented her with a beneficent Gandhi smile and added, "You stink."

Before Poe could protest, the vampire strode out of the room, leaving Poe to gape after him. She was shivering and utterly alone, surrounded by fussy vampires.

———————

Poe hardly enjoyed one of the few hot showers she had taken in fourteen years, which was a shame since the water didn't smell like fishy sludge, nor was it discolored and grainy. The roomy bathroom filled with tiles, mosaics, and mirrors was completely lost upon her. She didn't even appreciate the huge old-fashioned shower tub that surpassed the size of Goss'. How could she when images of her friends' demise flashed in her mind continuously?

"Awfully sorry, Sister and Goss," she said out loud, "I let you both down so bad."

Never had she unsuccessfully worked so hard to change her train of thought. If it hadn't been for phobia and cowardice, her friends might still have been alive. She didn't deserve to cry, but tears of frustration flowed anyway.

In less than twenty minutes, Poe hopped out of the great tub with a pile of dripping, freshly laundered clothes. She had used her raw fist to beat blood and dirt from her shirt and pants. She did as Sainvire said and dabbed peroxide at the nail wound on her leg, red, puffy, and swollen from the shower. She hung her wet clothes on the side of the tub.

After attending to her thigh and various lacerations, Poe happened to look up and jumped back in fright. Poe realized that the peeping tom looking back was her own reflection. She wiped the thin film of steam clinging to the surface of the mirror.

An unrecognizable face stared back. Huge dark brown eyes, almost black with very long, straight lashes, blinked. Her wing-tip eyebrows were raised in shock. A pinkish-white scar running from mid-forehead down to the left underside of her eye marred her smooth skin. Her small nose had a cut on the bridge. On either side of her face were thin red scratches, probably from when she jumped through glass. Her naturally puffy lips were swollen even more from a vampire slap.

"Boy, I look awful."

She probably deserved every scrape and bruise, too. After all, she was still alive. What a betrayal. The tiny mirror in her bunker only showed a third of her face at a time. This big contraption of a mirror was unwelcome because in her head she still had an image of herself having the ungainly body of a kid.

She could not stop, however, and unwrapped Sainvire's lush green towel beginning to bleach from the peroxide. Her physique sure had changed. Ignoring the welts and darkening bruises on her rounded hips, arms, legs, and chest, Poe gawked at her body, temporarily forgetting about her friends.

"What in the world happened to me?" She had felt the changes, especially the curvy bumps, had even stared down at them on occasion, but she had never seen them reflected on a giant mirror like this before.

Her full breasts with peach nipples scared the hell out of her. To think, she hadn't even considered wearing a bra all this time. *Embarrassing!*

"No wonder Morales became all pervy whenever he saw me." She made a mental note to scour the city for a brassier if she survived the night.

Her gaze traveled down her narrow waist to her stomach with barely a ghost of roundness. From there her eyes led southward, purposely skipping the vee of her privates, jumping straight to her curvilinear butt, then her slim but muscled thighs and calves. Poe squeezed her arm muscles, liking what she saw. Deep dimples appeared on either cheek.

"Good to see all the pull-ups, sit-ups, and muscle toning worked," she said, pleased. "Anything to avoid being a 'big head.'"

She had become obsessed after coming across a very disturbing book about kids locked up in the attic. They had big heads but tiny bodies. Having little exercise and no sun exposure for years, the littlest kids became deformed. The eldest brother and sister began an incestual relationship. It was quite troubling. *Never want that shit to happen to me, no siree.*

Letting her wet black hair fall from beneath the towel, Poe was surprised to see how long it had grown. She usually cut it about shoulder length, but her old scissors had clunked out on her months ago, and she was too lazy to look for another pair.

What'll I wear?

Poe spied a huge black robe hung behind the door. No doubt it was Sainvire's. She put it on and went outside. On the big bed lay several floral dresses, short, medium, and long.

"Yeah, right," Poe huffed. "Over my dead body."

She'd sworn off dresses when she was six. Her mother had to just about stomp her to get her to wear frilly little things for functions and such. The pressure had become so bad that Poe begged for a whacking on the butt rather than endure the humiliation of wearing a dress.

Poe opened Sainvire's closet and pondered the contents. She snatched a pair of black pants, a black t-shirt, and some socks.

"He won't miss these. He's got lots." Like Poe, Sainvire owned twenty pairs of the same outfits.

Taking the scissors from the medical tray, Poe planted herself on Sainvire's bed and cut away at his clothes. When the pant legs, shirt sleeves, and belt were sheared to her satisfaction, Poe finally allowed herself to think about how the vampire would react. She shrugged her shoulders, thinking that if she was going to croak tonight, might as well go pissing off the famous master of the city – in a pair of his pants.

———————

He wasn't pissed; he was merely amused.

The young woman didn't bother to conceal the newly filched bedroom weapons bulging in the pockets of her – his – butchered pants. One of his belts duly shortened cinched the ridiculously large pants about her tapered waist. The fabric crotch nearly reached her knees. Hooked onto the belt was a pair of scissors and three hastily sharpened lead pencils. His partly tucked black t-shirt hung loose and long on Poe's frame.

The ludicrous pants made him shake his head. The bottom of the slacks, accidentally cut high-water length, gave Poe a Huck Finn look, especially since she walked barefoot and one pant leg was shorter than the other. He noticed something different about her. Poe's once unfettered bosom was bound underneath the shirt. He smiled grimly. So the girl finally noticed them.

Sainvire watched her go down the third set of escalators with sharp vampire eyes from where he perched on a glass walkway smack in the middle of the library. He decided to let her explore before telling her what heinous part he had played in the deaths of Sister Ann and Goss.

———————

Poe imagined several scenarios of the master vampire mauling her to death upon discovering what she'd done to his pants. But after minutes of nasty internal debate, Poe finally decided to explore and perhaps find a way out. She donned her hastily fashioned weapons onto her belt. Her Adidas were soaking wet and made squeaky, squelchy sounds, so she took them off and left them to dry in the bathroom.

"Too slippery," Poe muttered, kicking off the vampire's huge socks once she'd reached the puppet theater. They made her clumsy on the tile and marble floors. Sainvire's clothes smelled like Snuggles fabric softener, the same brand her dad had used for laundry. Such familiar scents unnerved her. She shifted her attention to the problem at hand. Banking on her hunch that Sainvire had already claimed her for his supper, she prayed that the other vampires would leave her alone.

"I'm going to reconnoiter a bit, doggy. I can't get us out of here without proper weapons," she whispered to the battered dog still knocked out from drugs. "I don't know what Sainvire's game is, but I swear to you, I will knit his intestines into a sweater with number two pencils if it's the last thing I do."

Once satisfied that her dog was still asleep and breathing, Poe headed to the far end of the hall. The hall, cordoned off by a balcony, gave an awesome view below of two massive flights of escalators in between a sentry of towering columns thirty hands thick. Each floor led to different sections of the library.

"This place is smaller than I remember, but still massive," she mused quietly.

Below, Poe spied vampires, humans, and a sprinkling of adrenaline-rushed halfdeads, the latter noticeable by their healthy complexion, performing different tasks. And that was what it looked to be, humans and undead of differing ethnicities going about their work. *I thought minorities were turned into shit sweepers and laundry washers.* One particular section, the Social Sciences floor, appeared extremely busy.

"Hello, what's this?" she asked the post she was leaning on. Poe squinted, swearing that the floor had been converted into a laboratory. Despite the half-closed blinds, Poe could see microscopes and other lab equipment through the otherwise clear glass walls. Fear choked her. Could it be a blood farm? Poe swallowed hard and turned away.

"I hope that place isn't what I think it is," she boiled.

She tiptoed with her bare feet to the first escalator, disregarding the stares of two vampires coming from the opposite direction and carrying bags filled with clear liquid.

"What?" she hissed at them.

Emboldened as they did not lift a finger to stop her or alert the vampire security, Poe descended the second set of escalators. She winced at the cold bite of the metal steps that aggravated the myriad bruises and cuts on her body. She had found purpose again. If the Social Sciences section was a cattle farm, then she would find a way to destroy it.

"Goss and Sister Ann would've wanted it this way," she whispered.

There certainly was a bustle of activity in there. She hadn't seen so many living people since she was eight, and she felt intimidated. Clutching the rosary and minuscule dart blower around her neck for courage, Poe entered the lab.

At first Poe's uncanny appearance didn't cause an iota of controversy. A couple of dozen vampires and humans went about their work, not even glancing at the barefoot, oddly dressed young woman scoping the spacious converted floor for any signs of cattle blood-letting. Instead, only live and undead creatures in white lab coats fiddling around with vials and serums casually greeted her.

"Hello. Hello to you, too. Oh hi," she nodded at everyone who greeted her. Heartened, Poe ventured further inside the lab, occasionally reaching out and squeezing hanging plastic containers filled with thick clear liquid that seemed to be everywhere.

A vampire with atrophied veins on her face startled Poe by appearing electrically quick in front of her. The undead gave her a most benign, fanged smile and went about her work. Poe fretfully skipped to the next table that happened to be empty of supernatural beings. Some vamps were faster than others, but she preferred the slower ones.

Hanging on hooks was a dozen or so plastic containers of the clear, gel-like liquid. In the middle, though, a lone plastic bag containing red liquid looking suspiciously like blood stopped Poe in her tracks.

"Is that blood?" she muttered.

Disquieted, Poe reached for the bag for a closer look. Poe was heavy of hand given that she had never had the chance to outgrow the grabby reaction of a third grader. She did not gauge her strength and before she knew it, the bag of red liquid was off the hook. It slipped from her fingers like a fat balloon filled with water, crashing like a wave on the white marble floor.

A tepid, "Oh shit," was all she could say. The design left on the floor would have made Jackson Pollock applaud from the grave. Poe couldn't escape notice.

She was the center of attention, standing with her mouth open, eyes huge from guilt. She was crimson down to her toes. To her chagrin, the human contingent seemed more furious and outraged at the mess their fellow live person had made. Vampires had to restrain a particularly incensed man, cursing the newcomer cruelly, from rushing at her.

"You stupid little jerk!" the man with a goatee, a more annoying version of Jim Carrey, bellowed. "If you can't keep your sticky fingers from touching lab work, you're not welcome here!"

Like a goldfish ignominiously jumping out of its bowl onto a messy desk, Poe opened and shut her mouth several times before saying, "M-miserable leech."

"What did you say, you dumb bit–"

A woman wearing pajamas with winged yo-yo designs abruptly stopped goatee man from finishing his thought. "Enough, Ambrose. It was an accident."

"Yeah, but who'll fill up another bag?" he spat. "It's too late to round up volunteers. Most everyone's asleep. The little idiot will have to fill it up."

Poe's eyes widened then squinted narrowly like Dirty Harry himself. *There's no way any of these leeches, these traitors, are going to draw my blood without a fight!* Poe unhooked the scissors from her belt, baring her teeth. She had a nasty feeling that jeet kune do would be needed this evening.

Like mist taking shape, a figure appeared next to her elbow. Poe pointed the scissors at the form, ready to stab the dull blade into its heart. The grin on the figure's face, however, confused and disoriented her. There stood Joseph, wearing nothing but the dastardly leather pants that seemed to be two sizes too small, shaking his head at her.

"Sorry. No one's going to touch the Little Miss this evening. Boss' orders," he beamed, sounding extremely amused.

Ambrose, seething emphatically, barked, "Well I'm not giving any more blood tonight!"

"Hmm. But I don't think we've met before," commented Joseph with a yogi smile.

"No, but I've seen you around," Ambrose snorted disparagingly. "Can't miss the glaring dragon on your naked back."

"You're new, I guess," Joseph laughed with him, imitating Ambrose's donkey snort. "Otherwise you'd know not to speak snarky to me. I'm the boss' best pal."

"So does that mean I can't tell you to fuck off?" Ambrose retorted without fear.

"Sure you can, but I'm liable to misbehave and trip accidentally on your jugular."

The pear-shaped woman in her early forties smoothed down her yo-yo pajama top and stared warily at Poe. "I'll do it. I haven't done it for a while anyway."

"Thank you, Perla." Joseph gave the woman's shoulder a squeeze. "We really appreciate it."

At this, Perla looked miffed and more than a little annoyed. She mussed the vampire's soft, shoulder length hair and pushed him away. "You better get out of here, Joe, before I change my mind." She looked at Poe again, this time with a hint of amusement. "And take the barefoot contessa with you before I let her stab Ambrose's neck with those rickety scissors."

"What a dick," Poe mumbled as she left the lab.

But a vexing internal voice laughed pitilessly at her righteous anger. The voice grew in volume, contemptuously telling Poe, *You're only pissed at Ambrose because he acted more human than you.*

Even if she didn't want to admit it, Poe resented the older humans in the lab. They didn't have to spend their lives underground and alone like they were already dead. They didn't stutter or suffer countless phobias.

"Don't feel sorry for yourself," said Joseph, startling Poe. "You got away clean."

"I wasn't feeling sorry for myself!"

He threw her a knowing look to say, "Yeah, right."

"They were jerks. That's all."

Joseph stayed silent, but a smile lingered and riled Poe's injured pride. She kept her mouth shut, nevertheless, knowing she would seem petulant and childish in whatever form her answers took. She changed the subject.

"What were those clear liquid things?" she asked, not really expecting an answer from Sainvire's buddy. His half-naked, tattooed back and chest grated on her nerves. His bare feet reminded her too much of her Adidas-free feet, blood splotched and all. She especially couldn't handle his leather pants; they were simply too *Beach Blanket Bimbo* with too much cowhide for her. She knew that leather was the way to go in vampire literature and movies, but it grossed the living crap out of her.

"Genetically engineered plasma, saline, some funky fungal bacteria, a drop of blood, and a couple of other refined proteins I can't pronounce."

"What're they for?"

"Grub." Joseph let her pass before him up the escalator, following closely behind.

"What do you—"

"You'll find out soon enough," he interrupted, nodding his head and smiling politely. "I heard that you stutter. Why aren't you now?"

"You don't make me nervous. Your classy cow skin pants don't scare me."

Joseph guffawed heartily. It was no wonder Perla, the nice woman in yo-yo pajamas, treated him like a regular, likeable human. He knew how to take a slam. Despite herself, Poe smiled at the vampire's contagious laughter. She missed Sister Ann's unholy laugh and Goss' hilarious snorting giggle fits.

"Seriously, Joseph," Poe said, catching the quick sobering of the merry vampire's visage as if he expected another iffy question that wasn't for him to answer. "Are you Chinese?"

"What makes you say that?" he asked, his eyes full of mischief.

"Well, the Chinese character tattooed on your left booby." She pointed at the black, three-inch tattoo. "And the dragon on your back."

"Listen, the tattoo is on the left side of my *chest*. Number two, thousands of non-Chinese got the same kind of tattoos before the Gray Arma-crackin'. It was a craze for a while. And C, and most importantly, never assume a person's ethnic background in Los Angeles. It's rude and you'll almost always guess wrong." He smiled again, making Poe cringe even more. "I'm not Chinese. I'm Filipino American with some bastardized

Spanish blood, I'm told. Any other questions about me, my body art, or racial make-up?"

"No. Just the meaning of the tattoo," Poe said, thinking fast, hotly embarrassed.

"Well, I'm not really sure. I was told that it meant honor, but since I don't read or speak Chinese, I can only hope the tattoo artist didn't lie to me. He tattooed 'moron fashion victim' for all I know."

Poe forced a laugh, feeling a little less stupid. The vampire lectured her but in a funny sort of way, just how Goss used to do. She understood that she was hugely ignorant about social subtleties since Goss and Sister Ann had pointed them out often enough. PC she was not.

"I like your name, Joseph," Poe stated, surprised at what came out of her mouth.

"Oh yeah? Why?" he asked, arching an eyebrow as if expecting some more nipple references.

"Because you, um, have the same name as my brother." Poe said, looking away.

Joseph grinned, showing extremely white teeth with sharpened fangs. "That's funny. I may have had an annoying sister named Poe in my other life."

Was that an extension of friendship, or merely another one of his jokes? No matter, for Poe knew that she was screwed at that point. This charming vampire before her would not die at her hands. Unless of course he tried to kill her.

"Oh, my mother was half-Filipino, you know," she told him proudly.

———

Joseph, apparently, was her tour guide for the evening. He took her to the media room where quite a selection of movies was stashed. Several booths equipped with viewing equipment lined the walls.

As they walked down the lanes, Poe would point out the names of the movies currently playing. "That's *400 Blows*. Good movie. That's *Tarzan and His Mate,* and that's *Blacula*. Wow. *El Norte*. Good but a real downer."

"I guess you've seen a lot of movies in your time, eh?"

"Nearly every day and every hour since I was eight," said Poe. "That one's *Office Space* and the next one over's *Dong Dong Silver*."

Joseph shook his head as if he'd misheard the girl. "Dong Dong Silver?" He peeked over the last booth.

"Hey, mind getting your own booth, folks?" a vampire with his human honey complained. "Looking over our shoulder is not cool, man."

Joseph pulled the squirming Poe out of the media room. Once outside he had to sit down and clutch his stomach for support to keep from toppling over. "*Dong Dong Silver*! Ha ha ha!"

Poe just stood there, offended and truly mortified. She didn't discriminate when it came to movies. She watched them all.

A now sober Joseph ended his outburst at the sight of Poe's obvious embarrassment.

"Hope you're hungry," he said, changing the subject. He led her down a corridor into a huge kitchen with rows of tables and chairs.

She drank the sight of vampires, halfdeads, and humans supping together.

"So many people," she said in a whisper.

Then her nostrils picked up the most magnificent smells she hadn't sniffed in over a decade.

"A buffet," she said with awe, ranting out names of nearly forgotten all-you-can eat restaurants.

"Todai's sushi and seafood grab-a-lots, Raji's Indian foodtacular, Nyala's Ethiopian smorgasbord…"

She didn't remember being handed a tray. There on the slab of heated metal tins represented an amalgam of Angelino cultures. Pad thai, tamales, orange chicken, bibimbap, vegetable tikka masala, blintz, collard greens, kebobs, mashed potatoes, pork chops, sushi, teriyaki chicken, mac and cheese, and so much more! She stood where she was, staring as hungry humans passed her up.

After fourteen years of eating jellified canned food, she piled it on.

She scooped some rice and poured vegetable tikka masala sauce on it. Then some greens without bacon, mashed potatoes over jerk sauce, corn on the cob, stir fried veggies, eggplant curry, California rolls, and–

"Will you be needing another tray?" Sainvire asked, casually appearing out of nowhere, looking at the mound of food on the cattle runner's plate and tray.

"Oh. Sorry." Poe plopped down the rice pudding she was about to spoon into a bowl, embarrassed. Beaming down at her, Sainvire ladled some of the pudding in the bowl on her tray.

"She's suddenly the center of attention," Joseph commented, looking about him. Vamps and humans alike had ceased supping to stare at the stranger and her mound of food.

"Don't mind them," Sainvire assured her. "They seem to have forgotten their manners."

"It's 'cause my tray looks like the mashed potato mountain in *Close Encounters of the Third Kind*," Poe said quietly, not in any way deterred from the meal.

"I forgot to tell you that you can come back for seconds. Or thirds," Joseph said, his perpetual smile shining. He was holding orange juice and grape soda in his hands.

The two vampires led an extremely crimson Poe to an empty table. Joseph pushed the juices toward the girl.

"Hope grape and orange is fine."

Poe nodded her head and mumbled her appreciation. She didn't immediately dig in to her plate, thinking that this might very well be her last supper before she became someone else's dinner. Sainvire and Joseph sitting across the table made Poe uncomfortable. It was as though they wanted to watch her gobble down the tower of tikka and laugh at her expense.

Bastards. They finally ignored her and started talking quietly about Trench and his angry goons. Trying to remember proper fork and knife etiquette, Poe slowly dug in. The traffic cop in her head hollered for her to slow down. She slackened the pace for about a minute. Then it was suddenly about vengeance, like Lardass at the pie-eating contest in *Stand by Me*. Unlike Lardass, however, Poe paused now and then to appreciate certain dishes by closing her eyes and memorizing the flavor and texture, for she knew it could be another decade before she tasted anything so yummy and warm.

With her eyes closed, she reveled in the teriyaki sauce over rice. There were simply no words to describe the explosion of flavor. Even the orange juice got a fist-slamming show of appreciation. In the midst of the pauses, grunts, and lip smacking, Poe was oblivious to her surroundings.

"I don't think anyone's given our cooking such a resounding compliment before," Habib, one of the four chefs, commented while looking on.

Sainvire was careful to wave away certain humans who inched to their table for a closer look. Vampires who dared to hover too close received a quelling look from the master vampire. To all this, Poe was blind, lost in gastronomical delights and remembrance of her mother and father who believed sampling different kinds of food to be a privilege.

To everyone's surprise, Poe obliterated her plate, down to the last crust of bread that wiped the sauces clean. The tip of her nose dusted with sweat. Only when Poe swallowed the last spoonful of rice pudding did she become aware of the pain in her stomach.

Then there were hooting and clapping. The cafeteria audience had converted the meal into a cheesy reality show, the kind her parents didn't let her watch because it brought out the worst traits in the contestants. The voice police returned and said, *I told you so!*

Her stomach, tremendously stretched by the amount of food shoveled in there, gave a kick. Flame-faced Poe had no recourse but to extend her hand to the four chefs that encircled her: Habib, Janice, Petra, and Ray.

"What a show, what a show," random people said as they clapped her on the back. She didn't appreciate the gesture at all. The movement jarred her belly, causing terrible discomfort.

And to think, she had even briefly considered Joseph as a sort of friend. Sick jerk. He laughed the loudest. Sainvire, having had enough himself, extended his arm to Poe to hoist her up. The girl merely threw him a piss-off look and rolled herself out of the chair. The unnaturally large bulge of her stomach garnered another round of applause.

As she headed for the door, she ignored the laughter. On the right, Poe noticed a dreadlocked vampire sucking on a clear plastic bag bursting with thick fluid. The vampire winked at her, and the human girl sitting next to him clapped. This was such a strange place, definitely not how she expected a cattle farm to be.

———————

Poe shut out the conversation between Sainvire and Joseph as they walked ahead along the long corridor to the vestibule of the library. She could care less about them.

All those wasted years craving for human companionship. There were tons of humans, fifty at least in the cafeteria, and they treated her like a stain. The lab folks wanted to beat the crap out of her, not to mention turn her into cattle.

"Bunch of leeches," she gritted in a low voice. "Try living on cans of discontinued slimy green beans for a month and see how you act in front of a buffet table."

Who needed these obnoxious people? She certainly did not. It was no fun to be one of the Beverly Hillbillies when the jokes and jibes were thrown at her. *Shoot, Dad was a podiatrist, for crying out loud – a doctor! He knew everything about bunions, California Missions, and the Southern Pacific Railroad.* Her mom was a famous local artist and a great reader who owned fourteen portable record players and two rare Victrolas, the kind with a crank and wood horn.

As for Poe, she learned how to read when she was scarcely three years old. She received honors and awards for speed-reading by the time she hit the fourth grade. Her mom always said she was one sharp chickie who might one day become a reporter or comic book writer. She could solve math problems with her right hand and compose an essay with the left.

"Not many people can boast that they are ambidextrous, sweetie," her mother often reminded her.

Now these so-called living, breathing people treated her like garbage and made her the brunt of their jokes.

"Screw them," she fumed silently. "I'll never lift a finger to help anyone. May they choke on all the good cafeteria food they chug down! And they can just–"

"Poe, are you ready for our little talk?" Sainvire asked, leading all three up the escalator and forcing Poe to pay attention.

"Yes," she said huffily.

Joseph laughed, holding his muscled tummy. "You're not sore about the cafeteria incident, are you, Poe?"

Poe glared at him. How could this guy who shared her brother's name laugh at her, too? *Jerk!* "What do you think?"

"I've never seen the cafeteria so lively. It's usually like a morgue in there," Joseph continued, unmindful of Poe's wounded pride. "We have your appetite to thank for that."

One more crack and she would truly embarrass herself. She was on the verge of throwing up and worse, crying. She looked away, pretending to scrutinize some paintings from the Trash Can movement of the early 20th century. She could care less about them.

Sainvire stopped smiling, noting the girl's inability to take a joke. He motioned for his friend to stop the teasing.

"Joseph, it's almost three in the morning. Poe and I have many things to discuss before dawn."

Joseph sobered, understanding his flub. "Yes. I have to check on a couple things myself." He tried to catch Poe's eyes, but she wouldn't look up to meet his. "Goodnight, Poe. I enjoyed giving you the star tour." He gave a little nod to Sainvire and walked away.

Sainvire led Poe up the escalator, mindful of her space. Once they reached the domed lobby, the two headed wordlessly to Sainvire's private rooms. Poe didn't even ask. She just proceeded straight for the bathroom, locking the door behind her. She turned on the shower. What followed next was a tragedy. All the good food she'd imbibed gushed out in lumps as soon as she knelt on the tile floor before the toilet seat. Poe reasoned between heaves that the humans should have been cultured enough not to make a big deal of her gluttony.

At the fourth heave, Poe spewed out the very last of the good food. She cried silent but defiant tears. She grieved for Goss and Sister Ann, whose early deaths she could have prevented. She wept for the bruises and cuts she'd received that made her body sore and feverish. She stifled a sob as she remembered the stinging anger and ridicule from her own people. And she threw up the best damn food she'd had in years. In the end, she cried for one of the most god-awful days she'd ever had in her life.

Depleted, Poe blew her nose with toilet paper. She washed her puffy red face and tried to blink the redness away.

"Try to think of something happy, you big cry baby," she admonished her reflection and started to look for floss. She didn't want a repeat of a tooth pulling by a thick-fingered Goss using pliers meant for plumbing.

Brushed and flossed and eye veins shrunken to size, Poe felt confident enough to face the vampire. She needed to be scary to get some respect. She imagined hacking the smiling head of Joseph, the leather-loving vampire sidekick, and puncturing Sainvire's distracting orbs with sharpened pencils. If she really wanted to, she could kill all of them.

———————

Sainvire gingerly lifted the comforter under the sedated dog, hoping the poor mutt wouldn't wake up. As lightly as he could, he floated a foot above ground and glided back to his room. Penny twitched and whined as if stuck in a nightmare. Sainvire's jaw set hard.

He hesitated before placing the dog down. "Which would you prefer, little Penny?" he asked softly.

At first he was going to set her down on the bed, but he thought Poe might decide to sleep with the dog and injure the mutt further with the movements of the soft mattress. No. Penny would have to sleep on the divan by the bed. Sainvire's gestures bordered on non-movement. He made Penny's descent onto the divan a breeze.

Poe was still in the bathroom, her grief not hidden from the vampire's keen ears by the rush of shower water. At least she wasn't vomiting anymore. Sainvire chose a leather armchair by the window to sit in and waited for her to come out.

"I'm hoping you'll make our meeting less awkward," he told the wiry haired dog.

He was correct on that score. Immediately after entering the room, the young woman kneeled by the dog and whispered, "I'll get us out of here soon. Then we can start over."

Occupied with Goss' dog – hers now – Poe realized that Penny was by far more abused than she. Penny's beloved human companion, along with Legs, was gone. Poe forgot about the vampire momentarily as she tended to the dog. When she finally did look at him sitting as still as an empty church and watching her, Poe forced a look of nonchalance.

"Sorry I took so long," Poe began. "I'm, um, not ready for real food, I guess."

"I assure you, Poe, there's no need to explain." He motioned to a leather burgundy armchair across from him. "I quite understand. We really should begin our conversation about your friends since dawn is closely approaching."

And so began a narrative that left Poe reeling in its intricacy.

CHAPTER 4–REASON FOR TERMINATION

TO SAY THAT POE was nervous would be an understatement. Her slouched, constantly shifting figure could not stay still on the slippery leather chair. Her eyes flicked between Sainvire and the naked Modigliani painting behind him. Calamitously the bandage she had taken from the medical tray and wrapped around her bosom itched terribly.

At least the vampire looked as discomfited as her. His clear eyes heavy with secrets, Sainvire finally cleared his throat and began.

"Before I tell you what I know, I must first ask you to disclose what I'm about to reveal only to people you trust implicitly."

For a few seconds all Poe could do was stare incongruously at the master vampire. "Well, um, who am I going to tell? All my friends are dead. The humans here are so obnoxious, they won't get anything outta me."

"There's Megan and Morales," he said quietly, noting the stiffening of Poe's spine.

"H-how did–"

"You'll find out everything, Poe, as soon as I get your promise."

"Alright. You have it, but on one condition. You have to tell me who killed my friends." *Even if it was you*, Poe thought.

Sainvire nodded his assent, his face not betraying anything.

"I give you my word," he said quietly.

He looked intently at Poe's face for so long that the girl was on the brink of developing a much bigger complex about her scar. Then he spoke with a deep, gravelly voice.

"Before the Gray Armageddon, a contingent of vampires was already in search of a new, non-human food source. With the aid of some very gifted scientists, geneticists, phlebotomists, and a brood of other experts who knew about us, we initiated research. In two years, we made promising progress. But the gray matter came, destroying most of the human population and civilization as we knew it. And to this day, the poison winds still remain a conundrum for which we have many explanations but no definite answers. My personal theory is that we doomed ourselves with germ experimentation that succeeded in wiping out most everyone. Anyway, after the tragedy, vampires broke into factions to fill the power vacuum.

"The Vampire Council that had existed for hundreds of years set up a new working government in the cities with vampire concentrations." He touched his temple and looked away from Poe's dark gaze. "The Council in Los Angeles is composed of five very powerful vampires just as lost as the rest of us. Predictably most undead decided to go off alone and hunt the remaining humans for food and sport without thought of the future. It was a chaotic time as you may remember." He gave her a meaningful look.

"Looting and carnage ruled the streets for weeks afterward, eviscerating the already dwindling human population. Some of my scientists, the ones who had been working at an off-the-books underground location researching alternative food sources for the undead, survived when the gray miasma arrived. We salvaged the accumulated data and brought the files to this library. I moved the scientists here, and I have extended them my protection ever since. They and a few others have continued the research." He cleared his throat, letting his words sink in.

"Vampires have existed for thousands of years, so I've been told. Many delight in creating minions by boring holes through a victim's skull and pouring vampire blood onto the exposed brain or by repeated bites within days of each other. I had to do something about the steadily disappearing humans and the growing number of new vampires created each night. It didn't take a genius to do the math."

Poe sneered, "So you set up the operation, imprisoning humans against their will and turning them into a bunch of miserable cows to be bloodmilked."

Sainvire's gaze found hers. "I'm not going to deny anything, Poe. I am the mastermind of the whole sordid business. I deserve everyone's contempt for what I have done."

As if his guilt is going to right his wrongs! "Your life story is really interesting, but I'm too tired and vampire-prejudiced to care," Poe sniffed, disgusted at the presumptuousness of this Mengele. "How is this connected to Sister Ann and Goss?"

Sainvire hardly blamed Poe for her animosity. He felt the same way about himself.

"Sister Ann used to be a leech. She fed the cattle, prayed over them, and collected their blood for a certain master." The look on Poe's face stopped him. "Look, Poe. She wasn't a leech by choice. No one wanted to drink her blood because superstitious undead declared they would self-combust if they did. And no one dared to kill her, as some still believed in the idea of an afterlife and the wrath of God for harming a nun.

And despite the topsy-turvy times, Sister and I developed camaraderie. I managed to negotiate her release from the vampire she worked under and brought her here."

He sighed, remembering the sweet, lined face of the nun on the brink of madness. If Catholicism was dying when the world was normal, it was dead now. "We became good friends, believe it or not. She encouraged me to persevere in trying to find a new food source, and she commended me for not milking any of the cattle I maintained. Strictly volunteer blood donation or animal blood for me and my people." He smiled and said, "Joseph treated her like a second mother. He even taught her some jujitsu when she was up for it."

Poe couldn't help herself. She was entranced. Sister Ann had always been close-lipped about her previous life. What she did know of the nun, she had learned from Goss.

"One day Sister Ann asked me to grant her freedom." Sainvire pressed the palm of his hands to his forehead. "I was petrified for her. Without my protection, anything could happen, habit or no habit. The streets still crawled with rogue vampires who refused to stop hunting humans. They believed it beneath them to drink refrigerated blood. I tried to convince her that leaving wasn't a good idea, but she was adamant, telling me that she was going to rescue the poor cattle she had helped bleed. I'm sure you know how hardheaded Sister Ann could get."

Poe nodded. She certainly knew. The nun was unstoppable when it came to preaching against particular movies in her bunker.

"I knew I couldn't stop her. She would find a way to escape. So we made a deal. She had to train with Joseph and ammunition experts living here for a year.

Then she could go. Good thing she agreed because I thought I'd have to hog-tie the woman." He beamed at the memory. "After the year had passed, I introduced her to Morales and Megan who were experienced traffickers in the underground by then. Her task was to rescue cattle and bring them to the runners."

"Soon after, she met up with a very emotionally battered Goss who had just escaped from one of Trench's facilities. Sister comforted him over Daryl, and later, when he was stronger, taught him all she knew. She brought Goss over for sparring lessons with Joseph." He gave the barest hint of a grin. "He'd taken Aikido in college and proved to be an apt student."

"A month or two after Goss threw you against his wall, and Penny," he looked over at the sleeping dog, "bit you on the ankle, our researchers made a breakthrough." He forced himself not to laugh at Poe's reaction. She shivered at the things he knew.

"They found that by putting together particular synthetic materials mixed with plasma, a few drops of human blood, and a few other not-so-hard-to-find minerals, the perfect vampire food was created. After a few trials, about eighty-five percent of our test subjects preferred the Plasmacore, as it's now called, to blood. Results vary from vampire to vampire. It gave some vampires better night vision, staved off hunger longer than blood, and it actually enabled quite a number of undead to withstand some sunlight."

Poe looked at Sainvire a little differently. He had found an alternative source of food for vampires. Farms and cattle would no longer be needed.

"But when I took my trial results over to the Council, I was quickly censured."

"But why?" cried Poe, tucking her dirty feet in a cross-legged position and sitting straight back. "How could they want this, this…crazy thing to continue?"

"Damned if I know. They didn't even favor me with an explanation. I was threatened that if a single Plasmacore bottle is seen on the streets, then my charges and I would face the Council for treason."

"Treason? What the hell does that mean?" a seething Poe asked, digging her nails into her uninjured thigh to keep from letting out a string of curses.

"It means that my people and I will be hunted and executed by the Council's minions, and possibly by the Council itself."

Poe shook her head. "I don't get it. Wouldn't they want to feel a little bit of sun, or –"

"It's not as easy as that, Poe. The Council and some remarkably old vampires are shaken by this whole development. The councilmembers are ancient immortals who are strong beyond belief. The vampires that created them and the brood they have spawned all over the world have always enjoyed prestige and royal treatment. I'm not only talking about the Council in Los Angeles, either. I'm referring to all the councilmembers and Ancients who have profited from fear and reverence for hundreds of years around the world."

"I still don't get it." Poe scratched her head in frustration. "Can't their system take the Plasmacore or something?"

"They *can* drink the Plasmacore. That's the problem." With his hand, Sainvire stopped Poe from asking another question. "Put it this way, Poe. Imagine you are the Queen of England, set apart by blood, riches, and circumstance. You are told that if you drink a can of root beer, a soda that would take away all the perks and bring you on even footing with street cleaners, prostitutes, coal miners, and such, would you drink it?"

"Sure," Poe answered quickly. "I love root beer."

"Yes, you would. But you haven't tasted the birthright of a queen. Gold, crown jewels, palaces, maze gardens with peacocks, the rights of condescension." Sainvire stretched his long legs clad in black slacks, nearly touching Poe's foot which unwound at the same time.

"Our ancient, closed-minded vampires want the mystique of vampirism to stay. They want glory, awe, and fear from fellow vampires and humans alike. Strength used to lie in the strain of vampire blood where one was created from, as well as the vintage of the vampires themselves. But even supernatural beings can't compete with nature, science, and genetics."

Poe nearly catapulted out of her seat as Sainvire's extremely sharp and intimidating nails shot up fourteen inches, turning into deadly black talons.

"During the past hundred years or so," Sainvire continued as if nothing untoward had happened, "fledgling vampires springing from no discernible ancient bloodlines showed promise of power far stronger than many Ancients. Some could even walk in daylight, only needing to protect their eyes. Some could fly and some could unearth entire buildings with their bare hands. Some exhibited strengths far more advanced and complex than any ancient immortals from the earlier bloodlines."

He stared at Poe for quite some time before continuing. His gaze lingered upon her long, lustrous hair parted on the side and held with bobby pins, her naturally arched eyebrows, serious dark eyes, small perspiring nose tip, and down to her lips, still swollen from a punch. "In short, the old order started to crumble. Superstitious hogwash now had a basis for scientific study. Old and ancient didn't spell fear anymore."

"Are you an old vampire?" Poe asked, for she couldn't take his probing any longer.

Sainvire chuckled. "Yes, I suppose I am, only compared to you. I'm sure the silly war I fought in won't ring any bells. I left Chicago, my home, to fight with the Abraham Lincoln Brigade against Franco in Spain."

"This was before World War II, right? I know it. You were like Humphrey Bogart in *Casablanca.*" She smiled at history learned through the insightful textbook of films.

"I wouldn't put it quite that way. Rick Blaine ended up owning the Café Americaine in the Hollywood version, while I got to be food for a hefty Spanish vampire woman with foul breath who had been a prostitute at a seedy Andalusian whorehouse. Did I mention she was sex crazed? The war was a lost cause, and my idealism died when shrapnel lodged into my shoulder." He crossed one ankle over the other. "I was thirty-four years old when I changed into what I am today. We can thank the little señorita for lapping up the blood from my shattered shoulder and biting off a chunk of my noggin and spitting blood into my brain."

"So your nails grow and you can fly. Do you have any other talents?"

"I have many talents, Poe." His eyes left hers and stole a quick glance at her bound bosom. *What a shame*, he thought. "I will be sure to show them to you, but right now, I have to finish my tale. Where was I?"

Boiling from the vampire's suggestive words, Poe said, "You were talking about the ancient vampires and the new breeds."

"Yes, thank you. Anyway, the Ancients, when they found out about the talented new breeds, as you referred to them, they were naturally overcome with fear about the possible consequences. So like they had done for centuries upon finding freak vampires such as myself," he retracted his claws for effect, "they hunted them down and exterminated them. However, when the gray came, it seemed silly to kill off vampires without justification. The Council would've been exposed. So they allowed us to be part of the new society, never letting us forget the primal order.

"Imagine their chagrin when I came up to them and offered an alternative to pure human blood. They were livid to say the least." He sighed. "It was my fault, really. I thought everyone was going to have a fist-slamming celebration like I did. I also was foolish enough to assume that the Council owed allegiance to me for planning the cattle idea." He looked at Poe, wincing at the cattle reference. "Here we are at an impasse. We have the Plasmacore, but we can't let anyone outside this library know about it."

Again Sainvire lapsed into silence, lines appearing on his forehead. "If you must know, I…I'm the one who killed Goss and Sister Ann," he said, almost whispering.

Poe sat frozen, stunned at the abrupt change of subject. Pure anger seeped through her system like venom, and Poe bolted out of her chair. Before Sainvire could straighten his legs, Poe sprang on him, her knee on his thigh and the point of the medical scissors at his neck.

Her voice, deep and husky with pent up fury and melancholy asked, "Why?" She thought he was Sister's and Goss' friend.

Sainvire didn't change his relaxed position. He looked at her dark eyes, swimming with hate, guilt, regret, two inches from his own. Her breath smelled of wintergreen toothpaste.

"Because I wasn't there when they needed me," he answered, closing his eyes. His mouth set in a hard line. "I was out of town, secretly meeting with other vampires, giving them samples of the Plasmacore and the formula and components to recreate them."

Poe's hand wavered, the scissors shaking, but still she didn't let go. Her throat seemed parched and hollow.

"A master vampire shouldn't leave his people, and that's what I did," he continued, his voice deep and soft. "I found out that Goss and Sister hadn't arrived to turn over any cattle when I met with Morales and Megan in Pico Rivera." He opened his eyes and stared at Poe. "I went to see Goss and it was too late. Trench had already gotten to them. That was when I saw you jump out of the glass window while under attack by Trench's people." He sighed, yet again. "You see, it was my fault for overreaching my bounds."

Liquid fell on Sainvire's cheek. It wasn't his. Vampires were incapable of crying. He looked up to see Poe's eyes huge with tears. She clutched at his black shirt as if about to rip it to shreds.

"It wasn't your fault, not entirely." Poe's voice was heavy with grief. "It was mine, too."

Sainvire leaned forward and dug his hands on either side of her arms. "Don't say that," he commanded. "You went up to the clock tower by yourself to rescue them. You were surrounded by vicious–"

Poe shook her head. "No! I should've left my bunker sooner but…but–"

She cried hard, clutching at Sainvire's shirt. "But I didn't! I was too much of a coward!" She stabbed a number two pencil at his chest, but not hard enough to do any damage. "It took two weeks to convince myself to go out and look for them. At least you were off doing something important. While I watched videos and sat it out, my friends were being bled to death."

Sainvire put his arm around her, only to be pushed roughly away. Poe slumped back to her chair. With the back of her hand, she wiped the drops on her cheek. She kicked herself for being so damn weak in front of Sainvire. Some crybaby vampire killer she turned out to be.

Sainvire restrained himself from embracing the young woman fighting hard not to weep. Apparently they had two things in common: their love for their dead friends and the guilt they suffered over their deaths. No matter what the other said, the guilt would lie in both.

Quietly he rose.

"You can sleep on the bed. I thank you for listening to me. I know how tired you must be." He bowed and walked away, closing the door behind him.

Poe stared after him, her nose red and runny. *I must look disgusting and weak to him.* For some reason, this thought bothered her quite a bit, for shouldn't she have been dwelling on her guilt instead of what the vampire thought of her?

CHAPTER 5-POE ON CAPOEIRA

OUTSIDE, GRAY CLOUDS REJOICED as feelers of lightning pierced the sky, creating a smoky afterburn across the downtown skyline. Rain, not wanting to be outdone, poured out in great pelts. Wind came, slapping palm tree fronds and ejecting their rat inhabitants to the concrete jungle below. With a pillow over her head, Poe slept through the clutter. It was a little past noon. Just like the storm raging outside the window, she was oblivious to the figure that studied her sleeping form, the observer's fist clenching and unclenching. Satisfied with what he saw, the man made a hasty exit.

Inside the library was a bustle of activity not unlike the storm outside. If the comings and goings of the lower level were viewed from the air, ant-like figures in white robes would have been seen packing Plasmacore bags into crates. Once the boxes were filled and packed in bubble wrap and foam, vampires and halfdeads lifted them effortlessly onto the waiting trucks in the parking garage. What couldn't be seen from above were the newly awakened humans ready to replace the night shift workers. The operation was quite involved and organized. And every detail was recorded by memory by the ever-watchful eyes of a spy.

Down in the library basement slept about four dozen vampires, getting needed respite from the night's work and the sun. The spying eyes counted the vampires occupying the ground floor and made another mental note.

Lightning projected phantasmagoric shadow and light from the sundry stained glass and other windows of the library not covered by tar. The mole stopped within earshot of three beings talking intently by the elevator.

"I'm done with being a traveling salesman," said Sainvire. "From now on, I'm staying put. I'll never let anything happen to our people again because of a utopian dream."

"It's no dream. Many of your kind have already taken to Plasmacore," said Perla.

"You just want to stay because of the girl," teased Joseph. "She's a looker, that one."

The spy listened as Sainvire, Joseph, and Perla discussed the girl named Poe. As soon as Sainvire turned to study the pillar he was hiding behind, the operative pivoted and headed toward the escalator on the other side of the hall.

"Who was that?" Sainvire asked.

"Oh, he's the new phlebotomist," Perla volunteered. "He's the human our sweepers found wandering around Santa Monica few months ago."

"I have the oddest sense that he was listening to us from behind that column," Sainvire commented as he followed the man's descent down the escalator.

"How did he say he survived all this time?" asked the master vampire.

"With help from the clandestine community in West L.A. and Santa Monica, of course," answered Perla. It was well known that the small group of stragglers and survivors had formed a working community thereabouts. They'd dodged cattle round-ups routinely initiated by master vampires and councilmembers. Many of them were Sainvire's contacts.

"He's pretty weird," Joseph supplied. "He got on Poe's case for spilling a packet of blood. He almost tackled the poor girl. Would've liked to see him try. My money would've been on Poe, of course, after what Goss told us and what you witnessed yesterday."

"Just keep an eye on him," Sainvire ordered. "One slip and I want him gone, alright?"

His two friends nodded their assent.

"Joseph, will you escort Poe to the armory room this afternoon?"

"It'll be my pleasure," Joseph grinned. "Although I can't imagine a human so slight handling such heavy firepower."

"Friend, you haven't seen her at work," said Sainvire with a crooked smile. "She single-handedly killed over a dozen of Trench's troops and survived with only scratches and a nail wound."

"Sounds like Terminator Girl has a fan," Joseph mocked the much taller vampire.

Sainvire didn't deny it. He merely told the impertinent vampire to scram for he had something to discuss with Perla.

When they were finally alone, Sainvire turned to a smiling Perla, clad in yet another set of matching pajamas, only this time the yellow jammies bled with Voltron figures in various fighting stances.

"Not you, too, Perla," Sainvire despaired, shaking his head.

"Well, Kaleb, it has been years since you've had a woman, vampire or human at that." Perla hooked her arm in the crook of Sainvire's.

Sainvire squeezed his friend's arm and flashed a wry smile. "Are you sure about that? I've been traveling a lot recently, you know."

His retort made the round-cheeked woman chortle, and she pinched the master vampire's perfectly firm buns.

One of his dark eyebrows lifted. For the affront, he retaliated by placing a booming kiss on the top of her head. He was used to his friend's very touchy and sometimes shockingly irreverent but benign actions. Besides, Perla had a partner whom Sainvire adored and respected. "Were you able to procure what I asked for?"

"You bet. The items are already upstairs," she scowled, giving him a significant look. "Now I think I'll take a nap before I play babysitter today."

———————

Poe woke up to a crowd within the terrarium they called the library.

The bed's too comfortable. She'd lost command of her internal alarm clock. The presence of four creatures in her room – Sainvire's room – nearly spurred a heart condition. She bolted upright, her sore muscles and myriad injuries screaming. One hand explored her head for any holes and the other reached under the pillow for scissors, her hair falling in tangled disarray around her face.

"Good morning, Poe," Perla greeted cheerfully as she placed Poe's freshly dried clothes and shoes on the foot of the bed.

"You mean, good afternoon, don't you?" Joseph corrected. He flashed Poe a disapproving headshake, his trademark smile nearly surfacing.

Poe couldn't quite get herself to speak. She was afraid a string of gutter-stutter would come out, so she waited until her breathing settled a notch. She saw Sainvire give her a quick nod as he fed spoonfuls of what appeared to be mashed potatoes to a groggy Penny.

A tall and thick middle-aged vampire that was sitting at the far end of the room drifted a foot from the ground toward the bed. The woman simply smiled at the weapon in Poe's hand.

"My name's Maple," the vampire introduced herself, dropping a heavy sack full of bullets on the mattress. "These are for you."

"Huh?"

"Bullets, Poe. Not just marinated bullets but bullets filled with garlic oil. Or as Sister loved to say, blessed bullets." She extended her dead white hand. "Nice to meet you."

Poe stared at the hand and until she finally extended her own. The vamp's hand was softer and warmer than she had imagined. "Um, nice to meet you."

A little more than confused, Poe looked around the room, unsure of what to do. The huge bed dwarfed her, quite pathetic and rumpled. Her silence also added to doubts about her killing ability. Perla already had a preconception of the girl as a clumsy blood spiller. Joseph, although he enjoyed sporting around with his new pal, had his doubts that this little leaguer could kill supernaturals even with the aid of weapons. "She's just lucky," he told Sainvire.

As for Maple, the girl's inability to handle this simple social situation lost her some Kool-Aid points. But she did concede that Poe had lived a decade or so of her life alone, which would explain the warped social skills. And they had invaded her space before she had time to dress.

Only Sainvire had the utmost confidence in the girl's abilities. He'd seen firsthand what Poe could do under duress. She was also a damn fine shot, accurately able to shatter two vampire heads at once. He sensed the doubts around him, but they would just have to see for themselves. Besides, Poe's husky voice penetrated his senses like nothing else.

Perla was the first to break the silence. "Here are your clothes and shoes, dear." She smiled as Poe's eyes lingered on a Voltron figure on the woman's sleeve. "We have washers and dryers downstairs. Hope you don't mind." Poe shook her head, mumbling a thank you.

"You'll find a new toothbrush in the bathroom and some ibuprofen. You must be really sore by now."

Because Poe kept staring at her with those big eyes with a pinched look, Perla decided to be a little more specific. "You can take a shower now if you wish. You have a long afternoon ahead of you." She indicated Joseph with her head. "Joe there will outfit you with new weapons, and Maple will show you the vampire's most vulnerable areas, the ones Sister Ann neglected to teach you. So go on and get ready so you can have lunch beforehand."

Poe nodded once and slinked out of the bed barefoot and into the privacy of the bathroom. None of the vampires or Perla failed to notice the tattered condition of Sainvire's old trousers which overnight had sprouted little strings from the hacked hems. The four visitors held their urge to laugh until after the young woman had shut the bathroom door. Then they let loose.

If Poe did hear laughter, she ignored it, for among the folded clothes Perla handed her were three new pairs of cotton bras. At that moment, she simply wanted to get gobbled down by any miserable monsters looking to have a meal.

———————

Acutely aware of the prying eyes hoping for a repeat of the night before, Poe made it a point to eat more slowly, savoring the flavors of hash browns, pancakes, and veggie sausages.

"Are we correct in assuming you're vegetarian, Poe?" Habib asked in a prim British accent. He and the other three chefs joined the girl, Perla, Maple, and Joseph during brunch.

"Um, I never thought of that, but I guess so," Poe answered, drinking a draught of freshly squeezed orange juice. "My dad could drink a gallon of this stuff without taking a breath."

It looked like she would have three escorts for the rest of the day. As she finished her O.J., Poe surreptitiously checked out Joseph who poured some Plasmacore into two glasses, handing one to Maple. Her gaze turned to Perla, dipping a piece of toast in the yellow part of her eggs. She stopped her scrutinizing when she noticed Janice, one of the chefs, looking at her.

"How's breakfast, young lady?" she asked.

Poe swallowed and enthusiastically answered, "Delicious! You guys are the best cooks in the world."

The chefs beamed, promising dinner to be a truly lavish affair. Poe smacked her lips and rubbed her tummy in anticipation. "I can't wait." Joseph ended all the food talk, feeling rather hungry himself for something altogether different than his liquid meal.

"Enough about food already," Joseph begged. "We need to vamoose to the Dirty Harry Room."

Poe thanked the chefs again and took her leave, her belly round from the amount of food inside. She wondered about the Dirty Harry Room but decided to wait it out.

It didn't take her long to utter, "Oh, I get it." The Dirty Harry Room contained weaponry of all kinds from as early as the 1600s. The room used to be the special library reserve for newspapers, magazines, microfilm, and CDs. Now it carried hundreds of axes, knives, bayonets, crossbows, and of course, guns. The end of the long, bare room boasted nothing but three large target sheets tacked on a wall of wood and tough fibers to blunt the bullets.

Poe's eyes warily drank the sight of such magnificent weaponry. Her parents, avidly anti-gun, were probably looking down on her with terrible disapproval. But what could she do in such dark times?

Eyeing the row of axes, she quietly said, "I want one of those." She'd always had a hankering for a Hawkeye axe.

"Should we start with the guns? You'll need a few," Joseph suggested.

Poe followed him to the rows of perfectly shelved handguns, rifles, semi-automatics, and shotguns. Poe gravitated to the Walther PPK, hoping to replace her dear James.

"I prefer a Walther PPK and a Beretta."

"Try handling other guns first. You might be surprised," Joseph advised.

Reluctantly Poe inspected the automatic pistol that Joseph, uncharacteristically clad in a Watchmen shirt, handed her. It was a 10mm Remington, a bit heavy and large for her hands, but she just had to please the smile-heavy vampire looking over her shoulders. At least he was fully dressed this time. She didn't even bother to step at the shooting line. Poe fired from where she stood at the corner end of the room.

Perla and Maple, deep in conversation, were startled into attention by the blast, their eyes alternating between Poe and the target. Her shot was a few millimeters from the bullseye, but it was still in the red circle. They looked at the girl who made a face at Joseph and said that the Remington was too heavy. Their conversation stopped for good to watch Poe select several guns and fire them. Holding a gun in each hand, Poe shot at two separate targets simultaneously, hitting the center of both. The two women exchanged looks.

"I take back any doubts I had about her skills," Perla whispered to Maple.

"Ditto. Taken back."

As surprised as Perla and Maple, Joseph was decidedly awed by the shooting prowess of the young woman. He grinned as he handed the Glock, his favorite weapon, to Poe.

The pasted look of cynicism on Poe's face faded as soon as she held the small G-19 pistol that held 18 rounds of ammo. It felt feather light and fit perfectly in her hand. It was made out of synthetic polymer that was stronger than steel, yet was hugely lighter than most pistols. She took the other gun Joseph held out to her. It was a Glock 33, also known as one of the smallest .357s ever made. For such a powerful handgun, it was surprisingly buoyant.

Poe moved to the firing line. Extending both hands into fire position, Poe sprinkled bullets on the three targets on the opposite side of the room, hitting the bullseye over ninety-nine percent of the time. To her surprise, the Glocks proved better than her old guns. The change saddened her, but for safety sake, she chose accuracy over loyalty.

"I'm sold on these two," she said to Joseph.

"Wise choice."

Poe ended up with a Walther PPK and three Glocks, including a mini-Glock, a palm sized firearm that could be easily sheathed at her ankle. Maple also supplied Poe with a mini-Uzi that was more high-tech than the one sliced by vampire nails back at Goss'. For what it was worth, the manufacturer guaranteed that the Uzi wouldn't lock.

"No, really. I don't want a shotgun," she said adamantly. "I'll kill myself with the recoil. But I wouldn't mind a small axe and some knives."

Perla helped sharpen the chosen Hawkeye axe, while Maple and Joseph looked for the right-size shoulder and ankle holsters for the girl. Poe filled her backpack with ammunition. She was used to heavy weights on her shoulders.

Maple gave a brief but informative lecture about the vulnerable spots of vampires. Poe was surprised to learn a thing or two. For instance, she hadn't known that a vampire's spine could be severed if hit two or three times with blessed ammo. The bacteria in the garlic would prevent the bones from soldering back together. Since the vampire was nice enough to share such prime information, Poe felt more at ease. So much at ease that she asked Maple in a whisper if it was true that male vampires reacted like human males when kicked in the groin.

Maple didn't even bat an eye and answered her question as if it had been asked in a classroom. "A little, Poe, but not enough to bowl them over or keep them from doing their business. It's more psychological than anything."

For some reason, the conversation turned to sex. Joseph was the one who answered the questions most asked by humans.

"Yes, we can have sex with humans and vampires alike," he sighed. "No, we can't spawn any half-human, half-vampire brats – we're dead. But there are those pesky rumors that vampire babies begat by dead partners can sometimes take seed. Supernatural anomaly. Since I haven't seen any fanged vamplings with my own eyes, then they must be myth. And no, we don't feel sexual and turned on by drinking blood like what oversexed novelists insisted upon drilling into the public's head. Blood's just food. You don't want to have sex with your bowl of oatmeal, do you?" He looked at Poe, a little annoyed. "Any more questions before the lesson?"

Poe crossed her arms. "I didn't ask you those questions, you know." She looked at a mischievous Perla. Peevishly, she continued. "And what lesson?"

Joseph opened the door to a gymnasium and let the three in. "Just a little something so we can gauge your self-defense skills."

Poe's eyes widened. "Man, I'm all cut and bruised up from yesterday. I can't be thrown around and kicked by subcreatures."

"Don't worry about it, Poe. We know about your injuries," he smiled. "Besides, I'm not the one who's going to kick you around. That would be these gentlemen over here."

As if on cue, three humans – one thin, one burly, and one extremely muscular – wearing white sparring outfits appeared from around the corner. The lounging crowd clapped readily.

Poe had an intense urge to punch Joseph's gleeful mug. This wasn't funny at all. These guys looked like they belonged in *Bloodsport*. She limped from her nail wound, her cuts still fresh. And she was bursting from lunch, for Pete's sake. She felt like unlatching the safety of one of the Glocks and shooting everyone in the room who'd come for the spectacle.

"Poe, this is Jim. He'll be your first sparring partner." The thin but sturdy man bowed to her. His face screamed pain in Poe's opinion. She flared her nostrils at the man. She pulled down at her Pixies t-shirt. "If you would take off your holsters and backpack, the games can begin."

Poe scowled at Joseph, her five-inch scar turning white. *This isn't a gladiator show. Miserable fucker!* She threw her new guns unceremoniously by Joseph's feet hoping one of them would go off and shoot him in the ass. Perla gave her a squeeze, looking mighty nervous for the girl. Maple whispered in her ear, "Remember, anything goes, Poe."

Poe nodded at the two women, too tense to give a proper smile. Her butt was hurting, too. She thought she should just refuse, but she knew Joseph would never let her hear the end of it. And unbelievably, her new bra was giving her grief. Too stiff and itchy.

As if the whole thing wasn't painful enough, Sainvire came striding in looking cool and collected, ready to watch the bullfight. Poe's breath caught in her throat. *Why did he have to be so damn tall and interesting-looking? And those freaky eyes! Why didn't Joseph choose three women to spar with me?*

"Please, Mom and Dad, don't make me look stupid in front of Sainvire," Poe prayed silently. She squatted down to tighten the double-knot of her shoelaces.

As soon as Poe stepped on the mat, Jim circled her as if she were prey, and assumed a fighting stance not unlike Ralph Macchio's "Crane" from *The Karate Kid*. *Fuck me*, Poe thought as she stood. She couldn't remember any of the stances she had learned from

Goss and her videos at home, and she had no idea which style she would sport. *I'm dead.*

Economy of movement, Poe, said Bruce Lee in her head. Before his voice finished, however, Jim had already snaked a punch in her direction. Poe barely avoided the full impact of his fist as she did a Cassius Clay and stepped back, dancer style with her chin tucked in.

The smack she took instead of a punch served to piss her off since she knew at least a dozen folks were watching. Some she recognized from the cafeteria. When another punch came at her, Poe blocked with her elbow, trapping her opponent's hand. She returned with a back kick, cracking his kneecap. It was always a good move to go for the knee. As Jim fell, Poe continued to work on his hand, snapping back his wrist.

"That's what you get, jerk!" A dirty fighter, Poe didn't stop with the wrist. She kicked at the man even when he was down, concentrating on his face and privates. "Die!"

"Jim will never be able to have kids," said an onlooker sweating on a treadmill.

Maple had to carry the defeated man away from the still kicking Poe, while she let loose a string of *Scarface* lingo. Maple flashed Poe a one-down, two-to-go look as she handed Jim into the waiting arms of a medic.

Beet-faced and pacing, Poe smoothed back the long strands that escaped her ponytail. For some annoying reason, her sweat glands set their headquarters on the tip of her nose. She wiped the offending droplets with her lucky Pixies shirt, her mother's favorite band.

A burly man named Biff with long sideburns stepped on the mat. Poe urgently wanted a break.

Didn't boxers get five-minute rests? *Jesus, Mary, and Joseph!*

She snapped the many black rubber bands on her left wrist until the pain reminded her that it could be worse. Poe reluctantly stepped up to join Biff. *Better get used to something harder than a thwack on your arm*, Poe thought bleakly.

"Your dirty tricks ain't gonna work on me, missy," he drawled. "I learned from the same instructor as Elvis. You do know who the King is, don't cha?" Biff threw out, disgusted at the girl's lack of honor.

"Um, sure. Elvis of *Clam Bake* and *Kissin' Cousins* fame. King of cheese and swampy movies." She let the number one fan have it. "Oh yeah, he was into karate-choppin' and sequined jumpsuits, too."

Ticked off, the yoked man kicked at her bad leg, causing her to fall on one knee. "Never insult the King!"

I hate this guy, she thought. *C'mon, Master Lee. Give me a sign!* While she waited for inspiration from the Master, Poe stood up and blocked each kick with her left leg, positioned Thai boxing style. An elbow blocked each punch. Evidently she had not developed sufficient calluses on her leg bones and elbows. Lightly kicking a baseball bat while watching movies or reading books and chewing old gum wasn't sufficient training.

Each massive block caused her to clamp her teeth shut from pain. His bones were definitely gargantuan compared to hers. Finally the Master spoke, just in the nick of time.

Lesson A, Tape 2: *Playing with Human Instinct* stole into her mind.

"Thank you, Master Lee," she murmured, parrying Biff's punch and lashing at his ankle with a kick.

The burly man deflected the blow with his massive arm. Poe targeted his ankle again with her foot but was blocked by a knee. The third time, she kicked toward Biff's ankle, but she aborted the move midway and hit Elvis #2 with a jarring right to the face. *Faked out! The shit really works!*

Red and furious, Biff ran at her. He succeeded in grabbing the scrambling Poe from behind. He lifted her off the floor, her legs dangling uselessly. JKD move number 23: *Do whatever the hell it takes!*

"Um, there's something about you, Biff," Poe said with difficulty. "Being this close to you makes me realize that you smell rancid." She pried off a finger digging on a rib and snapped it back, breaking the digit with a pop. Biff immediately let go, falling on his knees and yelling profanity Poe had never heard before.

To shut him up, Poe released a high kick squarely in Biff's mouth, making him keel over and swallow a tooth. Once on the floor, Poe grabbed his thinning hair and rammed his already bloody face on the mat over and over until she was again dragged to the sideline. She cussed at the semi-conscious Biff who was having difficulty breathing from the blood oozing out of his broken nose. "And a blue aloha to you, too, fucker!"

"I thought you said she was no contest," the blubbering man, spitting out blood and teeth said accusingly at Joseph as he was escorted from the mat. For the first time, Poe noticed the shocked faces of the humans in the gym. Some of the bolder vampires acknowledged her with a nod, and a few didn't even want to make eye contact.

A second after the blood and teeth were wiped from the practice mat, the last sparring partner cartwheeled onto the mat in unbelievable speed, drawing applause. Poe felt a thrill of apprehension. She didn't know shit about Capoeira, the Brazilian martial arts that stocked a lot of dance and twirl movement.

Miserable Mission Impossible *with Tom Cruise. That's what I get?* Poe thought, searching for a useful defense maneuver.

"It's an embarrassing form of martial arts," Goss once said, shaking his head. "You don't need to learn that crap because it leaves you wide open. You don't want a ballet recital anyway, kid. You want something ugly and rough that will hurt your enemy something fierce."

But something was off about the man called Rufus, and it wasn't just his lack of shirt, either. He was too fast. As soon as the third contender landed on his feet and winked, Poe realized what it was. Rufus was a halfdead as indicated by his short fangs. *Fuck me. I'm dead.*

Poe gestured to Joseph for a timeout.

"Why? It's almost over, Poe. Do you think you'll get a break during a vampire attack?"

"This isn't a vampire attack! And that guy is a halfdead!" she screeched. "It's not fair–"

"That's how life is sometimes," Joseph smiled patronizingly. "Now get in there and fight the mutha!"

Poe held her tongue and gave him the finger instead. She looked up at Sainvire staring intently. The vampire looked nervous for her. For good measure, she flipped him one. *At least I'm not the only one afraid for me*, thought Poe. Taking deep breaths and exhaling slowly, Poe faced the half-vamp. *There are guns for these sorts of things.*

"I'm the Great Ali's daughter," Poe mumbled to herself. "I'm too pretty to…"

Rufus flamboyantly cartwheeled toward Poe, stopping directly in front of her. Quick as a flash, he kissed Poe on the tip of her sweaty nose. Everyone in the gym roared with laughter, except for Sainvire. Humiliated to say the least, Poe lashed out, slapping the beaming halfdead.

Rufus' expression soured. He grabbed Poe by the shoulders and hurled her in the direction of her three companions. Her shoulder blade hit the back of a metal chair, igniting an electric shock of pain.

"*Aray ko!*" she said in Tagalog.

From the floor, Joseph loomed over her with his yellow smiley Watchmen t-shirt, raising his eyebrows as if to say, "Well, what are you waiting for?"

Despite the pain, Poe got up and spat a thick one on Joseph's bare feet. She jogged to the bastard, Rufus, and snarled at him. Poe easily dodged the lead straight punch he threw at her, watching the cords on his neck instead of his eyes. The tightness of the neck was a more accurate gauge of where the next punch would originate.

As soon as Rufus retreated, however, Poe executed one of the dirtiest tricks she knew. She stomped hard on the tender part of his foot. Rufus' scream didn't matter, for she knew that the pain in his foot would keep him occupied. She made sure to maintain the pressure on her Adidas. One second, two seconds, a punch. The halfdead tried to pull away but couldn't. The girl hung on his neck, and he was stuck like an Everlast punching sack, just like in Lesson 32.

She was the most lowdown fighter the gym had seen yet. The halfdead had to grab Poe by the neck and lift her off the floor to pry her off of him. Poe's sore knuckles were worse than useless. She couldn't even pry Rufus' big fingers off her neck. From the corner of her eyes, she saw Perla and Maple looking tense, and Joseph, for once, didn't have a trace of a smile. But the weirdest of all was Sainvire. He was no longer sitting and looked positively murderous. Before the pressure around her neck could make her pass out, Master Lee's voice rang in her ear. *Remember the three-pound pressure rule.*

Her eyes widening, Poe grabbed Rufus' left ear, and with all her might, pulled down. She came tumbling on the floor, her fist grasping the halfdead's ripped ear. So it was true. It only took three pounds of pressure to pull someone's ear off. She did learn a lot from watching videos and reading books. *Who needs to go to school?*

Rufus' wail was deafening, as his hand tried to cover the gaping hole made on the left side of his head. Sainvire was beside Poe, helping her up. At least three people tried to calm the distraught Rufus, but he would have none of it. Poe dislodged Sainvire's hand from her elbow and walked toward her fallen nemesis. Rufus looked up at the small woman, five-foot-two and three-quarters to be exact, who had ripped his ear off and belted out a murderous series of curses.

Poe forced herself to smile sweetly and say, "This is for kissing my nose without my permission you disgusting halfdead!" She hurled the bloody ear in the daywalker's face and strode out of the gym.

———————

She didn't really know where to go, so Poe decided to go back to Sainvire's room. She could check on Penny and use the bathroom. Her hands shook. The rich meal and the bodily injuries she had received seemed to wreak mayhem with her already traumatized system.

"Everything is a joke with that moron," she seethed, talking to the air. "I could've been killed! But then again, he'd probably laugh his head off if I got pounced to death."

Her body ached from being thrown around the room and kicked repeatedly. *Punks!* As soon as she could get Penny out of there without injuring the mutt further, they would be off. This library was just too crazy for her.

Penny lay on her side, half awake. When Poe sat down to face the dog on the sofa, she whined. The area where her tongue had been was still swollen and the cut fresh, but because of her healing doggy saliva, Penny was happily on the mend. Poe exhaled on the dog's face. Penny seemed to find the warm breath comforting and gave a little sigh.

"Poor ratty dog."

With Penny safely dozing, Poe went into the bathroom with an old *Time* magazine in hand and did her business. She was one those people who could read or think on the porcelain throne until their legs turned numb. Her sister Sirena had taught her well. She did her best thinking that way.

When she came out a cool forty minutes later, Sainvire was looking out the Spanish-style window, patiently waiting for her. Oddly, the vampire wasn't affected in the slightest by the weak sunlight that struggled to emerge in the downpour. This revelation disturbed her strongly.

Instead of blushing at being caught using the commode for almost an hour, Poe pursed her lips and looked up at the ceiling. She was sick of feeling embarrassed. She'd already done her job as the freak gladiator of the day.

"What?" she asked the vampire who turned around to face her. He was wearing the same outfit as yesterday, black t-shirt and dark slacks.

"Just wanted to give you these," he said as he pointed to the bed. There lay an Uzi, an axe, three Glock pistols in holsters, and her favorite James Bond gun, a Walther PPK – the weapons she'd left at the gym.

Poe didn't even thank him. She just took the holsters and slipped them around her shoulders. The smaller one she strapped to her ankle. The Uzi and axe she threw on the bed. She demanded the time.

"Five-thirty," Sainvire answered in a calm voice, following Poe's every move with his unnerving eyes. *The girl has the right to be mad*, he thought. Joseph was a prankster who didn't know where to draw the line. His friend certainly overdid it with the sparring demonstration that afternoon. Since he had allowed the spectacle to continue, he blamed himself for the carnage.

Like those at the gym, he couldn't keep his eyes off Poe and her unscrupulous fighting skills. The combat was the closest thing to television he'd seen in years. A small person brought down three skilled fighters. The girl was intriguing him more and more.

"What time is dinner?" Poe asked hungry again after her vampire-slinging excursion.

"There's food around the clock. If you wish to have dinner, you can go now."

Not wanting to appear like a hog, Poe covered herself. "Habib, Janice, and the other chefs promised to make something really good in my honor tonight. I don't want them to think I'm rude by showing up late." She hurried out the room before Sainvire could say anything further. She smiled at the fact that she wasn't stuttering anymore.

CHAPTER 6-SKY'S BLEEDING DEAD

POE MADE UP HER mind. The cafeteria, with an exposed kitchen at the head of the buffet tables, was her favorite place in the library.

"Here's hummus flavored slightly with garlic and coriander. This dish is garlic okra," Habib described, pushing his black-rimmed glasses up his nose to magnify his eyeballs five times their size. "This is—"

"And here's a terrific eggplant and tahini dip called baba ghanoush, Poe," Janice interrupted, putting a ladle full of each dish on Poe's tray. The deep age lines on her face glistened from her cooking efforts. "Please try the Ethiopian lentil soup, Spinach adobo, tofu spaghetti, avocado and olive salad, and freshly made pita bread that I whipped up in your honor."

"Hey, where's the meat?" a fifty-something man with a limp complained. The buffet line wasn't moving at all and the trays bearing veggie dishes didn't appeal to his palate.

"Yeah," another butted in. "Weren't we going to have ribs today?"

The complaints fell on deaf ears.

"Okay, Janice. Quit showing off. My turn now," Ray said, shooing everyone with his get-outta-my-way gut. You mentioned you like pad thai, so I fixed you up a batch," he said, plunking a big orange serving on Poe's already teetering plate. "It was the only dish I could make because I had to grind rice into flour to make the proper noodles for the dish. Preparation alone took almost all day."

"Quit making excuses, old man." Petra tapped him on the shoulder to get him out of her way. She must have been in her seventies but still dyed her hair crow black. Traces of hair coloring stained her forehead and neck. "I made only two dishes, but you're going to love them," Petra assured the half-drooling Poe. "I made you some sayur lodeh soup – that's Indonesian vegetable soup with coconut milk – and some Guamanian red rice.

Poe had never heard of some of the dishes, but she was more than willing to taste. She beamed but avoided the eyes of her fellow diners. It dawned on her that with the exception of a handful of youthful vampires, the library was filled with people over twenty years her senior. Of course, true vampire age was impossible to guess from afar.

"You guys are some of the best people I've ever met," Poe said, and she meant it. "If you ever need anything…"

"Eat up, girl," Ray ordered the girl who was on the verge of sniffling. "You need to replenish after your little adventure this afternoon."

"Where did all this food come from?"

"From the Valley, of course," said Habib. "Haven't you heard of the holy roller farmers who supply meat and vegetables to Los Angles in exchange for some autonomy?"

Poe shook her head.

"Well they're vampires who drink only animal blood and farm at night. They stay away from the politics rampant around here. Occasionally they're called upon by the Council, but mostly they're left alone. They're responsible for feeding the humans of our city."

All five sat on a table with a reserved sign on it saying: *Sit here and DIE!*

Poe inhaled the saliva-inducing aroma, imagining all those years of eating cold, slimy canned nibbles. She shivered, hoping she would never have to suffer that fate again. Just to eat this feast regularly, Poe was almost willing to be Sainvire's gopher and occasional blood supplier. Almost.

She dug in, but before she could take her first bite, Maple and Joseph appeared by her elbow. She gave Joseph a nasty look and brought the garlic okra to her mouth. However, Joseph's seriousness made her fork waver. Something was wrong.

Maple, looking nervous, told Poe to follow her.

"But I'm eating." Poe said.

"Can't you wait until after our friend here has finished her meal?" demanded Ray, looking like a Hobbit with his girth.

"Yeah. She hasn't even taken a bite yet," Petra agreed, pursing her heavily lined smoker's lips.

"Poe needs to come with us now," Joseph insisted, his mouth tight with worry.

"But–"

"The Council has summoned her to appear before them," Maple announced quietly. This time, the chefs did not protest. Aghast, they looked at Poe with fear. Her appetite vanished.

Habib slid the tray away from Poe, saying, "I'll keep this warm for you, dear girl."

The other cooks nodded, looking suddenly ill. Janice had to disengage the okra-heavy fork from Poe's hand. She knew then that something sinister was going to happen to her.

The Council equals ancient vampires with crazy powers. She'd killed a few of Trench's people and lied about non-existent underground guerrillas. *I'm history, and I'm ethnic!*

The quiet trek to the first floor lobby was terribly funereal. Maple and Joseph didn't explain anything, but their grim mouths said it all.

By the entrance stood Sainvire, his long, dark coat already on. Perla fidgeted nervously beside the tall vampire and smiled weakly at Poe. She handed the girl a newly laundered coat, the armaments, and her pack that contained all the blessed ammo she was going to need for the night. Her new set of weapons seemed to follow her from room to room. Sainvire inclined his head at her, his unnerving eyes flashing with restrained energy.

"No doubt they've told you," he indicated Joseph and Maple, "the Council sent a messenger requesting your attendance this evening."

Poe nodded. Asking why would have been insipid and pointless, because everyone already knew that she was going to be tortured and turned into a bedpan emptier before morning. With a sigh, she put on her coat, thinking that this was her last night on earth, and she didn't even have a proper last meal. She stooped down to double-knot her sneakers.

Her self-pity ended when Perla locked lips with Maple. They were like Ginger and Gina, the lesbian porno queens, but older, more round, and definitely homelier. Holy cows, she had no idea. It gave her a nice, warm feeling. At least there were still lovers in the ridiculous world of vampires. Too bad for her; she was going to die a virgin. And a starving one at that.

Joseph had been ordered to stay near home base, and he was not a happy dead for it. Kaleb Sainvire was a friend, but he was foremost a master vampire who had the last say when it came to his people.

"Remember the three S's?" Joseph reminded his friend. "Speed, stealth, and suave? My retinue of expertise will be needed tonight." The words nearly made Poe gag. Joseph smiled facetiously. It was his last attempt to lighten the direness of the situation.

"I need you here to protect the fort in case of an attack."

Because he couldn't very well go against the master vampire, Joseph gave Poe a squeeze and mumbled an apology for the afternoon instead. Poe gave him a dimpled half-smile and said, "Buck up, Joe. You'd better wish I don't return, 'cause I'm going to kick your face in when I get back." She punched him hard in the stomach. Joseph grimaced and pretended he was cowed.

Joseph lifted the heavy wooden beam, pushed the door open for his friends, and said, "Godspeed to you all."

The door bolt clanged shut behind them. The three were on their own and they had to make it to the Herald Examiner Building on the south side of downtown.

———————

Unmitigated darkness blanketed downtown by the time the three had walked a block from the library. Unrelenting rain pelted the already gurgling streets. It had been three days since the downpour began. Rainfall had become more prevalent after the gray miasma. Poe thought a lot about the change and came up with the best educated guess a third grade dropout could concoct. Perhaps it had to do with the lack of industry and cars and the untouched natural resources. Nature was still purging itself.

The three figures cautiously listened to any sounds out of the ordinary, trudging through the overflowing streets. Their only illumination was the occasional display of lightning. A bout of nerves attacked Poe.

"Um, Sainvire," Poe began, clearing her throat.

"Yes, Poe?" the vampire answered in a low but alert tone. The young woman's silky voice unsettled him.

"I've been thinking. Would you consider letting me go so I can skip the meeting tonight?"

"I wish I could, Poe," he answered. "But keeping you under my protection is the only option we have."

"'Cause you know, I'm not all white. And they do bad things to minorities."

"I won't let anything happen to you," he said, putting a hand on her shoulder which she shrugged off.

Poe swore when she lost her footing in the dark. Her body was too rigid from her natural fear of darkness, lightning, and vampires. Wading through sewer water was no picnic. She cursed Sainvire and Maple for not carrying her into the air and making her stagger instead in unbelievable filth and cold. She thanked Sister Ann again for giving her tetanus shots, but they weren't going to do her any good if she contracted cholera and the plague.

"Hold on to my coat, Poe," Sainvire said, not asking. Poe was going to tell him off but decided against it. She held on to his sleeve.

When Maple tripped a quarter-mile into their trek and had to be steadied by Sainvire, Poe finally realized that the female vampire couldn't fly. She could only hover a few feet from the ground as she had after tumbling. At least she wasn't the only one hampering the journey. They should have been up among skyscrapers and away from the rank water with lots of rusted metal slivers. Her Adidas swam in fetidness that marinated her pruned feet in street sauce.

She did not want to die.

I could shoot Sainvire and Maple in the head and make my escape, Poe said in the muddle of her mind. *It'd help if I could see two feet from me.* Immediately the sweet scene between Maple and Perla came back to her, and she resisted her impulse.

Vampires were quickly becoming more three-dimensional, and she didn't like it. Nosferatu was so much easier to hate. The past few days made her realize that not all vampires possessed the inherent evil of their kind. The revelation made it all the harder to lump them together.

Sainvire's silence over the looming Council meeting didn't help. Poe would have been delusional to deny that she was more than a bit apprehensive. Shouldn't he have prepped her about what to expect and what to say before the oldest vampires in town?

"Over a thousand!" she spat in the rain, talking quietly to herself. "More like five and two of them are dead. I'll get tortured over semantics." She would not spill the beans on her friends hiding out in Pico Rivera. *But under torture? Waterboarding? I hate pain!*

"Shouldn't we discuss strategy?" she began. "Or at least tell me something useful."

"The less you know, the better you'll be," was the only thing Sainvire said.

She asked again.

"Can't you tell the Council that I got away, that I outsmarted you and Maple?"

"It's too late for that," he replied, his voice hardening. "We have company."

Poe opened her mouth to ask the vampire if she'd heard him correctly when Sainvire and Maple quickly flanked her on each side, their dead bodies tense. The family of rats swimming alongside them in search of solid ground was not the reason for their caution. Taking the hint, Poe took out both Glocks from her shoulder holster and readied herself. She could barely make out Sainvire now that he positioned himself ahead. He wore black like her. Maple was easier to spot because she had on a white raincoat that reflected in the dark.

Scuttling sounds and sloshing feet on the flooded streets were heard, followed by laughter. Like a formulaic diabolical laugh from Vincent Price in the Thriller video, the snickers and bellows were meant to petrify.

They worked on Poe, for she couldn't see a thing. She was ready for the plucking, alright. The only thing she could do was to tighten her hold on the newly acquired guns.

Sainvire's heavy arm draped around her shoulder and led her to the right.

"Be prepared for anything, Poe," he whispered in her ear. His cold lips so close made her shiver. *Great Ali, help me!*

Her two companions remained stalwart and silent despite the exaggerated malevolent laughter. Their reaction didn't make Poe feel any better. She would have liked to hear them fight back with dirty words. Gutter talk would have fixed it for her.

When finally the three resumed their trek in the midst of their unwanted entourage, Poe wondered why they hadn't been attacked yet. Then a voice, well remembered in its venom, addressed her personally.

"Even if you survive the Council tonight, Julia, we'll be waiting for you. To escort you back to our banquet table."

It was Pengle, the ugly vampire whose hand she had hacked off with the Rambo knife. She was in the shits. There were only three of them, and from the echoed sound of laughter all around, a contingent of vamps and subvamps from Trench's camp surrounded them.

"You hear me, Julia?" Pengle taunted. "After we feed on you tonight, until not even a drop of blood's left, your body will be hacked to pieces and stewed." He chuckled, "To feed our poor starving cattle, not that they would get more than soup from your brittle bones."

Poe swallowed hard. *Some visual!* She hated that Pengle. She should have finished him off, but he returned to mess with her mind. Hadn't she read a tedious paperback by Machiavelli she had found lying around the upstairs hotel? The man said something about never leaving enemies alive, no matter how young or old, for they might come back to haunt you. *The kook was right!*

"Maybe four or five of us will have fun with your body first. You've titillated us with your unfettered breasts–"

That was it. Poe could stomach talk about cannibalism and blood drinking, but *never* her top parts. Especially since she hadn't thought to wear a bra until the night before.

"How's the hand, Pengle?" she asked calmly when everything about her wanted to scream. Stuttering be damned. "Did the stump sprout some digits yet?"

The vampire took time to coherently answer, confirming Poe's thought that Pengle was as pissed as

Adam after biting on the apple at the behest of his woman.

"You bitch!" was the best he could do. "I'll send twenty vampires to stomp you, then—"

"Then you're going to suck all of my blood. Then you're going to make me into stew to feed your cattle," she finished. "You already said that, stumpy!"

Again, silence from the far end.

"You dumb bitch," he repeated.

"So you've already said. But if I'm so dumb, then how come I'm holding two pistols with my two bare hands?"

That did it. Pengle, the one-handed vampire, lunged at her in the inky darkness. Only creatures of the night could have detected the movement. Sainvire intercepted Pengle, taking hold of his sparse hair and coat. Without much effort, the master vampire tossed the angry Pengle five yards away. Poe laughed at hearing the splash.

"Poe, you better keep your mouth shut," Sainvire ordered. "We don't need you to antagonize any more vampires into ripping your throat tonight."

"But I didn't start—"

"Enough. Be alert instead of contentious."

His rebuke stung. The master vampire owed her no allegiance. He could just hand her over to the waiting arms of Pengle. Or worse, the Council. It was best to do as he asked, but if he ever told her to shut up again, Poe vowed to stab his eye with more than just a pencil.

Maple gave her shoulder a squeeze for courage, and the three walked the gauntlet to the headquarters of the Vampire Council. Taunts and jibes accompanied them.

It seemed an eternity before they reached the old Herald Examiner Building, a Mission Revival monument to a dead media empire. All three were drenched, but only Poe's teeth chattered from the cold, or perhaps, fear.

Two imposing sentries awaited them by the immense double doors, their yellowish fangs hanging half an inch past their lower lips. Everything in their pores screamed "old." Poe inhaled a deep calming breath before entering. The whole thing wasn't quite as grounding as she had wanted, for an honest to goodness Igor appeared out of nowhere with an elaborate bow. This bent creature had one giant eye and a tiny closed one, a flat but crooked nose, and thin lips hiding two rotten front teeth. And if that wasn't quite enough, his back was hunched. His name, as he introduced himself, went with the rest of him.

"Good evening, Mr. Sainvire. Ms. Brockhurst. Pleasure to see you both again," he lisped with a watered-down British accent. The one eye turned to Poe. "Milfred is my name, Ms. Julia." The butler's giant eye looked as though it winked whenever he blinked.

"If you would all please follow me to the Council's chambers, it would be duly appreciated." They followed the man's halting walk to the judgment room as Poe had labeled it in her mind.

Finally able to see the expression on her companions' faces, Poe asked, "What the fuck?" with her eyes. She received a tight smile from each vampire followed by a hell-if-I know shrug. If these old-fashioned Ancients still preferred to hire the Bram Stoker kind of lispers, then she was going to be worse than stew.

Unoiled hinges slowly creaked open as Milfred waved them inside the metal-studded doors leading into the circular chamber meant to instill old-fashioned macabre. It worked, grating on tightly strung nerves.

Even Sainvire's stoic composure slipped at the B-movie moment.

Oddly, Maple smiled and took something out of her pocket. "Figured you might need this, Milfred, since the hinges of this place seem to act up whenever visitors are around," she said, handing a blue canister to the butler.

"Much thanks, Miss Brockhurst." The butler inclined his head. "It was kind of you to bring an, er, WD-40 with you. The Council will be right along shortly."

The building was entirely illuminated by silver candelabras bearing dripping candles and crystal chandeliers heavy with wax and cobwebs.

"They have something against electricity?" Poe asked in a whisper for which she heard no answer. "Burning candles contributes to global warming. At least that's what my mom said."

These Council cronies knew how to feed off the fear invoked by old black and white Peter Lorre horror flicks. The candles created ghastly shadows, especially on the polished marble floors that intoned frightful clank-clank sounds when heels made contact. A grotesque painting by Titian covering almost an entire wall depicted a fallen angel under attack from a band of demons, the angel's pain-filled, bleeding eyes staring up to heaven for intervention.

"That'll be me," Poe muttered. "My prayers will be unanswered, too."

Underneath the painting stood a half-moon, elevated bench long enough to seat five councilmembers comfortably without elbowing one another. On either side of the bench stood two sentinels similar to the creatures that guarded the building entrance. These two looked fiercer, without a drop of pity like prehistoric things that didn't give two shits anymore. Shadows hallowed their eyes and made their unnaturally lengthy yellow teeth glisten.

"These walruses need to floss," Poe said too loudly.

"Shh!" Maple admonished.

Milfred led the three companions to the center floor that faced the bench.

"Wait here," he said with a raspy voice then limped away. His irregular footsteps made such morbid echoing sounds. The resonance halted abruptly by the door where he waited like the others for the Council to appear. The squelch of Poe's fidgeting wet shoes and dripping clothes were the only clatter that disturbed the silence of the chamber.

I bet they're going to make a grand entrance fit for the old, corny days, Poe thought and gritted her teeth to stop from chattering. She was freezing, and even the hundreds of chunky candles around the room didn't warm her any. To kill time and make herself feel better, Poe stooped down to untie and re-tie her sopping laces. She vowed to never stutter again.

They stood for almost twenty minutes. Purple-mouthed Poe turned to Sainvire and said, "They're not coming. Let's go home."

Sainvire looked down at her upturned face, white from the cold, and shook his head no. He smiled, however, at the verbal slip. He was surprised at how much he appreciated Poe's full lips and expressive dark eyes. The thought of her living at the library proved a pleasant one.

Poe shut her mouth. She had referred to the library as her home. *How embarrassing! He must think me a frikkin' parasite out to eat him out of home and library.*

With Poe occupied in a mushroom cloud of mortification, the sudden appearance of five ancient vampires didn't scare her any worse. Two entered from the main door, floating their way to the wooden seats. One fell from the high ceiling, landing gently on his feet next to his chair. Another seemed to appear from under the bench. And the last walked from behind the darkness of the room, her long limbs hugged by a flimsy Indian chiffon gown and her silver two-strap high heels clicking seductively on the floor. The statuesque immortal paused rather dramatically in front of Milfred and handed him her shimmering shawl.

"Zank you, Milfred dear," she said tenderly with the grating accent of Zsa Zsa Gabor. She patted his cheeks fondly and resumed her hypnotic trek to the bench. Poe bit down the urge to rub her eyes. She could have sworn that the leggy blonde was wearing nothing under the gauzy green material.

As she made her way to the bench, the very attractive blonde with periwinkle blue eyes stopped before the three visitors. She ignored Maple altogether and merely glanced over Poe's much shorter form, rudely lingering on the girl's scar. No, the woman had eyes only for Sainvire, who returned the stare with an uplift of his black brow. Because Sainvire didn't show any sign of backing down, the ancient vampire smiled then laughed, flicking her long tresses back. Fast as the eye could see, the blonde was leaning against Sainvire, her torrential breasts rubbing his chest while her hands tried to tilt his head down for a wet lingering kiss.

Poe and Maple could only stare open-mouthed at the two. They looked like models from old perfume ads. Poe mind-slapped Sainvire for being such a slutty vampire.

"Mono," she muttered.

He didn't even try to stop the vampire. In fact, he looked as though he was enjoying himself, as his arm had snaked around the woman's narrow waist. When

Poe was about to insinuate herself between the two very striking undead, Sainvire pushed the blonde away.

"Enough," he said evenly, black blood dribbling on the side of his mouth, his own fangs sharp.

Winded, the ancient vampire staggered back then collected herself, her mouth dewy with blood from the kiss. She had a fondness for biting, especially the tongue in mid-kiss.

"I see you still have inhibitions vhen it comes to public displays of affection," the vamp complained. "Pity."

With a flick of a look at Poe, the Ancient resumed her catwalk to the bench. And she really wasn't wearing underwear. Poe could clearly see the outline of two teardrop buns.

The blonde shrugged away the disapproving looks the other councilmembers gave her and sat down on the far left of the bench.

"Don't give me zhat look, Gruman," she hissed while arranging herself on the chair.

"And what look would that be?" Gruman Raspair intoned. As head of the Council and the oldest in appearance among the vampires, Raspair reminded Poe of an even more fucked up Hannibal Lecter.

"The Nazi I'm-going-to-torture-you-later look," she said without mirth.

Gruman waved his hand in dismissal and began with the introductions. Sainvire's tongue-mate was Gwendolyn Salam. The dark-featured man to her right was an Ancient named Rodrigo Jacopo. He looked to have been about Sainvire's age when he turned. His green eyes bore into Poe's dark browns during the greetings. He was the vampire who fell from the ceiling, apparently spying. And more than the others he caused Poe's heart to palpitate.

"How do you do, Poe?" said Wilhemina Dunne, the most affable of the councilmembers. "It is my hope that this meeting will adjourn soon so you can get out of those wet clothes." The short-cropped brunette was the only one who smiled encouragingly at Poe.

The man to her right, Umberto Dali, sped through the introductions and grumbled his request for the session to begin. "Do let's hurry. I can think of a hundred other things I'd like to do this rainy night." The ash-haired vampire with searing light-brown eyes looked young enough, but his actions and brusque manners made him an ideal no-nonsense judge of indiscriminate age.

Gruman Raspair, olden in looks and age, began the meeting by motioning Poe to step closer to the bench that loomed over her like Alice in Wonderland furniture. *So he can look down on me from above and make me feel like a tick*, thought Poe, as she complied with the order. The first step she took, however, was a complete failure, for she slipped in a pool of water from her soggy Adidas. Maple had to steady her to keep her from falling. Sainvire leaned by her side to whisper in her ear.

"The best thing you can do is be honest."

Honest my ass! Now he tells me. With that, Poe harrumphed and elbowed him away from her.

Gwendolyn laughed, obviously tickled by the daffy-footed vampire rustler. "Are you sure she's ze one Quillon vas talking about?" she asked no one in particular.

Poe squared her shoulders and resumed walking, ignoring the squelching sounds of her sneakers. She hated Sainvire's girlfriend with a fist of fury.

"Do you know why you're here, Ms. Poe?" Raspair's high-octave voice reverberated in the room.

"No," Poe answered, thanking her patron saints for not allowing her to stutter. That was all Gwendolyn would need to enjoy the laugh of a lifetime.

"No idea at all?" Raspair asked again, his bushy eyebrows furrowing.

"If this has anything to do with yesterday afternoon at the Eastern, then I have a clue."

"I think you have more than a clue, Julia," a voice from the doorway accused.

Poe's eyes narrowed at the sight of Trench. Shadows obscured half of his face until he stepped under the chandelier. His once unmarred skin now had Freddy Krueger crags on his right side from the holy water Poe had sprayed at him. *That's what he deserved for being such an asshole. But how did he survive the garlic bullets?*

These vampires had become too complacent and fat with their titles. Squirting Trench with holy water acid was easy for Poe, and the Council did not even confiscate her weapons. *If the sentinels and the five powerful councilmembers are expected to stay my hand, then they're idiots. If I shoot at least two of them before I'm stopped dead, I'll die smiling.* Their cockiness about living so long with ultimate power was going to be their undoing. Poe had her proof that they could all be killed or maimed after all.

"This little girl sprayed me with garlic water, as you can see. She also shot me in the chest. If you want to inspect–"

"No, thank you, Quillon," Rodrigo said dryly. "Your face is evidence enough."

Quillon winced at Rodrigo's flippant comment, but he continued. "And she killed fifteen of my people along with two cattle."

"You're the one who bled my friends to death, you freak of nature. As for your bloodsuckers, they had plenty of opportunity to kill me," she spat. "There was only one of me!"

Quillon took a menacing step toward Poe, but the lithe body of Sainvire blocked his progress. Poe swore she could smell the violence emitting from Sainvire's pores.

The Council merely watched. Gwendolyn chuckled, enjoying every tense moment. Raspair grumbled but said nothing. After living so long, any fracas that broke the tedium was welcome.

Finally Sainvire spoke, his vigilant eyes glistening by candlelight. "What is Julia Poe accused of, Council?" His deep authoritative voice rang and brought the room to attention. "Is it usual for the Council to state the charges at the end of the hearing?"

Wilhemina nodded and said, "You're right, Kaleb. How remiss of us." She looked at Poe, stating the charges from memory. "Julia, you are accused of willfully killing ten vampires and five halfdeads, as well as perpetrating the termination of two cattle with the help of your underground circle. A separate charge of maiming and/or permanently injuring nine of Trench's people will also be reviewed. The last and most important charge is one of murderous intent against the vampire race. You are accused of being the ring leader of thousands of guerillas compelled to kill vampires, steal cattle, and retake the city."

Poe felt ill. How could she defend herself against such fiction? Everything was untrue, except for the killing and maiming part. But guerilla fighters bent on retaking the city? She looked back at Maple and Sainvire who gazed encouragingly at her but offered nothing.

"How do you plead?" asked Gwendolyn impatiently, her bosom jiggling with every toss of hair.

Poe shook her head and blew out a terribly shaky breath. She prayed for strength to her Patron Saints of Decent Lawyers, Atticus Finch and Clarence Darrow.

"Before I answer any of the charges, I'd like to know if you make concessions for self-defense."

Umberto Dali, who hadn't uttered a word out of extreme boredom, grunted in the affirmative and added in a disinterested voice, "Technically you're food, and food cannot defend itself. But go ahead. Give your explanation so I can finish the second season of *Deadwood*."

"Yes, sir. I did kill those vampires and halfdeads, because they were trying to kill me. There were no guerilla groups in there. Just my dog and me. As you already know, vampires are way stronger than us humans, so it's romper room logic that I was outmanned, outnumbered, overpowered, and all that." She exhaled, conjuring the famous Scopes Monkey Trial in her mind. "So for the first charge, I have to plead not guilty."

"Then why were you at the Eastern Columbia Building?" Umberto asked gruffly.

"Because my two friends were up there," she said as her eyes flashed at Trench. "He had them bled." When her voice shook, she cleared her throat. "One of them was already dead. The other died during the melee. His men were waiting to ambush me."

"So you're telling me you went there by yourself?" Raspair asked.

"Yes."

"Trench, you told us that you came upon a dozen guerilla fighters."

"I was told that, Your Honor." He coughed. "I believe they all got away, except for this one who was picked up by Sainvire here. He now claims her as his, by the way."

"But there was only me!"

"Liar!" Trench accused.

"You're the liar, dick!"

"Enough!" ordered Raspair. "Sainvire, did you see anyone other than this girl?"

Sainvire stepped forward. "Other than Trench's men, Julia was by herself."

"What? You're going to believe him?" Trench bellowed indignantly. "He'll say anything to protect his little fuckwit mistress—"

Two gasped in shock. Gwendolyn, who had looked almost as bored as Umberto, now sat up straighter, looking over the dark-haired Julia more keenly. The other was Poe, who was nobody's mistress. *At least not yet!*

"Watch what you're saying, Trench. The Council can sniff a lie a mile away," Sainvire warned. Only the hard glint of his liquid eyes betrayed his feelings.

"Did you personally see any of these twelve vigilantes, Quillon?" asked Dali, his deep-set eyes penetrating Trench's.

Quillon hesitated. He seemed to recall that Umberto Dali could whiff out a lie like a trained hound. His unmatched skill was invaluable to the Council.

"No. I didn't. But my men did."

"Did you bring any of these *men* to appear before us?" Rodrigo asked, detecting the lie as well.

"No. I didn't think I'd have to." He shook his head.

"Well, about two dozen of your people were nice enough to follow us here. Maybe some of them can vouch for you," supplied Sainvire, the tension easing from his voice. "They're still outside, I'm sure."

"That won't be necessary," Quillon sneered. "Look at the facts. She admitted to me and my associates that she is leader to thousands of underground fighters bent on dousing sleeping vampires with garlic water." Quillon laughed sardonically. "She even said she was a queen to them."

To this, Poe paled, feeling sick. She was glad not to have eaten the nice dinner prepared by the wonderful library chefs. It would have tainted the white marble floor and further prejudiced the Council to her detriment.

"Vell, vhat do you say about zhis, girl?" Gwendolyn asked impatiently, her well-endowed bosom heaving dramatically. *Really! No need for the Jell-o effect.*

"I, I lied to Trench. There is no guerilla movement."

"More lies."

"Quillon, if you open your mouth again during this girl's testimony," Dali roared, "I will personally eject you out of here through the skylight." Everyone looked up to the murky glass showing nothing but stormy skies.

He turned to Poe. "Go ahead and explain yourself."

"Ok. Trench told me that my friends claimed there was an underground movement." She sighed. "I told him I only knew of the three of us. But crater face here insisted there was a massive resistance, so I let him believe it." Quillon exploded bazookas with his eyes. She prayed that her omission fooled Dali the truth sniffer.

The four councilmembers turned to Umberto Dali. He returned their gaze, nodding once.

Without warning, all five vampires stood up and headed for the second chamber door beneath the Titian painting.

To say that the atmosphere in the chamber was tense would be an understatement. It was bubbling with Quillon's ill will and Poe's bruised pride at being relegated to mistress level. Maple's face was about to crack from keeping such an emotionless face, and Sainvire was frozen where he stood thinking about the mob they'd have to endure outside if they survived the Council ruling. Poe was ready to collapse. The beating she had been taking since the night before, especially with the wet clothes that hung on her shoulders, made her body lash out. Poe looked around for a chair, but saw only the five high-backs behind the bench.

Sainvire laid a supportive hand on her shoulder. She didn't shrug it off.

Finally they emerged, a quarter of an hour later. Wilhemina Dunne was the only one with a smile, the clinking bob on her ears swaying jauntily. The rest were either stoic or dour, like Gwendolyn Salam.

"Ms. Poe," Gruman Raspair began. "All charges against you are dismissed."

Maple exhaled loudly, hugging the girl's shoulders. Quillon bared his fangs in ire. Since when did colored cattle supersede the rights of a master vampire?

"However," the head of the Council continued, "we are of one mind about the threat you present to our city. We are not unaware of your affiliation with Fred Beaver and Sister Ann, but being that they are no longer alive, you place us in a very difficult situation."

"Do we let you go unscathed and unpunished for past deeds, or do we ensure that you will no longer be a threat?"

"And technically speaking, you have no rights but to be fed vitamins and nutritious food," finished Rodrigo Jacopo.

"Or mop up after ze vhite cattle," Gwendolyn hissed, looking Poe straight in the eye. "My vote is to get ze straws out."

Sainvire spoke, his voice clear. "I will take responsibility for her."

"No. I think she should be under my care since she murdered so many of my people," Trench demanded.

At this, Poe raised her hand. "Um, I'd rather you kill me if you're going to hand me over to Quillon." She looked pointedly at her nemesis. "I can't promise not to kill any more of his vampires, and that would violate Council rules."

Wilhemina smiled wider. "Sainvire is the only option for her then."

Gwendolyn pursed her rather thin mouth but said nothing.

"Sainvire, we expect you to recover all the missing cattle ever taken by this girl within the month," Gruman Raspair snarled, clearly not happy about the leniency. "And heed my words, young lady. If I ever hear of any vampire killing or cattle kidnapping that reeks of you, then I will personally hunt you down and puncture your jugular with my 24-carat gold straw."

He turned his bushy gaze to Sainvire. "As for you, Kaleb. We expect this girl to become cattle, leech, or vampire. If you can't live without her, lobotomize her and spit blood into her brain. If you choose neither then every action she takes will reflect on you. For every vampire she kills, we will execute five of yours. For every cattle she steals, ten of yours will be handed over to Trench and other master vampires." He paused, relishing the pregnant silence. "And for your information, food like that with impure blood should not be carrying firearms.

"If she escapes, then you will personally face the Council for her crimes of treason against the new realm." He smiled, his yellow fangs glinting obscenely. "Do you still accept responsibility for this girl, or do you willingly turn her over to Trench?"

Without even batting an eye, Sainvire answered, "I accept." Gwendolyn, looking miffed, stood up abruptly and left spectacularly through the side door.

Poe felt her heart lurch. She would be a prisoner of Sainvire. *Should I just ask to be executed on the spot?* And yet she didn't want to die. Nor did she want to go back out into the world by herself. She had no one out there. It was too early to say she had friends like Joseph and the chefs at the library. To be friends with vampires at all would make her title of vampire killer a contradiction in terms. Like a rag doll slumped against the wall, Poe remained quiet.

———————

As if supporting the Council's decision, the rain trickled to a halt, and the moon slowly pushed back dark clouds to emerge in all its rock star glory. The smell of freshly ended rain lingered along with the squalid smell of the city. Like synchronicity, two dead hearts and a live one thumped with pleasure at the sight of the clear night. Poe tasted the cool air, savoring the freedom of being outside. And just like that, it was over.

Something nagged at her. Pulling on Sainvire's coat sleeve, Poe asked, "How come Trench isn't sludge? I shot him in the chest."

Looking into the darkness, Sainvire answered distractedly, "Must have been wearing Kevlar."

"Or he's drinking Plasmacore," added Maple. "They all do nowadays, the hypocrites!"

Before she could ask another question, Gwendolyn approached from the shadows, slowly circling the vampire killer. "I didn't know you liked zhem so young. And little."

Poe burned in the darkness at having been judged and found wanting. *Not everyone can have model legs and Betty Blow boobies like Gwendolyn.*

"Gwendolyn, leave her out of this," Sainvire asked politely. Too politely.

"Tell me if it's true or not," Gwendolyn purred, running a fingernail along the underside of her breast. "Is she your mistress like Trench said?"

"It's been over between us for years now, Gwen," the master vampire answered cryptically. Inwardly he could taste the disgust on his tongue. He couldn't believe he once had a relationship with such a spoiled, vengeful creature. "I don't have to explain anything to you."

"He's not my–" Poe tried supplying the truth but was cut off.

"I must take Julia home, Gwendolyn, before the rain returns." He was done talking. He gave a nudge to the small of Poe's back. Maple followed closely behind.

A furious Gwendolyn screeched, "And I vore zhis stupid dress just to complement your eyes." She huffed, "Vhat a vaste!"

"Face it, love," Sainvire threw over his shoulder. "You're just bored. And when you're bored, you're a soap opera."

Milfred appeared bearing a delicate shawl and put it around Gwendolyn's shoulders. The harsh lines of anger on her face dwindled away, smiling tenderly at the butler. All Milfred could do was blink continuously as though in love with the concept of servitude. Bathed in the newly emerged moonlight, she turned to the departing backs of Sainvire and his companions.

"He's right, you know. I need some stimulation and ze little girl vill do nicely."

With all the bitterness she could muster, she wished them ill luck going home and strode back inside the Herald Examiner Building followed by a very sycophantic Milfred, the only creature she could abide.

Once safely out of earshot, Poe squawked, "I don't appreciate you making her think I'm your love slave."

"She's going to think that anyway despite what you or I say. I was just trying to save time by leaving this place as quickly as possible," Sainvire explained.

"What's the hurry? It's not raining anymore and–"

Maple interrupted. "We've got to reach the library before Quillon's people show themselves. Kaleb was just trying to get rid of her. You don't truly think the Council is going to let you get away scot-free tonight, do you? They've got to appease Trench somehow."

Poe nodded, understanding at last. She survived the Council because Sainvire had claimed her as his. He was too powerful a vampire to cross. And so was Trench.

A small rock aimed at Poe's head began the bloody night. Sainvire and Maple safely deflected the first ten rocks or so, but there were far too many to block and too much noise to sort through. Poe received a third blow on the temple, bloodying her vision. Another hit her ear, her head, then her upper torso and legs. She could barely hold on to the Uzi because she was too busy crouching low on the ground and shielding her face. The fishy, metallic smell of her blood was overwhelming not only to her but the legion of vampires hiding behind the darkness of night, waiting to feed. She licked at the blood that dribbled down to her open mouth. Blood tasted nice and warm, but that was all. Completely overrated, like tonguing rusty metal. *Not worth getting killed over*, she thought.

"Maple, watch her," Sainvire ordered as he flew up into the hazy sky toward the stone throwers. His killer talons gleamed in the moonlight and his elongated fangs were bared in anticipation of the fight. Poe shivered, grossed out at the thought that she semi-fancied the fiend.

Maple and Poe heard scrambling and an occasional pain-filled scream, nothing more. The pelting stopped, but Sainvire did not return. Maple hissed and took off her white coat. Her forearms had become hard as steel with goose bumps until little deadly spikes appeared on the surface. The middle-aged vampire had turned into a bludgeon machine.

"They're coming," warned Maple.

Poe stood up from her crouch and readied her Uzi. Blood was still trickling from her ear and forehead, but she ignored it. She was more paranoid that disgusting gutter water would splash her wounds.

With the help of the bright moon, she saw shadows slinking their way. She thanked the bottles of beta-carotene she had been taking all those years for clear vision. The moon shadow made the band of over twenty vampires and halfdeads more sinister and frightening. Poe swallowed then fired a round.

Vampires who could fly took to the air. Those who could move with the speed of a bullet train attacked. The rest hovered, hissed, and sliced at them with talons not quite as long as Sainvire's but deadly nonetheless. Either way, Maple and Poe were outnumbered.

The vampire fought as if she were Joan of Arc herself, battering heads and severing spinal cords with her arms without even an expression on her lined face. She was frightful. No wonder Sainvire had chosen her to accompany them.

Poe had trouble. She had a hard time seeing with the moon intermittently ducking behind clouds. She had to contend with drops of bothersome blood dripping from her many head wounds, blurring her vision. She wiped her eyes with the sleeve of her coat for the hundredth time. Inattention cost her, for a vampire took the opportunity to tackle her from behind.

Her arm weight pinned the Uzi, and she couldn't very well get to the Glocks in her shoulder holster. So she went limp and pretended to be unconscious. She took the nasty punches the undead gave her. When the vampire was satisfied, he turned her over. That was when she blasted his mothersucking head off.

"You stupid piece of shit!" Poe yelled maniacally as vampire blood and brain showered her face. *No time to wipe them up*, she thought, as three more halfdeads surrounded her, guns at attention. She grunted and pulled the trigger.

Nothing happened. The manufacturer's oath that the Uzi would not lock was utter rot. She hated Uzis. She jumped behind a garbage drum to shield herself from the raining bullets. Before she could reach for her guns, Poe fell back, as a bullet went through both sides of the thick drum and missed her by a sliver. Steel-tipped bullets. *Yikes!* A shadow fell on her. Before she could look up, she found herself airborne.

Her arms were yanked by two leering vampires, her weapons out of reach. Unlike Sainvire, two undead flunkies were needed to lift her up in the air and not very high at that. With arm and shoulder tendons stretching like a twisted violin cord, Poe shrieked.

"That's right, girlie. Cry your eyes out," said the pudgier of the two. "Trench is gonna kill you tonight, and we're the ones who're gonna bring you in."

"That's a dozen janitors each, hombre," said the other vamp with crooked teeth that shimmered in the dark. "Mexican janitor neck or not, that's a fresh kill every night! Fuck that refrigerated shit."

"Besides, this little mutt killed our friends," said pudgy hombre, tightly gripping his hold on Poe's arm as an early round of punishment.

Poe forced herself to stay calm. She refused to make a fool of herself any more in front of these vampires by hollering like a coward. But in the end, she couldn't help it. She took a deep breath and screamed, "Saaainvire!"

Before she could even blink three times, she saw him silhouetted against the moon. His face was fierce and full of bad intent. His two-inch fangs frightened Poe more than she would admit. When the two bozos saw the master vampire, they let go of Poe and fumbled with their weapons. Three things happened at once. Sainvire caught her by the scruff of her coat with his left hand and dodged the deads' bullets by sheer speed alone. With a grunt, he threw Poe upwards until she almost believed she was a rocket blasting to the moon.

While Poe began her descent to earth, Sainvire busied himself by grabbing pudgy hombre's oily hair and cleanly severing his head with his talons. The other vamp with crooked teeth attempted to fly away but was too slow for Sainvire who skewered his heart Benihana-style. He finished just in time to catch Poe's fall and land her softly on top of a jeep Cherokee.

"Are you alright?" he asked, his incisors looking menacing.

"Uh huh," answered Poe, breathless and fearful of the vampire.

"Get your Glocks ready. There're still more of them out there." When the girl didn't answer, he said, "I can't babysit, Poe. You've got to pull your weight."

At this, Poe's nostrils flared, insulted. "I always pull my weight," she said, pushing him away. Unsheathing her Glocks, she jumped down the hood of the jeep onto the street. She ran to where Maple was busy bashing heads with her spiky forearms.

"Pull my weight, huh?" she muttered. She turned loose to ease Maple's burdens by shooting six vampires in the head before they even knew what was happening.

"Poe, watch out for the speedy ones. There are two of them," warned Maple. And just like a portent, one appeared to slam Maple against an ancient palm tree and again at the hood of a car like she was a mannequin.

The girl inhaled and aimed. "Help me, someone," she whispered. The voice in her head said, *now*, and Poe fired. The dead twitched on the ground by Maple's feet.

Before she could crack a smile, the wind was knocked out of her. Someone, too quick to identify, tackled her and was about to slam her. Even though she could not see Speedy Gonzalez hugging her at the waist, Poe pointed her gun at what she thought was its back and fired. She crashed painfully to the ground with a raging female vamp on top of her. The creature writhed in pain, screaming, "I'm going to kill you, bitch!"

Poe didn't want to hear it and aimed her .357 Glock at her blonde head and pulled the trigger. She walked a quarter of a mile back to where she'd left Maple. The fighting was over.

"You okay, Maple?"

"Yes." The vampire smiled reassuringly. "What about you? You look like you've been shot in the head."

"I was. By rocks."

They waited for Sainvire. When he flew above them and landed on his feet, his face was a scowl. At least his fangs had shrunk back to their manageable size. He told them to continue back to the library. He was going to fly up and watch for any more of Trench's people from the air. Then he was gone, swallowed up by the night.

Every single part of her body ached – even down to her hair follicles. She burned with a fever and could barely swallow the delicious barley soup Janice had made. Her head and ear hurt so bad that even a smidge of light gave her a tremendous migraine. However, Maple insisted that one oil lamp stay lit in case she needed to go to the bathroom. One more trip or fall would have done her in. The single comfort she had was the opportunity to sleep in Sainvire's soft bed again. She knew her occupation of the room would have to end, but since she was sick, Perla assuredly said that she could stay another night.

After a shower, Poe inspected the rock-inflicted wounds and winced. "I look like a demon trying to sprout horns," she said about the discolored bumps on her temple. Her left ear was stitched, as the lower earlobe had been hanging by a thread of skin.

"No peridot earrings for me, thanks," she told herself out loud.

Her naked torso bore silver dollar-size welts that were already turning blue. Without bothering to dry her hair, Poe slid under the sheets, wearing one of Sainvire's black t-shirts and Perla's voluminous pajama bottoms. Penny the dog was asleep on the divan, probably knocked out by painkillers. *Lucky dog.*

She wished somebody had given her something to kill the pain. Her sleep was brief before she felt a presence in the dark. The sole oil lamp that lit the room revealed Sainvire. Instinctively, Poe did not move, keeping her lids half open.

The vampire glided to the bathroom to minimize noise and gently shut the door behind him. Poe heard the shower running. Her heart thumped criminally. She didn't see Sainvire go in with fresh clothes other than the soggy ones he wore. It was a relief to know that he didn't have a dryer function under his clothes after all.

Could she actually be privy to a dead guy in the buff? Even though she felt a little unclean at the thought, Poe anticipated the possibility. She'd watched those crappy teenage flicks where 16-year-old girls were getting it on. *I'm twenty-two, for goodness sakes.*

"It's between him and Morales," Poe muttered about the men in her life.

But since Sainvire was closer and made her skin itch whenever he smiled at her, Poe wouldn't mind an affair, if she could just get over her distaste for the undead.

Her entire body hurt like hell. Doing it with Sainvire would be too much like having an affair with Tarzan on the vine. She was in no mood to be jarred and hoisted.

I'll just be a perv and sneak a peek, she told herself.

The vampire emerged from the bathroom, wearing only a towel around his waist. Poe could scarcely draw a breath. She studied him as if he was a rare butterfly and she an entomologist. He had the body of a day laborer that was marred by a twisted shoulder. She wondered how he had gotten such an injury.

Being a peeping tom proved to be too irresistible for Poe, particularly when he pulled the towel about his slim waist.

Poe couldn't help it. She gasped. Sheer terror enveloped her from the slip, but the vampire didn't seem to notice. She suddenly had the urge to pinch, touch, and explore. *No male porn star ever looked like this!*

"Are you enjoying yourself, Julia?" Sainvire asked, drying his upper body with the towel. He turned his back on Poe and presented her with his firm backside.

He knew that she was awake and devouring him with her eyes. Like it was going to make it better, Poe pulled the comforter over her head to hide her shame.

Sainvire chuckled at the sight of Poe hiding under the sheets. He put on a black t-shirt and straight-legged blue Dickies and approached the bed. He sat next to her.

"Will you face me or are you going to be immature about this whole thing?"

"Go away. I'm trying to sleep," said Poe in a muted and scared voice. Sainvire pulled the comforter and blankets down and tried to catch Poe's mortified gaze.

"Poe, look at me."

Poe shook her head.

"You know, I should be the one offended since you practically molested me with your eyes."

That did it. Poe's eyes snapped open. "What do you want?"

"Aren't you going to apologize?" he asked, his short black hair hanging wetly against his face.

"What?" Poe almost yelled out. "You were the one walking around naked in my room."

"I believe I have the right because this happens to be my room."

"Fine. I'll leave your room this instant." Poe sat up and winced.

Sainvire put his hand gently on her shoulder. "Don't worry about it. You can stay here as long as you want."

"Forget it, sicko!" Poe bellowed, pushing at his hand, the brief contact giving her goose bumps.

"Sicko?" Sainvire said with disbelief in his voice. "If I remember correctly–"

"Shut up about it," Poe burst. "So I looked. You were parading around naked like Harvey Keitel. Isn't that human? So what if I peeked? You think I've seen real naked people before?"

Sainvire's eyes widened, a grin quickly spreading.

"By the look on your face, Sister didn't keep her trap shut. Look, I didn't know porn was different from regular films until the nun told me, alright? I'm not a perv!"

"I didn't say you were," he said so gently that Poe was taken aback.

The vampire lost his grin and was staring at her lips like they were the last piece of pecan pie in the entire world. She couldn't help it; she licked her cut lower lip from nervousness. This movement seemed to embolden the vampire further, and he gazed lustily at her eyes. With a feather-light finger, he touched the bump on her forehead then lowered his lips to kiss her injuries, even the two-day-old scratches. One by one.

Poe closed her eyes, trembling from fear, lust, pain and a combination of things she couldn't explain. When the kisses stopped, she opened her eyes to see Sainvire's beautiful silver eyes that shone even in the semi-darkness. He looked at her with such need. Again she licked her lips and swallowed. *What will he do with me? Will I be able to say no?*

As if her fingers had a will of their own, her hand snaked up to touch his long eye lashes. They were so soft. Once the curiosity of her fingers was sated, they explored the cold skin of the vampire, touching cheekbones, nose, and lips. The feeling wasn't unpleasant.

She traced the scar above his mouth, her fingers lingering on his full lips. Boldly she inserted a finger to trace his teeth and fangs then traveled down to his strong jaws.

Sainvire couldn't take anymore of the girl's exploring fingers. He touched her hair, still wet from the shower and caressed a curl. He lowered his mouth and kissed her partly open lips.

Poe had never experienced anything like this first kiss. It was like eating good hot food after living off expired canned sardines for a decade. The kiss started out slow then deepened into an urgent need to hold, clutch, and embrace. When his cold tongue penetrated her mouth, Poe balked, not because it was cold, but because it felt too different, foreign. It was like tonguing sashimi. All she'd ever had in her mouth was food, utensils, gum, and toothbrush.

With much reluctance, her mouth allowed tongueplay. The soft caresses of his hands as they explored her smooth tummy felt too much like cold cuts skimming her flesh. She would have been a liar to say she didn't feel a thing. Sainvire's large hand cupping her breast left a trail of cold heat on her body, but it wasn't nearly scalding enough to let the matter go any further.

The cold call of distress doused the languid, mercurial heat inside her belly as the image of Sister

Ann's and Goss' dead bodies suddenly raided her thoughts. It was too much, too soon. Poe broke the kiss, shoving Sainvire away. She breathed heavily as if she had been underwater too long.

"I'm sorry," Sainvire apologized. "This isn't exactly what I intended. I'm old enough to know better than to lose control." The vampire forced a smile, albeit an apologetic one, and was gone.

I don't know if I can sleep with something dead, she thought with a shiver under the blanket. *It just feels wrong.*

CHAPTER 7-THE BICYCLE

POE WRESTLED WITH DOGGED images of the past days that would not give her rest. When she fell into an uneasy sleep, she did not quite reach the peace of mind she was after. The dream was the same thread of faces and events that made up an epic six-hour movie, full of beheadings, blood drinking, and fornicating nuns with breasts like Shady Melons.

She dreamed the night and day away, feeling more exhausted with each breath. Her body screamed to be woken at the slightest excuse.

Wake up!

The familiar voice she'd tagged as her utterly reliable half interrupted her dream. At once, Poe quickly snapped out of her slumber and sat up. The voice had never let her down before. Blinking awake, she barely registered a man hurrying out of the room before he completely disappeared.

"Who, who the heck was that?"

At first she thought it was Sainvire, but the man was inches shorter. The realization gave her a troubling feeling. She waved away the disturbing events from the night before and headed straight for the bathroom, taking her clothes, weapons, and pack with her.

In less than ten minutes, Poe came out decked in her vampire executioner outfit of olive green army pants and a Pixies t-shirt. She had twenty pairs of the same clothing in her bunker since she had found that bright colors gave her migraines. Her collection came in handy for someone who hated shopping despite the fact that everything in town was free.

"Not again, Poe," she reprimanded herself as she crouched down to check if she had double-knotted her Adidas. She knew she really had to stop that nonsense. Up she stood.

Penny's worried gaze silently followed her every move. Poe bent to look eye-to-eye at the dog.

"Hey there, doggy," Poe said awkwardly. The dog looked away, perhaps sensing the girl's discomfort.

"Look, Penny," she started, not knowing what to say. "It's just you and me now. Sorry about kicking you that one time. And for calling you ratty."

The dog stared into her eyes. "Once you can handle being carried, I'll take you to my house." Poe sighed. "I'll need company since I probably won't be able to kill vampires or turn cattle loose anymore.

"I'm retired, I guess. If I hunt, I'll be putting Sainvire and his people in danger." She kissed the dog's head that smelled like popcorn. "There's only foraging and movies for us now."

She gently pried open the mutt's mouth and checked the severed tongue. The swelling had gone down, and the wound had almost completely fused together. *Good!* Her legs, on the other hand, would take longer to heal. *Poor thing.*

Like an ant farm tossed around by a dumb kid, the whole library shook, explosions ricocheting down to the foundation.

"Shit! An earthquake," was Poe's first assumption. Tremblers seemed to have been more frequent the past few years. But the explosion and gunshots deleted the thought. She ran outside the circular foyer to find clots of people splashing into each other, completely disoriented and panicked. Poe ran down the side staircase, her unreliable Uzi at the ready. Because she felt nervous not knowing if the semi-automatic was going to jam on her again, Poe fired a shot at a potted plant on the landing, crumbling soil and roots everywhere. It worked. After an involuntary glance at her shoes, Poe continued downstairs.

Bullets zipped by her as a barrage of halfdeads wearing bulletproof vests poured forth from the black hole that was once Spanish metal-studded double doors and into the threshold, mowing down Sainvire's people with their semi-automatic weapons.

"This is like a bad Chuck Norris flick," Poe said over the sound of gunfire.

The chaotic sounds of running footsteps and screams curdled Poe's blood. Gun smoke raided her nostrils and stabbed her eyes.

"Please, Bruce, Ali, Xena, light my way and deflect any bullets meant for me." Positioning herself between the cold wall and a small hallway leading to the stairwell, Poe aimed for the heads of the invaders. She ruptured quite a few melons before the wall started dissolving chunk by chunk from each steel-tipped bullet fired. Poe had no choice but to run back up the staircase and blindly aim at the halfdeads that dared to follow. From the upper landing, she shot accurately through balcony grates at every head that appeared until the stairs below were littered with smoking skulls.

On the opposite side, halfdeads and vampires that could withstand the sun infiltrated her floor. A scream of warning clued her in.

"Watch out!" Poe swiveled back and saw a woman with sordid bruises on her face pointing at the escalators. Her eyes widened, realizing that the woman with the swollen face was Samantha, the nurse who had tried to help Penny but took a beating from Poe instead.

Cursing herself, Poe fired at the enemy ascending in droves by escalator and the opposite stairwell. In the time it took for her to shoot nine halfdeads, twenty of Sainvire's people were shot dead where they stood. Under the great painted sun dome twitched bodies beset and pierced by bullets. Samantha was not among them.

"Please make it, Samantha, so I can apologize properly and thank you for all you've done," Poe prayed, crossing her fingers.

Poe's arm shook from the force of the Uzi. Unconsciously she bit on her lower lip until it bled. "Mom, don't let the gun jam again," she entreated. She was alone among dead and halfdead, shooting every which way the enemy poured forth. A bullet pierced her triceps clean through without touching bone as she adjusted the grip of the weapon. It was her first gunshot injury, and it shook the shit out of her.

Out of the blue, Joseph appeared next to her crouching form, firing a semi-automatic from each hand.

"Go get the dog!" he screamed over the ruckus.

Shaken but fully loaded, Poe backed her way into Sainvire's room and bolted the door.

"Gadzooks, dog, I got shot," she said to Penny, shivering.

Penny's ears stood like satellite dishes at the disturbance. Poe tried to stuff the dog in her pack. Her legs stiff in a plaster cast wouldn't fit in Poe's pack. She wrapped the dog in Sainvire's dark blue sheets and taped two pairs of bulletproof vests Maple had given her about the dog. She slung the mutt on her backpack and reloaded, taping two magazines together to have more bullet reserves.

Gunshots still blazed outside. She could almost swallow her heartbeat. "Blast!" Poe took a step back. "I can't do it." She did not want to go out there.

She took a deep breath and carefully opened the door. With her guns ready, she stepped out. She spotted Joseph, floating barefoot halfway between the floor and the ceiling and plugging bullets at the enemy. Poe joined in, pounding a group of already wounded halfdeads.

Joseph lowered himself, dragging Poe behind the safety of a wall.

"Joe, what's–"

"No time, Poe," he whispered. "Listen to me. We'll try to find whoever's alive and evacuate. You're on your own, kiddo."

He spotted a head peeking at them from behind a defunct but decorative antique card catalogue shelf. He rested a hand on the girl's shoulder and fired. Poe jumped, grumbling that she was going to be deaf before her next birthday.

"We'll try to meet at 6th and Olive three nights from now." Again he glanced over her shoulder. "Hope to see you and Penny there." Careful not to hurt the dog, Joseph stuffed five pieces of paper in her backpack and kissed the top of her head before resuming his double-handed blasting. "It's the formula for Plasmacore, Poe. Spread it around."

Before she could beg him to take her along, the question vanished from her mind as a small incendiary device rolled in her direction. *Shit shit shit!*

Hardly thinking, Poe kicked the explosive like a hockey puck toward the escalator where vamps dressed in paramilitary uniforms were pouring out. The device exploded after hitting metal stairs, spraying limbs on the walls and ceiling and forever disabling the escalator. *There goes a Renoir, Van Gogh, and Rembrandt*, she thought. Poe fired at the remaining bodies flailing on the floor.

"Mom must really hate me now," Poe gritted.

It was clear. Poe ran down the stairwell, encountering a vampire more or less bursting from excess. His maw was covered in blood and pieces of meat where he had taken a chunk out of his victims' flesh. Apparently certain vamps became overexcited at the leeway given to them. Poe helped him out of his misery by shooting his engorged gut and spilling some of the load.

Downstairs she saw only litters of twice-dead corpses and human carcasses. It was so easy. The fighting had transferred to the other side of the library, and from the sound of gunfire and grenade blasts, the laboratory was the target. All she had to do was run out of the hole that used to be the front entrance of the library, and she would have been free. But stupidly she had second thoughts. Her feet turned toward the freight elevators at the rear entrance of the building. The level of noise and activity made it easy to find.

Her eyes squinted menacingly at the spectacle of Sainvire's slumbering vampires being carried and tossed outside like garbage bags, the sun incinerating them slowly and painfully. *Where are the clouds and rain now?*

"Get the hell out of here," Poe ordered herself. "The more bloodsuckers dead the better."

Poe's jaw muscles tensed. Sainvire's vampires hadn't treated her that badly. In fact, they treated her fine with the exception of the humiliating incident in the cafeteria. There was Maple, Joseph, and…Sainvire.

Knowing she would regret it later, Poe hoisted her Uzi and ran to the back elevator leading down to the basement where the sun-sensitive slept like stone.

Slick from gore she did not see, Poe nearly lost her footing around the bend. It was a wonder she did not crash into padded figures that took the horror out of vampires.

"What the hell do you think you're doing?" she asked the four outsiders covered in gray astronaut suits with tinted face shields to avoid the sun. "Drag those bodies under the stairs or I'll shoot your stupid Darth Vaders and microwave you to a crisp."

Once the vampires were safely under the stairs, Poe executed the four invaders anyway. It irked her that vampire slumber equaled truly dead for once.

When the elevator opened for another shipment of sleeping undead, Poe was waiting. Her jaw dropped as she recognized the man ordering the Pillsbury Doughboys about. His goatee and I'm-so-mean Jim Carrey face would always be in Poe's Asshole Hall of Shame.

"Ambrose, you fucking snake!" she hissed, blasting the three suited up vamps in the elevator, saving the Judas parasite for last.

The only thing the man could say was, "Fuck me!" as he tried to press the close button. Unfortunately the body of one of his bloated suit people blocked the elevator door from shutting.

"Hey, let me explain," he started. "I'm innocent. They forced–"

Poe shot off each of his kneecaps. Without taking a breather, she ignored his cries. She reached for the axe slung in her pack and hacked at Ambrose's pleading arms. It only took four strokes to cleave the traitor of his limbs, bones and all.

Convulsing from shock and the loss of blood, Ambrose cried, "Mercy. Please!"

"That's for calling me a bitch at the lab," she spat in his hysterical blood speckled face.

Poe shot the control panels of the elevator to make sure it wouldn't make any more trips that morning. She left, leaving a quaking, armless Ambrose, blood squirting out of severed arteries like overflowing cow teats.

She knew her cruel tendencies would bother her later, but for now she waved away the incident. The bastard deserved it, and she fervently hoped he would survive his ordeal so he'd be turned into a permanent vein tap for Plasmacore production.

Leaving behind the sound of bullets, screams, and breaking glass, Poe stepped out of the library she had loved and called home for three days. She looked west. It was barely 7:30 in the morning, and the sun shone brightly over the city. It was exactly the kind of sunny California day tourists used to pay big money to experience. A map to the stars' homes, shorts, visor, camera, and a double-decker tourist bus were all that was needed.

"Where's the smog when you need it?" Poe grumbled.

She hadn't seen the cloud of pollution in years, and it bothered her. After all, smog was a Los Angeles benchmark. It went hand and hand with the Hollywood sign and lusty Angelyne billboards.

"Sorry, Pen, but I gotta stop," she said lamentably having walked for miles. "Your fifteen pounds of fur is equivalent to the heft of an elephant right now."

With an elbow, she punched a hole in the front window of an inconspicuous Korean restaurant in the heart of the Mid-Wilshire district. Her head throbbed from an especially nasty migraine, the kind that had compelled her to vomit in the boulevard ten minutes prior.

"It's like staring at neon-pink biker shorts after leaving the theater," she complained about the brightness of the sun, letting them inside. Bamboo walls, pleasant Ikea lamps her mom would have hated, Korean calligraphy scrolls, and Jungi Ta'l shamanistic masks greeted them.

Without bothering to wipe the dusty seats, Poe sat down and placed the bundled dog on the table. She unwrapped the Kevlars and Sainvire's sheets. The little dog shook from the pain in her legs. Poe uncapped a Tylenol gel cap, tapped the powder onto Penny's half-tongue, and downed some for her own pains. She blew at the dog's face and rubbed her pink belly until she fell asleep. Reluctantly Poe forced herself to eat a protein bar for strength. It was indescribably disgusting after she'd tasted ambrosia at the library.

She cleaned up her wound and tried to sleep away the pain in her head by stretching out on top of one of the tables. The thought of those she left behind haunted her. She prayed to the only deities she knew: her parents.

"Perla has no supernatural powers. Please let her be alright. I never did thank her for washing my clothes. And those vampires in the basement. Don't let those bastards singe them. Look after Joseph and Maple. And Sainvire, too," she sighed. "Even though he's a vamp and his cold touch is a little repulsive, his heart's in the right place."

On that note, Poe fell into a feverish sleep for twelve hours until a clutter from the kitchen woke her.

Clutching her Walther PPK, Poe groggily headed to the kitchen area.

A cleaver missed her stitched up ear by a bead, landing with an evil thud on the bamboo wall behind her. An old man with a bloody apron over an immaculate white formal shirt stood weaponless, having discharged his cleaver. Poe, itching to pop his head, stayed her trigger finger.

"Did Trench send you, leech?"

"No! Nobody sent me," he said with a thick accent. "I came here to cook this."

The old man pulled out a dead rabbit from the sink. The floppy bunny conjured goose pimples from her flesh. She pointed the handgun at the man.

"Don't even think about sautéing my dog," Poe warned huffily.

The old man shook his head, disappointed. "You people all alike. You see Asian man, you think he eat dog." He shook his head again. "Only poor, hungry Asians, Africans, Europeans, Middle Eastern people eat dog."

Fine. She got lectured wherever she went, even at a wretched two-bit Korean restaurant. Being bloody ignorant is no walk in the country gardens.

"Alright. I get your point. Sorry," she apologized snappily. "But you did try to kill me with that crazy knife." She pointed at the cleaver stuck in the bamboo siding.

"You scare me," he sniffed.

"I guess you broke out from a blood farm, right?"

"Yes. And you?"

"Long story. I don't know you enough to waste my breath. Continue with your skinning and me and my dog will be outta your hair."

——— ———

Even without a coat, Poe sweated like it was raining. Her black hair acted as a conductor, absorbing all the heat in whacked out Los Angeles. She avoided major arterials like Wilshire Boulevard and cut through residential areas. She was distracted and feverish from her gunshot wound and the pounding she'd suffered the past few days.

"Choose a pad, any pad, Penny girl," she said tiredly, taking a right on Carondelet Street. The street banked up like she imagined San Francisco streets to be. The grade was so steep that it felt like climbing Mt. Everest. She was winded in no time. Cardiovascular activity only came up when killer vampires gave chase.

The hill led her to a row of old Victorian and Edwardian mansions. "Can you believe this, Pen? Amityville houses in L.A.?" The houses looked too well cared for. Some of the front gardens had tomatoes, snap beans, and eggplants growing from the vine.

"Gah," she mumbled, heading downhill again. "No vacancies in this neighborhood. We best chance it and head home, eh? We're too sick to sleep out here. We might get our necks cleaved by escapees who can mistake us for spies."

Her mouth dropped. An aqua Schwinn leaned impressively against a lamp post. Upon closer inspection, she found that the bicycle was oiled and in good working condition. Best of all, it had a basket on the front. Some runaway had looked after it with love. She carefully arranged Penny in the basket and kicked out the bike stand.

"Finder's keepers," she mumbled, not feeling an iota of guilt for the beaut of a bike.

Nearly twenty-four hours after the attack, Poe set off to her bunker. She was careful to avoid the streets known for master vampires and their farms. After a time, the heavy bicycle took its toll as her creaky limbs began shaking. *That's karma for you for stealing off with someone else's pride and joy.*

"Don't think about going there, Poe," she told herself upon returning to the edge of downtown. "The library's gone. Get your butt underground."

Her feet pedaled their way to the vicinity of 6th and Hope out of curiosity and subterfuge anyway. She just had to see if the landmark library was still standing with a distant hope that Sainvire had repelled the invaders.

Poe's musings ended as she passed the old building, gently applying the Schwinn's brakes. Most of the black painted and tarred windows lay in billions of sticky pieces on the ground. Black, soot-like burns licked the once immaculate exterior walls.

"Somebody was grenade-happy."

The front doors were completely smashed like they had been bazooka-ed. Missing chunks of walls left holes in the once beautiful Egyptian-eclectic architecture.

Poe squeezed her eyes shut for a moment, forcing herself not to think about all the priceless books inside. The only thing she could say was "Fucking Nazis."

Poe pushed back every thought of the tragedy and biked toward Little Tokyo. It was imperative to pedal double-time to get away from the scene of destruction. She didn't go a block before she saw a pack of dogs ravenously devouring a man wearing a bloody lab coat.

The urge to shoot the four feasting dogs made her hands shake. She knew, however, that gunshot would alert doped up leeches and sun-immune vampires. Reluctantly she let it go.

By the time she reached the Japanese American Museum, Poe was shaking from exhaustion. Her legs, not used to pedaling over three miles, felt like jelly. She parked the bike inside the museum where she normally stashed her moped and lifted Penny carefully out of the basket. Her wobbly legs walked the block in screaming rage. She couldn't reach the tiny, old hotel fast enough. The sweat on her brow, neck, back, and bra-encased chest added to her ire.

"You gotta stretch, or you'll be screwed tomorrow," she told herself.

All she wanted was to get Penny comfortable in her bunker so she could steal up to the third floor of the hotel and shower in cold, discolored water. Poe checked the undisturbed hair on the front entrance and stepped inside, carrying Penny like an infant. From the basement she pulled up a hidden door and descended the stairs to the bunker. She clapped twice and a weak light automatically switched on. *Good ol' Clapper.*

As she bolted the door shut behind her, the solar-generated bunker lights and air ventilation automatically turned on. She placed Penny on the futon mattress on the floor, arranging the dog comfortably with soft towels and sheets. Penny, unable to make any sound except for an occasional whine, let a sigh escape.

"No more rickety Schwinn basket for you!"

Only after she placed a bowl of water and stale Lucky Charms cereal by the futon did Poe expel a sigh of relief herself. She looked around her sorely missed home. Anime stickers covered one wall marking her adolescent years. Hanging on hooks on the opposite side was an alarming collection of handguns, pistols, semi-automatic weapons, and knives, complemented by a nasty machete marking the end of childhood. A smattering of Japanimation, Sanrio, and Totoro toys taken from the abandoned shops around Little Tokyo sat on top of DVD and book stacks.

Three sets of robot alarm clocks of Mazinger Z, Ultraman, and Doraemon were displayed on top of the television. Next to the small desk were a mini-gas stove, a fridge, and a milk crate full of canned goods, cereal boxes, and bottled water. A set of bullet tongs and bullet mold lay discarded on the floor. Clear barrels of silver and gold jewelry and sterling utensils lay next to the wall like sweets in a candy shop for bullet smithing. Another two barrels filled with lead pellets sat on top of the small fridge.

Poe's favorite possession, a replica of Yoshitomo Nara's painting of a little girl smoking, hung above her futon. Nara was her favorite artist.

"Sorry plant," she said while watering the browning Chia Pet. "It was outta my hands."

She was home, and it felt really good despite the awful day. She grabbed a pair of pajamas and sniffed to make sure they were clean. Just in case, she cut off a big piece of plastic cling wrap and wrapped the .357. Quietly as possible, she let herself out and went back upstairs to take a shower, the water as cold and goopy as ever.

———————

Poe allowed herself to veg out on the extra-long futon with Penny in petting distance. "We deserve this, Pen," she said emphatically in her Little Twin Star jammies while watching *Cool Hand Luke*. She devoured the last of the yummy Trader Joe's banana chips.

To live in her bunker away from vampire politics was all she needed in life. Thirty feet underground was as safe as she could have been.

"I hate Nazis," she commented randomly. "And vampires are true fascists, especially when it comes to the color of their food."

Oh no you don't. You can't think about negative shit. You're retired.

She squinted at the image of thick-necked George Kennedy on the screen and thought of some good points.

"Well, I'm a bit bolder now. I can enunciate well when need be. A few idiosyncrasies and ticks have been pushed back a little. I didn't even check my shoelaces before going upstairs to take a shower.

"I don't fear vampires or death that much anymore. If I die, big deal. There's Penny to think of, though. Then there's Plasmacore. It's the perfect symbol of hope. The idea behind it is well worth dying for. And let's not forget, I've tongue wrestled with a hot vampire."

To prove that her newfound intrepid self had little fear left, Poe crawled out of her futon studded with Bad Badz Maru and Iron Giant pillows and searched for the one DVD she had avoided all these years.

When she finally popped it in the player, Poe plopped back down on her bed, hugging a fuzzy Keroppi blanket around her.

After this, nothing can scare me anymore.

Nosferatu's creepy white face leered at her in the silent film classic. Poe was so hypnotized by Max Schreck's demonic image that she forgot to read the subtitles. The movie still creeped her out. But it made her realize how overrated and horrendously boring it was. Terrence Malick had proved that a beautiful metaphor-ridden film didn't necessarily spell a good movie. She had to violently shake her head to keep from dozing off.

The immortal undead scratching outside her bunker door with his deathly long nails, depriving her of many a good night's sleep, was nothing more than pasty complexion and bad teeth. She rubbed Penny's belly and blew out a calming breath.

"For ages I believed Nos to be the total shit. What a waste, huh, Pen? If the creature ever did show up on our doorstep, I would—"

Then it happened. There was a knock akin to a scratch from the outside. Poe thought the sound was part of the dramatic orchestral score until she turned the volume down. Penny whined, plunging Poe's heart thirty feet. Clutching the rosary around her neck, Poe inched her way to the weapons section of the bunker and seized a Colt .45 semi-automatic pistol. She wasn't about to just unlock the door without some sort of protection.

She cursed herself for watching the damn Nosferatu flick. *I just jinxed myself and summoned the fucker in the flesh!* Her false courage crumpled at once.

Most likely she had been followed.

The sham titanium door let out a scratching, knocking sound again. This time it was stronger, more urgent, and highly menacing. The gun shook in her hand. *My nightmare has come true*, she cried silently.

Goss had never drilled a peephole. The best thing she could do was to wait it out but the noise took a toll on Penny who shivered like she was covered in ice. Poe bent down to kiss the mutt's soft ears and whispered, "It's okay, little doggie. I won't let any bloodsuckers get at you. I'll kill you first before that happens." Such downcast words did not soothe the terrified animal.

The knocking became more urgent and sharp, hurting her teeth. The dog whined more violently. *Penny's going to have a frikkin' heart attack if this keeps up.* Poe wiped the sweaty tip of her nose with a forearm.

Her nostrils flared. Poe resolved to end this once and for all. Either she or Penny was going to perish in cast and flip-flops, or they were going to demolish Nosferatu once and for all.

Squaring her shoulders, Poe secured the chain lock and opened the door a crack, just enough for a quick glimpse. A squeal sadly eked from her mouth as an extremely bloodied vampire stood outside her door, carrying an oversized gym bag and a much-dinged Kalashnikov.

According to her three alarm clocks, it was only 3:50 in the afternoon. He should have fried out there in the sun. The master vampire was sun immune in addition to his many other unsettling talents?

Poe observed the vampire collapse wordlessly on her squeaky computer chair, peeling off his bullet-ridden shirt. A dozen bullets lodged in his body, arms, and face were pushed out by healing skin. Sainvire looked like hell, so diametrically unlike his usual indestructible demeanor. She guessed that even vampires got tired after a few rounds of bullets to the kidneys.

"What happened to you?" she asked, but he shook his head, too exhausted to speak. After a time, he asked where a working shower was located.

"Goss rigged up the rooftop cisterns to trickle down to the third floor. Head for room 305, but don't expect any water pressure," she told him. She watched his muscular, perforated back as he walked unsteadily out the door, holding a bag of Plasmacore and a shirt.

Like a girl with a purpose, Poe hastened to straighten out her bunker, stuffing used socks and underclothes in the laundry sack and folding the clean ones into a nice, neat pile. She tidied up the bed and moved the now calm dog to a stack of soft pillows on the floor next to the Froot Loops and water.

As if Paul Newman himself were going to pay her a visit, she swept the room with a long-handled broom. She picked up the bullets fallen from Sainvire's body. It was then that she noticed an odor. Poe sniffed the bullets.

"Garlic oil?" she mulled with fear. "And he didn't die or melt. Jesus, what kind of vampire is he?"

She set the bullets aside near the trash bin and washed her hands in the mini-sink with a pump-action water supply. She was petrified. Desire, lust, and virginal horniness were demolished with one sniff.

Almost an hour later, she heard the oddball scratching on her door. Sainvire was back. Poe ushered him to the same chair he had collapsed in before. He looked like his old self, with a little more color, perhaps. He smelled of Irish Spring, her soap of choice. His dark hair dripped on the same bullet-encrusted black shirt, revealing bits of flesh here and there.

Poe couldn't quite speak. His presence in her most prized bunker didn't exactly leave a minty fresh taste in her mouth anymore, and she felt foolish for cleaning up. So she stood over him until he spoke.

"In case you're wondering how I know about your home, Sister Ann and Goss told me," he said and cleared his throat. "I was to look in on you if something happened to them. Sister tried her best to teach me the secret knock-scratch, but being tone deaf and musically disinclined I couldn't quite remember it. So the rough scratches."

At least he finally sucked at something, Poe thought disagreeably.

"I want to thank you for letting me use your shower and bunker," he said wearily.

"Oh whatever," Poe waved his indebtedness away. "You let me sleep in your giant bed so it's only right." She added, "But I can only offer you that lump of futon on the floor. Sorry."

Sainvire's strained face eased. "It looks really comfortable, Poe."

She didn't know why her ears reddened at the manner he said her name because it was delivered in such a normal, non-suggestive way.

He stood up and walked around the 200-foot-by-50-foot room replete with junk, karaoke machine, and other perplexing rubbish. He read the titles of books strewn here and there.

"You like to read?"

"Sure. When I'm tired of watching movies. I can read a book a day," she said proudly.

"Impressive. I see you read all genres."

"Yeah. I read whatever I find."

He perused strange-looking stuffed animals and smiled.

"I like this one. What is it?" he asked, tapping the head of the bobbing ceramic toy.

"That's a forest ghost from Princess Mononoke. You know, Miyazaki," she explained. "It glows in the dark."

"Miyazaki? Can't say I've heard of him." He put the item down.

"Oh, he's a great animator and writer. His stuff's better than any lousy Disney cartoons."

Sainvire, truly fascinated, asked about the other unfamiliar toys until Poe's tenseness wafted away, and she became a willing tour guide of her own pad. How to explain the bluish Moomin, the pear-shaped Totoro holding a leaf umbrella, or a bobbing Mr. T from the *Rocky III* movie for that matter?

It was tough, but she tried her best until he came upon a near-naked fourteen-inch Rei Ayanami resin doll from the Neon Genesis Evangelion series. Blue-haired Rei only had a skimpy towel covering her most embarrassing body parts. Her perkies were completely at 12:15 attention. Poe evaded his questions and referred to her guns instead, then quickly turned to her movie collection and the subject of the giant poster of Jim Kelly.

"I had to borrow a ladder from the museum to get it down," Poe said with a sigh.

Since they were already on the topic of video stores, they pleasantly discussed Poe's favorites, such as *Harold and Maude* – great soundtrack – and *Croupier* with Clive Owen, both films sitting in the middle of the stack. Sainvire picked up a copy of *Mission Impossible: The Impaling* of which the cover had a long, thick, most amorally veined weapon of destruction ever conceived. And it wasn't Tom Cruise's exasperating toothy grin, either.

"I don't think I've seen this version before," he commented with a raised eyebrow.

It went downhill from there. The videos and DVDs, towering high, seemed to spit out awkward titles and jacket covers. Her attempt to drag him to the comic book pile was a no go. Not even her stacks of CDs and records were incentive enough. Poe had no choice but to leave the vampire to his own exploration in the guise of checking on the sleeping dog.

Sainvire's occasional cough, sniff, chuckle, and throat clearing nearly drove Poe to claw her way above ground for the creatures of the night to have a go at her throat. She was so damn mortified. *In my own home, too!* Even Sister Ann didn't make her feel that low. And cheap.

Poe gave Penny a heaping rubdown, complete with scratching, petting, and massage. When she couldn't take Sainvire's laugh at her expense any longer, Poe finally let out a defensive explanation about the amount of X-rated smut in her living quarters.

"I took whatever I could from the shop next door, okay? I told you, I didn't know this kind wasn't like other movies until Sister Ann told me they were bad." She glared at him from the bed. "Besides, I mostly put them in the player for the music!"

Sainvire smiled benignly, which pissed Poe off even more. "And how come you're not melted or dead anyway? You've been shot with garlic bullets!"

The vampire put down the tape he'd been holding, walked slowly to the chair, and dragged it to face Poe. Only when he comfortably straddled the chair, his arms leaning on the chair back, did he answer Poe's question.

"I've developed immunity," he said simply.

"Say that again?" Poe demanded with disbelief in her voice. His abilities were so damn much that he was starting to become scary. Was he indestructible?

"Perla has been using me as a guinea pig for the past fifteen years, even before the gray clouds." He rubbed his jaw. "She started giving me tiny amounts of processed garlic extract. It made me sick at first, causing rashes, singed skin, and break-outs. When the discomfort let up, she pumped the dosage up a notch. Eventually my body didn't reject the garlic's venom anymore. It took quite some time for my body to accept the poison, and it hurt like hell."

Poe cleared her head, thinking about Westley, a.k.a. Dread Pirate Roberts, from the movie *The*

Princess Bride. He drank poison until he became immune to it.

"What about the sun? Were you able to walk during the day the moment you were turned, or did you sunbathe in increments too?"

"No on both counts. A couple of scientists believed that most vampires developed a combination of HPS or Hermansky-Pudlak-Syndrome, also known as Albino syndrome, and red cell depletion a day or two after crossing over. However, the one percent who could stand a little ultraviolet rays tended to be from warmer weather places like California or desert countries." A hint of a smile tugged at the corner of his mouth. "Again, I volunteered to be experimented on even though I didn't know much about science and such. They injected me with an extremely high dosage of Vitamin C, beta carotene, melatonin extract, and other serums they concocted in the lab." He chuckled, "they even made me drink a pint of fresh orange juice for a week straight, making me so ill that I was laid up for a month."

Poe didn't see the humor. Vampires drinking orange juice and getting shots to be able to walk during the day was a freaky and sick idea. Not only would they suck the blood out of the crumbs of the human population, they would also pluck all the citrus in the state. *Fuck that.*

"You're a regular lab rat, Sainvire," she said, her voice hard. "If I didn't know you were from Chicago, I'd a thought you came from Beverly Hills, the body altering capital of the world." Her nostrils flared, "However did you convince your plastic surgeons to implant those insane extending talons of yours?"

Sainvire's smile didn't falter. "Those came with the original package, Julia."

"Bet they did," she sneered. "You're like that Michael Jackson I saw at the Hotel Otani a couple years ago, but instead of getting your skin bleached, you go to the tanning salon."

His face sobered, gripping the back of the chair. "You're wrong, Poe." Had she succeeded in irking his macho pride? "I get color from being out in the sun like most people. I travel a lot. Secondly, I'm not Michael Jackson, whoever he is."

"Oh, c'mon. Everybody knows who Michael Jackson is, you faker," said Poe, smacking the side of her head for emphasis. "What do you want then?" Poe gave a very derisive smile and asked, "To be human?"

Sainvire lowered his chin onto his arms resting on the back of the chair. "Why, yes," he answered coolly. "I wanted to fight a fascist government, not be dinner for some rancid Spanish whore who fed on me while I was dying from shrapnel wounds in the shoulder and belly. She left me to turn into one of her kind, spitting her black blood into the hole she punched into my head. That was out of my hands." His tone hardened. "I prefer a steak and rhubarb pie over drinking blood to live, Poe, even though blood's a very easy thing to get." To belabor his point, he stared at the throbbing vein on her neck and was on her in a blink of an eye, his fangs extending inches from her face.

"With our strength, our speed, and near indestructible ways, we can achieve almost anything." He tapped the pounding vein on her neck, causing an involuntary whimper in Poe. "We can easily drink from you humans after hunting you down for sport like Quillon Trench and his followers had imagined. So damn easy."

Poe tried to push the heavy body away from her own, but it was like nudging a car that was still in park position. "Get off me!"

"What's the matter, Poe? Don't you want me to be the vampire that you envisioned? A beast? A lecher? A killer?" He lowered his face even closer until Poe could feel his arctic eyes and his cold breath on her cheek.

He pushed her head aside for better access to the throbbing artery in her fine pale neck. Poe felt the tip of the fangs make contact with her skin, and she had no choice but to close her eyes and wait for the end. But only a cold tongue lingered at her neck, licking at the skin. Lips followed until Poe's fear turned into something completely different.

Sainvire's tongue traced a path to her collarbone, then down to the opening of her pajama neckline, burning a path in its coldness to the hint of fullness beneath. First the top button and the second, then the third were undone to reveal more of the milky softness of her breast, dusted with small bruises from the past week. When his tongue found an upraised peach nipple for his mouth to suck on, Poe let out a moan. Only then did the vampire release a flushed Poe, and he sat back down on the chair.

"I've hunted for blood for far too long," Sainvire said quietly, his face and body rigid from having to push away from the woman who incited a fever in his dead body. "To want to be what I was shouldn't be a sin."

Poe's hands shook as she buttoned up her pajama top. Cold sushi or not, the dead man conjured up desire, and she wanted to cry. To be doused in cold water after such heat was plain rude. *Why did you have to use my body to make your point?*

Because she couldn't look at him and there was nowhere to hide in the crowded bunker, Poe pulled a blanket over herself and hid from the vampire's stare. She had such an awful feeling of loss.

The vampire would have to sleep on the floor. She wasn't relinquishing her bed. How easy for him to throttle the passion then slam down the breaks. It wasn't right. She clapped her hands two times under the blanket, and the lights turned off.

Under the safety of the blanket and the cover of the night, Poe achieved some privacy. She didn't know whether to laugh, weep, or throw up from getting licked by a cadaver.

Sainvire didn't take long to figure out that Poe was hurt and insulted by his callous way of proving a point. No one in more than thirty years had made him feel so many different emotions in a span of seconds as the young woman with the five-inch scar.

Silently he shed his clothing and shoes and crept to the futon on the floor. Ignoring Poe's protest, he scooted his way under the blankets.

"Get off my bed, fucker," she snapped. "You can sleep on the goddamn floor!"

"Sorry, but I can't. I'm recuperating, you see," he apologized half-heartedly. "You did promise me your futon in exchange for sleeping in my bed, remember?"

Poe was so annoyed that she forgot to be sorry for herself, hissing, "Fine, freezer meat!" She tried to get up and dragged the blanket with her, but Sainvire had anticipated the move. The girl was sometimes so predictable.

"Let me go, you freak! You feel like an iceberg!" She tried to wrest her arm from the immovable grip of the master vampire.

"No."

"I'm sleeping on the floor! I could catch hypothermia being next to you," Poe screamed, panicking.

"No," he said again without humor. "Keep the insults coming. I'm starting to like it."

"Look, this is my bunker. And why are you naked?" she asked as she felt his bare thigh pin her belly hostage.

He put his right arm across her chest to make his edict absolute.

"I'm naked because I'm going to do what I've wanted from the first time I saw you."

Poe ceased struggling, her eyes wide in the dark. She clapped her hands once and the weak bunker lights turned back on. She stared angrily at the vampire.

"What do you mean?"

Without batting an eyelash, Sainvire answered her query with a smile on his face. "I'm going to make love to you all afternoon. And all night if you can handle it."

She swallowed and bravely met the hypnotic eyes bordered by dark eyelashes. All she could do was take another swallow. A weak "no" escaped her mouth followed with, "I won't sleep with a glacier guy."

Then Sainvire nodded. "Sister Ann told me that you were an honest person. She said you never lie. Is that true?"

"Of course it's true," she answered, not liking the mocking sound in his voice.

"Then if I ask you a question, you won't lie to me?"

"Of course not! I don't lie!" Poe insisted, despite the nagging recollection of a string of white lies told to both Goss and Sister Ann about certain DVDs.

"Fine then," he said. "Are you attracted to me?"

Poe balked at the trap. She should have smelled it coming. "Well I'm attracted to many people." She stared at his forehead to avoid his searing look. "There's Morales." Poe rejoiced inwardly when Sainvire's brow furrowed. "Then there's this guy I met yesterday at a Korean restaurant in Mid-Wilshire. He tried giving me his cleaver. He was a gorgeous halfdead."

"I'm not asking about them," he interrupted, sounding more than a little annoyed. "I'm asking about me."

"Sure, I guess." Poe looked at his face and lifted the blanket for a peek at his endowments, acting as nonchalantly as she could. "You're tall. Not as pasty as other jerkoffs out there," she said, crinkling her nose. "Your face is tolerable enough. Not handsome or anything. That scar makes you look like you once had a harelip, but who am I to talk, right? Your lower lip's a little too fat, but it's alright, I guess if you like that sort of thing. And your touch is cold, short of reptilian."

"Harelip?" Sainvire said irritatingly. "A piece of shrapnel smacked my face, kid." His eyes narrowed, "And fat lips? Reptilian?" He shook his head. "I hope you're kidding."

She couldn't help but see flashes of the naked body under the blanket. "Your body is tolerable, too sinewy maybe," she continued with the bashing. "That broken shoulder is an eyesore. Not very easy to ignore." She shook her head. "And if you think you're doing it with me, then you're a moron. You make me shiver, but that's because you're a walking icebox."

"I heard many things about you from our mutual friends, but none of them mentioned your mean streak," he said tiredly. "You can only kick a dog so many times, Poe. I've lost my lusty feelings toward you, so if you don't mind, kindly vacate the bed and sleep with your dog. It's been a tough couple of days."

Her ears burned. She'd certainly overdone it by describing him as a beastie instead of someone who could charge the march of her heartbeat. She was off the hook, but why did she feel so bad about scooting off the futon?

You're just as bad as the bigoted vampires running the show, dictating which tone of neck color they can pierce or what have you. Sainvire's a good guy, and you've just shat on him. You're a prejudiced heel, Julia Poe, accused the voice in her head.

"Sorry, Sainvire," Poe croaked, scooting to the edge of the mat. Apologizing hurt like heck. "I overdid it. Truth is I do like you, and I admire your work with Plasmacore. Maybe I'm too fond of you. And, um, I'm interested in doing it with you, but your, um, lack of heat sets my teeth chattering. So anyway, sorry for being such a dick. You can go to sleep now."

The vampire reached over and pulled her back under the blankets. Wordlessly he just held her in his arms. When her teeth began rattling, he quieted her with a kiss, brutal at first, then soft and languorous. Poe didn't resist.

She laced her fingers through his hair, becoming excited by its soft texture and freshly showered smell. *Kiss him like he's alive. He'll warm up soon enough,* advised her mental counterpart. Like a pro, Poe answered each cold tonguing with a few warm strokes of her own. The feel of his cold, naked flesh against her warm body became tolerable.

Once nothing covered Poe's body but the bruises, gunshot, nail hole and scratches she'd accrued the past few days, Sainvire simply stared, besotted by the full breasts, tapered waist, and nicely rounded hips. Her thighs and calves were sleek, and the tough calluses that ran down her shinbone were a wonder.

"There's still time to back out of this, Julia Poe," his hypnotic voice whispered in her ear. "Although I can't wait to feel your legs wrapped tightly around my waist, I don't want to pressure you and be wracked with guilt afterward."

"There's no pressure now," she said with haste, her own voice husky. "I'm used to your temperature, and really, I want you to put your thing in me."

Sainvire laughed. He couldn't help it. How he'd love to bottle her voice. "Since obviously you're new at this, let me give you a boring summary of what I'm going to do to you. If you're still interested, then I'd be happy to make love to you all day."

With his face pensive, he began, "It's important that you have several orgasms before I enter you. For lubrication and such," he explained, tracing her mouth with his finger. "Thereafter, I will devote some time getting acquainted with your nether region, especially this little bit here."

His finger honed in on her nub. She smiled. "Do what you need to do. Believe me I've seen enough foreplay thanks to the Black Yella Bruthas video store to bring Sister Ann back to life."

"Shall we see?" he challenged, parting her legs, determined to make the experience as pleasurable and pain-free as possible. With every thrust of tongue, her hips jerked upward, meeting the strangely cold, freely moving organ. And when she couldn't take it anymore, Poe moaned and found herself using porno vernacular from the hundreds of DVDs she'd watched.

Sainvire lifted his head from between Poe's soft thighs for a second, unsure that he'd heard the young woman correctly. With a smile, he brought her to an itchy crescendo until her body convulsed. Only then did he rise to enter her slick, still pulsing, opening.

They lay tangled until Poe's limbs cramped up and had to shift position. Sainvire draped his leg over the girl's bruised thigh, his elbow propping him up to stare down at her. He wiped the beads of sweat from Poe's nose, licked it, and grinned. He smoothed down her tangled hair. Not done yet, Sainvire enthusiastically ran his tongue on the sweat between Poe's breasts.

With her palm, Poe explored his misshapen shoulder, lingering on the scar where the shrapnel had embedded. Up to no good, Poe smirked. "I like deformed men."

"Why, thank you, Ms. Poe."

"You're so welcome, Mr. Vampiro."

His black-rimmed silver eyes danced. "You're beautiful, Julia," he said, adding, "You make my dead heart beat again."

What could she say to such sweet words? She simply blushed and looked up at the ceiling. "Apart from you being dead, you're not so bad looking yourself, Kaleb."

His eyes twinkling, he teased, "That wasn't what you said not so long ago. You made me sound like an ogre, third from your line-up of Morales and a Korean halfdead with a cleaver whom I am truly intimidated by because I don't know him."

Poe smiled, her dimples deepening. "You've been kicked up to number two, second to Mr. Cleaver. Now that I've had a taste of your talent."

"Mighty big of you," he said dispassionately, tracing her hips with his large hands that paused in the vicinity of her near-hairless sex. "Beside your head, you hardly have hair anywhere in your body."

"It runs in the family," said Poe, laughing throatily.

"Did I ever tell you how much I love the sound of your voice? How dearly I love your eyes? They're very expressive," he confessed. "I've wanted to undress you since the moment I plucked glass shards from your arms."

"You're depraved!"

"Hey, I know you molested me with your eyes that night."

She giggled then abruptly stopped. It was such an alien sound to Poe's ears.

"And you do know that you sweat mostly on your nose?"

"That's private stuff," said Poe, embarrassed.

"It's charming, like your luscious red lips."

Poe blushed and asked shyly, "What about my scar?"

He traced the five-inch scar. "It shows how courageous you are. I wouldn't change it for the world."

Tired of getting compliments, Poe pinched his nose. "I'd get rid of your lip scar in a second."

A little offended, he growled, tickling Poe until she was close to throwing up.

"Truce," she begged until he stopped and cradled her in his arms. After a comfortable silence, Poe asked, "Why are you so idealistic, Sainvire? You fought against Franco even though it wasn't your war, in another country for crying out loud. Then the Plasmacore thing. I don't understand you. With your powers, you could rule the world."

"Don't romanticize my life, Poe. I've done my share of killing. You can say I just don't like what I see, and I have the means and vision to change things. And to be truthful, you can blame Upton Sinclair for my so-called idealism. I read his work as a young man and was forever changed."

"Upton Sinclair, huh?" said Poe. "He wrote *The Jungle*."

"You read it?"

"Oh, don't act so shocked. I read everything I find on hunts. I'm not such a plebe despite the looks of me."

"I never said you were a plebe. In fact, I think you're one of the sharpest people I know," he said, kissing her hypnotic mouth. "That's why I think you should join us. I don't want you to be alone ever again."

Poe shrugged. She didn't want to reply. She knew, however, that he could hear the escalating beat of her heart.

He reached down to the moistness between her thighs. "Again?" Poe asked. "Don't you ever get tired?

"That's the beauty of being a vampire. We can go on forever," he said with a grin. Sainvire made love to her again until she agreed to boot him up to first place.

* * *

"Sister Ann and Goss never really trusted me." Poe blinked her droopy lids at the vampire. She was tired as hell, but she simply had to know. "You were in the ins so you can tell me."

"Sister and Goss loved you and were in awe of you for surviving on your own. Sister was especially impressed by your instinctive ability to hit the target, whether with a bullet, knife, or stone," Sainvire said, pushing strands of hair away from Poe's face.

"That's nice, but you didn't answer my question," she said with her lids shut. She was on the verge of sleep.

"They had some misgivings. You had survived vampires and leeches since you were eight. The probability that you were a plant hovered in everyone's mind."

Sainvire thought she was asleep for the silence stretched on, but he was wrong. "Sister never told me where she lived. That hurt. She trusted you, the vampire who organized the cattle milking."

The vampire winced. It was a sore spot for him. "True. I'm the one who masterminded the whole damn thing," he said morosely.

The girl's breathing deepened, falling into an exhaustive asleep. The vampire studied her slumbering face for a time. Her plump, slightly swollen lips tugged at his consciousness. He memorized the moment then rose. It was time that he left.

Several hours later, Poe awoke to find herself alone. If it weren't for the plastic daisy on top of a hastily written note, she almost believed she'd dreamed up her time with Kaleb Sainvire. The bold, old-fashioned script where the r's looked like s's said: I will see you at the meeting. Yours, K.

"Meeting. I forgot about that," she said, rubbing her eyes. She swung her legs off the futon and shrieked. Her inner thigh muscles burned like they were getting pelletted by B.B.s. Who'd have thought she had some unused muscles left to exercise? "Better stretch. Otherwise I'll be less than useless."

CHAPTER 8-CHEEK AGAINST FIST

SAINVIRE DIDN'T RETURN THAT night or the following morning. For all Poe knew, the whole episode could have been an extremely detailed hallucination, if not for the musky, metallic smell he left behind on her pillows and the bullet shells by the trash pile. She could barely walk.

She wondered if she was in love since she was feeling woozy and sentimental. He made her legs weak. She blotted his face from her consciousness lest she lose her concentration. *It's not very smart to fall for a vampire.*

Since she had several hours to kill, Poe decided to be useful. She collected the guns and ammo stashed by Goss on every floor of the hotel. The displaced residents of the library would need them.

"No use fighting the realm without guns," she said to Penny whose eyes followed her.

Once a healthy mound of firepower appeared on the floor, she tried being handy with a hammer and nails. Constructing a wheeled cart to attach to the back of her bicycle wasn't as easy as she had imagined. The only wheels to be found were from thick leather armchairs from the sixties. They were round novelty items that spun all over the place. She had no choice, however, because a large bundle of M-16 rifles, shotguns, and other long-bodied weaponry already burdened the passenger seat of her bicycle.

After twenty minutes of sketching, she came up with the idea of replacing the pulley rope with wood beams and plywood to fit the crate at the back of the bicycle. The design took another hour to construct. When put to the test, the pathetic looking contraption worked, but it slid sideways, sometimes unbalancing the bicycle.

"Miserable piece of shit!" Poe yelled, stopping herself from kicking the eyesore. Poe didn't care anymore, for she'd just about had it. Besides, she was running late. Cursing, she changed into her Sonic Youth t-shirt and doused herself generously with garlic water until she reeked like chicken adobo. She slammed the lid upon the crate and hammered nails with one resonant hit.

"I want my Vespa back!" she screamed before pushing off to her destination.

It was a nice, clear afternoon despite the trash-strewn streets blocked by rusted automobiles and nervous, salivating dogs rummaging for food. Even sickly brown birds and plentiful pigeons sunned themselves on electric wires, singing their approval with the crystal blue sky in the background.

"Disgusting, diseased birds!" grunted Poe, pedaling erratically beneath them. She could have cared less about the brightness of the afternoon.

She swerved left-right-left, not because of road debris, but because of the crate the bicycle was pulling. It was dancing to the tune of the young woman's cursing.

Maybe they sensed her frustration and helplessness, but hungry dogs circled closer to the old Schwinn, hoping to afford a nip or two of Poe's flesh as punishment for wandering into their territory. Too bad for them. Their drooling faces collided with the steel-tipped combat boots that covered her legs almost to the knees beneath her army pants.

"That's for even trying," Poe said gratingly as she kicked at a hairless dog.

Cool didn't always spell comfort, durability, or for that matter, maneuverability. *Damn all Schwinns to hell! Why couldn't I find a better bike?*

Poe wiped her brow, cursing herself for wearing a lightweight pea coat and a thick bulletproof vest over her t-shirt. The coat might have been light, but it was still black, absorbing the wrath of the sun and making her sweat like Albert Brooks in *Broadcast News*.

There was no time to stop and take off the damn coat or deal with the fly-ridden dogs that still followed her tracks. She was half an hour late.

The designated place was on the south side of downtown, a truly depraved area full of hirsute palm trees in need of a shave from a generation of inattention. Rats made the California trademark their nest. Even the ficus and jacaranda trees left uncut loomed over the street, creating an arbor of drooping leaves and bark so thick that they blocked out most of the sun.

Back in the day, that part of the city housed warehouses filled with bleak, underpaid workers, smog-spewing industry, drug addicts, hookers, and alcoholics. They also sheltered the ballsiest giant rats ever to be found. Twenty or thirty of them had chased Poe during one of her searches years ago for an alternative home. The rodents changed her mind about living there for they were ten times the size of any regular city rat she had ever seen.

She didn't exactly feel tingly and safe riding the worthless, heavy bike and its load to the center of rat hell. Her sore muscles were torturous as the sharp debris on the road prevented her from jetting out of there, and she still had about half a mile to go.

Then there was Sainvire's naked body. She'd always thought it was bullshit for women in books and films to throw themselves at their lover's mercy with no mind of their own beyond pleasure. To this, she muttered, "Still do. Sex is wonderful and exploding and all that, but after the last convulsion, life crashes to normal again. No big whoop. Sainvire would have a hell of a time convincing me to wear spiked heels and a cat outfit or to whack somebody for him."

She conjured up her West L.A. home in her mind, ten minutes from the Santa Monica beach. "It's time for me to go home. I've got Penny to think about. Sainvire will never leave his people, especially after Sister Ann and Goss."

Her concentration on the task at hand and the image of blue waves crashing on the beach paid off. Only forty-eight minutes late. Two more hours until sundown. She parked the bicycle near 16th and Olive and waited for an escort to appear and direct her to the chosen warehouse.

But no one did. She only encountered a welcoming committee of hissing rats the size of armadillos, utterly unafraid of anyone, least of all her. "Good ratties. Go on with your business and pay me no mind."

A contingent seemed to be headed somewhere more satisfying than Poe's meager flesh. Ordinarily she would have let out a sigh of relief, but not this time.

"Something's wrong," Poe said quietly, her heart thumping.

Outnumbering her a thousand to one, the rats should have attacked. Poe readied her Kalashnikov assault rifle Sainvire had left for her. Smaller than its more famous counterpart, the AK-47, the rifle was outfitted with a PBS silent fire device and a BS-1 underbarrel grenade launcher.

She took a deep breath and followed the hustling rats that surpassed her thighs in size. "Thanks, Sister, for insisting I wear steel-tipped boots for special occasions."

The stench of rotting meat, garbage, rat droppings, and something metallic and fresh assaulted her nostrils. She made an effort not to be sick as she stepped on bullet-sized rat shit that blanketed the ground. She shivered at the thought that she had actually considered hiding out in this rat-infested part of town. *I would've woken up a skeleton.*

The cavalcade of giant rodents led her deeper into warehouse row. The weight of the ammunition in her pack combined with her muscle aches and intense dislike of rats heightened her already tense nerves. Someone screamed, smacking fear into Poe. Taking a deep gulp of air, she ran toward the shouting without heeding the rat tail, snout, and bodies she squished.

"Please let the screaming come from rats getting stepped on," she prayed to her patron saints, Bruce, Ali, and Xena.

An assembly of rats was sniffing around a rusty blue warehouse. They appeared angry for being shut out of the fun inside. When she got close enough she heard the sounds of objects or possibly bodies getting hurled against metal walls.

"Please, don't do this," a woman's raspy voice begged from inside, her crying pitiful. *Please let Sainvire and Joseph be safe*, prayed Poe.

The sliding metal door wouldn't budge. It was locked from within. Desperate for a way in, Poe ran around the compound in search of a window. She wasted no time climbing a rickety pile of scrap metal and moldy wood beams to reach a tiny window twelve feet off the ground. Twice she nearly toppled from the unstable mound of debris but stabilized herself by holding onto corrugated grooves of the warehouse walls for support. She didn't lose a second shattering the opaque glass with the butt of her Kalashnikov until it was shard-free enough to crawl through.

Poe fell onto a pile of crates, not caring if her legs broke. She rolled to the ground and prepared to join the fight.

The weak light inside the warehouse made Poe pause until her eyes warmed up to the dimness. When they finally adjusted, she saw corpses with their eyes wide open, crumpled on the sticky floor littered with Scrabble tiles, playing cards, and Monopoly money.

"Poe!" a woman hoarsely said with relief.

"Samantha?" Poe asked, confused. The nurse she'd slugged for patching up her dog sat on the lap of an extremely ancient vampire with brown walrus teeth. His nicotine-stained hand was worming its way to Sam's crotch.

Three other vamps just as old smoking Cubano cigars and holding up cards turned their creaky heads her way. An undead in a burgundy tuxedo was sucking dry the neck of his win. With a burp that made his fellow rat packs chuckle, he flung the drained body against the steel walls. Crooked fangs dripping, the dead turned his attention to Poe with a smug look on his face. "And what do we have here?"

Samantha, quivering, was completely naked with the exception of a pair of yellow Chuck Taylor Converse shoes. Poe noticed similarly unclad cattle and humans standing behind each poker player. "What the heck is going on?" she asked. "What kind of meeting is this?"

"Ah, another fresh vein," a rather rotund dead commented. He looked as though he'd just inhaled twenty Wimpy burgers. "This is our lucky year. There ought to be more vampire wars. We'll have more exciting morsels to ante."

"Ante? You're using humans as gambling chips?" Poe asked with incredulity.

The whole table chortled.

"It's not funny, fuckers!"

"Please, the language," the more waifish of the four protested. "This is a gentleman's game designed to distract from the boredom of living forever. And you dare bother us?"

Poe bit her lower lip in contemplation. She answered, "Yeah. I guess I'm here to eke something out."

From her wrist, she slid a throwing knife slick with garlic oil between her fingers. In the bat of an eyelid, she hurled the four-inch Bo-Kri into the air. It squared the skinny vamp in the left eyeball. The shit really hit the fan then.

"Samantha, duck!" Poe yelled, letting the Kalashnikov dangle to her side. She summoned all hopes of accuracy to avoid striking cattle or the woman. The moment the blonde in her mid-thirties dove for the crap-encrusted floor, Poe took her first shot at the psycho-perv, catching him dead center in the heart.

"Get down, cattle!" she screamed, frustrated that two of the Ancients had time to scramble free because she hadn't taken the shot. *I could kill those bovine piss-shots myself!*

Poe tossed Samantha her extra gun and went in search of the two remaining vampires in the cavernous building. *For being so old, they can sure move fast.* They were so fast that she did not see one of them sneak up behind her.

A vampire hurled her like a sack of potatoes at the interior wall. Her already severed and stitched ear took the brunt of the blow to the side of the head. The moment she landed on a pile of scattered mah jong chips, she was yet again hauled by her coat and hair and tossed headfirst by a squat Ancient with a missing fang.

"You're that girl we've been hearing about, aren't you?" said One Fang. "The one who's thirty but's never been bit."

Poe yelped, already imagining the ridged metal on her face. She tried reaching for one of her guns, but her coat pinned her arms. Without meaning to, Poe cringed and made herself small in expectation of the impact, allowing herself to slip from the big pea coat and fall to the sticky floor with a groan. *Better fall than wall*, thought Poe, and grabbing her Kalashnikov, sprayed the ancient thug with blessed bullets.

"I'm only twenty-two, you dipshit!" she coughed, truly insulted.

Her ear was bleeding. The stitched lobe had dislodged again. Poe's hand shook from being so cursedly angry. Before she could scramble to her feet, Burgundy Tux Vamp flew straight at her and grabbed her ponytail.

"I don't care who you are," the debonair undead spit with venom. "You killed my friends. It's hard enough to live when packaged blood is everyday gruel. Now you've left me without my poker chums."

Airborne from a fistful of her hair, Poe struggled to pry the vampire's fingers. Her scalp was screaming to be left alone. "Oh boo hoo already," she cried. "If you're so bored and lonely, why don't you let me kill you?"

The vampire growled, his jowls salivating. His already long incisors shot up another inch. "I'll rape you, desecrate your body, then drink you until you're one of them," he said as he positioned Poe so she could see a view of the naked cattle standing around like animals, waiting to be turned into patties. "I'll turn you into my personal cow."

Feeling ill, Poe took out a butterfly knife from her pocket and flipped it into position. With one stroke, she cut off her ponytail. She made sure she had a view of the vampire as she fell fifteen feet to the crud-softened flooring. With hate, she plugged the undead until hot shells and vampire entrails decorated the warehouse, all before her back hit solid ground.

She didn't move. The vampire's body fell entirely lifeless by her feet. Tearing up, she kicked the cadaver away from her. "That's for even mentioning the word 'rape' to me, you piece of shit!" She kicked him again for good measure. "And that's for nearly breaking my spine."

She remained on her back and rubbed her burning scalp. She kept her stunned position even when Sam put a bullet through the vamp with Poe's knife in his eye. Her ponytail lay by her left hand. The sight angered her.

"Are you okay, Poe?" asked an exceptionally bruised Samantha who put on her pea coat without asking.

"My back is shot," Poe sniffed. "And I'm lying in squishy shit, but I'm all good. You?"

She extended a hand with a chipped coral manicure and helped Poe to her feet. "Oh, you know. I got beaten up again. That's my lot in life."

"Listen, I've been meaning to apologize."

"Rescuing me is better than an apology," said Sam, wiping her snot on the coat sleeve. "At least I wasn't raped by corpses."

"Yeah, that's something."

"We've got to find the others," said Samantha who dressed the three bitten, drooling humans with the loud clothing of the fanged departed. "I don't know where to go. I was taken before one of our people could tell me anything."

Poe sighed, seething inside. "We can't do anything now. You'll all have to stay at the Japanese American Museum while I track down Sainvire." *Joseph and Sainvire led me into a trap. I'm going to blow some kneecaps, Samuel Jackson-style.*

"I thought gambling dens were myths," Samantha said softy.

Poe kept her mouth shut. She wanted to cry and bludgeon Sainvire to pomegranate pulp. He fucked her a third time knowing she was going to be beaten and raped by Ancients the next day. "Can't wait until we see each other again, dick. My lower back for your gullet," she murmured quietly, looking surreptitiously from under her straight lashes at each of the surviving faces behind her. The two women and a white-haired man walked as quickly as their addled minds would allow, waddling in oversized shoes borrowed from the dead.

At their side, Samantha rode the wobbly bicycle bearing the crate of guns and ammo. She looked like

Tippi Hedren with scattered hair. The woman had outfitted herself with the works: a rifle and handguns galore.

Poe's ear had stopped bleeding, and the tiny earlobe flap held on to dear life by a stitch. *Definitely no peridot earrings for me.* Sister Ann had said not to trust anyone. *I should've followed the nun's advice.* She thought of Sainvire's unforgettable naked body and shuddered.

"You know what I'm gonna do, Samantha?" Poe said then interrupted the woman before she could speak. "I'm gonna rid this town of vampires. I'll just kill them all. Before, my heart wasn't one hundred percent into vampire killing and cattle running. Now it is."

"You can't mean that," said Samantha, who held back on pedaling a notch. "You can't seriously put Kaleb and his people in the same league as Trench and Gruman Raspair."

"Sure I can. Wholeheartedly."

"But–"

"But nothing. They all gotta go so humanity can be free again." She saw the disbelief in the pretty woman's face and raised her hand. "Let's not talk about it anymore. I gotta think about fixing up homemade explosives. *If I can find Goss' instructions, that is.*"

Poe caught movement in the periphery of her eye. She recognized the hip-heavy woman waving at them as one of Sainvire's cronies.

Skidding to a halt, Sam got off and let the bike fall where it stood. "Veronica! Don't tell me the gang's all here."

"I've been waiting for that one for like over an hour," the pretty brunette complained. "But nice to know you made it safe, Sam. So like what happened to you? You look like Joseph's dead toe nail."

"Long story. Can't get into it now. We've got to let these guys rest."

"Yeah, well, they can sit in the shade over there. Sainvire told me to haul her ass to the meeting, like over an hour ago," Veronica said, clearly displeased.

"To finish me off?" Poe threw out, equally annoyed.

"I don't know what you're talking about," the forty-year-old teenager said, zigzaging her neck like a turkey with attitude. "The meeting's started. Couldn't wait for you any more."

"What meeting?" Poe asked incredulously.

The brunette sighed in frustration and gave Poe a don't-play-dumb look. "Give me a break and just follow me in. I've been standing here for like ages and I'm missing out!"

Poe didn't budge. She wasn't going anywhere. Surely there was a second trap laid out for her in case she survived the first. *Fuck that.*

"Is Sainvire at the meeting?"

"Of course he is," the middle-age valley girl said as she rolled her eyes. "Can we go now?"

"No," Poe answered quietly but firmly.

"What?"

"No."

"Geez, you're one annoying little—" The woman, red from too much sun exposure, stopped herself from blowing up. "Kaleb said not to come back inside unless I bring you with me, so why don't you be a good little girl and follow me, huh?"

Poe shook her head, looking highly peeved at the patronizing woman who dared refer to her as "little" when she herself was short. "Why don't you tell Sainvire to come out here and get me himself?"

"But he's in the middle of the conference. There're over a hundred people in there."

"Look at my face," Poe said.

"What about your face?" the woman demanded, furious. Her eyes lingered upon Poe's scar and earlobe.

"Do I look like I care?" Poe raised an eyebrow for emphasis.

"Just do as she says, Veronica," Samantha nervously suggested.

Narrow-eyed, Veronica screamed, "Fine! And your ear is fucking gross!"

Poe was relieved to see the prissy brunette leave her sight. A few more seconds and her index finger would have ended all diplomacy. Just to make herself feel better, Poe fiddled with the AKS-74U, releasing its magazine only to push it back in place. She slowly checked the vicinity for possible snipers. The surrounding buildings had too many perfect hiding places. Poe shrugged her shoulders and sat down on the broken concrete steps of a forgotten park. She ignored Samantha who tried to speak with her.

Five minutes was all it took for him to exit from a high-rise. The master vampire had no discernible weapons, but then again, his long nails were all he needed. He reached the middle of the road before Poe ordered him to stop.

"Where were you, Poe?" he asked, clearly incensed. "Do you realize how much time we've wasted waiting for you? Now we're racing against the impending darkness, and on top of that you pulled me out of the–"

"Fuck you, *culo* bastard," Poe said coldly.

"If you're going to be childish about what happened–"

Poe almost snarled before she shot the master vampire in the gullet, but short of finishing his ability to speak.

Sainvire fell on his back, clutching at the wound on the right side of his neck. He looked up at Poe who now stood over him with a grim yet triumphant look on her face. Despite the pain he noticed the beaten condition of the girl for the first time.

"Poe? What?" he croaked his gray eyes aghast.

"So you're not only a fucking murdering slimeball with killer claws, but you're also an actor, too," she chortled. "Can't blame you there since we're a skip from Hollywood, eh?" She shot his left kneecap. Murky liquid oozed. She had to admit that shooting the vampire of her dreams gave her a satisfaction beyond therapeutic.

Amidst Sainvire's painful coughing and Samantha's hysterical yelling, Poe found herself encircled by over fifty humans, halfdeads, and vampires. She pointed the Kalashnikov at Sainvire's head.

"If you want to see this *kintama's* basketball explode, creep closer," Poe warned after she saw vampires, including Maple and Joseph, try to sneak around her blind side. To illustrate her point, Poe aimed at Sainvire's right kidney and fired. The master vampire yelped and writhed in pain in the middle of the street.

"Don't do anything!" Perla screamed to the others. "Get back over here where she can see us." She waved her hands to mark the line of retreat. "Okay, Poe. Don't shoot Kaleb anymore." Pushing the panic from her voice, Perla asked, "What's this all about? What has Kaleb done?"

"If you really don't know, Perla, then you're lucky. But jerkweed here," she began, gesturing at the master vampire on the ground. "And *joga*-face Joseph there…" On cue, she shot the tattooed vampire in the groin to illustrate her point. To say the least, the crowd unleashed a chorus of screams. "They both deserve to die." The wailing that came from the easygoing vampire almost drowned out all the shocked voices.

"Stop! Poe, I beg you," Maple pleaded, her voice shaking but determined. The lines around her face looked more prominent in the sun, making her look years older than forty-seven as she shielded Joseph with her bulky body. "Why are you doing this?"

"Why am I doing this, Maple?" Poe spat. "Good to know you're ignorant of the whole affair because I really liked you."

Sainvire tried to speak, but a steel-tipped boot in his mouth shut him up. "This–" she kicked Sainvire's busted kneecap. "This *pendejo* and his little *hine daikon* buddy sent me to a warehouse full of ancient cocksuckers to be done in." Foul words in multiple languages flooded her mind. She booted him in the injured kidney for good measure.

Sainvire, holding his side, tried to sit up and explain. "No!" he gurgled in an anguish-filled voice. "Not true!"

"Joseph there told me to go to 16th and Olive. And who do I see but Samantha and the cattle getting anted around like Frank Sinatra's broads."

Joseph, having a difficult time, sat up with the help of Maple and held on to his oozing privates. "I said, I said 6th and Olive, not 16th and–" Joseph collapsed back on the ground, cupping what was left of his manhood, apparently not as immune to blessed bullets as Sainvire.

"No, fucker. You told me 16th and–"

Poe's retort ended there, because Sainvire's claws shot up and sliced her thigh. In a wrecked voice, he said, "This was the place, Julia. No one tried to shop you." Poe toppled and yelped in pain, cursing like a salt dog. Before her eyes, the bullets lodged in Sainvire's body popped out like wine corks as he stood. Poe fired at the master vampire's face, but a fleet and angry Sainvire dodged the bullet.

She made as if she would shoot his face again, but she aimed instead at his other kneecap, eliciting a livid scream from her lover of one day. She rolled back to her feet and fired at the swarm of vampires and halfdeads that ran and flew her way. Completely pinned down, Poe let out a stream of bullets that hit two of Sainvire's people before sharp claws sliced the rifle into fragments.

Screaming, "I'm Billy Jack, goddamnit!" as loudly as she could, Poe reached for the pair of Glocks from her holster. One particularly malodorous vampire who tried to nip at her neck tackled her, but Poe, so high on adrenaline that she literally drooled, shot the creature's balls off. From the ground, Poe did a 360-degree spin upon her elbow while shooting a circle of bullets into the mob, like a violent breakdancer.

Only, certain vampires proved too quick for her. They started piling their massive bodies on top of hers like a skinny wrestler's worst nightmare.

"Enough!" Sainvire's voice boomed. "Let her up." He sneered, "If she tries to escape, you have my permission to have her for a snack. You five, guard her. Everyone else back inside the tower. We need to finish this. Gunfire is nothing new to this area, so we've got some time."

The bodies of the folks she killed were left breezily on the street beneath the canopy of wisterias. Before going in, Sainvire gave Poe a look that bordered more on pity than spite. She flipped him off with a smile for his condescension.

"Stupid bastard, giving me that look," she yelled, relishing the fact that he hobbled.

With four burly vampires and a halfdead guarding her, there was no need to be tied up. "Great, one of them's the three-pound pressure guy," she muttered. She couldn't forget a bitter face like Rufus', particularly since she had yanked off one of his ears. *Capoeira guy!*

Poe had a feeling that the guards wanted her to attempt to escape so they could avenge their dead comrades without repercussion. Like a good little kid, Poe sat down on the pavement and dabbed her bleeding thigh with the hem of her t-shirt. Unfortunately, Rufus wouldn't have any of that good behavior garbage.

"Get on your feet, girl," he ordered with a twinkle in his eyes. To avoid a confrontation that would most likely lead to her death, Poe obeyed. She couldn't stand to have another Capoeira moment with skewered thighs.

"That's a good girl," he mocked. The four other vampires smirked. She definitely wasn't going to get any help from those goons.

Her head came exactly up to the muscular halfdead's chin. She met his burning stare with a sweet look of her own, and Rufus frowned. Poe couldn't help it. She smiled. Big mistake.

"Ya think that's funny do ya?" As fast as a halfdead could, Poe felt rather than saw a sharp, staggering slap from Rufus. Poe had to shake her head to clear the circling birds and orient herself before returning with a whopping slap of her own, which only annoyed the martial artist more.

He encircled her slim neck with one hand, thick fingers squeezing the breath out of her. His other hand tugged maliciously on the dangling lobe of her left ear.

Poe was too shocked at the deed that all she could do was watch Rufus inspect the piece of meat like it was candy corn made of gold. He pulled out the stitches then winked at Poe. Gloatingly he popped the piece of ear into his mouth. Rufus chewed the meat as if it was the best piece of sushi he'd ever tasted and swallowed orgasmically.

"Now we're even," he said friendly-like and mussed her head. He joined the four chuckling vampires.

Still in shock and terribly grossed out, Poe huddled down on the pavement, touching her disfigured ear. For some strange reason, she didn't feel like murdering the halfdead. She could have easily killed him with the gun in her boot, but she stayed her hand. *Karma's a bitch. At least it wasn't my entire ear,* she thought. *But why did he have to eat it like sashimi?*

While stunned, she was approached by Perla who handed her a bottle of water. The head scientist, just for the meeting, wore a fancy Cookie Monster pajama ensemble, clashing with her unhappy countenance. She swept the fallen bodies on the street with her eyes, swiftly blinking them away. They were her friends.

"If you have the ear skin somewhere, I could sew it back for you," she offered, sitting companionably next to Poe. Her voice sounded edgy with forced cheerfulness.

Poe couldn't help it. She looked at the grinning face of Rufus before answering in the negative.

"Oh well. You'll just have to be without it."

"Guess so," was all she said, not feeling particularly chatty.

Perla tapped anxious fingers on her knee, fretting how to start. How could she begin to explain the complicated to a young woman so sheltered and ignorant? That the world was not black and white? The promise of a society without enslavement was so close at hand, she could taste its vinegary assurance. With a silent prayer, she rushed headlong.

"Poe, I know we haven't known each other long enough for you to trust me, but believe me when I tell you that Kaleb did not–"

"Perla, you're a nice woman," Poe interrupted. "You washed my clothes. But you don't know shi… anything about what happened. If you're here to convince me that your boss is a saint, then please take your water bottle and go back to your little jamboree."

"Fine. I won't talk about him," she said, giving Poe a tight smile. "Did I ever tell you how Maple and I met?"

Poe wanted so much to roll her eyes and say, "Of course not, you dumbshit," but didn't. She had respect for the woman and for that matter, Maple herself. In deference, Poe shook her head no.

"Maple was my mechanic for five years before she got the courage to ask me out. I was much younger then her so she was quite reluctant." Perla sighed. "I said yes, of course. She was shy, but she wasn't intimidated by the fact that I was a geneticist and making three times her salary."

Perla looked across the street at a giant faded billboard of Angelyne, the blonde breast implant icon of Hollywood, wearing a skimpy pink ensemble even in her fifties. Her face was pulled so tight that her eyes were slits. "She was proud of what I did. And I was proud of her."

Even though Poe was deathly engrossed, a nagging voice asked why Perla was telling Poe her life story. In order to move Perla along, she let out a rude sigh of boredom. But the scientist continued anyway.

"I found my soul mate." Her brows wrinkled. "Then the gray matter came and killed almost everyone. I was safe in an underground lab Kaleb set up for us while Maple was at home, dying." She cracked her fingers nervously. "I was on the phone with her, listening as her lungs filled with fluid on the second day of the nightmare."

Poe couldn't keep the look of disinterest on her face. She was hooked.

"Kaleb held my hand through the horror, comforting me. Then I asked him to do me the greatest favor in the history of favors." She looked at Poe. "I asked him to turn Maple into a vampire."

She bit her lower lip. "With much trepidation because he didn't approve of siring new undead, Kaleb sought out Maple and braved being out among the gray matter. You see, nobody knew anything about the poison. I guess we still don't. At the time, we had no clue that vampires were immune to the gray."

Poe scrunched up her face and looked away. It was about Sainvire again.

"I can't trash the man who saved the love of my life from certain death."

"Maybe he's nice to you, Perla, because he's your friend. Or maybe because he needed you to make him into a superhuman vampire with exceptional skills and a tan." Poe gritted her teeth. "But folks like me and the people that died today are nothing but pawns in a torrid game of downtown chess."

"I'll never believe that. He happened to confide in me when he returned from your bunker," Perla stated matter-of-factly. "He has feelings for you."

"Who gives a shit? I care more about my sneakers than him. I only used him for his body," Poe stated coldly, seething with shame about her business being shared with other people. "And you don't have to lie for him."

"I wouldn't lie," Perla said, looking angry for the first time. "Don't you think you could've gotten the numbers wrong? I mean six and sixteen in the middle of a deafening gun battle?"

"I have a photographic memory, even with my stupid stuttering," she lied. She really didn't know anymore if Joseph had said six or sixteen anymore. But she wasn't about to admit that. *In a perfect world, vampire hunters don't make mistakes.*

Perla sighed. "That area is known as a free zone where anything goes. It's not uncommon for some daring Ancients, vampires, and halfdeads bored of hotels and clubs to use the warehouses around there to gamble or play games with like-minded friends. Torture, sex games, what have you are commonplace there."

Poe abruptly stood up and limped to her bicycle. The image of scattered playing cards and chess pawns on the sticky floor of the warehouse flashed in her mind. *I fucked up something big.*

The five goons Sainvire selected as guards surrounded her. She had a mini-Glock tucked in her boot and a Walther PPK in the Velcro side pocket of her pants. She would use them if she had to.

"Let her go," Perla ordered Rufus and the four vampires. "And give her back her guns. We don't want anything to happen to her on her way home."

Reluctantly the five edged away from the bicycle. Rufus, a true sport now that he was happily digesting her ear, saluted her goodbye. Poe threw him a grim smile then nodded to Perla. She felt ill and slightly churlish. She was not mature enough to admit a possible mistake.

"Just remember that your boss was the mastermind behind cattle milking to feed the L.A. vampire population." Poe detached the crate of weapons and hopped on the Schwinn, but still trained her cold eyes on Perla. "Let your scientific mind stew over that fact."

With those parting words, Poe pedaled away, stinking like rat pellets and missing an earlobe. Shaken more than she would admit, Perla composed herself and didn't join the meeting until the girl was out of sight.

CHAPTER 9–A RECKONING

DESPITE THE NEAR DARKNESS, pink and orange halos raked the sky, brightly illuminating the moon's rays. Busted knees and mayhem gave Poe certain fearlessness. She could care less if she died, lived, or turned into a bloodaholic vampire. Her hate would always be with her, alive or as a walking dead.

All she knew was that there would be weeping, flagellation, and gnashing of teeth in biblical proportions if she didn't capitalize on the coconut-sized *cojones* she'd grown.

"I'll start with Trench. Then the Council," Poe vowed.

A rather deep pothole she'd neglected to detect on the road nearly unseated her. Her eyes watered. Her back hurt and so did her leg. Poe slowed the bicycle. She thought the goon blocking the road with his arms crossed was one of Sainvire's, until she saw the Wyatt Earp mustache and the pirate hook screwed in his hand.

Looking like she'd just swigged a tumbler full of vinegar, Poe announced with distaste, "Pengle!"

"What up, bitch?" he greeted with a hard grin. "Heard the shooting. Happens all the time in this cesspool, but just had to check." Equipped with nightsticks, sidearms, and wearing LAPD uniforms, five of his posse came striding up to stand with Pengle. One was an attractive female cop.

Lost all your fear, eh? the voice in her head taunted.

"Yes, I have," she muttered defiantly, reaching for her Glock and stepping off the moving Schwinn. Before the bike crashed on the ground, Poe had plugged bullets in the faces of two of Pengle's henchmen and flung herself behind a minivan.

"You better go back where you crawled from, Pengle, before I blast away your other hand," Poe jeered with confidence. "You know I shot your two pals in the nose and not their Kevlared hearts. I'm that good, muchacho."

Her megalomania was rewarded with steel-tipped bullets that whizzed through the van like heated knife on butter. She ate solid cement, slamming her face into a nosebleed. Poe ran her tongue along her teeth and sighed with relief that she hadn't chipped a tooth. Rotten and damaged teeth were something that could drive Poe to harikari. She was that obsessed.

"Jesus, Mary, and Joseph!" Poe cried as windshields exploded into hail around her.

She crawled away with a glass chip jammed just millimeters from her right eye. It was so close she could see the reflection of her lashes. She plucked it out, quickly dabbing at the drip. Poe aimed at a cop-vamp hopping on car roofs and hoods. Officer Freaky was showing off to what remained of his buddies.

With one squeeze of the trigger, Poe caught the creature in the throat and was disappointed in her accuracy. She had been aiming for his head. "Gotta do better than that, dimwit," she said to herself.

Bullets and glass exploded all around her. She was on the verge of howling from the shards slicing her arms, elbows, and knees. A hand that snuck out from under the car stopped all that. The extremely strong tug banged her forehead against the bottom edge of a car door, giving her an instant shiner.

"Son-of-a–" her curse ended midway as she saw the tiny hand grasping her t-shirt. The sight froze her blood.

"Yikes!" she shrieked.

The face under the car was that of a beatific boy not more than four years old. If it weren't for the glowing yellow eyes and the two-inch fangs that served as his canines, Poe wouldn't have believed what she saw.

"Jula. Jula. Jula," the devil boy kept repeating in a cute little-boy voice. Poe not only detested the new pronunciation of her name, it made her sick. Goss said there was nothing supernatural about the undead, but Poe, face-to-face with this entity with gleaming eyes, had to disagree.

The leering cherub with a purple tongue revolted her. "Let go, you little freak!"

She tried to pry away the tiny hands curled on the bottom of her shirt, but when she touched his skin, the devil tyke hissed and screamed like a roasting banshee, nearly blowing her eardrums out of commission. The kid withdrew his hand and Poe saw what she'd done. Smoke wafted from where Poe's garlic-marinated skin had left a perfect imprint.

Like a giant spider, the bloodsucking imp scuttled away as fast as he could. Unfortunately for him, Poe got over her disgust and shot the baby from under the car.

"That's just fucked up!" Poe shivered. Either the boy had been turned before he lost his baby fat or he was born dead. Either way, he unsettled the shit out of her. Vamp babies born of vamp parents were just too scary to contemplate.

Unless other men in blue lurked, by Poe's count only Pengle and his female bodyguard were left. The favorable count, however, did not distract from the barrage of gunfire that sliced through metal and popped already deflated tires. It was getting darker.

A growling Pengle goaded, "Not so easy when we have guns, eh, killer?"

A parked Ford Galaxy looking more like a boat than an automobile saved her hide. The thick car from the early 1970s took the assault with a yawn, shielding her nicely. Climbing over a skeleton in a faded muu muu, Poe hid inside the car. She really needed to retire from all this.

"Sorry about this, Miss," she apologized to the corpse. "I'll be outta your hair in a sec."

Metal-tipped bullets merely pinged little indentations off of the car's protected side, impressing Poe to no end.

If she could have hugged the immense vehicle, she would have. She made a mental note of the make, promising to get one for herself if she ever got out alive.

"What the—"

The Galaxy rose taller than any other car on the street. Poe snapped on the lap belt, even though she knew it would offer zero protection. The heavy car was hurled in the air, loudly crunching nose-first into a thin-veneered Japanese car that turned tortilla. The skeletal driver lost her skull. Her windshield didn't fare any better, cracking into a spidery-veined mess. Poe's queasy stomach continued to bob up and down long after the shocks stabilized.

"Er, Mom and Dad, looks like I'll be needing your help again," Poe prayed. "Sister and Goss, now's a chance to help out 'cause I'm in the shits."

Not for the first time that day did Poe find herself surrounded and beaten up. And she needed to pee.

"Cinco de Mayo!" were the words that escaped her lips. A gruesome baby vamp with an unhealthy bluish tint banged on the windshield until shattered glass rained down on Poe's lap. Two more babies who made Chucky seem cute as a button appeared, pointing their purple tongues at Poe. They were naked, cherubic, and obscene, chanting her name like a one-liner parrot.

"I guess these night galleries are real," Poe said in panic.

Fingers trembling, Poe unlatched the troublesome seat belt. Her eyes didn't dare leave the circle of faces. "I need my James," she whispered as she unsheathed her replacement Walther PPK from her side holster. She had no idea where her Glocks fell, and there was no way in piñata hell she was going to bend down and look for them.

"Try it, girl, and you fry," warned a one-eyed vamp wearing low rider jeans. He busted the driver side window with his elbow and wrenched her gun away.

There's more of 'em, goddammit! Breathing hard, Poe wiped away the blood from her dripping nose and the cut near her eye. She glared at the walking facial hairs that surrounded her. Pengle brought more friends than she had thought.

"Lookit, the mighty vamp killer's gonna cry," taunted a tight-lipped Pengle who adjusted his custom hook. "Kawana, would you get the door for me, pretty please?"

The group's most petite vampire, who had tossed the elephantine car like it was pizza dough, kicked open her door. The inscrutable female cop who must have turned when she was in her early twenties tore the door from the vehicle like she was pulling a wing from a roast chicken. Poe couldn't help it. Tears of frustration ran down her bloody face.

"What are you doing running with these fuckers?" Poe asked the pretty black cop with catwalk cheek bones. "They hate minorities like us!"

"Hey, don't start generalizing," Pengle answered for the police officer. "Quillon Trench only hates the ugly, unlike his mildewed counterparts. They think they come from that fictional motherfucker Dracula's bloodline," he continued. His predatory stride made Poe gulp nervously.

"Oh yeah? If that was true," Poe said with a grimace. "Then why's an ugly guy like you not in the pit incinerating dead food? Better yet, why aren't you wiping cattle ass right about now?"

Pengle reminded her of Han, the old villain in *Enter the Dragon* who almost made processed opium out of Bruce Lee's butt. He had a hard time controlling his temper. "Babies, feed now!" he ordered.

In a breath, all three babies clambered on the clothed part of her, pawing and biting where no sign of garlic spray could be detected. Tiny incisors pricked Poe's thighs and legs.

"Get off, you demonic kewpie dolls!" she screamed, having a hell of a time prying off the critters from her limbs. *It's like they're crazy-glued!*

"What? Are you praying, Julia?" Han number two taunted. "And lookit, she's really crying now!"

Poe's lopped ear tingled, a definite harbinger for further bad news. There was no Sainvire to pop out of nowhere or a Maple to bludgeon them to kingdom come. What a time to start bawling. Her heart pounded like canons. She didn't want to join the cattle herd, and she'd been bit multiple times already.

"This here's the girl that gave you that iron hand?" someone asked, laughing. "She's just a scrawny kid."

"I know you didn't just insult me, liver face," Pengle said, staring down the only vampire without a mustache.

"Nah, course not, Pengle. Just being stupid, I guess."

Poe swallowed the disgusting taste of fear and ordered herself to get a grip. The vamps were distracted. *I'm not leaving this earth fighting, not crying and begging!*

On the Japanese count of three, Poe pulled out a smallish knife sheathed behind her back and began committing infanticide with the devilbabes. Each stab was fatal for the blade was slick with garlic oil. The sweet moment was spoiled by all the kelpie squeals.

"She's killing 'em!"

"I have a clear shot, boss."

"If anyone's gonna do damage to that bitch, it's gonna be me," Pengle shouted above the ruckus to his remaining sidekicks. "She's mine!"

Poe pushed the demonic Garbage Pail Kids off of her as she crawled from the doorless car.

"Let's go, Pengle!" Poe yelled, tears still streaming down her face. *Quit crying, stupid! It's embarrassing!* "You and me, Clint Eastwood style. Let's get it over with."

Pengle looked over the girl and her pathetic little knife. He reached down his oversized cowboy boots and procured an eight-inch Bowie knife.

Poe rolled her eyes to the heavens. As a last resort she launched her own puny knife, tagging Pengle square in the heart. Unfortunately the blade, impeded by the vamp's wool clothing, didn't go deep enough to kill, and most of the garlic oil had rubbed off on the babyvamps. The slit of an injury itched more than anything.

"Unbelievable!" he growled at the girl who had made him a lefty, pulling out the wimpy knife and flinging it to the floor. "You're begging for a skinning!"

"Now you're going to get it!" chimed the mustacheless vamp associate, chuckling darkly.

In a snap of movement, Pengle was on Poe, twisting a fistful of hair and yanking her head back so she could see his face. The palpably electric loathing in the vampire's eyes left a rotten taste in her mouth.

"A whole lotta blood's gushing outta my nose and eye, man. Either lick it up or clean it up 'cause they're starting to bubble." She had no idea what possessed her to keep goading the vampire. *Better dead than bled*, she thought.

Thinking his hand was still attached, he slapped her with the hook. "You think you're a funny girl, dontcha?" Pengle hissed when Poe smiled. "Well how d'ya like this, baby doll?"

The hook caught on her shirt, puncturing the upper tier sinews of her right breast and came out of the fleshy middle. He dangled a stunned Poe a foot or so from the concrete.

"Jesus!" was the only word that came out of her mouth. The pain was so intense.

"How d'ya like them apples, eh?" he repeated, his triumphant face too close for comfort.

He yanked the hook higher, soliciting a scream from Poe. The tendons and flesh were beginning to snap. All Poe could think of was the movie, *A Man Called Horse*.

"Okay, Pengle, that'll do," said a silky voiced Kawana. "Put her down."

Pengle ignored her and continued to suspend Poe like a slab of meat. Kawana sighed and aimed her six-gauge shotgun at two of her fellow cops who were relishing Poe's torture as much as Pengle. They died confused and headless.

"What the fuck?" screeched Pengle, dropping Poe's body on concrete with his hook still caught in the flesh of the girl's chest.

"Sorry, Pengle, but your time is up, too," the photogenic vampire said. "Say hello to Milosevic and Pinoche for me." Kawana discharged whatever round was left in the shotgun. Poe shielded herself as best she could from black blood and flesh. The execution complete, Kawana unhooked the claw from Poe's breast and pulled her to her feet.

"Cancer," Poe gasped, clutching at her breast. "I'm gonna get cancer for sure if I don't become a bat head first."

"It'd take at least twenty baby bites to turn you. They're not that potent," the cop said. "That's what happens when a dead couple breeds something unnatural, disgusting, and useless. It doesn't happen that often, but it happens."

This fact revolted Poe more than anything. Dead breeding dead was gross. "You're a copper and a vamp," Poe shook her head as the officer of the law picked her up like a child and began running. They were about the same height. "Let me down, sell-out bitch, or I'll thumb your eyes out!"

"Shut it!" the vampire hissed. "All will be explained. And if you call me sell-out again, I'll flatten you!"

Despite the pain exploding in her chest and her pathetic baby pose, Poe remained defiant. "You're the freak who picked up the Ford Galaxy without breaking a sweat, right? What's wrong with this picture? I wish

Goss was here so he'd do a piledriver on your coco-Nazi ass!"

Wordlessly, the vampire stopped and swung Poe like a bag of soiled diapers onto a brick walkway. Her elbow and rear took the brunt of the throw. "Mary and Joseph!" Poe cried after she got her wind back.

"I saved your skin back there, Julia Poe, and I'll be damned if I'm going to take your lip!" the vampire roared without volume. "If I wanted you harmed, you'd be squashed already. Now you need to clam it shut so fuckers looking to claim the bounty on your head won't overhear us!"

"Where are you tak—"

"What did I just say?" The vamp asked her lips stretched white with frustration. "I'm taking you to Sainvire!"

———

"She was a double major at UCLA: history and black studies. Black studies at UCLA you say? Ha! What a joke! They accepted seven blacks for a freshman class of five thousand when the world was running normal," Morales said, finally able to take a peek at the girl's much maligned mammary glands. He was acting medic for the Chinatown triage station where a chunk of Sainvire's people who survived the siege laid low. "I can't believe you called Kawana a sell-out!"

"And a coco-Nazi," Poe supplied as another shimmering example of her stupidity. "I feel rotten."

"You should," Morales frowned. "She could've gone on to law school or some such but she was naïve enough to think she could make a difference in law enforcement. To right some of the wrongs, you know. Before she could even test her theories, the global snot smeared its ooze." He wiped the sweat off his brow and scratched his nose. "What the hell did this fucker do to you? You're going to be scarred terribly unpretty, I'm afraid."

"What's another hook-hole scar when there's this centipede thingy on my face?" She watched him douse the wound on her chest with oxygen peroxide once more before sewing a few stitches. The folks fondly called him T-Doc, short for temporary doctor.

"She's been a double agent since the very beginning, taking Trench's shit for the good guys," said Morales as he made a fist. "The poor girl is a favorite of his because of her unusual Mighty Mouse strength, and because she's a looker. Imagine doing someone like Trench for almost ten years for a higher calling? Takes brass *cojones,* don't you think?"

He patted the edge of the cot. "Now let's see that delectable thigh of yours," the attractive smuggler winked. "I have it on high authority that Kaleb outdid himself with his claw because he's smitten with you."

She propped her damaged thigh and winced, demurely covering the rest of herself with a stained sheet. "You really need to work on your bedside manner, starting with the chronic licking of your lower lip and your penchant to yap. Unprofessional."

"Godsmack! I was a real estate agent, not an MD. I was pushed into this. Anyway, imagine if the son-of-a-gun had been in love with you?" he blanched, dabbing the swollen wounds and cleaning the dry blood around them. "Word is the two of you did the deed the other day."

Poe choked, visibly upset about Morales' lack of tact.

"The answer's staring me in the face," he said, studying the spreading flush on her face. He looked upset. "Sorry for even asking. It's hard to be civilized when there's no civilization left, but Sainvire ought to know better."

Poe seethed. Sainvire had tattled, and it burned. Between the casualties of her berserker moment and the screwing of the big boss, she knew she'd be lucky to get a space on the Chinese restaurant floor.

———————

She looked old, maybe about 25.

"Serrated hair, chopped ear, scars, scabs, and bruises," Poe recited to the image in the mirror. "Great beauty secret you got there. You ought to bottle it."

The reflection was a far cry from the person she had seen naked in the mirror a week ago. The woman who stared back in the chipped mirror of a fungus-encrusted bathroom was uglier, meaner, and missing a lot of moral fiber.

"Anyway, teeth time. It's either floss or the plyers," Poe said dryly.

After brushing her teeth and flossing, Poe put on a clean t-shirt and dark blue Dickies as crisp as chicharones courtesy of a t-shirt warehouse a block away. She slipped her socked feet into the insufferable combat boots.

"Hurry up, will ya? That's like the only working bathroom in Chinatown!" somebody yelled, knocking on the door with a foot. "There's like, a line out here."

Poe compressed her mouth tightly. She knew that voice. "Hiya, Veronica," Poe said with a nod as she opened the door. "All yours."

"Oh hey," the woman said nervously. "I like, didn't know you were in there." The woman assigned to wait for her the day before had witnessed the carnage and did not want to be on Poe's bad side. "Take as long as you want. I'll stand guard."

"No thanks. I'm going for a walk," she said, careful to avoid the bodies reposing in scruffy sleeping bags, then added, "Weird toilet, that. It flushes counterclockwise."

The evasive, prying, and illicit looks she'd encountered the past days had been the hardest to take. *I'll be lucky to get eye contact. Violence is a turn off, I guess.*

Sleeping on the floor surrounded by tired souls ensconced in sleeping bags made her claustrophobic and antsy, especially when every single one was armed to the eyeball. She never would have thought that she missed being the only girl in the world again. She slipped out the back door that led into an alleyway.

With the way things were progressing, Morales seemed to be the only one who was glad she was on their side. Sainvire and Joseph were nowhere to be seen. Even Megan, her one good friend, gave her the cold shoulder and narrowed her green eyes at Poe during chance encounters. Like providence, she heard the tinkly voice of her former friend.

"Are you sure you've got your wiring on the tip top?" asked Megan who leaned against the alley wall, addressing Morales who looked to be running out of gas, the shadows under his eyes exaggerated by lamp light. Next to him stood a gangly black man in his late thirties vigorously wiping his spectacles on his Celtics t-shirt. Another man who looked like Jerry Garcia sat on a block of cement roasting cans of beans and SpaghettiOs on a camp stove.

"I might've been an office jockey, Meg, but I can follow recipes for destruction to the tee," said Morales. He massaged his temples. Wavy lines, the only indication of Megan's age, appeared on her forehead. "Rudy and I have been triple checking all night so we won't blow anyone's head off by accident. Anyone alive, that is."

"Yup, I know, T-Doc," she nodded. "Sorry for being a pain in the neck. I just don't want any hitches tomo–"

Morales cleared his throat and nodded toward Poe who strode down the alley slowly. From the smell of it, folks had been using the alleyway for whizzing purposes.

Megan swore under her breath at the possibility of being overheard, her pursed lips looking like a pickled plum.

"Hey guys, it's only Poe," Morales said with a tight smile, looking from Megan to the girl. "Kaleb said to–"

"Kaleb's said and done many stupid things," Megan said harshly. "And if you think you're going to spill it to her, the one who killed our own people, then you best tuck in your sea cucumber because I'm going to yank it out and machete it."

Without thinking, Morales shielded his manhood and clamped his mouth shut.

"It sucks to be the rotten egg in the batch," Poe said under her breath and took a warm tin of SpaghettiOs from the grill, daring the brooding cook to tell her off. Surprisingly the Grateful Dead handed her two plastic spoons and placed two more cans on the grill without blinking.

"The fuck do I care about their stupid plans?" she muttered as she rounded Alameda Street. "Who are they kidding? They can't win against the Council and the master vamps. They have too many Igors and leeches eager to please."

She hadn't seen Sainvire since she had shot his major organs. The vampire was too busy plotting to save cattle in Los Angeles to give her the time of day.

Poe shrugged, thinking about the master vampire she'd wronged. Guilt, a familiar companion by now, visited her thoughts once more. Sainvire didn't have to do anything for blood cattle. He could just sit back and enjoy the grand lifestyle accorded to vampires of his stature. But he didn't. Because of her, his plans may have been ruined. *Sainvire should have turned me over to the Council. Or to Trench.*

Poe limped to Olvera Street, the nearby historic street dating to Spanish and Mexican rule, with the hood of her sweater covering her face. Chinatown and Olvera Street had been looted so many times that it had become blasé to plunder it any further. Besides, most everything ethnic had come out of vogue. European antiques, especially Louis XIV and Rococo furniture, were all the rage.

The Mexican marketplace replete with an old Spanish church right out of a Sergio Leone film had always been one of her mother's beloved places. Poe found her parents' favorite shop bursting with fat candles, Dia de los Muertos papier-mâché crafts, hand tooled belts, and a variety of Frida Kahlo dolls.

Once she'd closed all the curtains and turned on her flameless lantern, Poe went in search of a belt. The pants she had been given were a tad loose about the waist. She found a simple leather belt tooled with a desert scene. The silver buckle was embossed with a large cactus wearing a sombrero. "Can't be a vampire killer tripping over my *pantalones*, can I?"

The life-size papier-mâché skeleton mariachi band holding their instruments would have been creepy if her mother had not taught her to appreciate the dead collectibles as something artistic and part of her heritage. However, the saints and Jesus candles freaked her out. Melted, they were downright creepy.

"Somebody's using this place as a distillery," Poe said quietly, sniffing the air. She flashed her pocket light at every nook until she located a hipbath full of fermenting garlic water behind the counter. The primordial ooze had the consistency of slime inside an aloe vera plant. The goopier the soup, the more acidic and lethal to vamp skin.

"Thank goodness for the Lost Boys." She inspected the shelves under the counter and found a slew of empty squirt bottles and an open box of night vision goggles, mouthguards, and two squirt guns. She snapped the goggles on and saw green thermal nothingness as no one living shared the room. "I've always wanted one of these."

So she wouldn't forget, Poe tossed the goggles in her pack and dropped the bag on the floor. She grabbed an empty spray bottle and submerged it mid-forearm until the surface of the soup bubbled. She did the same with the toy squirt guns and threw them in her pack. "This is a good sign. Could my luck be changing?" she asked without sarcasm.

As if in answer, Poe spotted a portable DVD player next to the cash machine. This made her pause. "Maybe my luck's changed alright." She wiped her sopping arm on her t-shirt. An index finger pushed the play button, and she was surprised to find the seven-inch screen cough static and blink back to life. The battery had some power left.

A familiar scene of Harold attempting to hang himself while a Cat Stevens song blared in the background wrenched Poe's fragile constitution.

"*Harold and Maude*. I can't believe it," she blinked dazedly and began to sniff. "I love this movie."

Melting on the floor cross-legged, Poe began in earnest to chomp down on her rust-flavored food without taking her eyes off the screen. There was nothing like a Hal Ashby movie to take away the blues. Shortly thereafter, she heard tapping from one of the two windows in the store. She barely managed to swallow her last mouthful mumbling, "I knew this was too good to be true."

She pulled out one of the 9mm guns issued to her. It was a 15-round Astra A-90 with a silencer attachment. "Can't a person eat in peace around here?" she grumbled.

The tapping continued while Poe browbeat herself about the many ways she had screwed up, like stupidly walking away from the group into the pitch-black darkness and for getting tailed.

"Just do it," Poe told herself. "It already knows you're in here."

She opened the domed Spanish window and aimed her gun at one of the most grotesque faces she'd ever beheld. One of its giant eyes pointed east while the other pale blue honed in on her face.

"The fuck. What the hell do you want, butler?"

Milfred's mouth was moving but she couldn't quite hear.

"Well? Which Council person is lurking in the shadows?"

"It is only I, m'lady, bearing news."

"Uh huh." Poe waved her gun. "I'm in the middle of dinner and don't have time for a chat."

"Would you be kind enough to give me a hand?"

She didn't know how it happened exactly, but Poe found herself helping the butler clamber through the window.

He was surprisingly heavy for a near-skeleton and his hands were deathly cold, making Poe question if the butler was indeed alive. As soon as Milfred hit the tile on all fours, Poe slammed the window shut. She sprayed the inside ledge with holy water slung from her new belt. She turned to the hunchback, nudging him to spread his legs so she could feel for weapons.

"So what do you have to tell me?" she asked tensely, expecting to be ambushed anytime, "Before I shoot your kneecaps off." Poe hated to admit it, but she had discovered immense pleasure in blasting people's kneecaps off. Especially Sainvire's.

With a leg shorter than the other, Milfred launched himself to his feet and managed to look like an underpaid house servant once more.

"She wanted me to prepare the way, m'lady," he started, snapping in place his tuxedo tails that were probably in vogue in the 1970s, like the outfit Steve Martin wore in *The Absent- Minded Waiter.*

"Prepare the way? What are you, some kind of John the Baptist?" She had seen the movie with Max von Sydow as Jesus twice. "Never mind. Who is it?

The unhinged front door plummeted to the floor in answer. A very shimmery Gwendolyn entered, wearing a see-through nighty that displayed her slightly drooping girls, au naturel, and a pair of Reebok running shoes. She looked about the place and sighed.

"Milfie, darlink, my shoes?"

Like a bound servant more than content with his lot in life, the butler reached into his tuxedo pockets and acquired Gwendolyn's silver shoes with four-inch metal chopsticks for heels. With much pomp and ceremony, Milfred removed the bespattered sneakers from the vampire's slim manicured feet and carefully replaced them with streetwalker shoes. Only then did Gwendolyn give Poe her full attention.

The vampire pulled out a slim *Breakfast at Tiffany's* cigarette attached to an elongated pipe from the delicate elastic of her black thong underwear. She looked incredible and sexy and she knew it. Not many people could pull off the minimalist ho look.

"No offense, but I'd hate to be the one to do your laundry," Poe declared, her stomach tightening in one horrendous knot.

"Offense taken, human trash," Gwendolyn hissed. "But I'm not here to rearrange your face, girl. I'm here for Kaleb."

"As you can see, Kaleb isn't here, so scram. I've got a thing with *Harold and Maude* and you're ruining our night."

"Hmph. An old voman like zhat vit a teenager is an offense," the vampire commented colorfully, obviously aware of the age-defying classic.

Poe rolled her eyes. "Yeah, well that's rich seeing that you're a thousand years old or something, and your former boytoy, Sainvire, is not even a hundred. Isn't that an equivalent of a mummy hitting on diaper rash?"

Gwendolyn, the Barbie of the undead, morphed into Cujo. Her blue eyes narrowed into slits and her incisors dripped into something long and sharp. The girl who'd never learned tact did not see it coming. Gwendolyn snuck out her fist and cuffed Poe on the cheek, hurling her a few feet and rendering her unconscious for a moment. The vampire wrenched the Astra A-90 from Poe's limp grip and tossed it to the alert butler who caught it without expression. The spray bottle she flung behind the counter.

A shadow slipped in from the gaping entrance. The stealthy figure clad in turtleneck and gray overalls was lost on Gwendolyn if not for the cautionary cough the butler let out.

"Gwendolyn, dear, what in all that's scalding and torrential in the rutting part of hell are you up to? I thought you were with us?" the usually cheery Wilhemina accused, her pointed face all glint and grit. "I was on my way to see Morales and Sainvire when I saw the two of you hot on the scent of Julia Poe. What am I to think?"

"I am loyal, Vilhemina. For zhat zhere is no question," explained Gwendolyn to her fellow councilwoman. "I really don't vant to drink Plasmacore as sustenance for eternity. My life is dreary enough. But I vill do it for ze plan. Kaleb is acquiring supporters all over California. Zhat's a very dangerous thing. But I embrace it." Her voice became gentler, "I love him enough to help bring down the lure of vampirism."

"Then what possessed you to pound a girl an eighth your strength? And for chrissake, don't say it's because of jealousy. Women have fanned the flame of that petty excuse for centuries now, and look where it got us, still living among the cave dwellers with extra pointy fangs."

"For godsakes, Vil, don't go into any more of your tirades," waved Gwendolyn. "I can't handle a lecture tonight about how vomen are raped in zheir sleep and forced to carry zheir pregnancy to term and like zhat. Ze girl insulted me, and I couldn't stop my fist in time. Period."

When Poe came to, the second thing she noticed after the pain in her cheek was the heated altercation occurring before her. How long had she been out?

"I am all for ze preparations, Vil. I vill kill Trench and anyone who continues ze barbaric nonsense right beside you tomorrow," Gwendolyn pronounced. "But you've got to give me ze girl."

"Gwen, don't be insane," Wilhemina nearly shouted. "She's part of Sainvire's circle and must be protected. We need everyone, and her ambidextrous skills are key. We've gone over the concept of emotional maturity, Gwendolyn. Petty revenge is not only silly, it's downright–"

"Pathetic," Gwendolyn finished for her. "I know all zhat, but the problem is I am insane. I need to get zhis girl out of my system in order to move forward. Zhis is vhat I do. I torture ze love interests of my ex-lovers. It keeps me from boredom and bolsters my reputation. Like you said, I am several times stronger and vill more than compensate ze loss of such as her. Vhat's one little girl over a force of nature like me?"

Poe got the shivers. *That's just too Glenn Close!*

"This girl survived downtown. That's miraculous in itself. It's wrong to sacrifice her to the mania of a vampire sociopath who has a de Sade complex. Besides, Sainvire won't let anything happen to her. If he ever finds out that you've harmed her, then God help you."

Wilhemina ran her fingers through her short-cropped brown hair and sighed. Before she could say anything more, Gwendolyn laughed.

"He'll never know, of course," said Gwendolyn. The long limbed goddess shook her head and winked at the butler behind Wilhemina. And just like that, a blessed bullet muffled by a silencer went through the councilwoman's heart and head, rendering her permanently dead.

The vampire in lingerie kicked the corpse to be sure it was nothing but a husk then blew a kiss to Milfred.

"My hero. You're such a good boy, Milfie," she cooed at the man's shooting prowess. "Now get her out of zis distillery lest someone find her."

Poe was like marmalade for witnessing the murder of Wilhemina who incidentally had tried to save her hide. Swallowing the fear that had clamped her throat, she watched Milfred drag the body out the front door. *I hope he gets an aneurysm.*

"I sink you're avake now, short-ugly girl," Gwendolyn said, her back to Poe.

The insult pushed out the wimpy from her veins. Poe took offense at insults from the top-heavy blonde who, under certain lights, looked like a used-up San Fernando Valley porn star. Again Poe ruminated on her fate, convinced that had she not lived such a flower-in-the attic existence, or rather, flower-in-the-bunker existence. If fresh veggies and soy milk had been in her life, she would have been at least five-foot-eight. *I shouldn't dwell on the negative. At least my head isn't bigger than my body.*

"I figured you out, you fascist dunderhead. You hate cute, petite girls because they stole some action from freak hags a million years ago when you were born." She swallowed hard. She didn't measure up to the voluptuous vampire one bit. "Weren't you like Andre the Giant back then?"

Speechless but about to blow up, Gwendolyn's mouth opened and closed, waiting for words of anger to erupt. The girl had hit a sore spot. "You, you..."

Poe sat up and eyed her pack peeking from behind the counter. It contained her only other gun. She dove for it.

Only a foot more and she could have snatched the pack. A luminous stiletto heel kicked her mid-back, making her eat carpet fuzz. She tried to get up but the point ground down on her lower spine like a cigarette getting snuffed of life.

"And vhere do you zink you're going, ugly moose?" Gwendolyn's shoe lifted its pressure, landing a blow on Poe's left kidney. Inexorable pain stung every nerve in her body, leaving her curled like a rolypoly.

"I've been vaiting for such a moment. I am obdurately bored and vouldn't you know it, dateless for two years?" She kicked the pack until it clanged against the small hipbath.

"So take up knitting," said Poe barely above a whisper. She yearned to give the dead wench a piece of her mind, but the kick to her side depleted her. "The butt floss is so over already."

"Can't hear you. Vhat's ze matter, short and ugly, you don't know how to speak English, or vhat?"

Poe took a deep breath. *This fucking S.S. troll is such skidmark!* Poe was about to answer her until a kick on the side of her head made her much-abused left ear ring. All she could manage was a pithy curse and a grunt.

"Vhat vas zhat?" Gwendolyn demanded. "Vhat did you just say?"

Poe shook her head to clear her hearing and tried to rise on all fours. "I said who'd want a used up hag like you when there's a fresh, minimally used thing like me around."

The good trait about Gwendolyn was her inability to deliver a quick repartee. For one so old and wise with experience, she was easily stumped. Then again, her ready use of violence to shade her shortcomings nearly always saved the day. With a terrible scream, the vampire grabbed a fistful of shorn hair and pulled Poe to her feet.

"You...you..." Gwedolyn began. "You ill conceived, revolting half-breed!"

Poe almost laughed if it weren't for the burning pain in her scalp. She was going to lose whatever hair was left on her head.

Tearing up, Poe replied, "Quadra-breed, thank you very much. There's nothing uglier than an outdated racist bitch whose pea-brained head can't figure out that this is *California*." She inhaled a sharp breath as follicles screamed for mercy. "This is our state."

With much discomfort, Poe twisted her body around until she faced the much taller dead. Follicles began ripping. Crying, Poe hugged the walking corpse like she was her sweetheart. Gwendolyn's cold, jiggly breasts cushioned her face to near suffocation.

"A lesbian!" Gwendolyn screeched, trying to separate the girl from her. "Let go of me, you dyke!"

There was a hissing at first then smoke eased out from between their intertwined bodies. Gwendolyn with a look of panic in her eyes and bleated out in the language of her mother country, "*Umri v layna!* You vitch!"

Through the flimsy material, the vampire's flesh burned as if chemicals had been thrown at her. Her perfect breasts and stomach hissed from contact with Poe's shirt, still wet from when she had wiped the goo off her arm. *Sometimes it pays to be a slob.*

"I love your goat, too, Gwenny!" Poe untangled her hair from Gwendolyn's grasp and dove behind the counter. The portable DVD player crashed into the hip tub while Poe hit her funny bone along the tub handle.

"You fire zhat thing at me and bid adieu to your friends," Gwendolyn cried while pulling off the gauzy material of her nighty from her singed skin. "Haven't you noticed how quiet it's been ze past two days? Leeches are forbidden to shoot. It's so zhey can pin point vhere any noises are coming from."

Weak and vomitous from the kicks to the kidney, Poe dipped her hand in the slimy water and crossed herself in half-mock. She staggered to her feet as soon as the Astra, missing a silencer, and the spray bottle of blessed water were in her hands. Her scalp burned from the patches of hair yanked out by the undead who wept tearlessly.

"You, you vill die mercilessly for zhis!" Gwendolyn vowed, as her nicely manicured hands traced the damage to her perfection. She'd never been treated so by anyone in her nearly three hundred years. It was beyond humiliating. Her fangs tripled in length, giving her a feral, supernatural look.

Poe unscrewed the bottle and stuffed it in her pocket, paying the liquid no mind as it sloshed around her thigh. "I don't have any friends so I don't have a problem exploding your pie hole with this." She lifted the Astra for emphasis and walked slowly toward the vampire.

A cocktail of wailing and screaming escaped from Gwendolyn's beautiful Betty Blow lips. "You'd turn on your own people?" she asked in outrage.

"Sure. You see, they don't like me much," Poe forced a yawn. "And I'm not too happy about the patch you yanked from my cranium."

With a quickness that took the vampire by surprise, Poe leaped at Gwendolyn. Her boot aimed at the taller woman's ankle, landing a cracking blow.

Both of them tumbled, with Poe's arms still clutching the vampire's icy thigh. Poe's hold slipped down to the ankle once they hit the floor. She ended up with a four-inch heel, but it was enough.

The enraged vampire screamed her loathing of Poe as she tried to stand on a broken ankle. "You vitch! You horrid vitch." The vampire didn't look so pretty anymore.

"No arguments there," Poe nodded in agreement, straddling the tortured councilmember who most probably had never met defeat. She pulled the half-full bottle from her drenched pocket and slammed the opening into the shrieking mouth of Gwendolyn. She squeezed the bottle until its contents pumped into the vampire's mouth as Poe fought the naked woman's buckling. On reflex, Gwendolyn bellowed painfully and swatted the human sitting on her stomach, but to no avail.

The nemesis' mouth dribbled with black blood as she genuflected on the floor.

"Do unto others," Poe gritted, disgusted at how the liquid eviscerated the undead's mouth and throat. "I doubt there's a skilled plastic surgeon around for disgusting vampires like you. Even in Beverly Hills. So it's gotta be beauty or nothing." She dipped the heel into the slime and pounded it into Gwendolyn's chest.

The Nosferatu lay still after the fifth stab. To make the humiliation complete, every vein in her body surfaced black and hissing. The beautiful Gwendolyn was no more, and the butler was nowhere to be seen.

———

"I gotta get outta this city," Poe whispered to the cool night air. "I'm sick of this shit." Eyes stinging from garlic stench and self-pity, she trudged back to the temporary base. This time she was keener, more aware of recon necessities. No more lollygagging. Every bus bench, garbage bin, and post was suspect.

It was in this limping surveillance mode that Poe noticed movement inside a snugly parked Jeep Wrangler with deflated tires half a block from the restaurant. She took cover behind the doorway of an apothecary shop swimming with bottles of pickled roots shaped like grotesque, blobby humans.

The door opened and with only the light of the moon to guide her, Poe recognized the medium-height figure whose flaming orange hair sparked briefly as she scooted out of the vehicle.

"Megan?" her lips formed. Behind her ex-friend emerged a huddled man in a long coat. The figure appeared composed and at ease unlike her friend who fidgeted nervously and turned her head about for possible onlookers.

The two shook hands awkwardly and went their separate ways. The night was so still Poe could hear the pulsing in her ear. *What're you up to, Megan, consorting with a councilman?*

She remained in the doorway until the two disappeared from sight. Poe walked the two blocks to the restaurant with a heavy heart. Who should she tattle to in case the raid tomorrow – which she wasn't privy to – was compromised? She could not believe Megan to be a fink. Besides, Gwendolyn and Wilhemina seemed to have rallied behind Kaleb. Why not Rodrigo Jacopo?

"Hello, Julia," an accented voice said in the alleyway leading to the back entrance to the restaurant. Poe jumped. "I noticed you standing by the apothecary shop and thought you might have some questions."

"Rodrigo Jacopo," Poe said, blanching. "You must have great eyesight."

"It's one of my best traits," he smiled. "Come sit with me."

Poe hesitated at first but decided that it was safe enough to sit on a crate in the alleyway with the well-groomed vampire. One scream and the people inside would come running. She clutched the gun in her pocket to let him know she was no pushover. Over twenty bicycles, which weren't there when she went for a walk, leaned against the alley wall.

"Are you with Sainvire?"

"Yes. I am," he answered clearly but dripping with sarcasm.

"Um, what was that?" Poe asked, cocking her head with interest. The vampire sounded so caustic and rancorous that her eyebrow ascended a few notches on its own volition. "Care to elaborate?"

"We despise each other," he explained flatly, shrugging his shoulders, "but we implicitly trust each other."

Poe slapped her forehead as if conveying that either Jacopo was an idiot or she didn't understand English. "Um, my years underground must've zapped my brain's ability to decipher cryptic nonsense. Explain yourself."

"I apologize for the confusion, Julia. My last remark didn't make any sense." He laid a thick hand on his thigh. "I detest Sainvire because the woman I love has given her heart to him, and he refused it."

"Oh, now I see," Poe remarked, her eyebrows arched like a pair of wings. "What a prick! He should've accepted the gal's offer and remained your best friend, eh?"

"Something like that," Jacopo smiled. "And there's also the rub that I nauseate him. Sainvire abhors my very presence."

"Why does he hate you?"

"Because, because I broached the idea of milking the cattle to the Council."

"But I thought he came up with the idea." Poe sat up straighter, forgetting about keeping the gun still.

"It was his idea. He told me about it in passing, but more as a joke," he sighed. "But I told the Council about it without Sainvire's consent. The Council had already voted to pass it as law when Sainvire learned of it. He never forgave himself for telling me. Our friendship has never been the same since."

Jacopo sat in silence mulling the past.

"I'm no longer involved in vampire business, Jacopo," Poe flatly declared. "I'm on my own now, and that's how I want it to be. So there's no need to spill your guts any further."

Jacopo added a twig to the fire. "That's the reason I'm here. To tell you to lay low for a while. Something big is going to happen within the next couple of days."

Poe's ears reddened in anticipation despite her pretense of disinterest. "What's going to happen?"

"You've not been told of it, and I'm not about to betray another secret," Rodrigo Jacopo said with finality. "I merely warn you so you may not do anything foolish and inadvertently cause harm to my friends."

"Oh please," Poe said, insulted. "I already know. I have ears."

"What do you know?"

Poe shrugged. "You're planning to raid the three biggest blood farms in downtown on the same day." She'd heard snippets of conversation at the restaurant when people thought she was asleep.

"Apparently I'm not the only talebearer busybody around here."

"Guess not. The restaurant is crawling with them. Can't get it in their heads that a person with their eyes closed can still hear," Poe sighed. "I still don't know how you all plan on freeing and stashing over three hundred cattle in one day."

"Planning's been in the works for over a year now. It's been hastened by the library fiasco. And that had a lot to do with you." Jacopo's jewel eye glinted. He could almost see the girl flush in the dark. "We'll take Union Station and use the trains to transport the cattle."

"You mean the produce and meat trains used by the holy rollers and farmers?"

Jacopo nodded. Even he was impressed by the boldness of the plan.

"But the train routes only go to food farms. Lots of fanged farmers will be around." She swallowed hard. "That'll endanger your people unnecessarily, won't it?"

"Sainvire and I have been supervising the clearing of alternative rail lines of cars and other debris for the past few months. The tracks should be completely repaired and clear by tomorrow. And if they're not, on board the trains we'll have vampires and halfdeads that can toss a car or two out of the way while laying down new rails."

Poe was too overwhelmed just contemplating the gutsy plan. She remembered Kawana's awesome strength. "And you have real farms where cattle can go and recuperate?"

"Yes, Julia. I believe Sainvire and your friends Morales and Megan have been arranging the halfway ranches to accommodate cattle."

The way he said her name felt like hot silky chocolate going down her throat on a chilly night. Because Poe was staring intently at her boots, she didn't notice the vampire smile down at her.

"So can we count on you joining us?"

Poe shook her head. "No one asked me. And I haven't seen Sainvire since the big meeting."

"The meeting where you killed some of his people? And shot him several times?"

Poe flushed shame red in the dark. She tossed her serrated hair out of the way. "I tend to get innocent people and good vampires killed. That's why I'll never be included in your future world."

"Well, can we at least get your promise that you won't try to blow up Trench's hotel for the next few days? We really don't want any of the master vampires and councilmembers tightening up security and making it more difficult for us."

Poe nodded, her mouth clamped shut. Jacopo stood up and prepared to leave.

"Um, one more question, Jacopo," she asked. "Did the Council order the raid on the library?"

Only one thing betrayed his poker face. It was the engorgement of fluids on the largest vein on his forehead that pulsed erratically. Poe couldn't make up her mind whether the telltale pounding was an indication of dishonesty or truth.

"I'm not sure."

He knew about it. Poe's heartbeat raced, her face heating up. She rose. Her index finger itched. "There are three of you on Sainvire's side and you didn't know?"

He shook his head, "It's complicated. I can't elaborate anymore at this time."

The hand holding the gun wavered, but she stood up and stepped deeper into the shadowed corner away from the small fire. "One more thing, Jacopo," she said, stopping the vampire from leaving. His face bore the expression of a person in a hurry.

"The woman you like, is it Gwendolyn?" If Jacopo knew she'd just butchered the goddess vampire of his dreams…

The councilman forced a grin. He hovered in the air with one of those smiles that was indescribably guarded and far from comforting. Poe watched him disappear in the dark purple sky. Like Sainvire, Jacopo could fly.

CHAPTER 10-A SHOOTOUT LIFE

SLEEP EVADED HER. THE cloying stench of garlic hurt her eyes. Stupidly she'd doused herself with sticky garlic juice before hitting the sack. It was her cross, her amulet against fiends of the night. Her battered body needed protection even if she smelled like foot sweat.

It was open season on the girl who had killed a councilmember and a score of others at different stages of death. A platter awaited Sainvire's head for allowing Poe to go on a binge. Her battered ribs hurt which made breathing laborious. But she had to rise and put on her gear. A shower was out of the question.

Only the very sick and injured remained. The rest had slipped out before dawn. Poe could taste their fear even with her eyes closed. The plan was so audacious that casualties were inevitable.

A series of explosions shook the underbelly of downtown not one hour later. They originated from random, dispersed corners. The first thing Poe thought of was Penny who lounged alone in the bunker. She'd left the lame dog enough food and water for a week, but she still felt sick with guilt.

"Holy cow. It's started," Poe said and rubbed her nervous tummy. "Look after all of them," she prayed to her parents. Her heartbeat was surprisingly steady.

By six, Poe emerged from the building, Kevlared and heavy with artillery. From where she stood, the triangular roof of Parker Center was gone. Black smoke rose from the gutted building that housed many of Trench's police goons. It was as if downtown had lit giant incense sticks to flavor the air. Union Station, a quarter-mile from Chinatown, was intact, however. Jointly administered by the Council and a handful of master vampires, it was the best defended of all the cattle farms.

"Better go get Penny," she muttered to herself.

Poe helped herself to one of the leftover bicycles in the alley as her limp slowed her down. She pedaled speedily down Broadway, the voice in her head becoming vicious. *You need to help them*, the voice urged. *Some of them are your friends. You can't let them be slaughtered.*

"Shut up, you," Poe said. "I don't owe them crap. If they eat it, it's on their own heads. Now get the hell outta my head!"

———————

The plan had looked so clear and logical on the blueprints with pewter Monopoly tokens representing strategic placement of their people. Megan didn't count on fellow rustlers catching bullet wounds in the neck and noggin. "Body armor is useless to sharpshooters," she said in a panic. The Bonaventure Hotel had an elevated walkway gently spiraling in the middle of the hotel, perfect for unseen snipers who were picking them off one by one. Megan estimated there were only two shooters, but they were deadly nonetheless. Trench's henchmen were definitely skilled.

"We should've been out of here ten minutes ago!" she cried, tears of frustration and dread gathering in her eyes. "What's taking so long?" she asked Morales for the tenth time.

They expected stoned leeches and snoring vampires when they exploded grenades in the doorway of the Bonaventure Hotel. The hotel, used as a nightclub by Quillon Trench, also housed a premier blood farm to accommodate thirsty guests. The plan didn't account for accurate snipers or the number of undead able to defend the fort due to the lack of sun. The glass walls of the spherical hotel had been doused with tar to suit the undead.

"Keep the line moving, people," Megan ordered her voice already hoarse from screaming commands. "Fill the elevators and head to the lobby area now! Morales, how're you doing with blammie?"

"I can't set her off until you guys are out of here. Claude's set up two cases in two decommissioned elevators on the 20th floor. They're set to explode after this one," Morales answered tensely, his wrinkled brow swimming with condensation. He fiddled inside a large ice chest. He could smell the nutty, calcified smell of the plastique.

"Are you sure that thing's gonna work?" Megan asked for the umpteenth time as she pushed another three cattle into the cramped elevator and sent it downstairs where their people waited to escort them out of the building. At least the lobby was a blind spot for the snipers.

The slow progress of the cattle and the gunshots ricocheting around the cylindrical hotel floored her. "We're not here on a picnic, you know."

Morales wiped his brow and snarled, "Meg, if you ask me that one more time, I'm going to set the timer to ten seconds."

"Fine," she huffed. "Just do it soon or we're all dead."

"We're done for anyway if those snipers aren't handled," said Morales who kneeled on the floor to hide his precious head. "Those two bastards are butchering us." He gestured to his vampire assistant. "Squat behind me, Claude. If you get hit, there's no one left to carry this shit. I have a back problem. Might as well be dinner."

"If I get any closer to your behind, folks will start taking pictures," said Claude dryly.

The ice chest, the last of three, contained sixty pounds of C-4 with enough velocity and density to cut through metal beams. Questionable wiring and explosives connected it to a simple detonator, battery, and kitchen timer.

Claude, wearing a black turtleneck, carried coils of cabling. The pinched-faced halfdead had been an accountant in the old life. If his dead pores were still active, the day vamp would have been dripping from stress.

The kitchen timer in the shape of an apple didn't exactly solicit any trust. But Morales followed the Incendiary Bomber's Recipe Book to the dot. He'd done his job. Any calamities that occurred were out of his hands.

The farm, located on the fifth floor and surrounded by posters for cheesy '80s movies filmed at the hotel, was easy to reach. Any higher would have posed problems. One of the most photographed buildings in the world stood a measly thirty-five stories, towered over by a slew of downtown skyscrapers. Three of its main glass pod elevators had been disabled, and the stairway splashed with garlic water. It was the flying critters that they had to watch out for. Fortunately there didn't seem to be any at the hotel.

Foldable hospital beds where over sixty cattle were penned were configured in tight rows within the exposed atrium. The trick was to get the sluggish and rickety limbed down the elevator without getting hit by sniper fire. Already, Sainvire's vamps and eleven humans were thinning.

"Get down!" a human named Gina screamed at Megan who missed a bullet by an elbow. "Jesus, that was close," Megan complained. Before she could thank the woman that rescued her, two shots exploded, hitting Gina in the mouth and cheek.

"Shit! Gina's dead," Morales cursed, taking refuge behind a cement pillar. "Guys, hide behind the cattle. They're precious to the vampires and won't be in any direct danger."

"This is the last of them," Megan declared, her voice raw. Around fifteen cattle milled around waiting for the elevator to take them to the lobby.

"Good. I can set the clock to go off in ten minutes."

"Do it, but we're on our own. I've sent most of our people down with the cattle." Her breath froze. "I hear shots below. I hope you're wearing a vest, Morales."

"Hell, I'm wearing ten-year-old underwear," he said with a forced a laugh. "If that won't give me luck then I don't know what will."

Desperate leeches forcibly shook and kicked the hard-to-awaken vampire residents, even resorting to setting fire to their arms with lighters until conscious. Those who could crawl down the glass panels and the concrete walls did, looking like slugs. Flyers went straight for the rustlers.

The longer the cattle thieves stayed in the hotel, the more cretins crawled out of the woodwork. Infuriated vampires eager to stop the cattle rustlers hollered in their toughest voices.

"You think you can steal from us?" one of them shouted, pissed at being burnt and forced from bed.

"Don't you know that you can't go against the new order?

Rapid fire bounced around the hotel, poking holes in tarred glass walls.

Morales didn't see the human gecko on the post directly above him and screamed like a girl when wrestled to the floor. Claude, the accountant, tried to pry the lizard-like foe from his friend, but the slime hurled him against the elevator door. Pushing the cattle out of the way, Megan aimed at the creature pinning on Morales' chest. Before she could pull the trigger, a flying vampire with dried drool marks on the side of his mouth wrenched the gun away from her.

"Morales!" Megan squeaked as the vampire backhanded her.

The elevator dinged, and the doors opened.

"Anyone call for pizza?" a deep, throaty voice asked.

"Poe?" both Megan and Morales recited incredulously at the same time.

"Yup. Come to crash your party," Poe said with a smile that fizzled as a halfdead rammed at her with his speed. Sidestepping the creature, Poe happily planted a booted foot on his back and put a bullet in his skull. She followed with a left-handed chest shot to the undead that sat on Morales. Without missing a beat, Poe aimed for the flying beast that tackled Megan and shattered its face with the gun in her right hand.

"Hey, Poe," Megan said weakly, rubbing her face. After staring at each other for what seemed like the length of a Kurosawa epic, the Titian-haired woman broke eye contact. She reached in the elevator and pulled the stop button.

Behind Megan was an exodus of wobbly-kneed cattle that needed to be crammed in the elevator. Some had soiled themselves from all the shooting. "Hey, Megan."

"Ladies, a suggestion. Talk later. We got eight minutes to clear outta here," urged Morales. "So hussle!"

Sniper fire missed Morales by a thread.

"Holy pantalones! I almost lost my left hemisphere."

"Give me your rifle," Poe asked the temporary doctor and bomb maker. Morales slid the weapon across the floor. From behind a beam, Poe cocked the rifle in readiness and waited. "Do me a favor, Morales. Stand up real quick then duck back down again."

"With no helmet?" Morales protested, his sense of humor unsnuffed. "Alright, but you better not let them ding me. I have some underwear shopping to do after all this excitement." A second after bobbing his head up, gunfire from two separate directions shattered the glass elevator walls.

"Got you now, misters." Poe fired into the shadowy balcony two floors above them. She fired another two shots on the ninth floor balcony. The bodies of two snipers plummeted onto the lobby pond, the only indication that she'd hit them.

"That's my Poe!" howled Morales, clapping her on the back.

Poe jumped into the waiting elevator with the cowering cattle and her friends. They squatted low in case more snipers lurked. Morales was the first to step foot from the elevator when it reached the lower lobby to check if the area was secure. He motioned for Megan and Poe to ease the cattle out.

Bodies decorated the lobby area. Some were Trench's toked up leeches and vampires who had died in muddled confusion. Many of the dead, however, were rustlers.

"Hurry! Get these people outta here!" Morales yelled. Two humans wearing overalls marched in to lend a hand. "Claude, keep the wires moving. We're almost there."

Busy coaxing an ornery blood cow who refused to budge, Poe failed to see a group of groggy vampires leaving the monitor room. They were armed with matching silver 9mm Browning specials. When one of Sainvire's vampires directing people outside the automatic doors hit the ground dead, Poe snapped out of her reverie. She yanked the poor human survivor to the ground.

Mean and lean with her swollen cheek, Poe did a 180 and shot the three vampires dead-on in the heart.

"Right on!" yelled Morales who'd just stepped out into the street.

Unfortunately all three pissed off undead were wearing body armor. The three vamps trained their weapons on Poe, who dove flat on the floor, taking cover behind the thick slab of cement that enclosed the circular water fountain.

"Stupid, stupid!" Poe berated herself. "Always aim for the head."

Water and koi fish met angry bullets for what seemed like hours. Losing interest in Poe, who'd probably caught one in a major organ, Trench's vampires mowed down cattle to get to the rustlers retreating outside. They could care less about what their master would think.

Like a baby chick taking her first peek, Poe raised her wet head for another look at the sure-shot vampires. A hand touched her shoulder and Poe jumped. She let out a wild shot, almost pegging cattle in the ankles.

"Calm down, for chrissake!" Megan scolded. Poe wanted to elbow her friend in the gut and tell her off for stealing up on her. "Let's sneak out the side entrance there," she said. "There are plenty of cattle rescued already, and the explosives are gonna blow anytime now."

Megan's face had a strained, almost scared expression. Poe tried not to be annoyed at her friend and recalled Megan's traumatic retelling of her long internment with Trench. Now being under Trench's roof took guts.

Poe, however, narrowed her eyes and flared her nose. "No one's getting left behind."

Instead of swearing, Poe looked away and cocked her Astra. She popped her head up, just enough for a clear aim. In three consecutive shots, Poe managed to hit the goon triumvirate smack in the back of their skulls.

She blew away the imaginary wisps of smoke emanating from her gun. Megan's surprised gasp she ignored. "Let's go."

"Thank goodness for the vests," Morales cried, rubbing his stomach where a bullet had hit him. He ran back inside to check on his friends. "Get the hell outta here, every last one of you. The building's gonna blow in three minutes!"

Only when the last cattle stepped out into the winking sun did Poe go outside herself. Sainvire's day vamps piled on the slowest and weakest upon their shoulders and ran as far as they could. From two blocks away, they watched the Bonaventure Hotel implode on the lower levels and collapse sloppily, leaving more than a few sections burning but intact.

"Hey, I'm no explosives expert," Morales shrugged, chucking the extra wires in his pocket. "I was a realtor for goodness sake."

Sainvire flew alongside two Metro buses filled with cattle stolen from the Walt Disney Concert Hall. The plan, hatched over a year ago and put into effect after the library siege, looked to be working. Three groups targeted the Bonaventure Hotel, Disney Hall, and Parker Center at the same time. Once the cattle were safely led underground in the subway tunnels, Sainvire's people would converge and infiltrate Union Station, the "Last of the Great Railway Stations," and now the ultimate cattle farm. The sound of explosions around town was music to his ears.

Most enemy undead were asleep, and the halfdeads were no match for Sainvire's force. Sainvire's nocturnal vampires had been transformed into day vamps over time by Plasmacore.

Casualties were inevitable, however, and he was powerless to prevent them. The sight of Paul Robb getting an arrow through his chest pained him. His longtime friend that marched with Dr. King was one of his heroes. Robb was turned into a vampire in the 1970s and Sainvire had crossed paths with him soon after. He didn't delude himself. By sunset, more of his people would die. Union Station would prove to be their biggest hurdle. Just getting into the well-barricaded place would take a miracle.

He looked at the drooling faces inside the buses. The poor things were once animated and alive. He ran a hand through his black hair and said, "We're going to get you back to normal."

He thought of Poe, so full of passion and brimming with life. He'd never known anyone like her in his long years on this earth. The girl had shot him! Several times at that. Yet he couldn't stop thinking of her. He'd been told that Pengle had clawed his hook into Poe's chest and let her dangle in the air. Seething hate filled his thoughts. If Kawana hadn't killed the bastard, he would have hunted him down and shred him like Watergate files.

"Be safe, Julia Poe. We have unfinished business," he whispered in the wind.

"You've changed," Megan said accusingly as she tossed Poe a sandwich. The girl was winding down next to Morales in the underside of a set of stairs inside the 7th Street Metro Station platform. Megan had been supervising the welding shut of the station doors until she decided to ladle out lunch. The next objective was to hide confused cattle underground and follow the subway tracks to Union Station.

Poe winced at Megan's comment, purposely spoken within earshot of Morales. Averting her gaze to a group of cattle eating their food oh-so-slowly, Poe took a deep breath. For the first time, she noticed a tiny girl with oily brown hair about five or six kneeling on the platform. The girl wearing what looked like a potato sack was the first child she'd seen in over ten years. She seemed lucid as she was looking at Poe with curiosity.

Poe smiled at the child as she peeled back foil and chewed off a corner of a potato salad sandwich. She hoped Megan would shove off before she could say anything that could potentially end their friendship. Before she could swallow, Megan made another searing remark.

"I don't know if I like this new Poe or if I can trust her," Megan spoke as if Poe was not present. She deliberately exhaled, catching Morales' eyes for support in the weak camp light.

"Meg, what's with you?" Morales demanded. "She just saved our butts back there."

As slowly and as articulately as she could, Poe asked, "Which person did you like before, Megan? The stuttering girl who wasn't told about Sainvire's operation, even though she killed for him for years? Or could it be the girl who wasn't told that it was time for a bra at age twenty-two?"

Poe looked at Morales who scratched his nose without expression. "We all know which you'd pick, Morales."

Flustered, Megan tried to recast her words. Poe had never been contentious with her before, and it was more than a little disconcerting. "I didn't, I just don't like to see you with bloody cuts and bruises." She ran a hand through her red hair. "And the way you killed those vampires. You were so clinical."

Poe, laughing without cheer, held her belly. "Goodness. Sorry about that." She stopped mid-laugh and looked pointedly at her friend. "I should've asked dead folk to take it easy with their fists so I could stay pretty." Then she breathed deeply and counted in Japanese for calm.

"And as for me killing clinically, I was taught by the best. A nun and a giant who apparently didn't trust me one bit." She glanced at Morales whose jaw clenched and unclenched. "I've killed for you people. I freed cattle so they could be on a real working ranch, somewhere far from the city. Somewhere a fourteen-year-old would've been best suited."

Megan didn't even bother looking up anymore. All Poe glimpsed were her red ears as she stared down at the roast beef sandwich on her lap. So Poe continued.

"And I truly do apologize for being so hard." She gritted. "Goss is gone. To keep it that way, I had to chop off his head and throw it down the garbage shoot." Poe swallowed at the lump in her throat. "And Sister? She was stabbed in the eye next to me, and I couldn't do anything about it."

"I didn't mean—"

"Sorry if the change in me offends you, Megan," Poe continued, "But to tell you the truth, I like me better this way. Tough shit if you don't trust me. Like you ever did."

Poe stuffed the sandwich crushed by her fist into her pack. She stood up and headed toward the cattle quietly eating lunch. She plunked down in the middle of the platform lit only by a few camping lanterns. She ignored the garbage and dirt and rested her hurt back. "I need to take a nap," she mumbled to herself and tried to yoga away her grief. "I don't feel so good."

An hour later, Poe had her gun cocked and pointed even before her sleepy eyes focused into the face of Morales.

"Whoa, Poe. It's me, Sam." The handsome, easygoing man actually looked panicked.

Poe retracted her gun and wiped her dry mouth. Not for the first time Poe felt embarrassment about her shoddy looks. Her uneven-to-missing patches of hair, mislaid earlobe, and multiple scars and lacerations made her self-conscious. She said a quick prayer for her straight teeth to remain unchipped. Morales, sensing the awkwardness of the moment, took out a moist towelette packet and handed it to Poe.

She accepted it with thanks as she sat up creakily on the bench. "I feel like shit." The towelette was as dry as tissue after a decade of disuse.

"And you've looked better," he said with a nod.

Poe shuddered at this side of Morales. *No perverted winks and leers? No sexual innuendos? Boy,*

I must really look hell-nasty for him to be respectful all of a sudden. Or maybe it's the bra.

"Thanks, Morales," Poe said, blowing her nose and tossing the soiled wipes on the platform. "Say, why's it so dark in here? Where's everyone?"

Morales flaunted a crooked and irresistible smile. "Just wanted you to know that the last group marched in the tunnels almost an hour ago. If we don't vamoose now, we won't catch up." His smile disappeared, locking eyes with Poe. "I don't want to sound yellow, but it's dark and damp in the subway tunnels and the thought of rats and insects kinda loosens my bowels. I'm not stable enough to be in the rear of the procession. We gotta follow the tracks now."

Poe surveyed the empty platform and the darkness ahead. She inclined her head and said, "Why didn't you go with them?"

His brow drew together. "Ask me later," he sighed.

"Well sorry anyway."

He ignored the guilt dripping from her words. "The plan is to march the cattle through the subways tunnels to avoid the Council and the rest of the bloodsuckers until our transportation's ready. "In the meantime, we're crossing our fingers that all the cattle are physically and mentally able to make the trek."

Poe bit the inside of her lip trying to gauge the plan. "So we're really heading to Union Station?"

"Yep, yep. While you slept, we injected the anemic bunch with vitamin B_{12} shots. Liver sandwiches, water, and vitamins helped revive some of them. I saved a shot for you if you're interested, but we really gotta go," said Morales.

"Thanks for thinking of me, T-Doc," Poe smiled gently, her dimples showing. "But I think I have enough energy to carry me through. Between you and me, I'm downright weak-bellied when it comes to needles. How's Sainvire going to rustle up transportation for all these people anyway?"

"By hijacking the trains at Union Station."

"What?" Poe bellowed, spitting accidentally where Morales sat. "That's the mother lode. There'll be tons of vamps, cops, and the rest."

"Yeah," Morales nodded, looking distractedly at his Indiglo watch. "If anyone can pull off this lunatic idea, it's Sainvire. We gotta go, kid."

She nodded. "One more question. Did Megan ask you to stay behind?"

"No," he answered too quickly. "I was concerned about you. I thought you could use a nap. Problem is I dozed off, too."

Reeling that her only girlfriend didn't see to her welfare pissed Poe off. She did the next best thing; she picked on Morales. "You should've been that concerned eight years ago when you found out I lived alone underground. It would've counted more."

"I know."

An awkward silence filled the air. Only Morales had the balls to break it. "Don't think bringing you in and sending you to the recovery ranch didn't cross our minds." Morales rested his hand lightly on Poe's arm. "It's just that you had never been cattled up, and you survived the city on your own all those years. Then you showed up at Goss' building. We were suspicious that you were a plant."

"For nearly a decade? Hundreds of rescued cattle later?" Poe quipped, removing her arm from under the man's hand. The thought of Goss and Sister Ann whom she'd loved unconditionally not trusting her broke all comfort and Christmas cheer from her heart. That was why Sister Ann kept mum about where she lived all those years. "You all used me. To think I was working for a damn vampire all that time!"

She jumped down the platform to the dark, gravelly tracks beneath and began following the rails using a small flashlight she'd retrieved from her pack. Her leg ached, but what could she do?

"I'm sure I'm speaking for everyone," he said, following the girl into the tunnel, his Adam's apple bobbing. "We're all sorry about what we did. Especially Megan. Especially me."

"Don't give me that, Morales," Poe huffed. "It's a bit too late. As for Megan, she let me know what she really thinks of me."

"Think of me what you will, but Megan has always loved you, Poe."

"Nice way of showing it."

"She was just jealous of you."

Poe's head swiveled so fast that Morales actually heard her neck tendons crack a little. "Jealous! Jealous? Gimme a break! She's pretty and intact for crying out loud!"

"She heard about you and Kaleb. About the night he spent in your bunker."

"Who blabbed?"

"Kaleb did," Morales laughed without glee. Then he corrected himself. "Alright. To be fair, Claude, the biggest mouth in the west, heard Sainvire spilling his guts out to Joseph. Within ten minutes, the underground was abuzz with the news."

Poe wiped the spittle that spewed from her mouth. *Is nothing sacred anymore?*

Morales shook his head. "He could've laid low in Pico Rivera after the raid, Poe. He went searching for you instead. He hid out for hours near your bunker, hoping you'd show up. He was gunned down by day vamps for crying out loud. So when Kaleb finally came back to HQ a day later, Megan confronted him about it."

She asked the million-dollar question. "Why is it so important for her to pry into other people's business?"

"Must I spell it out for you, Poe?" Sam's brow drew together, cursing when he tripped over an empty paint canister. "She's in love with him. Always has been."

Poe hyperventilated thinking about best friend etiquette. Everybody knew how wrong it was to snag a friend's boyfriend. *Crap! I'd hate me, too, if I were in Megan's shoes.*

"Well, you know, I didn't know. Nobody told me." She shook her head. "But, um, she can have him. Never liked the bloodsucker anyway." Her heart felt like it was being ground by a handheld fruit juicer. Fact was, she lusted for the vampire, but she hated him too.

"She can never have him, Poe. That's the problem." He expelled a breath reeking of liver and onions. "Megan is Sainvire's great niece. She's his brother's granddaughter. He'd always taken care of the Sainvire family in some way even when the world was normal."

That's a mouthful, thought Poe. Sainvire's brother's granddaughter. *What the hell does that mean? Goodness, the apocalypse is over. What's a little familial intermingling in this crazy city anyhow?* But the thought of doing it with her own grandpa's brother made her want to hurl.

"Kaleb thinks of her as family and not as a potential mate," he continued. "But she still holds out hope."

"Gee, wouldn't want to touch that one." She sighed somewhat relieved to know that Sainvire had some scruples left and that Megan's feelings weren't reciprocal in any way. When Morales raised an eyebrow at her audible sigh, she quickly added. "I, I've had a feeling for a while now that you kinda like her, too."

At this, Morales laughed. "Poe, I like all women. Pretty ones, most of all." He shined his flashlight on her face and beamed, "My true weakness." He pointed the light to the ground.

Poe looked away, flattered by the hint, but she didn't take it as truth. She'd seen herself in the mirror, and she was scary as hell. She was missing pieces of herself, and that fact was difficult to gloss over.

"Who made her into cattle?" Poe remembered seeing the bite on Megan's neck.

Morales scratched the stubble on his chin. "That's a long story, Poe. I think we should pay more attention to what we're stepping on. Avoid that opossum ahead."

Determined to know the truth, Poe laid a hand on Morales' forearms and looked into his face, silently conveying that she deserved to hear some truth for once. She pulled out a headlamp and adjusted it on Morales' head. Quickly Poe put on the night vision goggles from her pack, giving her momentary vertigo. Everything became Tron green.

"Alright," he sighed. "A year or so after the Gray Armageddon, the cattle round-up began. Sainvire's ideas were put into play. Trench's roughnecks swept the Echo Park area. Megan, who was holed up in a hill house, was taken away. I met her in the same cattle truck bound for the Bonaventure Hotel that had been claimed by Trench."

Poe slowly withdrew her hand from his well-muscled upper arm as they resumed their walk. "Why didn't Sainvire rescue her or something?"

"He tried when he found out. Only, Megan opened her big mouth and threatened Trench by saying that she was related to Sainvire." Morales shook his head. "Calling it a blunder is big understatement. Trench made her his personal fountain, drinking her blood through straw hook-ups every night." He pursed his lips at the memory. "There was bad blood between the two masters, you could say. Trench wanted people as prey to be hunted. He didn't want to drink cold farm blood."

"What did Ka…Sainvire do?"

"He met with Trench several times, but the vampire only toyed with him. Trench stuck an intravenous hose directly into Megan's forehead veins and drank her blood like a cocktail in front of Kaleb. Sainvire almost killed him on the spot but Joseph stayed his hand. To kill a master vampire wouldn't have been a prudent thing to do." He glimpsed Poe's scar in the dark. "Eventually the Council stepped in. But they voted in favor of Quillon's ownership rights."

"How did she get out?"

"With the help of a councilmember."

"Rodrigo," she uttered under her breath.

Morales looked at Poe strangely. "Yes, Jacopo. He was the one who actually approached Kaleb about a plan to steal her away from Quillon."

"Were they chums, or what?"

"That was the strange part. They weren't even friends." Morales focused on her bug- eyed goggles. "He just offered to snatch Megan away and have her stay in his place until it was safe to deliver her to Sainvire."

"Hmmm," Poe nodded in understanding, eyeing the fungus-laden walls of the subway. She shivered at the sheer number of cockroaches commingling on the walls. *Rodrigo loved Megan enough to get her away from Trench.* Poe stopped asking questions and let Morales concentrate on the tracks.

Morales spotted an abnormally large rodent near his foot and squealed like the end was near. The muscular man was scared of the dark.

For one so cunning, Morales was a bit of an airhead. His ridiculous penchant for choosing the worst weapons because they looked "manly" irritated Poe like nothing else. He carried two extra-long Dirty Harry Magnums that took up far too much space on his fishing-jacket-slash-battle-armor. The loose bullets jangling in his pockets weren't practical at all.

"You know, reloading two-cylinder six-shooters bullet by bullet in the middle of a fight is gambling with fate," she told him.

Morales just rolled his eyes and muttered under his breath, "Kid, just leave it to the pros," in a voice similar to a scathing Clint Eastwood.

She offered to lend an Uzi she was reluctant to use and an automatic she carried in her pack. He scoffed at her generosity, brushing off her criticisms and suggestions.

"Suit yourself." She shrugged and kept her mouth shut.

Aside from the headlamp, Morales had a boxy flashlight with an emergency radio attachment. Poe rolled her eyes at the fancy station knobs, as there was nobody alive to broadcast. *Amateur!*

"You wouldn't happen to have another pair of fancy goggles on you, would you?"

"Nope."

"Rat shit! Clumps of them!" she heard Morales whine after he slipped on moist tracks, nearly eating crumbs and other goodies on the ground. "Oh yuck," he cried when he rested his hand on the mossy wall to heave himself up. It was crawling with life.

Morales wiped the slime on his pants, the hairs on the back of his neck still standing. He clicked on his square flashlight that flickered weakly. "Damn batteries! Can never find a working set these days." Poe could have sworn T-Doc sobbed when the lights finally flicked off.

"Goss told you to use rechargeable batteries years ago, so don't complain." Poe adjusted the goggles to her eyes and warned her companion, "And don't you point your headlight at me. It'll blind me!"

"Yes, yes," he answered, irritably. He muttered that his light wouldn't reach her anyway, because she was so short.

Poe shut her mouth and didn't say a word. If she were to exchange words with moron man, she'd be forced to shoot him. Her temper had been awfully short lately. She bet that Mr. Manly Man never studied the tunnel maps like Goss and Sister Ann had insisted she do.He certainly was no Kaleb. She shuddered at the memory of exploring those luscious lips, those sensuous eyes with dark eyelashes longer than hers.

"Don't go too fast!" ordered a disturbed Morales, who kept slipping due to his low traction Pumas.

"Look, I'm limping. How can I go too fast?" Getting p.o.'d at Morales was better than thinking about Kaleb Sainvire. She owed the vampire an apology. He wasn't responsible for cattle milking. Rodrigo Jacopo was.

Poe forgot about Sainvire and Morales when a large creature trotted across her foot. She screamed and so did Morales who was tapped by the creature's tail. Poe, in turn, tripped and twisted her right ankle, the one Sainvire had punctured.

She seethed. Not everything appeared clearly, even with night vision goggles, especially if the opossum was coming from the rear. Not only was her ankle hurt, she was blinded, too, as Morales' light trained on her.

"You good, Poe?" Morales asked, giving her a hug and halfway lifting her off the ground. The concern in his voice was genuine. Poe was truly touched, but not to the point that she'd let him drag her around.

"No, I'm not! It's my frikkin' ankle," she fumed, tearing up. "Hell of a time to fuck up."

"I can carry you."

"No need for that," Poe said, chuckling a little. Then she winced at the pain. "I'll be well enough if you'd just point your light somewhere other than my face."

Instead of moving the light, Morales squatted down. He took out two red bandanas from one of the many pockets of his fishing jacket and bandaged Poe's right ankle tightly. The man was a better doctor than a killer.

"Of all the days for this to happen," Poe complained.

She appeared oddly ethereal, like a human fly with her enormous night goggles and hacked hair of different lengths. He gave her boot a light tap then stood up. Without asking, he took a small flashlight hanging from her pack to sweep the platform for possible obstacles. Finding no slippery mounds of rat droppings, he put his hand under Poe's armpit and helped her walk, keeping the flashlight pointed in front of them.

"I can walk, Morales," Poe hissed. She could feel the twisted ankle expanding. "Get your hand–"

"Forget it," he said firmly, holding her more tightly. "We need to catch up to the rest, *entiendes*?" Poe counted to three in Japanese: *ichi, ni, san*. "Fine!" she relented.

Poe hopped on one foot, testing the rocky tracks.

"Don't even think about molesting me in any way," Poe said as a bitter afterthought.

"FYI, this Petri dish of a tunnel has shrunk my manhood to dandruff size. Relax," snarled Morales.

They walked in silence, inching together ever so closely as they progressed deeper in the heart of the dank tunnel. Morales' robust Christian Dior perfume plagued Poe's nostrils. Strong artificial scents did not agree with her.

Morales' cologne intermingling with little creature crud and piss-ammonia kindled an awfully bad premonition. *Christian-fucking-Dior and my swollen ankle make me want to shoot someone.* She had to stop for she was hyperventilating.

"What's wrong, Poe?" Morales asked out of concern. "Is the ankle bothering you?"

She shook, sweating cold water. "Nothing. Yes, sumfin." She inhaled deeply, but away from Morales. "Get away from me."

"What?" Morales mouthed, completely taken aback.

"I mean your cologne is making me sick!" Poe reached for a glove from her pack and slipped it on her right hand. "Never mind. I'll lean on the wall."

Unhooking one of the two bottles of garlic water from her Mexican belt, Poe sprayed Morales in the face until he yelled an expletive. "Don't be mad. I'm allergic," she said when Morales remained silent. Poe hung the bottle on one of the hooks of his fishing jacket.

"This kind of perfume I approve of. I'm sure you'll need it today," Poe added. "And if I were you, I'd squirt myself with holy water as much as possible to drown out that problem."

"You know, if I didn't respect you so much, I'd strangle you right now."

"Just you try," she said, grinning. To assuage his ego, she mentioned how fit he was.

"You should see me without a shirt."

All talk skidded to a halt as terrifying screams and gunfire erupted farther up the tunnel. The mutual look of stark horror they gave each other in the dark was enough. Poe took off the sodden glove and threw it on the ground, hobbling faster. Morales handled one of his Magnums and half-supported Poe with his free hand.

Between the two of them, they hustled a consistent pace toward where the pealing screams originated. Each step and bang of gunfire made their pulses beat even more wildly. Finally Morales ordered Poe to get on his back.

"No way!" said Poe.

"People are dying, Poe. You've got no choice on this."

She hopped on his back and wrapped her legs around his waist. As a precaution, Poe stuffed his ears with tissue in case she had to shoot from above.

"Just make sure I can still hear, okay?"

"Yeah."

The man practically ran in the dark. Poe's extra weight didn't seem to hinder him. His lung capacity was impressive. Poe, clinging to his neck and head, was truly grateful that he was in such good shape. Her personal pony.

A couple times, Morales stumbled, but he corrected his balance without incident. The desperate voices grew shriller as they pushed on.

A movement from the ceiling caught Poe's eyes. As the objects drew nearer, Poe recognized three toddler babies with sharp fangs and darting tongues slithering on top of them.

"Oh, Jesus!" Poe coughed her skin alive with goose bumps. She unlatched the safety on the Astra and prayed that she could aim with the frog glasses on. Her hands trembled from fear.

"What's going on? What do you see?" Morales asked, scared shitless from being so blind despite their portable lights.

"Babies on the ceiling," Poe said, swallowing deeply. "Brace yourself. I'm going to shoot them down." She added, "Whatever you do, don't flash the lights in my eyes."

Because she didn't want those creatures any closer than they already were, Poe shot at all three from twenty feet away. The first two bullets went awry but by the third, Poe's instinctual shooting skills kicked in. The creatures squealed demonically as they fell to their deaths.

Even Morales shrieked, as Shaft would have put it, like a motherfucker, when the babies with sharp yellow nails fell on the tracks. From that moment on, both of them were alert like rabbits, scouting every wall nook and cranny for more of the same vermin.

"I heard they exist," Morales said, cringing. "Some were sucked by greedy vampires when they were babes and turned, and the rest are products of vamp-on-vamp love. Some stay in baby bodies and some actually grow up, so I hear. Disgusting!"

"I can walk now, Sam." Poe tapped his head. Ahead was a wall of babies, child vampires, and deformed halfdeads herding cattle into a nook. These cattle laggers were the slowest and weakest, the ones left behind by their group. The babies formed a monkey chain, looping their elbows together until they could torment the humans from inches away. She saw a particular hanging baby dart out its reptilian tongue and lick at a cut on the forehead of one of the cattle hanging on a thread of consciousness. Even in the dark, Poe could tell that the toddlers were filthy little fiends, bred and born in the tunnels because of their parents' shame.

Sainvire's people decorated the sticky ground. Cattle or not, some of the humans were awakening from their heavy languor. The sight of a demonic baby lifting and sucking an adult body dry could awaken anyone.

"Okay, Poe, but if you need to run, let me know and I'll give you a ride," Morales said, his voice at the breaking point. Mr. Macho was scared shitless. He shook like an old washing machine on rinse. Like Poe, he had never seen anything like that before. He had always been the planning and logistics guy, not a vampire and dead baby killer. While Poe was on his back, he had actually felt safe. Now he was close to pissing his pants.

A munchkin vampire spotted them, opened its mouth, and let out a sharp hiss that alerted the other beasties. Soon the group of impish kids, babies, and adult vampires re-grouped, surrounding cattle and using them as human shields against possible retaliation.

Poe slid to the ground, ignoring the pain in her ankle. "Morales, can you shoot dead on?"

"Wwhat?" Morale stuttered. "I'm not a crack shot. Not in the dark. No, not at all!"

"Are you comfortable enough to shoot those baby things instead of the big cretins circling the cattle?"

"Nnoo!"

"Then just aim for the ones on the ceiling, okay?" she ordered, taking the holy water from his jacket and handing it to him. "And when they get close, spray them until they fry."

With her own bottle, she sprayed a circle around them. "Just remember, they're barefoot and naked.

This stuff is like boiling oil to them. Spray the ground if you have to. And don't leave the circle."

She hooked the bottle back to her belt. In her left pocket, she took out a plastic water squirt gun shaped like a neon pink turtle. Procuring a plastic mouth protector she found at the Mexican shop, Poe stuffed it in her mouth. "There's no way I'm getting a chipped tooth today." She took the high-pressure gun and squirted the ceiling. Two babies fell screeching in agony.

"Shoot, Morales. Shoot!" Poe ordered her seemingly frozen partner.

With much trepidation, he did, the flashlight in his other hand shaking.

She grunted her approval and stuck the plastic toy gun in her left pocket again. Her eyes never leaving the thick wad of bodies on the ceiling that were carefully avoiding the holy water line, she shot her automatic upward. Many fell hissing, but the creatures were like ants, reforming and continually prodding on.

Her breath caught in her throat. The little girl she had seen earlier was snagged in the air by four linked baby vamps. The girl, used to a hellish existence, did not scream, but her dirty face looked petrified as if stuck in a nightmare.

"Ready?" Poe asked, fearful for the child.

"Yes," Morales answered. His voice was a little stronger and less nervous after he'd damaged his first two vampire babies.

"Now!" Poe shot at the linked vampires until they lost their hold on the girl. Poe prayed that the child did not break any bones. She looked so brittle.

Next she went after a throng of adult vampires that looked like the siblings of the Elephant Man surrounding about twenty cattle. Her automatics blasted at the first line of defense, and with the Glock in her left hand she aimed at the rear guard, babies and adults using humans as shields.

She took out the vampires and babies shot by shot with deadly accuracy, replacing clips as she went. A bullet rent the arm of a human. Poe's concentration faltered at the error and for the unmistakable human wail as he fell.

Next to her, Morales shot upwards, mostly hitting his targets. Some of the enemy, however, moved so swiftly that they were able to dodge the Magnum's force.

"I'm out of bullets," Morales cried in panic. "Need to reload!"

Cursing, Poe reached for the Uzi from her partially opened pack and threw it at Morales. She did not see the three-link vampire baby chain looped behind her. By the time she realized it, two of them had jumped on her head, and another set of six fell on Morales.

Both toddlers scratched Poe's scalp and neck with their grimy nails before sizzling from contact with her blessed skin. She wasn't aware of her advantage, however, because she was so disturbed by the close proximity of the baby vampires to her face that she lost it. Morales' blood curdling screams didn't help. Flicking out the oil-blessed wrist knives on either hands, Poe stabbed the two devilish chubbies over and over until their little hearts were punctured. Only when the smoke cleared did she fall back to earth.

She looked over to Morales, trying to disengage the little claws of six fiendishly uncute cherubs that had dug into his skin. The only problem – the hands were welded to him because of the recent application of holy water. Poe hobbled over to where he lay.

"Get off him!" yelled Poe. She squirted the creatures, and they bawled like chicken on the slaughter wheel. The blessed water melted flesh like candle wax.

With one fat thumb she pulled the hammer of her Glock, stopping any more babies from jumping on them. With the other hand flashing her sparkling new Rambo knife, she sliced away the parasitic vampire hands stuck on Morales' flesh. Morales scrambled to his feet.

"Scrape the hands later, Morales!" Poe yelled over the gunfire, the mouthguard garbling her voice. "Grab the frikkin' Uzi and kill vampires!"

Despite his state of shock, Morales did as he was told. He fired at the slithering abortions with desperation and surprising accuracy. Poe resheathed her gummy knives and reloaded her firearms. She hobbled closer, careful to avoid Morales' bullet shells and the small bodies that plunked down like melted icicles from the ceiling.

She targeted the deformed vampires clumped on cattle arteries. "One head. Two heads. Three heads," Poe recited out loud until she decimated the rank lot. Hearing her own voice helped her concentrate.

Poe nearly retched as her mind separated itself from the killing.

After a layer of bodies covered the floor, Poe handed Morales another clip and showed him the release. Catching on, he loaded the cartridge into his empty weapon.

Terrified cattle huddled together clutching flashlights, candles with paper drip catchers, and oil lanterns. As leery of Poe as they were of the supernatural beings, the cattle shied away from her. *That's what you get for shooting one of them in the arm.*

"Morales, you stay with these people," Poe ordered. "I'm going ahead." Gunshots could be heard a few yards away, and Poe was determined to see to the other batch.

"I'm going with you," he insisted, his voice unstable.

"No. If both of us go, these folks will be easy prey," she said adamantly. "They need you." She squeezed his arm then let go when he winced at the burnt hand glued to his forearm and neck. "We'll take care of those later." She opened her pack and handed out five handguns to the most alert of the bunch. She had swiped as many firearms as she could at the restaurant. Her pack was certainly getting lighter, and they weren't even at the destination yet.

"Just point and squeeze," she instructed the awakened cattle.

She hobbled as fast as her injured body would take her. "You have Penny to take care of. You can't die just yet," she whispered. There was no way that she would allow her dog and only family to starve to death. Besides, the ocean was waiting for them.

She hopped over debris. With the goggles on, the sound of her breathing, screams, and gunfire in the background were amplified like Darth Vader's asthmatic wheezes. Poe was stuck in a nightmare, a bilious, underwater dream full of unwanted swim partners with fingernails that had raked their own dead asses.

Every two seconds, she'd glance up the moldy ceiling to look for Gerber ghoulies. Just remembering those creatures made her feel foul and truly grossed out. She found herself saying, "Sainvire, be safe."

The trail of dead cattle and vampires gave her the impression that she was nearing the batch. She recognized one of the vampires lying dead on the tracks as one of the library chefs.

She was looking down at the fallen Petra when the body next to it sat up and karate chopped Poe's good leg until she fell on her butt.

Next thing she knew, her opponent yanked off the goggles from her face and flung them against the moldy wall. She was blind. Highly aware that she was in big trouble, Poe pushed herself to remember where the goggles landed, praying that she wouldn't get disoriented.

The whole world became one dark mess. Every time Poe tried to stand, a very silent and unseen enemy would trip her up. It was toying with her.

"This fight is unfair," Poe accused lamely.

The creature didn't even gloat or make noise, so she had no idea where to aim her weapons. Her backpack was yanked from her back along with the knives on her wrists. Because it was a matter of life and death, she glued her fingers to the Astra.

It occurred to her that she still had a miner's lamp around her neck. She pulled it to her forehead and clicked it on just when the creature's foot smashed her mouth, nearly cracking her jaw. She fired, but at the empty, dank air. Groaning and slurping her bloody spit, Poe stood up on wobbly legs. The creature wasn't done with her. It savagely smacked the side of her head. Dizzy as hell, she forced herself to point the light.

What she saw was worst than the Nosferatu of her dreams. Before her was a drooling malevolent beast with an enlarged eye and one tiny imitation of a normal eye that sported a blood red pupil. Its movement screamed hate. *I'm going to die!*

The creature was Milfred, the Council's butler, standing straighter than usual with a deranged look on his face. His one bulbous eye was horrific, blinking and winking at her light. His hunch did not protrude from his back anymore, and his tiny eye was no longer closed.

"Milfred, you faker," she accused, sounding garbled. Poe shook her head. "You've chucked the meek and supplicating act, I see." Before he could come at her again, Poe pulled the trigger, striking him in the chest.

The impact downed him, but he quickly recovered. He straightened his stained cloak and picked up his stride toward Poe. *The butler's impervious to bullets*? Poe shot him twice more on the same spot, but he continued walking. Fear tasted salty. Saline tears, together with blood, runny nose, and garlic sweat resembled the flavor of death.

Milfred tackled her, screaming a fleet of rubbish. His severely aged claws encircled Poe's neck. The back of Poe's head collided with slimy gravel. She would have passed out if it weren't for the words that came out of the butler's mouth as he squeezed her neck even tighter.

"Mum mum mum. Ya killed me mum, ya stupid girl. I'll fukin' kill ya till ya can't be killed no more ya–" he droned like a foul-mouthed British sailor in the movies.

Poe kicked his shin, kneed his balls, and pegged a bullet at his left lung, but he just kept on squeezing. Wanting a slow death for Poe, Milfred alternately slapped and punched her. He even hit her in the stomach to keep her conscious. The cretin was stronger than some of the vampires she'd offed before, and bullets bounced off him. He was going to kill her.

With nothing more to lose, Poe vowed to stare her killer in the eye until the very end. The headlamp projected a weak beam which made it easier to stare at the big and small beady eyes with hate. Since the gun was useless and her other weapons were strewn on the ground, Poe tried one last assault using the last of the arsenal – her hands.

Because the blowfish eye miffed her to the point of desperation, she stuck her left index finger good and hard in its orbs, as if she were penetrating a soft-boiled egg. And since the small beady eye with bloody pupils disgusted her, she punctured it with her right thumb.

Imagine Poe's surprise when the butler let go of her neck and clutched at his eyes, screaming and cussing like he was Kevin Smith. He had a weakness after all. Milfred tripped on Poe's fallen pack and stumbled backward. Providence at last.

"Your mum?" Poe coughed. "This is about your mom? Gwendolyn?"

She did not know whether his blinkers were going to heal themselves, so she approached Milfred with a knife she picked up off the ground. On the tracks, Milfred lay on his back. Underneath his coat revealed a vest.

"Bulletproof vest," Poe said with derision, spitting out her blood-flavored mouthguard. "The punk!"

Poe lifted an old Luger lodged in Milfred's pants. "Nazi weapon. How come I'm not surprised?" With an unsteady grip, she emptied the Luger into Milfred's face until pulpy meat was left. He died screaming, "Mummy, mummy, mummy!"

The hand that reached for the goggles on the tracks trembled. She'd shot a human.

And a bug-eyed butler toyed with me. Milfred hadn't straight out tried to kill her. He had amused himself by kicking the shit out of her first.

Looking sharply about her with the headlamp, Poe located the goggles and wiped them with her t-shirt.

She put them on, still sniffling, tasting the blood that leaked from her split lip. *I must be some sight. Mash meat isn't far off. Good thing my teeth are in good shape. Otherwise I'd shoot myself dead right now.*

At that moment, Poe despised the dark as much as Vincent Gallo's pompous films that irked her like no other. She hated vampires. She hated rats. She especially hated babies with fangs. Now she was in a dark tunnel surrounded by all of the above and more. And she was alone. She clicked off her light to stew in darkness. It seemed to be the story of her life.

Tired sobs escaped her mouth. "What the fuck was that all about?" She fired at the remains on the floor just in case.

She wiped the continuous dribble of blood and snot with the back of her hand. Because her nasal passages were congested, Poe blew her nose like it was the last well in Australia.

Hear that? That's the sound of bedlam up ahead. Now quit feeling sorry for yourself and join the party of the year!

Mostly hopping and relying on one leg, Poe managed to reach a group of cattle. What her green, hazy vision revealed made her shudder. *Xena help me!*

"After this horror, I'm taking Penny to the beach. We're retiring for sure!"

Sniffling, she aimed her firearm at the adversaries huddled together like one centipede body. The little creatures were using cattle to shield themselves against Sainvire's people who were dropping like baby teeth. Briefly she glimpsed Megan, aiming her gun at a wicked toddler, buck naked and filthy.

How many babies did these vampires crap out? Haven't they heard of abstinence or birth control? Even she knew about them. The unprovoked image of Sainvire performing coitus interruptus flitted in her mind to accuse her of hypocrisy. *Sainvire didn't happen. The whole thing was bogus and gross.*

"Down, cattle! Now!" she ordered in her harshest and loudest voice. More than a few dropped to a squat in fear of their lives. *Sex with the dead is so fucked up.*

Poe pulled the hammer and shot adult and baby vamps, picking them off like clockwork until the rest scrambled away from the huddle. Megan and a handful of rustlers followed her lead. The critters were so swift and reptilian that it took skill and deep breathing to plug bullets into their tiny bodies. Most of Poe's clips had been emptied. She reached back to the side pocket of her pack for more but found none.

Babies and toddlers scampered up the ceiling like Spiderman's spawn. One in particular had flying abilities. Softly padded like a plump two-year-old, it soared toward her with such animosity that it sent her reeling back. The little beast raked her scalp, claiming some flesh.

In the distance, she heard Megan scream, "Poe, I'm coming!"

While humans and Sainvire's vamps concentrated on the thick cluster of babies on the tunnel ceiling, Poe was busy rifling for ammo. The flying imp headed her way once more, screaming the most god-awful gibberish. The baby's mouth looked like shark teeth with one sharp incisor up front.

Poe screamed until she ran out of air. Squeezing whatever was in her hand, Poe yelled, "Fuck!" The holy water in the squirt gun caught the baby in the eye. The orb gurgled, expanded, and exploded.

"Here, catch!" Megan hollered, throwing her a fully loaded Walther PPK. With the combination of holy water spray and gunfire, Poe and Megan's people scattered the babies back into their hidey-holes.

"Thanks, Megan," Poe began out of breath. "We need to talk after–"

"Poe, watch out!" Megan screamed as a halfdead with melted skin and an asshole for a mouth rammed her from behind. The creature pounded Poe's back and shoulder with her fists. Pinned, Poe couldn't get up. The halfdead straddled her from behind. She lost her firearm in the shuffle.

"Get off of her, you sick bastard!" Megan shrieked, blasting the creature with Poe's neon squirt gun she found on the ground. The redhead was a mediocre shot. She wasn't about to fire at the creature at the risk of hitting Poe. "Five o'clock from your right hand, Poe!" she yelled. The gun by the tracks was within Poe's reach.

She could barely breathe let alone reach for the weapon. Her kidneys had taken a monstrous pounding. The halfdead punk stopped her assault on Poe and shrieked at Megan who had inched closer. Megan, having no choice, shot the halfdead with a bullet through the head.

Flipping over with difficulty after the limp body had slipped from her back, Poe held her position and kept her back rested. Every little turn and movement was a stab to her spine. The feeling was nothing she had ever endured before, not even with her many training injuries.

She curled her hand on the firearm a foot from where she lay. As best as she could, Poe tried to help out Megan and Sainvire's foot soldiers by guarding their blind side while they duked it out with little babies and vamps. Surprisingly she could hit just as well from ground level. When she couldn't provide cover because of her limited view, Poe barked warnings against approaching danger. But the day was won when cattle jumped into the picture.

At first, the weak, rubbery bunch, slowed by vampire bites, merely cowered in lethargy. Then a woman in her sixties stepped up. She pried away a ravenous infant from one of Sainvire's human scientists.

"Go, cattle!" Poe reveled on the ground. Somehow the label didn't quite fit anymore. "Go, lady!" she corrected.

The infant vampire overpowered her in strength alone, and it turned on her. The others, however, did not let the suckling devour their fellow unfortunate. With the combined counterforce of ten cattle, the infant was pulled away from Remy, the brave captive, and was stomped on. By then, even the weaker of the cattle was reenergized enough to protect each other.

———————

Megan found Poe on the ground staring up at her.

"You okay?"

"Nuh uh," answered Poe, whose back was on fire. Since she could still wiggle her toes, she figured that all was not lost. Fifteen of Sainvire's men, bringing with them about ninety cattle, had joined them from connecting utility tunnels along the way.

"How about these cattle, eh?" Megan said excitedly. "They slaughtered most of the deformed gremlins this side of downtown."

"Yeah, I know. I only had to fire once or twice to even out the odds."

"Are you going to lay there for the rest of the afternoon, or what?" Megan smiled in the dark, but the concern in her voice was unmistakable.

"Nope. Just until Morales catches up." She hugged her knees to her chest until she was seesawing on the pebbly ground to stretch her spine.

"Shit! I forgot about Sam!" Megan didn't waste a moment to send agile vampires and humans, newly arrived, to fetch Morales then turned back to Poe. "Thanks for helping out."

"I didn't do much. Just laid here," Poe said, avoiding the flashlight glare from Megan's head.

"Sorry about that," said Megan, moving her light to the side.

"Thanks." Poe was overwhelmed. This fighting over a boy, or rather, a great uncle, was silly. She wanted her friend back.

Megan squatted next to Poe and inspected her scratches and mouth wounds with a pen light between her teeth, cleaning them with less-than-moist towelettes.

"Megan," Poe began, "I didn't know about you and Sainvire."

"I know," Megan answered. "It doesn't matter now."

"I guess." Poe couldn't leave it at that. "But I just want you to know that it was a mistake, and it's over between us."

Megan looked her directly in the face, knowing that Poe would be able to see her countenance clearly through the goggles. "It doesn't matter, Poe. Whatever happens, you'll still be my friend, and he'll still be my great uncle."

Poe opened her mouth to speak, but Megan stopped her with a gesture. "I'm really sorry about how I treated you before," Megan began. "You're right. We should have trusted you enough to let you know about Kaleb and the Plasmacore."

Poe's eyes brimmed and everything turned green and hazy. The week had been emotionally taxing for both.

"I should've stood up for you and insisted that Goss and Sister clue you in to what was going on," she sniffed, her voice breaking. "I should've stood up for you as my friend, period. And your eye gear is weirding me out."

Poe ignored her injured back and sat up. She took Megan's hand and squeezed. The two embraced. They stayed this way until a humungous rat walked over Poe's ankle, causing both women to yelp and killing the moment.

"This is a really disgusting place to have a maudlin heart-to-heart," Megan proclaimed. She hoisted Poe to her feet and wiped away rat droppings clinging to her clothes. Without preamble, Megan unhooked her bottle of holy water and sprayed herself.

"So the objective is to smell like you, and I'll live through all this unscathed?" she asked.

Poe shook her head. "Well, not entirely unscathed. But I guarantee you'll make it. I'm mystical that way. Keep the squirt gun. I have two more in my pack."

"Mystical? Where'd you learn such a fancy word?"

"From that crumpled up Madame Elmira psychic poster by your feet."

"That's for when the pain really gets bad," said Megan who placed four tablets on her friend's dirty palm. "Take one tablet every four hours. Don't take them all at once, though. They might be expired, but they're still killer strong."

Ten minutes later, Morales and cattle comprised mainly of the elderly and the sick arrived bruised but intact. He immediately sought his two friends, giving them wet, lingering kisses on the cheek.

"Sam, you're going to give me zits, dammit!" Megan complained, pushing Morales away. She patted his shoulder fondly then left to organize the group. "I thank you all for your courage – humans, vampires, and everyone in between. There's still more to go, so we've got to book. The uninjured, make sure to find a buddy to support. Let's cross our fingers that we make it safe and sound to the trains. We all deserve a new life."

CHAPTER 11 – JIM KELLY COTTON CANDY

EVERY STEP WAS A spike rammed through each screaming groove of vertebrae. The other injuries she'd endured paled in comparison to the pain in her lower back, so sharp that her twisted ankle didn't even hurt anymore.

"Even the old geezers are moving faster than me," Poe complained.

"Ever heard of the word 'ageism'?" Morales mockingly asked while holding up his buddy of the day.

"Fine. Be like the rest," Poe said resignedly. "I know I fuck up a lot, and I'm the biggest politically incorrect moron there ever was."

"Well what can I say to–"

"That's why I need you to educate me," Poe finished her thought to the relief of Morales. The man was nice enough to pal up with the irascible near-cripple during the march.

Not that he resented Poe's extra weight or the reek of her sticky marinated skin. He just couldn't stand being the last person. Anyone or anything could pick them off and the group would be oblivious since they were lagging at least fifty feet behind again.

With the help of her night vision goggles, Poe could see the half-mad look Morales sported in the dark. The tenseness of his muscles and the constant beaming of his flashlight up the ceiling, on the walls, behind his shoulders, and down on the ground were big indicators that he was petrified.

"Has it been four hours yet?"

"Not even close," Morales sighed. "And don't even think about taking another pill. That stuff's intense."

"Intense? My back feels worse now," she whined, reaching in her pocket for two more pills. "These things have been expired for how many years? I think they've lost their potency."

When Megan came back to relieve Morales, Poe still had yet to feel any better.

"We're here. Union Station is above us," Megan said, slinging Poe's arm over her shoulder to relieve some of the weight. "We'll stop a few feet from the station's platform just as a precaution to keep from being heard up there. I don't think the invasion's begun yet." She pointed up at the ceiling.

"If they skip Union Station, we're in deep shit, right?"

"Burnt toast," Megan answered gravely. "So cross your fingers that our guys will come down and give the signal, stat."

Poe nodded, too tired to speak. Megan ordered the meandering cattle to take a load off and keep quiet. Like Poe, most just wanted to rest. Many had lost the ability to speak.

"Is it my imagination or are they looking more animated?" Poe observed tiredly.

"Don't know if you can see the quarter-size brand on their hands with that schmanzy eyewear of yours. They're basically symbols of the different blood farms they've been interred. Some have been traded and passed around. You can tell by the progression of burns on their arms," Megan explained sullenly. "Most surely remember the biggest farm of all, the Union Station blood factory above us. I'm sure they're not too happy about it."

Poe had seen the branded image of a fox, Trench's signature symbol, between the fork of the thumb and index finger on Megan's left hand. She'd never thought to ask.

The station was famous for the endless rows of cots placed to maximize space for more bleeders. They endured an eat and bleed routine – eat liver steak, greens, vitamins, and milk and then attach the intravenous needle. This cycle was repeated every three days, leaving the cattle to eat and nap most of the time. Some gained weight, but most lost pounds from stress. Women suffered the worst with leeches rutting on them when bored.

"Listen, Meg. I know you have tons to do," Poe began. "No need to babysit me. I'm feeling better already."

"Are you sure?"

"Yup. Just need a nap is all." Poe thanked Megan and shooed her away.

She took off her pack and slid it down, careful to distribute the weight. Ignoring the wet fecal droppings, Poe laid her back flat on the rough ground. She stretched her muscles again by seesawing her legs and back the way Goss had taught her. It was imperative to get her lower back in good condition. Otherwise, little Penny would starve to death in her bunker.

Before leaving Penny behind, Poe had plunked down Polaroid pictures of Goss next to the doggie bed and taped an extra-cute picture of Legs smiling on three legs. She could have sworn that Penny looked sadder.

The thought of Penny, mute, lame, and alone, nearly made her cry. "Keep it together, Poe. You'll get her back," she whispered in the darkness. After a thorough stretch and some tentative rolling exercises, Poe laid down on the floor exhausted. She took the last of the pills Megan had stored, eventually drifting asleep into a sweet and sour lemonade dream full of Jim Kelly and his cotton candy hair. Above the subway tunnel was the mother lode herself. The infamous Union Station.

"Poe. Poe," Megan whispered in her ear, nudging her to life. "You better wake up now."

Poe shook her head, pried open her heavy lids one by one, and found darkness. Her body ached, especially her back, but for some reason, she felt much better. She felt around, touching tracks.

"Something's going on up there." Megan pointed at the ceiling on top of which was Union Station. Gunfire echoed and ricocheted. "Get your things together."

"What time is it?" Poe asked, finally hearing the faint sound of gunshots from above.

"It's about four-thirty."

At the mention of the time, Poe's eyes widened. "Four-thirty! You mean I've been asleep all this time?"

"Shh!" Megan warned her. "You don't want to alert them that we're here, do you?" She ruffled Poe's shorn hair and left.

Poe sat up. Her rickety lower back caused her to chomp down on her lower lip. *Four-thirty! That means I slept for hours. Impossible!*

Somebody must have slipped off her goggles when she was conked out. Slowly she put them back on and busied herself by refilling empty magazines. She took out a water bottle from her pack and drank deeply. Something was different about her, but she could not put her finger on the change. Was it disorientation or some weird flurry in her tummy?

Your place is on the roof, said a soothing voice inside her head.

"I think I'm a little stoned."

She forced herself to eat an ancient granola bar with extra-wiggly protein for strength and to down a generous libation of water. She liked the detached, floating feeling, like being in a Bullet Time reality where spectacular movement happened at a mind-blowingly slower pace. No tension whatsoever.

Morales waded through a herd of cattle to seek her out. He chatted about nothing of substance, giving Poe the impression that her friend with the Adonis body was a nervous wreck.

"I wish you'd brought one of those Anakin goggles for me," he said after touching on Chinese take-out. "Oh, and Sainvire finally sent a messenger, a really skittish one."

"Morales," Poe sighed, a sure sign of annoyance. "What did the messenger say?"

"They're laying low. They can't make a move until the third strike force gets here to cover us. We don't have enough fighters to beat them back until then." He wiped a trickle of sweat from his forehead. "Sainvire didn't expect the number of sentinels sent to protect the depot after Trench's hotel and Parker Center were decimated."

"What's the strike team? Where's Sainvire?"

"The strike teams are escaped custodians and ex-cattle rehabbed in the California Central Valley. They're emptying Union Station of cattle as we speak. Sainvire and his vamps are with them."

Poe could tell that Morales wanted to be around her for the evacuation. She couldn't be his security blanket at that point because she wasn't sure her back and ankle were going to hold, even with the help of amped-up drugs.

"Get back to the front of the line, Morales. I need to pee." She held up her hands near his light to show that the discussion was over. "I can't protect you. I'm too whacked."

Poe was in the midst of zipping up and discarding a travel-size tissue pack when the order came from one of Sainvire's vampires to climb to the subway platform. She buckled her drunken sombrero cactus belt quickly and arranged her pack and weapons for easy access. By the time she hobbled back to the end of the line, she found that most people had been coaxed forward to be hauled up to the platform. With her tweaked back and ankle, it was almost impossible to squeeze past the crowd. She sat down, stretched some more, and waited.

"Sufferin' succotash," Poe said drowsily. "You have to be positive like Goss and Sister Ann used to be. If you've gone this far, then your odds are better than average," she said in the dark. "The pills'll help you perform better." She wasn't even nervous.

Watching cattle wiggle their way to the front gave her a bad feeling. *At least I'm packing heat. The poor dolts can't even protect themselves.* Her attempt at optimism ended with a bang.

Several bangs, actually, seemed to originate from the platform above where vampires and subhumans of different factions clashed. The odds were getting lousier by the second, and with her injuries, Poe had an unpleasant premonition that she was going to die that evening. And she wasn't ready one bit.

——— —— ——

"Pull 'em out! Haul 'em up faster than this for fucksakes!" a croaky undead yelled from the platform. From the looks of him, things weren't going as smoothly as his boss had envisioned. Now that there was the possibility of whizzing bullets damaging him for ages to come, he didn't seem so gung ho about rescuing a bunch of food.

"It'll be hella faster if somebody'd give some boxes or ladders for the cows to step onto, you idiot," somebody replied from the tracks. "Pushing their flabby asses up is getting old."

It was taking far too long to get the one hundred-plus cattle to climb to the high platform. A ridiculous amount of bullets reverberated around them. The chaperones practically heaved their weakened charges up. Careful handling of the humans was crucial since their bones were brittle after being bedridden for so long. The half-hour leeches gave the cattle to stretch out and roam each day wasn't enough.

Flying to the platform with an impaled dead in his talon, Sainvire ordered, "Esper, make sure the cattle stay behind the riot shields until they're deposited on our train." He stabbed the wiggling vampire youth in his clutches one more time and let him slip to the floor. Several bullet holes punctured the master vampire's clothing. He'd been busy rustling cattle at the biggest blood farm in the city.

"We'll do our best, Kaleb," said Ezperanza, a tall woman dressed in black riot gear accented with a yellow beret. Part of Sainvire's Chicano army forced to hide in the Central Valley, the woman bristled with intensity. It was her moment to avenge her people who'd been ill-used by the vampire conspiracy from the very inception. "But I gotta tell you, there are only a handful of shields available and they weigh more than most of us." Cut from industrial equipment like coke ovens and furnaces, the metal deflected bullets rather nicely. However, the weight proved problematic for non-vampiric folk.

People assigned to protect the transfer of cattle from the subway tunnels to the above ground train had to contend with the bombardment of bullets and batons while keeping the line moving. The train was on the opposite side of the station.

"Just try your best," the gray-eyed vampire said grimly and disappeared into the throng that fought the Council sentinels.

Megan gasped, having pulled a 120-pound woman using her back and leg muscles to the platform. "Hey, you there with the baby face," shouted Megan to a vampire who worked for Sainvire. Her uncle had disappeared to help hold the line.

"Are you talking to me?" asked the blue-eyed vampire that looked sixteen with a Sonny Rollins goatee and a red beret. He gave the redhead a cursory glance. He was too busy scanning for men in blue.

Megan's eyes narrowed, but she did not let go of a bony elderly hand. "If you guys want us to hustle then you'd better get more men to pull these people out of the tracks! We're getting hernias here."

"Sainvire said that we should keep a sharp lookout," he said defensively. "An' we're keepin' a sharp lookout." After his statement, an errant bullet grazed his left temple, heightening his distaste of the situation.

Megan used her leg muscles to heave another blood heifer out of the tracks, praying her back wouldn't snap. "Well I'm a relative of his. If you don't do what I say, I'll personally get Sainvire to kick your head in!"

Her chest heaved from exertion and annoyance. Megan stared down the insolent vampire that finally lauded her with eye contact.

"Resorted to dropping names, eh?" Morales said despairingly, sapped by cattle pulling himself.

Maybe it was because those red-lashed eyes showed no sign of relenting, the baby face vampire told his cronies, the Red Berets, to help out with the body extraction pronto. He, however, stayed glued where he stood. Sporadic gunfire danced dangerously down the metal-paneled halls of the station.

The undead joined them in lifting the bodies out of the subway tracks, and the line moved swifter and thinned just as quickly. Until, of course, the wind in the platform started picking up.

At first, nobody noticed the change.

Megan's mouth went slack, and her eyes took on a look of abject fear. She turned to Morales who looked as terrified as she. *Train!*

"Poe!" they both mouthed at once.

It was a nice breeze, but she thought nothing of it. Not until one of the cattle from the back snapped out of his stupor and began wailing and violently clawing his way toward the front. The man was saying, "Train's coming. Help. Train's coming!" End-of-the-world chaos battered the crowd as the remaining cattle caught the electric fear of death in the air.

Poe quickly took to her feet, looked around, and touched the slimy walls. Sure enough, she felt vibrations.

Her mouth opened and closed, unsure of what to do. She looked at her hand clutching a weapon to ward off her opponents and almost wept.

"Guns are useless against a train!" she reasoned, her pill-muddled head clearing.

She fumbled for the whistle around her neck and blew, hoping that the cattle would stop stampeding. She had already witnessed three older folks get stepped on and used as stairmasters. The shrill warning had the opposite effect upon the scene of panic.

"Calm down!" Poe yelled. "Don't trample each other!" But her efforts fell on deaf ears.

Her lower lip trembled then relaxed as the number of cattle thinned. "Megan and Morales will get all of them up the platform," she said out loud. She allowed herself the luxury of a smile for bravery that disappeared far too quickly as a train's high-pitched whistle hooted twice, stripping her of daring. There were at least twenty souls left, mostly elderly. Poe stepped closer into the light until she saw the high ceiling of the station waiting area. Her head was four feet short of the platform above.

"Fuck me," she grunted as she pushed a crouching man up at the expense of her lower back. "Thank goodness for drugs! Get up, you! You don't want to mess with a train."

The whistle sounded nightmarishly closer. The Metro Red Line was supposed to be a dead route.

"Poe! Are you down there?" Megan screamed over the sound of cattle crying to be helped and the blaring of the train.

Poe shook her head before answering. "Yeah, I'm here." She elbowed her way to the front, lowered her goggles to her neck, and sheathed her gun. The station lights blared into her cornea. The mob scene reminded her of a Laker championship game she once saw as a kid where crazed fans trampled a basketball player's spouse.

"Take my hand," said a voice she recognized to be Morales'. Poe clutched his arms. As she was getting pulled up, two or three cattle hung on to her legs. They were screaming above the train whistle for help. The whoosh of wind extinguishing the last of the candles many cattle still held added to the madness.

Stuck, Poe hollered, "Let go! Stop it!" But her voice was drowned out by Morales and Megan's desperate bellows and the frenzied cries. She gave her throat a rest as she glimpsed the headlights of the train emerging from the dark tunnel.

Half of her body was suspended where the cattle hung on to her legs. She could feel their bony ribs as they hugged her limbs.

But it was the desperation on Megan and Morales' faces as they tried unsuccessfully to pull her to safety that made her sob. She opened her mouth to tell her friends about Penny, but there wasn't enough time. She closed her eyes and prepared to be separated from her lower extremities.

That was when her belly hit the platform, sprawled between the exhausted bodies of Megan and Morales, her boots missing the train by a hair. The three remained panting as they watched the train slow.

"Poe, you crazy girl," Megan cried, embracing her friend.

Morales joined in by taking Poe's face between his large hands and planting a slapdash kiss on the mouth.

"What are you trying to do, suffocate me?" said Poe breathlessly but with mock anger.

"Sorry to interrupt the love fest, but you three better get up and head for Platform C," urged a familiar voice with a linty edge. "As you can see, the Council just brought in a trainload of reinforcements, and from the looks of it, they came from North Hollywood."

"Sainvire?" said Poe inaudibly. Perhaps his keen ears heard her whisper for he looked directly into her face, drinking in her unkempt, beaten appearance. He was there. All would be well.

"Poe," he nodded then glanced at the tracks. "Glad the train didn't get you."

With those words, Poe lost her concentration and looked behind her. Pieces of body parts decorated the edges of the tracks. She gagged. The scene reminded her of a magazine her sister had smuggled into their house when they were kids. It was the print version of *Faces of Death*. There was a whole section on Japanese salarymen who threw themselves in front of moving trains.

Megan gave her shoulders a squeeze. "C'mon, Poe."

Morales cocked his Magnum and asked, "Want to ride piggyback?" Poe shook her head and thanked her friends for pulling her up just in time.

"It's nothing, Poe. You'd do the same for us," Megan answered. "Besides, we were doing a poor job of it. My uncle, here, had to give the extra tug."

Poe looked to where Sainvire stood, tense and bloodied. Bodies were stacked high for the day and Sainvire was aware of each and every one. He stared unsmiling and said, "Get a move on. Platform C is on the other side of the station, where the long distance tracks pick up."

"The train is loaded with overseers and vampire farmers," said Rodney, an African American soldier, walking briskly alongside Sainvire.

"The best-laid plans gone to seed," said Sainvire with flint. "So the Council's secret weapons turn out to be farmers and rancher vampires with sun immunity? They could've used them earlier when the sun was still up." He allowed himself a small victory, though the working subway spur used by cattle that afternoon, thought to be decommissioned long ago, rankled him.

The subway train that nearly flattened Poe originated from the Universal City Metro stop. The once renowned Universal City Walk that used to thrill tourists despite the steep parking price and over-hyped storefronts was now an agrarian vampire community where vegetables appeared in neat rows and animal husbandry thrived alongside Jaws, T-Rexes, and Shrek. The harvest was grown for human cattle to consume in downtown Los Angeles.

The heavy sound of concentrated gunfire goaded Sainvire's people to move faster as they crossed the upper platform to the trains. "They must be disembarking," Megan cried.

"Load everyone on the trains quickly! We've overstayed our welcome here," Sainvire pronounced, his eyes resting briefly on Poe who was too busy hobbling along with a cattle buddy. He turned and flew toward the line of demarcation.

Most cattle were dehydrated and weakened. Armed guards left opaque bottles of Gatorade on the seats of the train. Boarding them onto heavily graffitied trains bound for the Central Valley proved to be a bother after cattle emerged to the ground floor by the escalators. Council vamps shot and slashed at the strike force trying their hardest to escort cattle to the train cars.

"The people with white bandanas on their sleeves aren't fighters," Morales told Poe. "So don't shoot 'em. They're here to feed, guide, and guard the cattle. They were trained with knives, axes, and machetes – weapons that don't ricochet in trains."

"This siege is really organized," she said, gazing at the fierce fighters sporting different colored berets and fending off the enemy in riot gear. They followed the plan blueprints to the dot. "I had no idea."

White bandanas proved to be the most able soldiers against the Council's minions who tried to infiltrate the herd of cattle and kept them from boarding the train.

"Um, Sainvire," Poe hailed, seeing the master vampire return from the front lines with a supply of Kevlars and guns ripped from the bodies of the enemy. She and her friends were about to board the train, but she just had to get something off her chest. "Sorry, but I have some information that might be useful to you," she lied.

"Of course," Sainvire said. He inclined his head politely though the tenseness of his face and the rigidity of his movements urged her to talk fast. "Megan. Can you distribute these please? And get on board. We're set to leave." He added as an afterthought, "While you're at it, help Morales find a more functional sidearm."

"Right," said Megan with a nod, hopping up to follow Morales. The door latched closed behind them. Knowing it's always better to unburden one's self in the face of death, she just wanted to apologize. "I'm sorry for shooting you."

Sainvire ceased his constant shifting and looked at Poe. "You're forgiven," he said then took her face between his hands and gave her the gentlest of kisses.

Before she could enjoy the moment, the nagging voice inside her head said, *You belong on the roof!*

As if sensing danger, Sainvire let go of Poe, pulled her close to the ground, and roared, "Poe, stay down!" He sliced at the air above her head. She had ducked just in time to avoid the swampy arm of a vamp intent on doing her ill. Her only new injury was a slight bump in the head from where the sliced arm clunked her.

They were done for. Slavers chipped viciously at Sainvire's lines of defense. They were surrounded. Many of the attackers were carrying old-fashioned pistols while others carried mallets and hatchets. The San Fernando Valley farmer folk were old school vampires who abhorred gun violence. Sainvire's fighters were simply too outmanned to keep their position.

"Ah, I think our little talk will have to wait, Poe," Sainvire said with clenched jaws as his eyes honed on five flying undead headed toward the train.

"Sure," Poe nodded. *And what's this about the roof again?*

To his men, he yelled, "To the train. Now!"

She was encircled by friends and the resolute Sainvire, and she hadn't thought to arm herself just yet. It was a grave mistake. Before she could take the first step inside the train, Poe was yanked back by the straps of her pack where her weapons were lodged.

When a gun barrel appeared millimeters from her ticker, Poe's heart rate didn't fluctuate. She made a mental note to ask Megan the name of the wonder pills she had taken if ever she survived the night. Sainvire was gone, fighting his own battles.

"Oh, please no!" sobbed Poe, her shoulders quaking from grief. Poe belted out the worst kind of weeping worthy of Brenda Blethyn, Halle Berry, and Sally Field. The pestilence to the ears would have sunk the Titanic a day sooner. The train engine coughed back to life. She could feel its power emanating along its sides.

The vampire holding the gun to her could do nothing but look for aid from his companions who were busy fulfilling the Council's decree. He would have been more than willing to shoot her had she not begged, "Don't shoot me, mister! I'll be your personal food bank. I'll shine your coffin. Just don't shoot me!"

"Hold on, girl," the bald, medium-height jelly belly of a vamp called out. "No one's going to do you in. You're the one with the virgin neck they're looking for."

"Virgin neck?" Poe whimpered dramatically. "I'll be drained by the Council?"

"Unfortunately, yes. I believe they might torture you first for the things you've done. Honestly my hands are tied. All I can do is pray for your salvation."

Poe took the opportunity to grab hold of the gun's muzzle and tipped it up and back, breaking his trigger finger. "Take that, you corn-fed son-of-a-bitch," cursed Poe, abruptly stopping her weeping. She had learned that particularly dirty trick from Goss himself, though he couldn't picture such a tree of a man blubbering to any dead to save his life.

Evidently the years the farm hand had labored in the fields had chiseled him into one impatient vampiric machine. He merely grunted, saying, "Forgive me, Lord." He began throwing punches at her, broken finger and all. Poe covered her face with her elbows, tightly deflecting blows. This was one of Sister's favorite muy thai defense shields for close combat.

Theoretically, the person throwing the punches would believe he is beating the crap out of his enemy but underestimates elbow strength, which can deflect even the hardest of blows. If the farmer had been human, his fist would have bruised for hitting rock-hard bone. Too bad for Poe, her head was beginning to reel.

But she waited. The moment the farmer slowed, Poe swung a vertical elbow to the cheek, followed by a horizontal strike to the temple and another on the nose. The vampire face was laden with veins pumping dead liquid to the eyes, skin, mouth, and roots in the scalp. The more she pounded with her elbows, the more damage she inflicted on the face.

"I can't handle vampires!" she gritted when her clothes snagged on an incisor the length of a toothpick. "Even an abstainer one like you!"

The brackish liquid luridly seeping out of his face surprised Poe and completely stupefied the vampire. Both Poe and the farmer had no idea of the amount of pseudo-plasma in a vampire's face.

While the vampire stared fixated at his hands covered in squid ink, Poe bent down and picked up his fallen six-shooter. She was in the midst of a melee where every sentient being seemed to be bashing and shooting each other. Her elbows hurt, but she was hoping the meds would numb the pain just like the other injured parts of her body.

Poe cocked the gun and pointed it at the farm boy's chest.

"I can't believe it," he said, his voice fading. "A girl's killed me," he spoke with surprise. He looked pitiable reaching for his antiquated hoe, goop pouring out of his face. It would be a real shame to kill him, but what could she do?

The vampire gripped the handle of his hoe, determined to perish with it in his hands. He squared his shoulders and faced his fate without complaints. It could have been the lingering effects of the drugs, but the leather-skinned vamp reminded Poe of Elzeard Bouffier, a simple man who only wanted to plant trees in a barren land. Perhaps her mind was addled.

"You're a farmer?"

The vampire nodded, jaw working. "From Iowa originally."

"Look, I don't want to kill you. Most likely it wasn't your idea to come here today. And I heard rumors that farmers only drink animal blood." The man did not move, perhaps from angry pride.

"If you promise to go back to your farm this minute, I'll let you off the hook. Are we square?"

Poe repeated the question, but this time she lowered the gun. The man looked as though he was losing an inner battle, from bruised dignity perhaps. He had been thrashed by a human girl. After a few interminable seconds, the man nodded.

"We're square."

———

The vampire farmers were a hard bunch to manage. And to kill. Most carried deep convictions that couldn't quite blend in the new bite-and-suck order. They were left alone to produce a regular supply of meat and fresh produce for the city cattle. The price of autonomy was to side with the Council if ever the new order was threatened.

The stalwart Council had also bused a delegation of ancient guards who looked intractable and impossible to hurt. The eternally extended yellow teeth and the line of inky drool on the side of the mouth were fearsome enough to scare off potential enemies.

But even more alarming than the Ancients' yellow walrus teeth were another round of infant vampires crawling out of every grate and vent to add to the carnage. They worked like a circus act, tossing each other at the nearest halfdead, human, and vampire like psychotic apes. At least they didn't discriminate.

Poe followed Sainvire with her eyes, willing him to be unharmed. She watched him slash a vampire from shoulder to hip and skewer a particularly nasty baby with his other hand. Three babies dropped on him at once and tried to gouge out his eyes, making him easy prey for lurking ex-LAPD officers bearing bulletproof vests, tazers, and guns.

A few feet from Sainvire was Joseph, gleefully kicking and stabbing vampires with garlic oil-soaked stakes. From the look of things, Joseph had bullet holes on his shoulder and stomach area that hadn't yet fused. He wasn't as quick a healer as Sainvire. But he was still grinning. Nothing, it seemed, could keep the vampire from showing his pearly whites.

"Mom. Look after that loco grinner. He reminds me of my brother," Poe prayed as her nose rested on a windowpane, fogging it up. "And look after Sainvire. He has good intentions."

You're needed on the roof, a voice impatiently said.

The cattle who'd woken up impatiently awaited the diesel locomotive to pull out of the station, away from the fighting. Poe pried herself from the window and the human cow she had squeezed between. The only thing she heard from them were sighs of relief. "What am I, stupid?" she told the voice.

"You know," she addressed the cattle. "It's okay for you to tell me off *Scarface*-style for parking on your body." It occurred to her then that she could be the only person alive to think Pacino horribly overacted in the film.

Poe walked the length of the train a step at a time, searching for Megan and Morales. She sidled against anxious cattle scrambling for seats and vampire guards yelling orders to keep the aisles clear. The little girl sitting between female cattle waved at her as she passed by. *She survived the fall back there!*

"You okay?" Poe asked awkwardly, having never dealt with a child in a while.

The girl in potato sack with large wary eyes and a dirty face nodded but did not speak. Poe smiled shyly and continued with her search for a familiar face. She found them in the third car standing in a queue to use the toilet. Poe's eyes blinked rapidly. Megan and Morales whispered briskly with Perla and Maple. The older women were armed for war.

Instinctively Poe tightened her grip on a Calico 9mm one of the white bandana guards had handed her on Megan's order. The funny looking piece, not much longer than a standard issue gun, held up to 100 rounds. Except for the hard recoil action, the gun was perfectly workable.

"Poe! Glad to see you safe," said Perla, rocking G.I. Joe pajamas and a protective vest. She was the first to approach Poe and give her a big hug. Maple followed. It was so unreal, especially amidst the cattle cries and the combat outside.

"I think you've just jinxed me," Poe coughed. "Now I know I'm gonna eat it for sure."

A noticeably uneasy Morales peeked out the window to watch the battle and briefly waved at her.

"Seriously, what's the plan? The train's barely moving," Poe asked, pondering what warranted all the hugging.

Apropos, the train lurched forward, throwing Poe halfway down the aisle and banging her left funny bone on the metal seat bars. Before she could get her bearings, the train pitched backward and hurled her toward the toilet. She screamed, "No!"

As the train pulled at a snail pace away from the platform, gunshots sprayed the train. Enemy dead clung to the side of the trains like barnacles. Sainvire's chaperones appeared, spraying holy water on the windows and waving lethal sabers slicked with garlic oil at the vampire foes trying to break in. Some scraped the vamp barnacle away with bullets and clubs hanging from broken windows.

Perla drew near the window and fired at the closest ones to her, saying, "Shoo!"

The bathroom door slammed open and a woman in her late thirties named Georgette shuffled out. She wore chain mail down to her knees. It looked to be an authentic hauberk relic, looted along with her club purported to be William Wallace's.

"Whoa, Gimli!" Poe said in awe, still on the floor and collecting her bearings.

Georgette walked over Poe's legs and slammed open a window to let herself out. *The woman can fly!*

"That's Georgette. She's from up north," explained Perla.

"Everyone down!" Morales yelled. Perla shoved a slow-to-react cattle down forcefully.

Two elderly cattle suffered from cardiac arrest. Their hearts could no longer take the stop-and-go stress. Morales went to the next train car with Poe and Megan close behind to check on other passengers.

The compartments were poorly lit. Poe kept her goggles in hand. The train chugged away from the station into the violet and pink-streaked evening sky, and Poe's good leg almost buckled over in relief. She made her way to the next compartment to check for casualties but was beset by an earsplitting noise.

"Jeez! What now?" complained Megan.

"That would be six really evil airborne vampires mocking us from the window outside," Morales answered, harassed. Two enemy vamps held on to the window ledge while running along the train like Clark Kent in the comics. One of them punched the glass and tried to snatch a passenger within.

"Get down!" Maple calmly ordered two shaking passengers. "Watch out for hot shells and glass." She fired out the window, hitting a fanged one, and watched him tumble out of sight.

Poe followed Maple's example and fired at the other audacious vampires. Despite the bad gun recoil, she was able to shoot down two peskies. The dead that got away gave Poe the finger and punched and kicked in more windows before flying away to the next car. The cattle sitting by the cracked windows scrambled on all fours down the aisle, a little slow on the take, blocking Poe's way.

"Shit! They're on the roof!" said Morales in panic. The one-two gallop of feet landing could be heard.

Get on the roof! The voice in her head returned.

Poe fired skyward with her Calico, showering hot shells on those closest to her. "Sorry!"

She was almost positive that she had shot someone. Pandemonium kicked into high gear among the beleaguered cattle who rushed to the aisle for safety. Before she could fire again, Poe pitched forward as the train braked to a scratchy deceleration.

Slammed against the connecting door, her shoulder suffered agonizingly on impact. It was the drugs. They made her clumsy and hear things. A dark figure punched the window closest to her open and swung in feet first, barely missing the seated cattle who yelped in alarm. For the second time that day, a large pair of hands picked her up and dumped her on an empty seat.

"Are you okay?" asked Sainvire.

"Uh huh," Poe answered, looking away. "If you try to pick me up again, I'll shoot you."

"You've done that plenty." He took a handkerchief from his coat pocket and wiped the brown glop seeping from a thigh wound. "Do me a favor. Try not to shoot at the roof for the next five minutes," Sainvire advised. "Some of us might want to keep our members intact."

"Maybe I can go up there–"

"Don't be daft. You can barely walk as it is."

Poe belligerently assented. She knew the roof would equal a swift death – hers. Before she could vilify herself about shooting the master vampire, however, Sainvire frowned at Morales and said, "Get a better gun, Morales." With that, he dove out the window.

"Whoa, Poe. You shot the master vampire again," said Morales glibly. "Don't you know he's on our side?"

"Put your Magnum away, Morales," Poe said testily. She imagined the man blowing up cattle or her at close range. "And get yourself a decent gun."

"You two follow me," said Megan. "The train's stopping."

The three tensely made their way into the engine room. The conductor was an ex-cattle by the telling bite marks on his neck. Unlike the other ex-cats she'd seen fighting around the station that made it a point to hide the marks of former servitude with bandanas, the dark man with pronounced Pacific Islander features displayed them proudly. Perhaps they were reminders himself of the importance of his job.

"Evenin'." He tipped his colorful fedora. He was busy slowing down the noisy locomotive to a stop. "Trees and shit blockin' the tracks."

"And drums, too," Poe added, pulling on her night vision goggles.

The driver made tsk tsk clicks and placed his .22 within easy reach. From the roof came the sound of running footsteps, bodies getting slammed, and a bevy of angry epithets. Some sections of the roof showed indentation from the weight of undead bodies getting walloped.

Two vampires landed right in front of the train, the crank headlights spotlighting them.

"My God!" Megan exclaimed. "That's Kaleb!"

"And Joseph!" added Poe.

Acrobatic vamps in black ninja outfits pursued the two.

"It's a good night for a costume party," grinned Morales.

Sainvire stuck his talons at an overweight dead while a black clad Joseph finished his enemy with swift Double Dutch blows to the heart. Apparently Joseph had fists of fury. The two friends kept a sharp lookout for anyone trying to disrupt the cleaners who ran or flew ahead to clear debris off the tracks.

When all was clear, Sainvire half-carried Joseph by the shirt collar back to the roof. The handsome and affable vampire could not fly one lick. On the way up, Joseph paused to wave at his rapt audience.

"Poe, go! Shoot them!" Morales pointed at three extremely tiny vampires sweeping the tracks.

"You crazy, man?" the driver said. "Our mission lies in the hands of that sun dead and two vamps. They're the sweepers. The littlest guy's named Ed. He can probably lift this train car with no problem."

Sure enough, the creatures hauled debris away with their bare hands. Ed, the runt vampire, tossed an uprooted oak trunk with a flick of a wrist. Poe whistled in awe, damaging further her split lip.

"Amazing," Megan said, staring at a female vampire lift a sand-filled drum and fling it twenty feet away from the tracks. "I've heard about these guys, but I thought it was all BS."

Then it occurred to Poe. *I should be up there.*

The train hadn't gone far at all. They were still perilously close to Union Station, the biggest cattle operation in the city. And City Hall, inundated by ex-LAPD goons, was just around the corner.

Don't know what it is, but it's the same head-voice that tells me where to point my gun with supernatural accuracy, Poe said in conversation with herself. "The voice I trust more that any other," she muttered.

"They're almost done," the driver said. "Then we can hightail outta here."

"I need to get to the roof."

"That's not funny, Poe," muttered Morales, punching her shoulder lightly. Poe's face remained determined.

"Poe, you can't possibly go up there," Megan began, knowing that Poe had already made up her mind. She reverted back to her nervous habit of tracing her bite marks with her fingers. "Your back is banged, and you'll need to balance up there when the train moves."

"I gotta. I can shoot real good, especially with that rifle," she said with a nod at the driver's Winchester.

"That's my good luck charm."

"Yeah, but you can't use it in this little room while driving a train. You got your .22 for that."

"It's suicide, you dummy!" Morales argued. "Sainvire and Joseph will stop them."

Checking her gear, she chucked out heavy ammo and weapons that were dead weight. There were half a dozen sidearms lifted from the makeshift headquarters. "Hope you can use this stuff," she said to the driver.

"Sure, kid," he smiled. "I can always use some firepower now that you're taking my good luck rifle away. By the way, I'm the only one who knows how to handle this bucket, so maybe one of you ought to guard me, eh?"

Poe made sure her pack was light and her guns loaded and ready to go. She sheathed throwing knives on her wrists holsters.

"I took some of the pills you gave me, Meg. I should be fine." She glanced at the grim-faced Morales. He was stubborn in his silence on the topic. He did not want the weighty responsibility of sending Poe to her death, and he was far too faint-hearted to go with her.

"But Poe–" Megan started. Poe didn't let her finish but gave the woman a quick hug.

"The train's not even moving." Poe wanted to quote Sister Ann's view on precarious missions: When there's adrenaline and danger, there's nothing you cannot do. But it wasn't the time to be a wise ass, especially when hardly a trace of adrenaline trickled in her veins.

It's the right thing to do, the voice whispered in her ear.

"This is for you," she said to Morales, placing a Sig Sauer 9mm in his hand. "It has fifteen rounds, and here are extra magazines."

"You keep it. You're the one dumb enough to climb up the roof to have your neck broken."

Poe sighed. "Morales, this is your shit here. I lifted the bunch from your HQ. Hidden in the oven, you know. It's been dead weight all this time. Old Dirty Harry there will get you popped quicker than Orville Redenbacher. And besides, you gotta protect, um–"

"Chamba," the driver supplied morbidly.

"Um, Chamba. Can you please open your door?"

CHAPTER 12—A TOUCH OF IRON

"ROPE LADDERS?" POE MUTTERED and pushed the last of the mouthguards across her teeth. Her life was one long funeral. "Figures."

Flimsy ladders of the homemade variety hung limply on the side of the train, slapped around by the night wind. They were for suckers who couldn't fly. Like Poe. She shoved the goggles into place.

"You just can't let it go," Poe berated herself for listening to a dodgy voice in her head that could very well be a precursor to a schizoid meltdown. She took hold of the nearest ladder and swung her left foot on the first rung. The jiggly, unstable cords of rope assured that she was a step away from a pebbly grave. *I ought to turn back, knock on the conductor's door, and beg him to let me in.*

It seemed like hours to climb halfway up the shivering ropes. Cattle eyes watched her lumbering moves like ho-hum spectators of a turtle race. "What're you staring at, dunderhead?" she asked an especially vapid cow whose window she banged against.

By then Poe itched to bash her against the metal exterior of the train. Her back and ankle felt as if twenty gargantuan acupuncture needles were deeply embedded in the skin.

"Just my luck," Poe cried. "The drugs are wearing off."

Her ears clung to the sound of vampire flesh colliding with its own kind. From the corner of her eye, she saw bodies plummet down the side of the train.

Another rung and she would have made it to the top, if only the train hadn't chugged back to life and started moving. All Poe could do was hold onto the unsteady rope ladder swinging with the air stream.

"Oh, c'mon! This day just won't quit." She closed her eyes and silently cursed the vampires who cleared the roadblock for doing such a quick job of it. "And that voice I hear, the one that says 'now' a second before I pull the trigger. It wants me dead."

Even though it pained her like nothing else, Poe yelled out, "Sainvire, Joseph, I'm kinda in trouble and need a hand."

It took three repetitions of their names before a hand snaked out to cover her arm and heave her up onto the roof.

The green halo effect from her goggles was disquieting. Lime-colored Joseph had fished her out of the predicament.

"Nice of you to stop by, Poe. Hold onto this vent. We're a little busy at the moment." The tattooed vampire ruffled her hair then quickly joined Sainvire, Maple, and Georgette in staving off some seven undead, three of which were Ancients. She crouched by a ventilation shaft and held on.

Movies with fighting on top of trains are bullshit! No human could throw a punch when a train was moving at 80 to 100 miles per hour. This train was not even traveling anywhere near that fast, and Poe was on all fours, holding on for dear life. With trembling fingers she adjusted her eye gear.

Poe watched Sainvire square off with a Schwarzenegger-of-a-cop who could out-fly the master vampire in every way and was at least ten stones heavier. The ballistic vest covering his barrel chest added to his hulky appearance.

Joseph, whose quirk was to appear and disappear in a flash, snuck up behind a fierce but achingly slow Ancient with a sword having it out with Maple, the bludgeon-armed undead. Garlic marinated weapons weren't needed if a blade decapitated a vampire. Poe watched the tattooed Pinoy busily lending his assistance to his comrades.

"Need help?" Joseph asked. Before Maple could answer, he snapped the Ancient's neck by lifting the creature from the knees and pile driving her head. Downed, Joseph punched her twice in the chest until her heart burst. Her limp body wafted away in the wind.

"You are a traitor to your own kind, Sainvire," the boulder in uniform said, swinging a metal club with six knives welded to it. "You've lost what little respect I had for you, you greedy bastard."

"Think what you will, Marvin," Sainvire said, inching back to avoid the deadly morning star weapon. "Bottom line, wrong is wrong. No one deserves the life of cattle."

Poe could imagine the club cutting her down as Sainvire inched back closer to where she crouched. "What the hell are you doing, Sainvire? Go the other way!"

"Isn't it a little too late to start having a conscience?" Marvin laughed acidly, swinging his weapon wider. "About how many people have you eaten since turning? A hundred? A thousand? Four thousand?"

Without looking at her, Sainvire stopped where Poe cowered and slowly bent his knees. "I've had plenty. But I think the operative idea here is that it's never too late to quit."

As quick as a powerful master vampire could be, Sainvire hunkered down and lifted one of Poe's sidearms. He aimed the Astra at Marvin's face. Sainvire had fired three shots before Poe knew what had happened. Marvin's Kevlared body tipped backward and rolled off the train, taking his vicious contraption with him.

"Thanks for the loaner," he said with a wink. He resheathed her gun. "But you don't belong up here."

Before Poe could say anything, Sainvire fought against the wind currents to pry a female officer from Joseph's back. He stabbed her in the heart with one elongated talon.

Georgette, covered in chain mail, swung at the dead that came her way with a spear whose tip was oiled with garlic essence.

Everyone but Poe had a task to do; namely, to check for hanger-ons. Sainvire once again approached the girl, his face deadly serious. Poe's presence unnerved everyone on the roof. She was a definite liability.

Sainvire landed noiselessly, grabbing hold of her arm. The undead wasn't in the mood to negotiate, and Poe knew it.

"You better climb back down, Poe," Sainvire ordered with barely concealed impatience. His face was grim with tension.

"Can't." Poe tightened her hold on the air vent, her mouth drooling from the mouthguard. "If you haven't noticed yet, the train's moving!" There was no way she could make it down and climb inside a window. She was human, after all, and was subject to the forces of wind and inertia.

"I'm tossing you through a window if I have to," he stated in a steely voice, tightening his hold on her arm.

"Forget it!" shouted Poe, twisting her arm from his grasp. *Stay firm and stay on the roof,* urged the internal voice. The movement nearly led to a very nasty fall if the Master Vampire hadn't righted her in time.

"Poe!" Sainvire thundered after she had taken a more tenacious grip on the crown-shaped air vent. "I can't promise to protect you."

"Who's asking you?" Poe threw back, trying to forget the feeling of vertigo with a touch of bladder pain from her near fall. *How dare he make it seem like he's protected me all this time? I saved my own skin 99 percent of the time.* She impatiently tucked stray hair that thrashed wildly in the wind back into her ponytail.

"Get rid of that girl, Kaleb, or I will," threatened the vampiric Gimli. "She's a distraction. I heard she got Goss and Sister Ann killed."

"Shame on you, Georgette! You ought to know better not to trust everything you hear," Maple reprimanded.

"Poe is a lot of things, but Goss and Sister were family to her," added an offended Joseph. "She's just trying to help–" Before he could further defend the girl, Joseph's eyes grew as large as tires. He pointed at bird-like figures in the sky. "Dark spots on the horizon. They're coming!"

The pairs of eyes turned to the shadowy specks in the darkening violet skies. A squadron of Council reinforcements headed their way by air, and on the ground, those who couldn't fly sprinted. Two of the sprinters were master vampires with bones to pick. Poe could almost smell the dread wafting from dead pores. Not many on the train had the ability of flight. Poe looked away and took a deep breath. She did not want to focus on her imminent bloody death at the moment.

"There's no time. Brace yourself and get that rifle ready!" Sainvire ordered. His free hand cutting the circulation from her arm loosened. "Let's see that skill of yours in action."

Joseph added, "Sis, this is the time to do it. We're done for if that many flyers catch up to us. Only six of us can fly, and I ain't one of 'em."

"Okay," Poe sighed, feeling pressured. Georgette and three others with long-range rifles began firing. Out of twenty or so who fired bullets, only one hit a vampire.

Poe took a deep breath and aimed. Within ten seconds, Poe downed five of their fifteen. *It's just like Duck Hunt, only the trigger's better.*

The calming voice gently guided her to cut the enemy into a manageable size. She hit two more before running out of bullets.

"Here," said Georgette who handed the girl her own Springfield. "Don't put stock in what I said before. Everyone here knows I have a nasty mouth on me."

Poe took the rifle from the vampire and nodded grimly. *Lady, if you only knew how right you are.* Crouching, she aimed and hit a few more pesky birds flying hither-thither to dodge her bullets. She allowed herself a grin when only four remained on the course.

"Go eviscerate them, sis!" Joseph yelled, dancing a jig on the roof.

"Oh no. I think I see Gruman himself," cried Maple.

The fun ended when three fallen vamps rejoined the flock. "Um, chain mail woman, are these blessed bullets?" asked Poe.

"It's Georgette, dear," the older vampire shook her head. "I can't be sure. I picked the gun up at the station 'cause it looked pretty."

Poe sprayed the two remaining bullets with her squirt gun, reloaded, and aimed. She hit one in the leg and another in the head.

Poe inhaled like there was poison in the air. Then she exhaled shakily, saying sayonara to the last of the bullets. "Now what, Voice? Can I get killed now?"

"Georgette, get the others ready," Sainvire ordered. "Gruman is a good ol' boy and hard as flint to erase."

Sainvire gazed at the unmistakable sight of running and airborne vampires looming closer by the second in solemn search of their food source. Vampires from Sainvire's camp climbed out from the windows to the thin rope ladders leading to the roof in expectation of the fight to come. Those assigned to guard the cattle inside the cars rechecked their weapons as the hoards gained momentum.

The train drove Poe crazy. It chugged to life then slowed down to a snail pace intermittently. A mile ahead were uprooted palm trees and tin drums filled with cement. Anyone that did not conclude that the whole situation was an ambush was either addled or cattle. The palm trees had been uprooted from far away and strategically placed to block the tracks. The approaching figures and the slowing train proved to be a real dampener and setback to the cattle robbery.

"I can't help but think there's a mole here somewhere," Sainvire said dispassionately.

"The slugs are crawling in," Joseph said with uncharacteristic vehemence as he stared down the group of runners trying to infiltrate the train. "I'm going inside." The barefoot vampire swung his legs through a window, landing safely in the aisle and showering cattle with glass. Winking at startled humans, Joseph used his extraordinary speed to run through the three separate train cars, punching vampires that crawled in through the windows before they knew what hit them.

"They're here! The fuckers are here!" he yelled, rallying the white bandanas to kill faster as more and more windows were shattered by the infiltrators. "Don't give an inch. Do not lose any cattle. Just bust their balls!"

Then it was all over.

Two purple-haired vampires landed on terrified cattle, the impact of their steel-toe shoes crushing delicate bones and eliciting the most god-awful screams from a sixty-year-old. They had two directives, to murder everyone that got in their way and overtake the train.

"Geroff my train, you lughead!" Joseph hollered, wielding a short-handled machete at a vamp halfway inside the train. With two slashes, the vamp's lower half fell off the window.

"You split me, man!" complained the undead who resembled Brad Pitt, but shrimpier.

"Well say hi to your legs for me," Joseph said, gleeful as he pushed the rest of the sundead out the window.

He didn't see them coming. A nightstick whacked the machete out of Joseph's hand, crunching bones in the process while another blow landed on his skull, the impact of which cracked his pony-tailed head. To add to the insult, the legendary grinner was hurled to the back of the train. Like Poe, Joseph narrowly missed getting dunked in the putrid toilet bowl. "Just barely," he muttered, quickly recovering on his feet.

He would've been A-okay but for a faint-happy cattle who tripped him on her way down.

"This is the infamous Joseph?" A third attacker joined the fun and howled. The mustached cop with a thick neck and cheek piercings jabbed a baton outfitted with a four-inch spearhead into Joseph's side to keep him down. "What a Nancy! This ninety-year-old cow could kick his butt. Huh, old cow?" he asked the trembling woman nearest him, knocking on her nearly bald scalp.

"You know something, officer? I have yet to meet a cop with honor. Goodness knows how many times I've been profiled driving under the speed limit," Joseph said flippantly as he was impaled once more with a nightstick rigged with a pointy blade.

"Well I ain't ever met a brown homey I trusted either, so I guess that makes us even, you bean."

"End this," one of the purpleheads ordered. "We've got Sainvire and Maple to off."

"Bean?" Joseph coughed. The crack on his skull was leaking fluids. "If you're going to insult me then at least get it right. I'm Filipino, ass cruds!"

"So I'll call you a dog eater," the hulking cop said and stabbed him twice more in the chest area. With the help of the purpleheads, he lifted Joseph's twitching body horizontally. They tossed him out the window into the rocky fields below. They knew Joseph couldn't fly.

Clinging to the mushroom vent and uselessly watching the fighting heat up around her, Poe noticed a body tumble into the rocky ground from one of the side windows of the train. It took her a few seconds to recognize the corpse.

"Joseph? No!" Poe choked, pushing up her goggles. She was half-hidden behind a fallen body that looked suspiciously like Rodney Dangerfield.

Adrenaline coursed through her system and overpowered mawkish emotions. *Fuck my back and my goddamn aches. No more excuses!* Assuming a 1980s Charles Bronson vigilante stance, something potent pumped into her spine.

"That was my brother somebody tossed out the window," she bellowed, tightly gripping the Calico. She shot two of Trench's vampires in the back. Their uniforms and shiny badges made them easy targets.

"You buncha Gestapos!" Poe cried. She aimed for the flying rats swooping in like hawks in the night sky. Joseph was the type of guy who made the very worst day seem like a field trip. *Shouldn't've shot his crotch.* The nasty way he bit the bullet proved too much for her. She lurched forward, banging her knees on the metal roof.

"Georgette! Duck!" she ordered the veteran fighter who quickly followed instructions and squatted low. With clear access to the ill-looking fanged one with nicotine-stained teeth, Poe fired by the vent. The bullet hit the vampire through the ear, and the vampire rolled off the roof.

"Thanks, young'n," a grinning Georgette said before flying off to the last train car. "I was wrong about you."

Poe aimed for a three-nostril, cross-eyed baby crawling on the roof like it was playtime. Its black hooked nails scraped the metal roof, putting Poe's teeth on edge.

"That's quite enough, young lady," a rumbling voice told her.

Before she could shoot the creature, the gun was pried away from her hand. Poe found herself kneeling before Gruman Raspair, the Council Chairman himself. The aristocrat of bloodsuckers wore a burgundy smoking jacket and gloves, protecting him from her marinated skin. Clearing his throat, the top honcho fired at Sainvire twice before the gun clicked empty then bent the pistol nozzle with his hand.

"Sainvire!" Poe yelled, crawling skittishly toward the downed vampire. She pulled out a 9mm Browning.

"How I despise guns," he sighed, twisting her gun away and pulling the girl to her feet. "So vulgar. That's quite a load you have on you, Julia," he shook his head, tugging off sundries like her whistle and rosary hanging about her neck. He tossed them overboard. Her pistols and clips tucked in holsters and belt followed. "I really ought to order a strip search for I will not put it past you to stash an armada under those redolent clothes of yours."

"Just try it, pops," she gritted. "You're overdue for retirement."

Before Poe could say more, the gray-haired vampire guffawed at her asinine comments, indicating with flair the newly arrived. Six ancient vampires that jumped up, landed, or flew down on the roof silenced her. Walrus teeth shone even in the early evening. They were surrounded and outnumbered.

"Crap," she said defeatedly.

There were only Maple, Georgette, Sainvire, and a handful of their co-conspirators in striking distance. The rest were busy fighting inside the train or spread out on the roof of three train cars. Many had fallen into the hands of the enemy. Poe accepted that Sainvire was the only viable match against Raspair and his old world tricks, but her guy didn't look so hot. He'd been hit near the heart and kidney before halving a swollen-faced undead. The bullet wounds fused achingly slow. The fool had given his Kevlar away. His martyr complex sickened her.

Maple bludgeoned fatally away with her forearms, catching chests and heads with calculated viciousness. Though fierce and thorough, the vampire lacked the gift of flight. She would've been crushed if she were to come to blows with Raspair. Georgette may have put up a nasty fight with the head of the Council, but she lacked accuracy. She fought like a madwoman, slashing wildly here and there in hope of catching flesh between her blades. Unfortunately she slashed air more than bodies, scattering her foes between the three train cars. For someone as cool-headed and methodical as Gruman Raspair, she would have been easy prey.

From the corner of her eye, she saw thin arms clutching a wind-whipped rope ladder. The wiry limbs belonged to a vampire named Ed she'd seen clearing the rails. He'd abandoned the other lifters to clear tracks to lend a hand. Though small and unassuming, the little fellow could toss uprooted trees as easily as chucking celery stalk. His wimpy appearance seemed feeble next to the substantial girth of the ancient undead who resembled Bib Fortuna.

He's the reinforcement? Poe swallowed, more than a little discomfited. *I can barely shoot with all the dancing going on. Then there's the wind factor. The little guy's all they can spare? And he isn't carrying a weapon!*

Her eyes watered from frustration. There was her unfortunate self, a human with a limp and lower back problems. She was left with only a six-shooter boot gun and a plastic water pistol tucked in her left pocket. The old coot didn't have time to put down her stash properly. The last puny knife holstered in her right wrist sheath was not discovered either. With such paltry weapons, she was a quarter of a soldier, but a soldier all the same.

In the distance, she could see an outline of about seven latecomers, and none of them was Trench. *The yellow livered cretin!* The weasel was shirking his responsibility. *Thank goodness for small favors.* The vampires that flew erratically their way were truly horrid flyers.

"Did I not say that I would personally hunt you down if this girl kills any more of our people?" Raspair asked a very solemn Sainvire who was on one knee, doubled over with pain. The master vampire had given up the pretense that he was the bulwark of strength. "I personally witnessed her shoot five vampires."

"Maybe you weren't looking closely enough. I shot ten plus two more before that. And I don't know if those little mini-freaks count for something, but I shot a whole playground of them in the tunnels," Poe interjected, turning up the smartass at the wrong time.

She was scared shitless, but she thought she could bide Sainvire more time to heal.

Raspair tightened his hold on Poe's upper arm, digging his gloved finger in the healing bullet wound from days before until blood trickled like sap again. "Interrupt me once more, I will gladly tear your jugular then toss your dead, inconsequential carcass in front of this worthless train."

Poe made a face and debated whether to say something snooty. Sainvire's pained look of warning made her feel tortured and helpless.

"Since I'm going to become flapjack anyway," she said, yanking her arm imprisoned still in the vampire's grip, "I might as well tell you about a few more folks I killed."

"Poe, be quiet!" Maple pleaded harshly, fending off two Ancients at the rear of the first car. She received a baton blow in the cheek for the distraction.

"No, Miss Maple. Let her speak," Raspair encouraged. "It is apparent that she thinks nothing of vampire lives, including those of your friends." His eyes rested on Sainvire who met the accusation stoically.

Poe caught Sainvire's blazing eyes with her night vision goggles. It was the only thing she could do to avoid thinking about the leaden thumb burrowing into her wound. She had to buy Sainvire some more time.

Her arm felt like it was getting stabbed by pointy glass chopsticks. *If only he didn't have those gloves on!*

"You'll need to appoint a new councilmember, because I killed Gwendolyn." She inhaled sharply from the pressure. She was going to tear up and possibly cry within the next few seconds.

The train stopped altogether. *Did the Council's men take over the railway?* She couldn't help but say a prayer for the poor Pacific Islander driver she had intimidated earlier.

"That's enough, Poe," said Sainvire hoarsely, holding on to his chest. He looked into the dark lenses of her goggles and silently implored that she keep her trap shut. Poe looked away. Her chest constricted with guilt. Kaleb Sainvire was her first real love outside of John Cusack, Paul Newman, and Steve McQueen. She knew his strength improved with every second.

From the corner of her eye, the little Latino guy named Ed quietly injected hope back into her heart. In his unassuming way, the debris hauler began a cleanup of his own on the roof. Without any weapons save from his hands that were smaller and more delicate than Poe's, he received every blow from taller opponents only to pounce on them with enough force to puncture holes through their chests and stomachs. He brandished an easy Mona Lisa smile.

Go, Ed! she silently rooted.

A solitary figure landed on the roof, swathed in an old-fashioned cloak. Poe's heart rejoiced. It was a feeling so foreign and devoid the past few days that she was at a loss. They weren't alone anymore. She thanked the stars that Raspair's back was turned and he couldn't see the intruder. *Vampires are seriously defective*, Poe thought bitterly.

"And I flattened your butler, too." Poe swallowed, continuing her cockamamie story until she felt brash.

"He's in the tunnels butlering hungry babies. Some I'm sure are your very own spawn."

For the insolence, the Council Chairman cuffed her across the temple. The blow nearly obliterated her sight.

"As I was saying, Sainvire," Raspair continued, "I will strike permanent death to you and those who insist on continuing their allegiance to the proliferation of Plasmacore. Did I not declare that you would pay for every vampire this girl has killed? Isn't that so, Rodrigo?" he said without turning around. He knew that Rodrigo Jacopo was there.

"Yes, sir." Rodrigo answered. "I believe we've done that twice over this night."

For the traitorous act, Georgette quickly swung two babies off of her so she could hold a spear tip against Rodrigo's heart. "Son of a bitch! You're the one that blocked the tracks—"

"And did I also not say that Sainvire would die if we ever found a trace of Plasmacore anywhere near downtown?" said Raspair as if Georgette hadn't spoken.

"Yes, you did," Rodrigo stated boldly, staring down Georgette who looked upon him with disgust, the tip of her sword inches from his heart.

"That's beside the point now, isn't it? Cattle theft is a drawn-and-quarter offense at the very least."

"I've always known you were crooked," Georgette accused.

"Georgette, you think everyone's crooked." Jacopo flashed a smug smile.

"But you, I'm sure about," she laughed bitterly. "You set us up."

"Hush, woman," said the Council Chairman. "This entire charade reeks of greed. You and a handful of idiots want to herd our food source." He turned around to look at Rodrigo and then found Sainvire's eyes, "So, Rodrigo Jacopo, councilman in these parts, what do you think we should do with a turncoat drug trafficker, vampire killer, and cattle thief in our midst?"

Every pair of eyes looked expectantly at Rodrigo.

"Councilman, that is a very difficult question." Rodrigo quelled Poe's disbelieving look with a smile and rested his green gaze on Sainvire. Ancient undead surrounded the downed vampire. "But I believe death by impalement would suffice – from mouth to orifice." In a blur, Rodrigo broke the spear aimed at his heart and stabbed the jagged edged handle into Georgette's chest. The force penetrated the rusty chain mail easily.

"Georgette!" exclaimed Sainvire, attempting to stand. The pain in his chest was still too great. The bullet was inches away from his heart.

The vampire, who looked like she had fought the bloody Crusades, collapsed instantly and was borne by the wind to fall on the rocky ground below. Full of good tidings, Rodrigo walked to the Council Chairman and patted him on the back.

Poe tried to pry away Raspair's hand, muttering the most terrible epithets she could remember directly at Rodrigo. She didn't care that her arm wound began bleeding again. "You *pinche* cocksucking roach!"

"Poe, enough!" Sainvire ordered. "It's alright. I imagined a worse death for myself. Be patient and wait."

He wants me to stall for more time. She inhaled deeply and exhaled slowly, counting to three in Tagalog, Japanese, Spanish, and English. Only then did she find hope in what Sainvire had said. *His wounds must be mended. It just has to be!*

The yoga breathing exercises didn't quite work when she stood face to face with a very smug Rodrigo.

But she did place certain perplexing pieces together. Like a bright bulb flickering to life, she understood. She had to play this right.

Just say it, the inimitable voice instructed in her head. She shivered. There was no way she could be wrong.

She shook her head at Rodrigo. "You're a pathetic, simpering, lovestruck blowhard. Megan will never love you, especially if you off her uncle."

Rodrigo Jacopo's smile vanished, and he yanked the girl's shirt. Raspair relinquished the girl to Jacopo, saying, "She killed Gwendolyn and your son, Milfred."

"The loony slut I could care less about, but a loyal son like Milfred..." Jacopo backhanded her face. She would have rolled off the train if he hadn't kept his hand clamped on her shirt. His hand sizzled from Poe's marinated skin, but he did not notice.

Poe licked the blood from her lip in fear that Rodrigo might get hungry. With a grateful sigh, she thanked providence for her mouthguard. She whispered something in the wind, meant for Rodrigo's ears only. With fury, Jacopo grabbed her much abused hair and prepared to toss her overboard.

Their pursuers were catching up quickly. Tense fighters on the roof of the three cars could almost smell them coming. "And Megan, too," Poe added. "Shot her in the head myself. She was honing in on Sainvire and me."

Like adding lemon juice to an open wound, Poe continued to talk, taunting anyone who could hear. "And I gutted Megan, chopped off her luscious candy corn hair. Didn't you see her headless corpse at the station?"

Before she caught Sainvire's gaze, she received another punch in the mouth, opening up old cuts and tearing new ones. *Not the teeth again!* Crawling on the roof, blood leaking on rusted metal, Poe looked up at Sainvire.

"None broken," she said with relief about her teeth. It was a pain to get the six-shooter out of her ankle holster without looking suspicious. She itched to blast these vampires who wanted to beat the shit out of her and her friends. But Sainvire wasn't ready yet.

A young woman getting beat to kill time on his account wasn't an easy feat to take. While she was on all fours a few feet from where he knelt, Sainvire flashed a look that said *get ready*.

"You do that again, Jacopo, and I'll annihilate you," Maple warned, blocking his resonant kick with her mallet arm. Maple, quiet by nature, was something to behold when angry. Even Rodrigo took a step back. For her effrontery, Ancients and young vampires alike surrounded Maple. Like a domino effect, Sainvire's people rallied to protect their own. The tense situation boiled over.

No fewer than six limbs splintered, and two heads rolled to the ground. The latter, courtesy of Sainvire. He could fight once more.

To this melee, Rodrigo was deaf and blind. The councilman shook from the urge to hurt the human who had dared kill his beloved, his reason for the ultimate betrayal. He had been looking forward to a new life with Megan without the domineering presence of Kaleb Sainvire. But all this plotting and planning was for naught. The person he most wanted was dead. And all he could think about was killing the human crawling on all fours in front of him. The pest had even killed his only full-grown son. With renewed fury, he lashed at Poe.

"What are you saying?" Rodrigo bellowed, clutching her vest.

Poe slapped his hand away and cussed him out in a whisper.

If she hadn't been wearing her night vision goggles, Poe would not have seen Rodrigo's eye vein plump up. He raised his hands to prove that he wouldn't touch her.

"Megan squealed and begged like a dumb mule. And rest assured, you were the one who tipped me off about her." Jacopo was upon her. Luckily Poe had rehearsed beforehand what he might do to her. "Fuckin' sick, digging her uncle that way!"

She exposed only her left arm. Rodrigo grabbed it and yanked her up, unaware that Poe's skin was erasing his fingerprints. *He's too angry to feel the holy water!*

Before Rodrigo could do any more damage to Poe, Sainvire appeared from behind and perforated his lungs with his talons. The councilman dropped to the roof with a look of blind hatred on his face. "You killed the woman I love," he hissed at Poe.

Poe retrieved the pink plastic turtle water gun from her pocket and said, "I lied. She's one of my best friends. I'd never harm her." With a harrumph, she squirted concentrated holy water into his mouth. Jacopo's face sunk in like rotten grapefruit. Slipping a four-inch knife from her wrist, Poe sliced his neck from ear to ear.

"He's dead, Poe," said Sainvire, helping her to her feet. "Can I leave you alone?"

"I've taken care of myself since I was eight, Sainvire," she said, insulted. "Go do your thing."

As soon as Sainvire flew to the next train to lend a hand, an Ancient advanced near her, walrus teeth drooling. *Oh shit*, she thought. Before she could consider running, Ed went to her rescue, grabbing the marble-skin Ancient by the ankle and swinging him around like the sling that cut down Goliath. The little man pounded fist-size holes on his back.

"Domo arigato, man!"

"No prob," said the taciturn man to a grateful Poe.

Breathing rapidly, Poe reached down to her ankle to retrieve the sole remaining gun.

Despite her conversation with Sainvire, she kept as close to Sainvire as she could. No one would have guessed that he had just been seriously injured. He turned a circle, slicing off the tips of the spears of the Ancients that surrounded him. *Such old-fashioned buffoons*, Poe thought. *Spears and swords instead of guns?* Sainvire damaged a breastbone and hacked off a shoulder before getting Poe out of the way of a short sword meant to disembowel her.

Maple fought like an executioner, back to back with Sainvire, pounding heads with her lethal, swollen arms. The middle-aged vampire looked fierce and positively dribbled with hate. She was a real warrior when it came to an all-out brawl.

A new flock landed, and the group of vampires seemed to multiply.

That was when Sainvire's vampires assigned to guard cattle inside the train climbed out the windows with sabers, guns, wooden stakes, and other hardware cutaways in their hands.

"Make way for the black folks," said one red bereted warrior as he fired his Astra at every cop he saw. Maple picked up a fallen axe from the rooftop before it clunked off the train, her hardened forearms ready to make mincemeat out of anyone who got in her way.

Ed, slight though he looked, snapped vampire heads like his favorite munchy – Butterfinger candy bars.

"Helluva time to discover I have an equilibrium problem, eh?"

"That's alright, Ed. Let's just spot each other," said Maple.

Poe glimpsed two vampires from Sainvire's camp duking it out with the Council's warriors. On the ground, a shirtless and shoeless vampire was taking care of three undead with a combination of martial arts and undead savvy. Two of the dead were master vampires who dressed like they were going to a club. Each fist he threw destroyed bones and hearts. He was so amazing that Poe lost all caution and looked down again.

"Joseph?"

Poe couldn't help it. She whooped happily. To give her friend the upper hand, she aimed her turtle squirt gun at his foes and fired. She sprayed all four, but Joseph didn't seem to be affected by the garlic water.

When the three black clad fighters paused to wipe at their hissing faces, Poe shot one in the neck and let Joseph finish off the other two. He raised his hand to her.

"Thanks, sis," grinned Joseph, saluting the kneeling figure of Poe on the roof.

Not too far away, Gruman Raspair, the unrepentant Euro-supremacist, was having the fight of his life. Ironically the two rustlers he clashed with turned out to be a gay woman and a Latino man. Maple nearly succeeded in throwing him off the train with her magnificent bludgeoning skills by catching him in the stomach. Ed, the slow but pouncing jackhammer, had broken more than a few enemy ribs. If it hadn't been for Raspair's ability to fly, he would have been pulped long ago. He had weaknesses like everybody else. Gruman Raspair flew away until traffic subsided on the train roof. Cursing, he patted the small gun tucked inside his robes. "It would seem that I must resort to using you tonight, little uncivilized thing. Ah well. I am surrounded by louts. It would be fitting."

Like a bird of prey, Raspair's eyes rested on Poe who was busy gushing over Joseph's recovery. The stream of water coming out of her ridiculous pink plastic gun made him shiver. He was going to kill her face to face, but he did not want to risk getting disfigured. "That pain in the ass!" he muttered as he plunged back down to the train when the spray gun finally squeezed empty.

Only, Sainvire, drenched with black blood, saw what was about to happen.

"Sorry, Poe," Sainvire said as he promptly kicked Poe in the back and barked for Joseph to catch her. A moment later, Raspair's shot struck Sainvire in the arm. Once again, the master vampire collapsed on the roof.

"Finish the son-of-a-bitch!" Raspair ordered the flaxen haired-twins who turned their sights on Kaleb Sainvire.

By the looks of it, the day was a victory for Raspair's people. They outnumbered Sainvire's forces two to one. Gruman took to the air, thinking his work finished. He was now a spectator to a death match.

As soon as one of the shockingly ethereal vampires positioned close enough to plug a bullet in his skull, Sainvire elongated a thumbnail and impaled the woman. The brother fired a clumsy shot while retreating to the sky, but Sainvire was on his tail, having extracted the bullet from his stomach. The long mane of hair became the undoing of the vampire with a Seraphim's face. Easily side-stepping the man's scythe, Sainvire was presented with a fistful of hair. He